中央高校基本科研业务费专项科研项目（NR2013055）

The Multiple Dimensions of the Other in J.M. Coetzee's Novels

库切小说“他者”多维度研究

石云龙 著

南京大学出版社

序

李维屏[①]

石云龙教授是当前国内研究库切的几位重要学者之一。他的这部新作以中国学者特有的目光，有效地借鉴了当代后殖民理论，对库切小说的“他者”问题作了全方位、多层次的研究。我以为，这是一部颇有学术水平和理论价值的学术著作，其间不时闪烁着作者的创新精神和智慧火花。

所谓“他者”，首先是个哲学命题。德国哲学家托尼逊(Michael Theunissen)在《他者》(*The Other*)一书中指出，“他者”问题是 20 世纪第一哲学命题。“他者”最初作为一个哲学范畴为现象学所论述，其后又在弗洛伊德(Sigmund Freud)和拉康(Jacques Lacan)的心理学、布伯 (Martin Buber)的犹太哲学、后现代主义等思想中得以深化。“他者”理论首先要表述的是“非同一性”的原则立场，认定他者是在我之外的另一个，不能被同一。从古希腊哲学智者派到德国法兰克福学派无不强调差异性思想。法国哲学家表现尤为突出，无论是早年的萨特(Jean Paul Sartre)、梅洛-庞蒂(Maurece Merleau - Ponty)、列维纳斯(Emmanuel Lévinas)，还是后来的阿尔都塞(Louis Pierre Althusser)、拉康、德里达(J. Jacques Derrida)、德勒兹(Gilles Louis Rene Deleuze)，都曾对他者理论有过论述。

然而，文学中的“他者”并不简单地等同于哲学研究中的“他者”，文学批评中的“他者”命题实际上与当代后殖民理论密切相关。后殖民理论家赛义德(Edward

① 上海外国语大学二级教授，校英语学科学术委员会主任，博士生导师，英国曼彻斯特大学荣誉研究员，中国教育部“跨世纪优秀人才”，《英美文学研究论丛》主编。

Said)在其著作《东方主义》中论及欧洲与东方关系时明确地提出"他者"概念，认为"东方"并非自然存在，而是欧洲最常出现的他者形象，欧洲与东方因而是主体与他者的关系。在后殖民语境中，前者处于具有强势话语的书写地位，而后者则处于弱势话语甚至话语缺失的被书写地位。他在阐释两者关系现状基础上强调，他者的重要性在于衬托主体，因为在西方理论家眼里，没有被书写者的"杂乱"、"矛盾"和"混乱"就无法凸显书写者的"理性"、"逻辑"和"科学"。在后殖民理论中，西方人往往被称为主体性的"自我"，殖民地的人民则被称为"殖民地的他者"，或直接称为"他者"。

后殖民理论的杰出代表之一、后现代主义和后结构主义者福柯(Michel Foucault)在讨论知识和权力关系时提出，两者其实是一对共生体，知识为表象，权力是实质。这意味着知识与权力并不客观中立，而从来就是权力之下的强者声音。强者声音即为主体、主流话语，而被主体遮蔽的总是"他者"。他者的缺场、沉默已是习惯使然，然而，在后现代语境中，"他者"开始以不同方式出场。作为以语言文字为工具形象化地反映客观现实、表现作家心灵世界的文学，在强调人类性、社会性、民族性、人民性、阶级性和真实性等特征的同时，必然参与知识和权力的游戏，必定关注到主体与他者的关系。平民化的"他者"角色作为多视角和多元的性质特征受到作家的普遍关注。作家往往把"他者"作为想象的存在，这种想象的存在是对文化形象的渗透，成为异国或异族的文化形象，如英国后现代主义作家约翰·福尔斯(John Fowles)在小说《法国中尉的女人》中"想象"了一个维多利亚时代的"他者"文化形象。

文学批评对他者的关注，按照美国罗德学院谢弗(Brian W. Shaffer)教授的说法，仅开始于20世纪，但近年来有了深入发展之势。文学批评界运用不同理论从意识形态、心理探索、叙事分析等方面对他者进行研究，例如，后殖民女性主义当代先锋斯皮瓦克(Gayatri C. Spivak)就在其批评实践名篇《三个女性文本与帝国主义批判》(Three Women's Texts and a Critique of Imperialism)中深入文本叙事和美学交织的网络，从后殖民角度解构了勃朗特(Charlotte Brontë)小说《简·爱》中女性他者伯莎的形象，约克大学教授阿特里奇(Derek Attridge)在《伦理现代主义》(Ethical Modernism)中则解析了诺贝尔文学奖得主库切(John Maxwell Coetzee)

早期小说中的仆人他者形象，等等。

石云龙教授于 2009 年涉足他者研究，其耗时 5 年的新作《库切小说“他者”多维度研究》是他近年来最重要的研究成果。该书根据近 10 年来脱离本土的所谓流散作家屡获国际大奖的独特现象，在查阅大量资料基础上，选取 2002 年移居澳大利亚东南部港口城市阿德莱德、2006 年 3 月正式入籍澳大利亚的南非英语作家库切作为研究对象，通过对其代表性小说《等待野蛮人》、《迈克尔 · K 的生活与时代》、《耻》和《伊丽莎白 · 科斯特洛：八堂课》的研究，从殖民霸权时代、后基督时代、后种族隔离时代、后现代语境等不同维度系统地探讨了库切小说中的“他者”形象。

石云龙教授的著作选取的视角新颖，主导理论明确，尤为可贵的是，该书在占主导地位的“他者”理论贯穿全书的情况下，根据实际需要引用了包括怀特(Hayden White)的新历史主义、福柯的权力话语理论、博埃默(Elleke Boehmer)的后殖民理论、赫尔曼(Judith Herman)的创伤理论、弗洛伊德的精神分析理论、波伏娃(Simone de Beauvoir)的女性主义理论、巴赫金(Mikhail Bakhtin)的复调小说理论以及相关叙事学理论等多种理论。这些理论的运用自然贴切而且不露痕迹，与深入细致的文本分析相得益彰，不仅增加了论著的理论深度，而且使得文本分析结论更具说服力，这充分表明论著作者宽阔的研究视野和娴熟驾驭理论的功力。

我认为，《库切小说“他者”多维度研究》是一部原创性研究成果。作者在书中多维度地探讨“他者”在库切文本中的表征、他者的内涵、他者群像背后的意蕴、历史的渊源、与现实的关系，展示了库切偏好呈现他者群像的缘由、库切的哲学反思等。作者以翔实的资料证明，库切塑造的他者群体对后殖民理论的发展、对后现代理论的充实、对文学创作与批评皆具启发意义，认为库切的文学创作实践对世界文学从主题到样式都做出了卓越贡献。该论著以其富于新意的立论、严密的逻辑、充分的论证表明，其研究已经处于国内库切研究的前沿，代表了学术界库切相关研究的最新成果。

石云龙教授在这部专著成书过程中，十分注重与学界的交流。书中观点在数次国际会议上经过交流与碰撞后得到后殖民理论、批评界专家学者的认可。他在武汉“库切研究与后殖民文学”国际研讨会上主持库切研究专题讨论时，与牛津大学博埃默等一批国际知名教授深入探讨，其小说他者论点得到充实；在雅典"语言与文学"国际研讨会上与包括开普敦大学教授们在内的库切研究者的讨论，丰富了其库切的书写为南非英语文学非传统性创作的观点；他在上海英美文学国际研讨会上的主旨发言以及同与会代表的讨论，得到同行专家充分认同。石云龙教授积极参与国际会议、敢于展示自己的研究观点，与学界同行充分交流，不仅使其开阔了研究视域，而且使其专著提出的观点更具说服力。

石云龙教授还在该著作后面附录了较为详细的库切研究资料。这些资料是他为库切研究而多次出国悉心查阅的结果，其中包括专著、博士论文、期刊论文等。这些研究资料为今后中国库切研究者们的继续研究提供了有益的参考。

我相信，这部难能可贵的著作不仅能使石云龙教授成功地建构其清晰的库切研究者的学术面貌，而且能进一步促进我国的库切研究及后殖民文学批评的发展，并在学界产生积极的影响。

2013 年 8 月 30 日于上海

目　录

附录：

前　言

2002年旅居澳大利亚阿德莱德、2006年入籍澳大利亚的南非英语作家约翰·麦克斯韦尔·库切(John Maxwell Coetzee)以其特立独行的风格，写出大量"既具有知性力量、文体从容，又具有历史远见和伦理洞察"①的文学作品，受到学界高度关注，英国诺丁汉大学文学教授多米尼克·黑德称库切为"最受尊敬、最频繁地被研究的当代作家之一"，因为"他的小说在南非文学，广义地说在20、21世纪小说发展过程中占有特殊地位"。② 库切的文学创作所取得的成就有目共睹，瑞典作家佩尔·沃兹伯格在库切2003年被授予诺贝尔文学奖时的发言，高度评价了他的文学对于荡涤人类灵魂、提升人类道德水平方面的伟大成就："库切……捍卫着诗歌、文学和想象的道德价值。如果这些缺失，我们将会什么也看不清，成为灵魂的盲者。"③正因为如此，英国著名文学评论家简·波因纳提出，"说库切是20、21世纪最具影响力的小说家之一并非夸大其辞"④。

库切的文学创作往往以出其不意的创新性而著称于世，他以超凡脱俗的他者姿态，创作出12部"篇幅有限而范围无限"的小说，被称为是能够"想象出无法想象的东

① Attwell, David. Editor's Introduction. *Doubling the Point: Essays and Interviews*. Cambridge, Massachusetts; London, England: Harvard University Press, 1992. 1.

② Head, Dominic. *The Cambridge Introduction to J. M. Coetzee*. Cambridge: Cambridge University Press, 2009. ix.

③ Wastberg, Per. Presentation Speech for the Swedish Academy quoted in "He and His Man the 2003 Nobel Lecture." *World Literature Today*. May-August 2004. 16－20. 18.

④ Poyner, Jane. Introduction. *J. M. Coetzee and the Idea of the Public Intellectual*. ed. Jane Poyner. Athens, Ohio: Ohio University Press, 2006. 1.

西"的"后现代寓言家"。[①] 早在《幽暗之地》1974 年发表之时，南非著名评论家乔纳森·克鲁就在南非文学杂志《对比》上刊文热情地称其为南非第一次出现的现代小说。评论家黑德则走得更远，他在《剑桥库切入门》中直接宣称，"后现代主义据说是随着1974 年 J. M. 库切第一部小说《幽暗之地》发表而来到非洲的。"[②]这种评论是否精准可能有待商榷，但是，库切的小说处女作带给南非文学的影响决不能低估。

既然评论家将库切的小说发表与南非文学创作的后现代主义联系在一起，那么，我们有理由相信，这部小说应该给南非文学带来了推动性力量，这种力量必定与南非文学传统不相一致但却与世界文学发展趋势合辙。库切研究专家斯蒂芬·沃森的评论不仅重新界定了克鲁的说法，认为后者说的"现代小说"实际上应该是"现代主义小说或后现代主义小说"，而且旗帜鲜明地支持了黑德的观点，认为"从来没有一部南非小说如此明显、甚至有意识地摆脱现实主义传统，如此坦诚地宣布自己的非真实性、虚构性"。[③] 众所周知，南非 50 年代文学通常不会显露政治意识形态，作家们善意地期待着各民族之间的对抗会导致产生一个多民族和平相处、共生共存的和谐局面；60 年代南非文学倾向性较为明显，自从臭名昭著的沙佩维尔惨案[④]发生后，文学作品大力表现的是黑人反抗种族歧视，探讨的是作家们的共同感受——他们不再试图维持那种由善意的白人和耐性的黑人共同努力来改善政治生态的虚妄幻想。其实，南非文学在相当长时间里就是在采用现实主义手法表现幻想与幻灭，主题较为局限，形式较为传统，用库切的话说"[南非作家的]艺术太缓慢、太老套、太间接，无法对团体生活或历史进程产生哪怕是最细微、最迟到的影响"[⑤]。

《幽暗之地》的问世，不仅为南非文学界带来全新的主题，而且带来别样的文学样

---

① Wästberg, Per. 2003. Award Ceremony Speech, December 10. Accessed March 30, 2012. <http://nobelprize.org/nobel_prizes/literature/laureates/2003/presentation-speech.html>

② Head, Dominic. *The Cambridge Introduction to J. M. Coetzee*. Cambridge: Cambridge University Press, 2009. ix.

③ Waston, Stephen. Colonialism and Novels of J. M. Coetzee. *Critical Perspectives on J. M. Coetzee*. ed. Graham Huggan & Stephen Watson. London: Macmillan Press Ltd., 1996. 13-36. 15.

④ 南非白人种族主义政权大规模屠杀非洲人的惨案。1960 年 3 月 21 日，南非德兰士瓦省沙佩维尔镇的非洲人举行大规模的示威游行，反对南非白人当局推行种族歧视的"通行证法"。南非当局出动大批军警镇压示威群众，致使 72 名非洲人被枪杀，240 多名被打伤，造成了震惊世界的"沙佩维尔惨案"。

⑤ Coetzee, J. M. Jerusalem Prize Acceptance Speech (1987). *Doubling the Point: Essays and Interviews*. ed. David Attwell. Cambridge, Massachusetts: Harvard University Press, 1992. 98-99.

式。这部小说首先突破了文学范式、叙事模式的制约，采用将相隔两个世纪仿佛毫不相干的故事并置，以隐喻的方式展示“厌恶人类的两种形式，其一为知性与夸大狂式的厌恶，另一为充满原始活力的厌恶，两者之间互为映照。”①库切的小说因而跳出了南非传统文学创作的禁锢，突破了狭隘的南非黑白之间争斗的主题，突破了小说创作的头身尾线性发展模式，作家审视的目光不再仅仅注视着南非本土黑白的争斗，而是投向世界，关注人性疏离异化等人类共同的话题。库切将以元小说特征明显的文本与他性充分的虚拟译本并置，因而便穿梭在两个世纪之间、穿梭在美国人与布尔人②之间，这种具有典型后现代文学特征的小说出现在 20 世纪 70 年代的南非，无疑对南非文学造成震撼性影响。库切能写出当时堪称如此先锋派的小说，恐怕与他本人此前的经历和所受的影响不无关系。在英国工作期间他于 1962—1963 年对著名作家福特的研究③、1965 年赴美国德克萨斯大学采用计算机语体分析方法对荒诞派戏剧创始人之一和集大成者塞缪尔·贝克特的研究④、博士毕业后在美国纽约州立大学的文学教学经历、作为南非人在美国反越战抗议以及随后的遭遇、长时间内浸淫在英美文化中的感受，使库切对当代意识形态、文学创作理论与实践产生了独特的认识，尤其是他对贝克特的潜心研究给他留下的沁入骨髓的影响，使他在尝试文学创作伊始就站在了时代的前列。

从库切的回忆来看，他研究福特是因为美国著名现代派诗人、意象派代表人物埃兹拉·庞德认为福特是“当代最优秀的散文文体家”。库切经过研究后发现，“福特给人的印象是，他从英国统治阶级内部写作，但事实上，他是作为一个局外人、作为一个对此有点渴望的局外人在写作。”⑤这种局外人书写的视角，确实也影响到了他的文学创作。不过，这种影响并没有让库切在创作中模仿福特的风格，而是启发他注意到如

---

① Engdahl, Horace Oscar Axel. Press Release. 2 October 2003. Accessed September 5, 2012. <http://nobel prize. org/nobel_prizes/literature/ laureates /2003/press. html>

② 南非的荷兰、法国和德国白人移民后裔形成的混合民族。来源于荷兰语“Boer”(农民)一词。今布尔人的后裔多指阿非利堪人(Afrikaner)。

③ 1963 年，库切以一篇研究福特·马多克斯·福特的论文获得开普敦大学文学硕士学位。其英国经历后来出现在自传三部曲的第二部《青春》(2002)中。

④ 该研究论文于 1969 年帮助库切获得德克萨斯大学语言学博士学位。

⑤ Coetzee, J. M. *Doubling the Point*: *Essays and Interviews*. ed. David Attwell. Cambridge, Massachusetts: Harvard University Press, 1992. 20.

何更有效地利用局外人立场，使他站在他者的立场上书写，而这种站在他者立场上进行他性书写的风格在其以后的文学创作中一直占有重要的地位。

其实，影响库切最大的应该是贝克特。库切在博士论文之外还曾写过一系列文章专门谈论贝克特，这些评论性文章清楚地表明了他对贝克特的认知与欣赏。阿特维尔采访库切时曾对后者说，"你对贝克特的评论似乎不仅回应了设计重复的活动，而且回应了你的虚构"①。库切明确地告诉阿特维尔，"贝克特对于我自己的写作意义重大——那一定是毫无疑问的……我对贝克特的评论不仅是学术训练……而且是企图接近一种秘密——我想要拥为己有的贝克特的秘密"②。其实，库切通过严格的学术训练获得了贝克特思想的精髓，而且，在汲取、运用这些精髓时得到了无比的快乐。"贝克特的散文……给了我感官的快乐，这么多年来这种快乐一直没有暗淡过。我对贝克特所作的批评来源于这种感官反应。"③这种快乐潜移默化地影响了他的小说创作，而后他创作大量的寓言体小说虽然说与南非政治生态不无关系，但是，最重要的还是与他的贝克特研究相关。

上述讨论可以看出，库切的《幽暗之地》创作别出机杼有据可依，而初试身手就在南非文坛引起反响，激发了库切的创作热情，也促使库切走上了一条不断挑战自我、挑战文学模式和叙事方式之路，而且每一次新的尝试都为阅读大众和创作者、评论者群体带来惊喜。他的特殊身份④使其一直站在局外人的立场冷眼看世界，而体现其不断追求的文学创作则永远给人以别样的他性感受。结果，"他尽管每一部小说都聚焦于南非，但是，他对后现代小说、超小说的关注无疑使他比大多数作家更加国际化，使他获得世界范围内认可。"⑤

库切破冰式小说《幽暗之地》虽然触动了南非文学界，但第一次真正使库切获得国

① Coetzee, J. M. *Doubling the Point: Essays and Interviews*. ed. David Attwell. Cambridge, Massachusetts: Harvard University Press, 1992. 22.

② 同上，第 25 页。

③ Coetzee, J. M. *Doubling the Point: Essays and Interviews*. ed. David Attwell. Cambridge, Massachusetts: Harvard University Press, 1992. 20.

④ 库切是南非出生的荷兰人后代，自小在南非黑白对抗的环境中接受英语教育，开普敦大学毕业后去英国做计算机程序员的工作，后去美国德克萨斯大学攻读博士学位，后留美担任大学文学教师，因抗议越战而导致绿卡申请被拒，回到开普敦大学教授文学。他的成长经历造就了他一直处于边缘、局外的感觉。

⑤ Canepari-Labib, Michela. *Old Myth-Modern Empires: Power, Language and Identity in J. M. Coetzee's Work*. Oxford, Bern, Berlin: Peter Lang, 2005. 14.

际声誉的小说还是诺贝尔文学奖颁奖词中提到的“有康拉德遗风的政治惊悚小说”[①]《等待野蛮人》(1980)。该小说在出版当年就获得英国最古老的文学奖“詹姆斯·泰特·布莱克纪念奖”,次年又获得英国费伯小说纪念奖。这部在库切获得诺贝尔文学奖后被企鹅丛书收入“20 世纪伟大图书”的小说深得贝克特等人真传,“《等待野蛮人》在很多地方与卡夫卡(《在流放地》)、霍桑和无处不在的贝克特的文本产生互文”[②]。毫无疑问,这与库切所受影响相关,也与他追求独特的他者写作风格有关。正如库切研究专家多维所说,“库切小说利用拉康被割裂的主体的观念(在文本与叙事之间割裂),设法达到逃离与主流话语共谋的目的。”[③]小说采用后现代政治寓言形式,“通过将野蛮人建构成精致而荒唐的想象而破解了‘文明/野蛮’二元论”[④]。从传统意义上看,文明人建立在假想野蛮人存在的基础之上,而文明的标准通常是由主流权威话语者制定,欧洲白人与非洲有色人种因而被轻而易举地建构成“文明/野蛮”二元论的两极。小说中,库切站在南非被欺压、被蹂躏者的立场,通过暴露欧洲白人文明者的野蛮行径形式,表现霸权时代的种族他者、性别他者和身份他者的遭遇,揭秘殖民霸权时代帝国文明的真相。这部形式特别、寓意深刻的他性小说为南非文学、世界文学提供了切实可行的小说样式。

三年后发表的小说《迈克尔·K 的生活与时代》(1983)堪称库切文学成就的第一个高潮,该小说甫一出版便不同凡响,被认为是“肯定生命的小说”[⑤],进入决选名单后击败呼声最高的萨尔曼·拉什迪的《耻辱》,一举获得当年英国文学最高奖——布克奖。该小说明显地受奥地利作家卡夫卡影响,将寓言体小说发展到一个新的高度。黑德的评论代表了学界的观点:“很清楚,库切处理边缘化和异化的手法与卡夫卡相

---

① Engdahl, Horace Oscar Axel. Press Release. 2 October 2003. Accessed September 5, 2012. <http://nobel prize.org/nobel_prizes/literature/laureates/2003/press.html>

② Newman, Judie. Intertexuality, Power and Danger: *Waiting for the Barbarians* as a Dirty Diary. *Critical Essays on J.M. Coetzee*. ed. Sue Kossew. New York: G.K. Hall & Co., 1998. 127.

③ Dovey, Teresa. J.M. Coetzee: Writing in the Middle Voice. *Critical Essays on J.M. Coetzee*. ed. Sue Kossew. New York: G.K. Hall & Co., 1998. 19.

④ Ashcroft, Bill. Irony, Allegory and Empire: *Waiting for the Barbarians* and *In the Heart of the Country*. *Critical Essays on J.M. Coetzee*. ed. Sue Kossew. New York: G.K. Hall & Co., 1998. 107.

⑤ http://www.themanbookerprize.com/books/life-times-michael-k. Accessed June 3, 2012.

似。"[①]库切在小说中对局外人或者说边缘化他者的处理到达了几乎出神入化的地步，为南非后现代文学注入了新的范本，同时也为其小说的经典化奠定了稳固的基础。库切本人并不否认卡夫卡作品对小说《迈克尔·K的生活与时代》创作的影响，在一次访谈中，他曾经明确地说，"你问到卡夫卡对我小说的影响，我承认这种影响。"不过，"字母K并非只有一种解释"。[②] 库切的说法真实可信，确实，他的小说受到过卡夫卡的影响，受到过贝克特的影响，但是，正如前文所述，这种影响是库切在深入研究过这些作家后沁入骨髓并化为自己意识的影响，没有任何模仿别人的痕迹。他从局外人视野解读南非种族隔离制度下社会的动荡、人民的苦难，为被边缘化他者化的普通人仗义执言，为话语权缺失的人们呐喊。小说蕴含丰富，寓意深刻，任何一种单向度的解释都会流于片面，给南非文学界带来的启示重大，意义深远。

库切接下来推出的小说《福》(1986)显示出鲜明的后现代主义特征。作者采用去经典的方式将英国启蒙时期现实主义小说家、被誉为"英国和欧洲小说之父"的作家笛福(Defoe)姓氏前缀"de"[③]去除(有趣的是，"de"本身除经常与贵族姓氏相连外就有"去除"的意思)，大有去经典、去贵族化、去规范化、去传统性的意思，使作家"笛福"还原成作家"福"。当然，《福》与笛福的《鲁滨逊漂流记》之间存在的明显互文关系无法否认。虽然它紧随在布克奖获奖小说之后出版，不免使读者对其存在更多的期待，因而使一些人感到失望，但是，这部"去"字当头的小说显现出非同寻常的他性特征，用哈根与沃森的话说"他[库切]的小说好像有意这样建构，以图逃避任何一种阐释框架"[④]。他选取白人女性苏珊作为主要叙述人物，引入女性声音以填补笛福小说中缺席的声音，试图以此与男性声音相抗衡，尽管"性别与[苏珊]缺乏叙事权威相关"[⑤]。除了在文本中

---

① Head, Dominic. *The Cambridge Introduction to J.M. Coetzee*. Cambridge: Cambridge University Press, 2009. 56.

② Coetzee, J. M. *Doubling the Point*. ed. David Attwell. Cambridge, Massachusetts: Harvard University Press, 1992. 199.

③ 笛福原姓福，1703年后自己在姓前面加上听起来如同贵族的"de"的前缀，形成笛福(Defoe)这一笔名。

④ Huggan, Graham & Stephan Watson. Introduction. *Critical Perspectives on J. M. Coetzee*. ed. Graham Huggan & Stephen Waston. London: Macmillan Press Limited, 1996. 1.

⑤ Hutcheon, Linda. The Politics of Impossible Worlds. *Fiction Updated: Theories of Fictionality, Narratology, and Politics*. eds. Calin Andrei Mihailescu and Walid Hamarneh. Toronto: U of Toronto P, 1996. 218.

重构女性话语、挑战白人男性作家权威以外，作者还特别注意表现沉默黑人男性的觉醒，揭秘历史写作中的权力结构，试图解构父权与殖民霸权，为女性群体和殖民地弱势群体寻求话语权。在文本中，作者采用诸如拼贴、互文、超小说、开放式结局等后现代主义创作手法，展示历史的多面性、复杂性并提供解构历史的新路径。小说为读者提供多重阐释空间的同时，为南非文学提供了文学新品。

1994年因为种族隔离制度被废除而在南非历史上十分重要，而库切这一年发表的《彼得堡的大师》也“标志着库切文学生涯的转折点”。库切的这种转折体现在他在作品中表现的与前一部小说《铁器时代》一样的“政治相关性与迫切性”①，正如毕晓普所说，“在这部作品的进程中，库切对政治身份的关注变得越来越明显”②。同时，这种转折还表现在他对创作手法的运用上。他借用自己从美国回到南非开普敦大学教授文学时的俄罗斯文学研究成果，尤其是陀思妥耶夫斯基专题研究成果，在小说中创造了一个具有自主意识的陀思妥耶夫斯基形象。库切将这位文学大师设计成因继子巴维尔(Pavel)亡故而来到彼得堡，而在调查中，与巴维尔相关的一些人物包括无政府主义者涅恰耶夫(Nechaev)、帝国警察马克西莫夫(Maximov)自然都进入陀思妥耶夫斯基的精神生活，使作者无法不与政治相牵连。此外，库切在叙事形式上进行大胆革新，他采用现在时共时叙事向传统叙事规约提出挑战，使包括陀思妥耶夫斯基在内的人物具有独立的声音、开放的他人意识，不断发出有价值的议论，与作者形成多重平等的对话关系。巴赫金在谈到陀思妥耶夫斯基长篇小说基本特点时曾经说“有着众多的各自独立而不相融合的声音和意识，由具有充分价值的不同声音组成的真正复调”③，而《彼得堡的大师》不仅具有所有这些特征，而且将陀思妥耶夫斯基拉入对话关系之中，故被认为是复调的复调，库切的创作因此而表现出独特的他性特征。

帮助库切第二次获得英联邦布克奖的小说《耻》(1999)代表着作者创作的第二个高潮。与作者早期作品相比，该小说现实意识更强。作者站在他者的立场，冷眼审视

---

① Head, Dominic. *The Cambridge Introduction to J. M. Coetzee*. Cambridge: Cambridge University Press, 2009. 72.

② Bishop, Scott G. J. M. Coetzee's *Foe*: A Culmination and a Solution to a Problem of White Identity. *World Literature Today* 64(1990): 54-57. 56.

③ Bakhtin, Mikhail. *Problems of Dostoevsky's Poetics*. ed. & tr. Caryl Emerson. Minnesota & London: University of Minnesota Press, 1984. 6.

南非社会转型时期——后种族隔离时代的严峻社会现状。长期以来的殖民主义、种族隔离时代产生的历史伤痛记忆在人们心灵中已经留下难以泯灭的创伤，这些创伤恒久留存，并不会随着白人统治结束而被人遗忘。当原先的主体与他者之间的关系被人为地颠倒后，如何认识历史变迁后新时代中的黑白关系，失去殖民政策护佑的白人殖民者后裔如何与这片黑人聚居地上的原始居民和平共处，饱受种族隔离历史创伤之痛的南非人怎样才能走出心灵创伤的阴影，是小说关注的重点。作者以"耻"为引，展示耻的内涵，这里既揭示了个体层面之耻，更暗示着群体层面之耻。他不仅探讨帝国主义殖民造成的历史旧账与殖民者后裔个体应当承担的责任问题，而且在设法探究如何解决问题的途径。不过，在探讨人类和解之途时，小说《耻》沿袭了《铁器时代》和《彼得堡的大师》中的宽恕主题，而宽恕通常与忏悔联系在一起，然而，"忏悔当时成为管控社会禁锢个人意识的一种工具，其真实目的因而被消解。"作者明白工具性忏悔无法得到真正的宽恕，永远达不到和解的目的，故而，"库切一直在试验着忏悔模式，而在这里他采用不同的方式接近这个问题。"[①]他从被颠覆的他者视角出发，表现自己对黑人文化取代白人文化并没有带来观念进步和社会和谐而感到的困惑，在展示后种族隔离时代南非的矛盾冲突之时，注重呈现殖民者后裔在白人统治结束后沦为地位被颠覆的他者的境遇，通过人物露西和受害女生之父的言论与行为，反思殖民者的作为，寄托和谐之愿望。

移居澳大利亚阿德莱德后，库切发表的第一部作品《伊丽莎白 · 科斯特洛》(2003)他性特征更加鲜明，这部可谓是讲座式小说或小说式讲座的作品是库切为文学长廊提供的新画卷。在此式样新颖的画卷上，他者作用得到更加充分的发挥，在他性十足的女作家与不同角色的不断抗争中，在对其进行质疑挑战的过程中，库切不仅讨论了非洲文学创作、非洲人文学科问题，而且讨论了人类、自然界诸多热点问题，在这部篇幅不大的作品里，库切讨论哲学、伦理学、心理学、人类学、诗学、动物生命等充满思辨色彩的众多话题，涉猎之广，令人诧异，他似乎想利用作品人物告诉读者，哲学语言或许并非女作家科斯特洛的强项，她在讲座中不能自如地运用哲学语言说服听众纯属正常，但是，学术讨论并非仅有哲学语言，采用诗学语言、虚构故事形式讨论哲理性问题

---

① Head, Dominic. *The Cambridge Introduction to J. M. Coetzee*. Cambridge: Cambridge University Press, 2009. 77.

同样能够帮助思考、探索真理，并且可以取得意想不到的效果。这部引起学者和批评家争论其文类归属的作品，以其特有的他性色彩，为文学创作和批评拓展了小说范畴，增加了新的样式。

如果说《伊丽莎白·科斯特洛》在小说样式上进行了富有争议的创新的话，《凶年纪事》(2007)在叙事模式上的革新则应该是标新立异之举。因为，前者采用了将讲座与故事相融合的方式来构建新的小说样式，这种建构虽然他性明显，但依然具有小说的基本要素，即作者创造了一以贯之的人物，讲述了她在不同时间不同地点讲座的经历，这里有人物塑造，有情节发展，有矛盾冲突，有高潮有结局，有对话关系有心理活动等等，当然还有传统小说所不具备的成分，即作者通过不同的"课"来明确传达讲座之内核；而后者虽然也不乏传统小说的基本成分，但作者表现这些成分时采用的手法出乎读者意外，他为读者刻意设置了阅读障碍。库切在作品中采用的是以技术手段来造成视觉冲击的手法，以鲜明的他性视图——在书页里加平行线，在叙事中形成客观上的共时特征，即上中下三栏同时发生、共时发展的方式，边发表言论、记录思想边推进故事，在众声喧哗中完成创作意图。作者因此为读者与评论界留下了不穷尽小说样式誓不停止文学创新实验的印象。

库切自投身文学创作以来，共发表 12 部小说以及大量其他作品①。这些作品不仅奠定了他在南非文学中的地位(三次获得南非最高文学奖"CNA 奖")，更重要的是获得了世界文学的认同，先后两次获得英联邦最高文学奖"布克奖"(1989，1999)，还获得法国费米娜奖、以色列耶路撒冷奖、《爱尔兰时报》国际小说奖等国际重要奖项，并于 2003 年荣膺诺贝尔文学奖。诺贝尔文学奖颁奖委员会在评价库切时以高度凝练的语言评说他是"一位审慎的怀疑者"，认为他"以无数姿态表现了局外人令人诧异的牵

① 发表《男孩》(1997)、《青春》(2002)和《夏日》(2009)等传记 3 部，2011 年以《外省场景》为名将 3 部传记结集出版；发表非小说类作品 5 部，其中包括《白色书写：论南非的文人文化》(*White Writing: On the Culture of Letters in South Africa*, 1988)、《双重视角：散文和访谈集》(*Doubling the Point: Essays and Interviews*, 1992)、《冒犯：论书刊审查制度》(*Giving Offense: Essays on Censorship*, 1996)、《异乡人的国度：文学评论集》(*Stranger Shores: Literary Essays, 1986－1999*, 2002)、《内心活动：文学评论集》(*Inner Workings: Literary Essays, 2000－2005*, 2007)，计划发表作品《此地此时》(*Here and Now*, 2013)；出版翻译作品 3 部，为丹尼尔·笛福、索尔·贝娄、塞缪尔·贝克特等人的 6 部经典著作再版撰序。

连","无情地批判了西方文明中残酷的理性主义和肤浅的道德观"。[①] 库切的获奖说明他的小说创作已经融入了现代小说主流。

确实,"库切常被人贴上'与众不同'作家的标签,他的小说常常会引起评论家们的直接反对意见。"[②]他自己在大众面前最常见的形象是"难以捉摸"、"难于描述"。他常常把自己置于大众视野之外,以旁观者/局外人的身份来审视南非殖民主义、后殖民主义、后种族隔离制度,审视当下这个荒诞不经的世界,揭示在非正义制度下的种种暴力行为,揭示被边缘化他者所遭受的压迫与痛苦,揭示人类生存的困惑、焦虑、孤独以及现代社会中人们丧失自主意识后的悲哀。在表现自己的哲思时,库切不断试验新的文学样式、叙事方式,故而其作品充满了他性,为读者、批评者增添了解读空间。文学评论界运用各种不同文学、哲学理论对库切作品进行了大量的解读,然而,无论哪一种文学、批评理论都无法涵盖其全部作品,因为他用不间断的文学实验创新永远走在超越自己的道路上。他的文学成就因此在南非文学史上占有重要的地位。

库切与众不同的小说,开始并没有引起太多关注,"直到第三部小说《等待野蛮人》(1980)在英国获得费伯奖和詹姆斯·泰特·布莱克纪念奖以及下一部小说《迈克尔·K的生活与时代》(1983)获得布克奖,才引起世界评论界足够的关注和承认"[③]。库切研究随着他在世界上频获文学奖项,尤其是他获得诺贝尔文学奖以来而不断升温,俨然成为一门显学,近年来有关库切国际研讨会[④]相继召开,使库切研究达到高潮。然而,用库切研究专家托尼·墨菲的话说,"对于所有读者,不过可能尤其是对南非人来说,这种作品[库切作品]面世时具有挑战性、不同寻常而且读起来有困难,在经历了将近30年时间评论与探讨后情形并没有改变。"[⑤]这为库切研究持续升温提

① Engdahl, Horace Oscar Axel. Press Release. 2 October 2003. Accessed September 5, 2012. <http://nobel prize. org/nobel_prizes/literature/ laureates /2003/press. html>

② Canepari-Labib, Michela. *Old Myth-Modern Empires Power, Language and Identity in J. M. Coetzee's Work*. Oxford, Bern, Berlin: Peter Lang, 2005. 15.

③ Kossew, Sue. *Critical Essays on J. M. Coetzee*. New York: G. K. Hall & Co., 1998. 2.

④ 根据可以查证的资料发现,2009年澳大利亚在悉尼召开库切研究国际会议,2010年中国在武汉召开库切与后殖民文学国际研讨会,会议分别出版了研究论文集。

⑤ Morphet, Tony. Reading Coetzee in South Africa. *World Literature Today* 78.1 (2004): 14-16. 14.

供了依据。

国外库切研究呈现多视角、多层次、多维度等特征。大量研究者根据库切的南非荷兰人后裔身份，结合南非的种族隔离制度对南非人民造成的伤害以及南非后种族隔离时代黑人政府试图揭示真相并实现种族间和解[①]的现实，对库切小说，尤其是对《耻》进行持续的批评性解读。德里克·阿特里奇经过研究后断言，库切小说无法逃离政治、社会与历史，虽然他出于无法言说的原因在不少作品中采用寓言形式来表达隐含意义，但是，他对待南非种族隔离、殖民主义传统的态度是明确的。“尽管他的小说没有采用直白的‘抵抗写作’形式，他对 1948 至 1994 年间执政的南非国家党的政策和实践及其政策建立的基础——更加古老的殖民传统持强烈反对态度。”[②]这种意识形态自然会引来评论家的关注。

文学批评家们发现，在对待南非种族和解是否能实现的问题上，库切持有明显怀疑态度，他在小说《耻》中设计的白人卢里拒绝忏悔的情节在某种程度上无意识地暴露了他的思想，这在山姆·杜伦特“后殖民叙事与哀悼作品”提出的那一系列问题中得到了印证。“什么样的真相、什么样的工作方式会带来和解？种族隔离受害者的证词和种族隔离加害者的忏悔之间是什么关系？讲述真相与发现事实真相之间的关系？”[③]这些共鸣式问题说明，评论界发现库切对妥协、忏悔、和解并不持乐观态度。与此同时，简·波因纳以“库切小说中的真相与和解”为题进行的讨论，针对库切之关注找出问题的症结并就解决方法提出自己的看法，“新南非面临的问题是黑人与白人如何能在一起生活，这个问题可以通过与前压迫者和解而非反诉得到部分回答”[④]。她认为，库切小说对真相与和解虽然有疑虑，但却对此保持持续性关注，而且，其关注的方式还呈现出多样性特征：“《耻》涉及所有这些问题，与此前作品相比，这部小说在后种族隔离时

---

① 南非大主教图图曾经说过，南非本应起诉那些在种族隔离时期犯下滔天罪行、但又拒绝忏悔的作恶者。然而，他们于 1995 年 12 月 16 日成立真相与和解委员会，为南非种族隔离制度的受害者提供了一个控诉种族隔离时期白人统治者暴行的平台，一般认为，真相与和解委员会改变了南非的历史，抚平了南非人心中的怨恨，为南非的稳定与和解奠定了基础。

② Attridge, Derek. Age of Bronze, State of Grace: Music and Dogs in J. M. Coetzee's *Disgrace*. *Novel* 34. 1 (2000): 98 – 121. 99.

③ Durrant, Sam. *Postcolonial Narrative and the Work of Mourning: J. M. Coetzee, Wilson Harris, and Toni Morrison*. Albany: State University of New York Press, 2004. 23.

④ Poyner, Jane. Truth and Reconciliation in J. M. Coetzee's *Disgrace*. *Scrutiny 2* 5. 2 (2000): 67 – 77. 67.

代再现并修改了这些关注。"[①]瑞塔·巴纳德(Rita Barnard)则通过对库切的《耻》及其他文本之间的关系分析,认为"在这部招惹麻烦的后种族隔离时代作品的核心,存在着界定、关系与责任的危机"[②]。

鉴于后种族隔离与殖民话题紧密相连,评论者常常采用后殖民理论视角,运用葛兰西的"文化霸权"、福柯的"权力话语"、杜波依斯的"文化身份"等理论,对库切作品中体现的对话语霸权的解构、对身份的不确定、地位的边缘化和声音的沉默化等课题进行研究(Spivak 1990[③]; Waston 1996[④]; Pechey 2007[⑤]; Post 1986[⑥]; Boehmer 2006[⑦]; Brink 2009[⑧]),认为库切的创作语境决定了其后殖民主义文学特征,因为哺育他成长的南非土地使他产生难以割舍的情愫,他在这里见证了人民的苦难、见证了白与黑的冲突、主体与边缘关系的颠覆与变化,与此同时,这块土地上先后发生的殖民浪潮和帝国时代留下的遗迹使他与殖民先辈们有着挥之不去的感情维系,加之他在英美文化环境中的长期浸淫,强化了他的这种情感。故而,他在小说创作中,常以独特的视角表现黑人的遭遇与反抗,呈现欧洲中心、白人中心语境下处于边缘地位的南非黑人的命运,再现后种族隔离时代白人在失去权威话语权地位后遭遇的被边缘化的困顿处境。库切小说的这些主题应该是后殖民主义和后现代主义共同关注的主题。

① Poyner, Jane. Truth and Reconciliation in J. M. Coetzee's *Disgrace*. *Scrutiny 2* 5.2 (2000): 67-77. 67.

② Barnard, Rita. Coetzee's Country Ways. *Interventions: International Journal of Postcolonial Studies* 4.3 (2002): 384-394. 384.

③ Spivak, Gayatri Chakravorty. Theory in the Margin: Coetzee's *Foe*—Reading Defoe's "Crusoe/Roxana". *English in Africa* 17.2 (1990): 1-23.

④ Waston, Stephen. Colonialism and Novels of J. M. Coetzee. Critical Perspectives on J. M. Coetzee. ed. Graham Huggan & Stephen Watson. London: Macmillan Press Ltd., 1996. 13-36.

⑤ Pechey, Graham. Coetzee's Purgatorial Africa: the Case of Disgrace. *Interventions: International Journal of Postcolonial Studies* 4.1 (2002): 374-383.

⑥ Post, Robert M. Oppression in the Fiction of J. M. Coetzee. *Critique* 27.2 (1986): 67-77.

⑦ Boehmer, Elleke. Sorry, Sorrier, Sorriest: The Gendering of Contrition in J. M. Coetzee's *Disgrace*. *J. M. Coetzee and the Idea of the Public Intellectual*. ed. Jane Poyner. Athens: Ohio University Press, 2006: 135-147.

⑧ Brink, André. Post-Apartheid Literature: A Personal View. *J. M. Coetzee in Context and Theory*. ed. Elleke Boehmer at al. New York: Continuum International Publishing Group, 2009: 11-19.

学界对库切的寓言体书写给予了持续的关注(Dovey 1988①; Wright 1989②; Gallagher 1991③;Gitten 1993④;Wenzel 1996⑤;Hayes 2010⑥),早期评论中将其寓言进行过度政治化解读的做法曾经引起库切的反感,后期评论家们一般联系后现代语境进行解码,认为库切是世界性作家,他的创作可能涉及南非故事,也可能涉及南非以外故事,采用的背景有时是当代有时是过去。这些以寓言形式表现的故事无需简单地与南非联系,而应该与人类处境、人类本性相关,库切作品主题中普世价值通常大于对南非的意义。阿特维尔对库切寓言有深刻的见解,认为作者利用卡夫卡、贝克特式寓言有其现实意义,而且提出,库切在《等待野蛮人》之后转向卡夫卡符合逻辑发展规律,在《福》中直接转向边缘化处境亦属自然。⑦

评论界对库切的关注、对其作品的解读还因其创作视野开阔、涉猎广泛而呈现出视角多样的局面,几乎所有的文学与批评理论都在他的文学创作中得到验证。库切研究中不可忽略的是与其他作者之间的对比研究(Kossew 1998⑧; Chapman 2009⑨; Diala 2001 -

① Dovey, Teresa, *The Novels of J.M. Coetzee: Lacanian Allegories*. Cape Town: Donker, 1988.

② Wright, Derek. Fiction as Foe: The Novels of J. M. Coetzee. *International Fiction Review* 16.2 (1989): 113 - 118.

③ Gallagher, Susan VanZanten. *A Story of South Africa: J. M. Coetzee's Fiction in Context*. Cambridge, Mass.: Harvard University Press, 1991.

④ Gitzen, Julian. The Voice of History in the Novels of J. M. Coetzee. *Critique* 35.1 (1993): 3 - 15.

⑤ Wenzel, Jennifer. Keys to the Labyrinth: Writing, Torture, and Coetzee's Barbarian Girl. *Tulsa Studies in Women's Literature* 15.1 (1996): 61 - 71.

⑥ Hayes, Patrick, J. M. *Coetzee and the Novel: Writing and Politics after Beckett*. Oxford: Oxford University Press, 2010.

⑦ Attwell, David. *Doubling the Point: Essays and Interviews*. Cambridge, Mass. Harvard University Press, 1992. 9 - 10.

⑧ Kossew, Sue. Colonizer/colonized: Paradoxes of Self and Other. *Pen and Power: A Post-Colonial Reading of J.M. Coetzee and André Brink*. Amsterdam: Atlanta, GA, 1996.

⑨ Chapman, Michel. Coetzee, Gordimer and the Nobel Prize. *Scrutiny2* 14.1 (2009): 57 - 65.

2002[①]; Strode 2005[②];Durrant 2004[③];Yeoh 2003[④];Szczurek 2009[⑤]),经常被用来做比较的有南非另一位诺贝尔文学奖得主纳丁·戈迪默(Nadine Gordimer)、诺贝尔文学奖得主、爱尔兰、法国作家塞缪尔·贝克特(Samuel Beckett)、南非著名阿非利堪斯语和英语作家安德烈·布林克(Andre Blink)、印度裔英国作家萨尔曼·拉什迪(Sir Ahmed Salman Rushdie)、捷克裔法国作家米兰·昆德拉(Milan Kundera)等,这些研究从内容到形式进行对比,肯定库切故意规避种族叙事、在纵深层次上拓展人与人之间复杂难描的关系和冲突所取得的成就,肯定库切在小说形式实验上所取得的伟大成就,充分肯定了库切小说创作的价值。

随着后女性主义、后殖民主义和批判种族理论的发展,批评家们开始结合库切文本对男性/女性、文明/野蛮、白种人/有色人种、主人/奴隶等二元对立论进行拨乱反正性研究,出现了零散的主体/他者关系研究论文[⑥]。

国内库切研究起步较晚,《外国文学》2001 年发表的论文《越界的代价——解读库切的布克奖小说〈耻〉》通常被认为是早期库切研究中较有价值的研究成果,因为论文作者利用库切在文本中使用的 Cronus(篡越)这个词为切入点,解读不同层面的篡越,得出较有说服力的结论。浙江文艺出版社在 2003 年库切获得诺贝尔文学奖后迅速推出的库切小说系列译本,虽然译文稍嫌粗糙,却为库切作品的传播和研究提供了难能可贵的基础。迄今为止,根据互联网上统计,自第一部库切研究博士论文《永远的异乡

---

① Diala, Isidore. Nadine Gordimer, J. M. Coetzee, and Andre Brink: Guilt, Expiation, and the Reconciliation Process in Post-Apartheid South Africa. *Journal of Modern Literature* 25. 2 (2001-2002): 50-68.

② Strode, Timothy Francis. The Ethics of Exile: Colonialism in the Fictions of Charles Brockden Brown and J. M. Coetzee. New York & London: Routledge, 2005.

③ Durrant, Samuel. *Postcolonial Narrative and the Work of Mourning*. Albany, New York: State University of New York Press, 2004.

④ Yeoh, Gilbert. J. M. Coetzee and Samuel Beckett: Ethics, Truth Telling, and Self-Deception. *Critique-Studies in Contemporary Fiction* 44. 4 (2003): 331-348.

⑤ Szczurek, Karina Magdalena. Coetzee and Gordiner. Coetzee in Theory and Context. ed. Elleke Boehmer, Katy Iddiols, Robert Eaglestone. New York: Continuum International Publishing Group, 2009.

⑥ Marais, Michel. *Death and the Space of the Response to the Other in J. M. Coetzee's The Master of Petersburg*. Athens, Ohio: Ohio University Press, 2006; Chapman, Michel. The Case of Coetzee: South African Literary Criticism, 1990 to Today. *Journal of Literary Studies* 26. 2 (2010): 103-117.

客》[①]发表以来，截至 2012 年 12 月，国内已发表博士论文 10 部；截至 2012 年 12 月，国内出版库切研究专著 4 部[②]。2001 年至今，中国期刊网上发表库切研究论文 400 余篇，其中核心期刊论文约 50 篇，其中外国文学研究领域的主要刊物[③]为库切研究做出了重要贡献。论文由刚开始时集中对《耻》进行研究，逐步扩大到其他作品研究。

鉴于多方面考虑，本书仅对中国外国文学研究专刊上刊载的约 50 篇论文进行分析归类，结果发现，国内库切研究相对来说还较为局限。这种局限表现在主题讨论多与后殖民、后种族隔离制度相关(此类论文有 10 篇)，讨论中基本涉及后种族隔离时代忏悔、宽恕、和解等话题，涉及帝国理念、自由言说问题，还涉及创伤书写等问题；文本研究通常集中在《耻》、《迈克尔·K 的生活与时代》等小说[④](关于《耻》的论文就有 12 篇)上；而叙事讨论则多数关注《凶年纪事》和《福》上。评论者们虽然也对库切的其他作品进行了零星的研究，人们在研究中也采用不同的理论视角。他们既讨论主题，当然也讨论库切小说叙事策略问题。不过，放眼世界，放眼国外已有研究成果，国内成果有时显得原创性不足，有些成果与国外已有成果相比有鹦鹉学舌之嫌疑，诸如忏悔、宽恕、和解话题的讨论，将已有观点改用不同语言方式传达给读者；有些成果套用相关理论，以库切作品为例来阐释某种并非新的理论，在不断展示论文作者的理论水平的同时，让人感到论文的启示性稍显不足，仿佛换一个案例可以同样达到相同目的。

库切作为一个身份特殊、经历非凡的作家，评论界感知到他的异样书写，发现库切作品中反复表现的边缘人物、被边缘化的人物，有些评论家根据后殖民后现代理论开始从他者角度去探索他的写作策略，如阿特里奇就以《铁器时代》为例讨论过库切小说的他性问题，认为“他的小说可以被读作一种持续而艰巨的塑造他性的事业……这些

① 王敬慧. 永远的异乡客——库切后殖民流散写作策略研究. 北京语言大学，2006.

② 高文惠. 后殖民文化语境中的库切. 北京：中国社会科学出版社，2008；王敬慧. 永远的流散者：库切评传. 北京：北京大学出版社，2010；段枫. 历史话语的挑战者—— 库切四部开放性和对话性的小说研究. 上海：复旦大学出版社，2011；蔡圣勤. 库切研究与后殖民文学. 武汉大学出版社，2011.

③ 截至 2012 年 6 月，根据中国期刊网上数据统计，《外国文学》与《当代外国文学》分别刊登库切研究论文 10 篇，《外国文学研究》刊登 8 篇，《外国文学评论》刊登 6 篇。

④ 经对比研究，中国外国文学研究专刊上的论文选题与全部期刊网论文选题成正比，如有关《耻》研究论文，专刊上 12 篇，约占总数 24%，而期刊网上 108 篇，约占总数 24%。故以专刊论文为例，具有典型代表性。

小说中出现的他性人物，通常是从居于支配地位的第一世界文化视角来看是第三世界个体或团体的替代性人物"①。科休在对比研究了库切小说《等待野蛮人》与布林克小说《干涩苍白的季节》后指出，"库切的小说探讨了殖民者——行政长官面临的道德、政治和个人困境，这位行政长官自己被贴上了'他者'的'内部敌人'的标签，因为他抗拒不变的帝国话语与实践，并且在其跨越帝国与野蛮他者之间的界限时表现出来"②。不过，这种视点研究论文很少，而且较为零散。国内学界也有少数几篇论文从他者视角观察库切小说，除本人的他者研究论文外③，有一篇将库切与鲁迅对比研究的论文④讨论了他者化流变形态，认为鲁迅的流变形态为传递，而库切的形态为逆转。应该说，迄今为止，尚未有研究者从他者视角对库切进行全面分析，分析其小说他者的形态，分析其小说他者在不同语境下的表现，探讨作家库切运用这些他者形象对文明、正义、帝国所进行的反思，对工具理性进行的拷问；未有人对库切刻意塑造这些他者形象作系统的梳理，对他将人物他者化的意图作深入探究；未有人对他的他性小说、人物他者化过程、作者自我他者化等课题作出理性的阐释。

对库切小说中的他者进行研究，就必定需要首先解决作为社会科学研究的核心命题之一的他者问题定义。经过追溯性研究发现，哲学家黑格尔较早地发现了"他者"的哲学价值。众所周知，这位思辨哲学代表人物解决哲学问题的路径是追求"总体"和"同一"，不过，他并不排斥差异的重要性。他求"同一"是求世界"差异"中的同一，这为"他者"的出现开辟了空间。海德格尔对于此在"在世"的论述是一大创新，他用独有的"共在"概念来表达"此在"在世是与"他人"同在。"'在之中'就是与他人共同存在。"⑤这种主体与他人的"共在"关系论述，消除了现象学家胡塞尔通过"移情作用"将他人建

① Attridge, Derek. Literary Form and the Demands of Politics: Otherness in *The Age of Iron*. Critical Essays on J. M. Coetzee. ed. Sue Kossew. New York: G. K. Hall & Co., 1998: 198-213. 204.

② Kossew, Sue. Colonizer/colonized: Paradoxes of Self and Other: *Waiting for Barbarians* (1980) and *A Dry White Season* (1979). *Pen and Power: A Post-Colonial Reading of J. M. Coetzee and André Brink*. Amsterdam: Atlanta, GA, 1996. 86.

③ 石云龙. 他者·他性——库切研究. 外语研究 2 (2011): 95-100; 约·麦·库切——为他者化的他者代言. 英美文学研究论丛 17.2 (2011): 67-80.

④ 石杰. 鲁迅与库切小说中的他者化比较. 渤海大学学报 4(2010): 59-67.

⑤ Heidegger, Martin. *Being and Time*. Oxford: Basil Blackwell Publisher Ltd., 1962. 112.

立在自我基础之上的唯我论嫌疑，为“他者”成为其哲学的一部分铺平了道路。而莱维纳斯反对本体论，借助“他者”批判西方本体论传统并企图超越，但他并不否认传统意义上“他者”的存在，只不过认为那是“相对他者”，是可以转化成同一或自我的他者，而他的哲学强调，要打破“同一性”，必须建立一种“绝对他性”哲学，提出一种无法还原为自我或同一的“他者”，与我“相遇”而完全不同于我的“彻底他者”或“绝对他者”①。在莱维纳斯看来，西方殖民主义、帝国主义、资本主义在对资本的贪婪与追求过程中所体现的那种单一权力意志，正是“总体”、“同一”理念在现实社会中的投射，而其发展到极致便是暴力和战争。他一针见血地指出，“作为第一哲学的本体论是一种权力哲学”②，认为这是西方文化危机的根本所在。

对他者的研究以及对文学作品中的他性研究，在后现代后殖民研究风起之后，渐成当下研究热点，给他者定义者往往是主导性主体，如德国著名哲学家、评论家西摩尔认为，他者“是超越远近距离的‘局外人’。这种人是群体本身的一部分，形似各色各样的‘内部敌人’，是群体既与其保持距离又要直面正视的成分”③。而著名英国学者、后殖民批评家艾勒克·博埃默则指出，“‘他者’这个概念……指主导性主体以外的一个不熟悉的对立面或否定因素，因为它的存在，主体的权威才得以界定”④。由他者衍生出来的“他者化”，则指人类通过将负面特点加诸于他者(其他群体或其他个人)而获得自我身份认同的过程。人们假设“他者”不如“自我”复杂深奥，“他者化”的施动者常把“他者”视为卑微劣等的对方，从而获得心理上的满足和优越感⑤。这里的他者研究通常涉及种族、性别、身份等差异，如白人叙述者眼里的“他者”往往是有色人种，“他者”的生活总是与混乱、懒惰、肮脏、放纵、愚蠢、邪恶、道德责任感匮乏等联系在一起，这就从反面证明了主导性本体的文明、秩序、修养、道德。正如弗雷德里克·杰姆逊所说，“人们对他产生

① Levinas, Emmanuel. *Totality and Infinity*. Pittsburg: Duquesne University Press, 1969. 35.

② 同上，第46页。

③ Simmel, Georg. *Georg Simmel on Individuality and Social Forms*. Chicago: University of Chicago Press, 1971. 144.

④ Boehmer, Elleke. *Colonial and Postcolonial Literature*. Oxford: Oxford University Press, 1995. 21.

⑤ Holliday, A. et al. *Intercultural Communication: An Advanced Resource Book*. London: Routledge, 2004. Accessed June 3, 2012. <http://www.themanbookerprize.com/prize/books/22.>

恐惧并不因为他邪恶,而是因为他是'他者'——异己、不同、奇怪、肮脏、陌生"[①]。对于与理论相关联的他性的各种不同阐释,是后殖民文化研究的历史前提。

被诺贝尔评奖委员会称为"后现代寓言家"的库切,在其文学创作中以典型的库氏寓言、迥异于南非文学传统的他性书写方式,多元化多层次再现强权政治语境下主导霸权话语形成的规律,展示后种族隔离时代权威话语者对被殖民者他者化的过程以及他者化的结果,以冷峻的笔触叙述话语权缺失的他者的生存与心理状态。

库切笔下的他者,与拉康主体间话语理论中的他者(L'Autre)极为相似,指异己、陌生、危险的"在者"和权力话语上的"不在场者"。这些他者缺乏辩解机会,通常只有沉默的形象。从"深入异己者与憎恶者内心"的南非最高文学奖——中央通讯社文学奖(CNA)获奖小说《幽暗之地》(1974)到"承继康拉德手法的政治恐怖小说"《等待野蛮人》(1980),从"根植于笛福、卡夫卡和贝克特"文学的作品《迈克尔・K的生活与时代》(1983)到"阐释陀思妥耶夫斯基生活和小说世界"的《彼得堡的大师》(1994),从展示"白人至上观念瓦解之后南非新形势"下人们际遇的《耻》(1999)到表现"作者与邪恶争斗"的著作《伊丽莎白・科斯特洛:八堂课》(2003)[②],从文体与视角各异的三栏式小说《凶年纪事》(2007)到探究真相的自嘲式自我重估小说《夏日》(2009),库切推出的他者形象不仅包括异族部落有色人种(如"思想者"尤金・唐恩计划中的越南人、"行动者"雅各・库切心目中的布须曼人和霍屯督人、帝国少壮派军人眼中的"蛮族"人等),包括"逃离动荡不安和战争迫近局势"的像迈克尔・K一样的沉默无语、苦苦挣扎的卑微残缺生命,包括在自然界任人宰割、受人虐待、毫无意义地牺牲的动物,也包括在后帝国、后殖民、后种族隔离语境中不再享有特权、丧失主导话语的白人以及似与时代环境格格不入的人。

本书选取库切小说中代表性作品《等待野蛮人》、《迈克尔・K的生活与时代》、《耻》和《伊丽莎白・科斯特洛:八堂课》为研究文本,根据库切作品发表年代将其小说背景整体定位为后现代,根据作品内涵从殖民霸权时代、后基督时代、后种族隔离时代、后现代语境等四个维度系统地探讨库切笔下的他者意蕴,涉及的理论包括拉康的

---

① Jameson, Fredric. *The Political Unconscious: Narrative as a Socially Symbolic Act*. New York: Cornell University Press, 1981. 115.

② Engdahl, Horace Oscar Axel. *Press Release*. 2 October 2003. Accessed May 6, 2012. <http://nobelprize.org/nobel_prizes/literature/laureates/2003/press.html>

他者理论、海登·怀特的新历史主义、米歇尔·福柯的权力话语理论、后殖民理论、朱迪丝·赫尔曼的创伤理论、弗洛伊德的精神分析理论、波伏娃的女性主义理论、巴赫金的复调小说理论以及相关叙事学理论等。

本书认为，库切作为布尔人接受的英语教育、亲赴宗主国都市伦敦的寻根经历、徜徉在“自由”美国所经历的异样感受、回到后种族隔离时代开普敦后精神的流散、移居澳大利亚在超越梦想的栖息地阿德莱德的思索，造就了他作为西方“他者”的作家特质；作者通过对霸权与暴力、践踏动物权利、压抑性权利、宗教信仰的负面作用等主题的揭示，表现出库切的他者对西方文明中残酷理性主义和肤浅道德观的批判；库切在作品中展示的宏观历史与微观历史的关系、人与历史的关系、事实与历史的关系、寓言体表述等，表现出他者对历史的权威及其背后的意识形态基础的解构；库切作品呈现的超越文学传统的实验，表现出鲜明的他性特征。

本书分四章讨论库切的小说“他者”：

第一章讨论库切小说《等待野蛮人》。该章首先采用后殖民和他者理论，通过对小说故事产生的背景考察，发现库切在小说中采用虚拟帝国形态，展示了殖民霸权时代帝国文明的本质特征。作者采用寓言体书写方式，呈现作为强势话语者的帝国的霸权行径，而霸权的行使则通过作为虚构帝国国家机器的军队来完成，与其处于对立关系的是处于偏远地带的“野蛮人”，亦即作为帝国刻意设置假想敌的他者。库切通过为处于强权话语的帝国安排种族他者，展示霸权时代他者的苦难，在表现他者受难的同时，揭示出作为主体话语掌控者的本质特征：他们这些任意地将不同种族的人打成另类他者的“文明人”，恣意凌辱种族他者，不仅与文明毫不相干，而且还暴露了自己是大自然异已的本质，是真正的野蛮人，真正的人类他者；库切还通过种族女性的处境描绘，表现了帝国文明的父权社会里，任人定义的女性他者：她们遭受种族和性别双重欺压，在帝国卫士的眼里，她们是可能会对虚构帝国利益造成威胁的野蛮人，作为女性，她们除了如其他同胞一样既没有任何身份特征，也没有任何标签式的显示符号外，还默默地遭受着男性“野蛮人”所没有过的苦难。这两种人同时都缺乏发声的机会，在身份上也都处于他者地位。最重要的是，库切在小说中安排了故事叙述者或小说代言人的边缘化和他者化，安排他的双重他者身份：对帝国而言，他是一个被疏离的边缘人，一个异化的他者；对“野蛮人”来说，是一个非自然的他者，处于中心与边缘、主体与他者的流动状态。

该章接着运用海登·怀特等人的新历史主义理论，考察历史记录者的资格，发现叙事者与帝国关系暧昧，既执意抵制帝国意识，是帝国的异己和他者，又不自愿地与帝国同谋，是自然的异己和他者；同时，利用原属帝国利益代表者，后被帝国边缘化的他者的自我质疑，对法律与帝国政治共谋关系进行解码。库切还利用被当作他者的老人死亡案例，揭露缺乏见证的历史事实任由权威话语者单方面篡改、虚构而被赋予历史合法性的情况，利用木简解读为例，说明历史阐释作为特定历史话语下的知识运作，存在着历史阐释者的不同关注与不同阐释结果。

该章还根据莱希特的正义定义，利用霍布斯和洛克等政治理论家的观点，研究库切笔下故事叙述者的冷静观察和亲身经历，发现了帝国"正义"内涵的实质。帝国为维护统治秩序，充分利用国家掌控的正义体制，对不符合帝国利益的他者进行惨无人道的镇压，实施霸权统治、暴力政治，达到的是非正义、非人性的结果。库切还利用帝国异化他者老行政长官遭受的肉体折磨，在暴露失去人性的帝国加害者们恶行的同时，向帝国权威话语提出挑战。

第二章讨论库切小说《迈克尔·K的生活与时代》。该章首先根据西方现代哲学家尼采的名言"上帝死了"，考察所谓后基督时代——基督教衰落、基督教理念淡化后的南非局势和库切刻意设计的暴力冲突场面，研究库切笔下呈现的暴力社会的他者形象：这里既有被边缘化、整天生活在无名恐惧之中的安娜，更有天生兔唇、智力发育不全被打入另册的他者迈克尔·K。

接着，该章采用福柯的权力话语理论，讨论南非种族隔离政策逐渐成形继而猖獗的乱世之中，边缘化他者在逃离社会过程中貌似消极实为有效的应对策略——沉默，用黑德的话说"沉默既是被剥夺公民权的标志，也是抵抗的表现形式"①。该章讨论了他者在维萨基农场、警察局、营地等不同场合下沉默的话语意义和心理活动，还讨论了他者从拒绝话语到对食物抗拒性的物理反应，认为这些举措既表现了卑微他者对权威话语者的反抗，也使人类持续追求的自由理想在沉默中得到张扬。

最后，该章依然利用权力话语理论并借助创伤理论，讨论了库切在作品中对创伤、历史、权力、规训等方面所作的反思，认为卑微他者迈克尔·K以独特的沉默方式对威权话语势力所进行的抗争，表现出作者在揭示人类社会的残忍暴力、相互隔绝、彼此仇

① Head, Dominic. *J.M. Coetzee*. Cambridge: Cambridge University Press, 1997. 98.

恨、愚昧自欺，检视西方文明理性正义本质、批判其道德伦理的同时，为遭受压迫和蹂躏的边缘化他者弱势群体仗义言说，为南非人民在历史社会中所经受的创伤、南非沉重的历史、权力话语、规训与惩罚等话题进行深刻反思，提出常人能否在历史社会中沉默隐身，他者在与环境的冲突中能否有自己的诉求等问题。

第三章讨论库切小说《耻》。该章首先通过对后种族隔离时代的黑白关系研究，讨论在种族隔离制度被废除后黑白关系的变化，发现民主制度的实行并未消除南非种族之间长期存在的矛盾与冲突，种族隔离制度的废止无法消除人们精神上存在的种族隔离。黑白之间并没有做到"尊重差异，包容多样"，南非政治版图上的黑白分明，依然是其鲜明的特色，不同的是，南非白人被边缘化他者化。

接着，该章借助权力话语理论和女性主义理论，讨论在失去偏袒性制度规则保护后以卢里、露西等为代表的白人少数族裔的命运。卢里在白人失去权力话语后依然我行我素，丑闻暴露后却拒绝忏悔，这种思维方式使他付出了不断被他者化的代价，最后自觉边缘化，从城市中心撤离，走向地处偏远的农场；而崇尚独立自由、自我支配意识强烈的白人女性露西却清楚地知道，后种族隔离时代白人优势地位已经不复存在，她在受辱后选择面对现实、接受妥协，表现了库切为实现种族融合而应多元宽容的思想。

该章最后借助资本主义契约原则、巴塔耶的欲望身体观、尼采的权力意志理论，检视过去曾经居于主导话语权的白人自我放逐、自我他者化的必然命运，因为他们没有意识到本能的性欲满足与人类道德和性伦理之间的冲突，没有适应护佑白人特权利益、维护白人霸权话语的律法已经废止的新形势。库切利用后种族隔离时代被颠覆了特权、沦为新时代他者的卢里的经历对性伦理和人性道德进行反思，利用卢里的女儿露西被抢劫轮奸事件反思了跌落到边缘他者地位的白人应该为历史的记忆付出何种代价、承担何种责任问题。库切怀着南非大地黑白种族应该和谐的信念，提出了宽恕和解、共存共生的希望，通过白人对动物观念的转变，传达了物种平等、和谐自然的思想。

第四章讨论小说《伊丽莎白·科斯特洛：八堂课》。该章首先根据巴思的《枯竭的文学》、利奥塔尔与哈贝马斯之争以及哈桑的概括性理论阐述，分析后现代主义的缘起，然后，结合约瑟夫·海勒的《第二十二条军规》、卡尔维诺的《宇宙连环画》为例，解读了后现代作品消解中心、游戏意义、颠覆主体的特点。

接着，该章根据后现代语境以及上述后现代作品表征，对库切的作品进行审视，发现库切深受法国结构主义、贝克特的荒诞派文学、普洛普俄国神话分析、纳博科夫以评注为主体的互文结构小说等的影响，其文学创作显现出鲜明的独立个性和迥异的他性特征，这种他性有时表现为将缺乏关联的独立文本组合，呈现元小说特征，有时采用碎片式的心灵独白，构建孤独他者的心理狂想；有时采用卡夫卡式手法展示混乱的精神生活，有时又采用戏仿的方式，影射西方经典；有时采用复调小说方式，形成与作者的多层次对话关系，有时又解构线性叙事模式，显现出无限制的开放性、多元性和相对性。

对库切移居澳大利亚后发表的《伊丽莎白·科斯特洛：八堂课》中女主人公的研究，则是该章的重点。论文根据作者对人物的定位、对人物文学观念的呈现、对人物在具有强大控制性力量的主流话语面前的表现设计，发掘出在后现代语境下特异他者的具体形象。本书认为，该形象在凝视与被凝视的过程中，在与作者设置的不同对话关系中，显示出特异他者的真面目。伊丽莎白·科斯特洛虽然行动怪异、性格怪僻，但是，真正使她成为特异他者的倒是因为她不遵守权威话语者既定的规则，不断对传统主流话语进行质疑，针对不同问题不应声附和，而是独立地发表自己的见解。作者借用这种他者形象，为的是诠释自己对文学信念、文学模式、小说本质、文学接受、区域文学、文学语言等问题上的认知，通过小说中非洲作家对比性讲座、哲学教授辩论性对话、小说家韦斯特语言沉寂等不同的对话关系来论证伊丽莎白的特异他性。

本书认为，借助代表性作品系统研究库切他性小说中的他者，从小说中他者的不同形态、不同属性、不同内涵，发现作者利用边缘化他者所揭示的内容、所表达的意义，不仅可以增加解读库切作品的维度，探索文学发展与后殖民时代知识分子迁徙的关系，对于探究世界文学发展趋势，研究无国界文学具有极其关键的意义和重要的参考价值。

Introduction

John Maxwell Coetzee, a South Africa-born English writer who migrated to Adelaide, Australia in 2002 and became a naturalized Australian citizen in 2006, has written in his unique style 12 novels of high quality and a number of other works[①] in the postmodernist context. As a writer "who in innumerable guises portrays the surprising involvement of the outsider" (Engdahl, Press Release, October 2, 2003), Coetzee has elaborately contributed to world literature a series of images of the Other. By revealing through the group images his profound reflections on the issues of common concern such as human civilization, human nature, equality and justice, moral ethics, etc., he becomes known for his being "ruthless in his criticism of the cruel rationalism and cosmetic morality of western civilisation"(ibid).

Coetzee's work with "a unique combination of intellectual power, stylistic poise, historical vision and ethical penetration" (Attwell 1) establishes his position in South African literature by winning three times Central News Agency (CNA) Literary Award — South Africa's highest literary honor. And more importantly, his work gains him worldwide

① Coetzee has published besides fiction three biographies, five non-fictions and quite a few translations, etc.

recognition in literature by winning successively the Booker Prize (twice), the French Prix Femina Étranger, the Commonwealth Writers' Prize, the Jerusalem Prize for the Freedom of the Individual in Society, the James Tait Black Memorial Prize, the Geoffrey Faber Memorial Prize before he received in 2003 the Nobel Prize in Literature, making him the seventh African to be so honoured①.

Coetzee thus becomes the focus of the academia②. The title "postmodern allegorist" "to imagine the unimaginable" (Wästberg, Award Ceremony Speech, December 10, 2003) has been widely accepted by literary critics and readers once declared by the Permanent Secretary of the Norwegian Nobel Committee. Dominic Head, professor from Nottingham University, calls him "one of the most highly respected – and most frequently studied – contemporary authors" because "His novels occupy a special place in South African literature, and in the development of the twentieth-and 21st-century novel more generally" ("Cambridge Introduction" ix). Swedish writer Per Wästberg's Award Ceremony Speech in 2003 pays high tribute to the great achievements Coetzee's writing has made to the purification of human souls and the promotion of human morality. He asserts that "Restrained but stubborn, he [Coetzee] defends the ethical value of poetry, literature, and imagination. Without them we blinker ourselves and become bureaucrats of the soul" (Wästberg 18). Taking the same view, a British

① He is the seventh South African Nobel Prize winner following Nelson Mandela, F. W. de Klerk (Peace Prize) in 1993, Nadine Gordimer (Literature Prize) in 1991, Desmond Tutu (Peace Prize) in 1984, Albert Luthuli (Peace Prize) in 1960, and Max Theiler (Medicine Prize) in 1951.

② Roughly estimated, about 22 monographs and collections of essays have been published since Teresa Dovey published in 1988 the first work *The Novels of J. M. Coetzee: Lacanian Allegories* and hundreds of research papers can be found in different journals within which 88 papers are found in the important literary journals such as *Critique*, *Contemporary Literature*, *Literature Study*, *Contemporary Poetics*, etc.

literary critic emphasizes, "It would not be an overstatement to say that J. M. Coetzee is one of the most influential novelists of the twentieth and twenty-first centuries..."(Poyner 1).

Coetzee study has become popular in the West today and one of the focal issues in China since the twenty-first century. Critics have studied Coetzee at different levels from multiple perspectives including ideology, psychoanalysis, narratology, etc. However, in the postmodernist and postcolonial context, the study of the Other in Coetzee's novels remains superficial without in-depth or systematic exploration. An intense study from multiple dimensions of the Other in Coetzee's novels with the application of postmodernist and postcolonial theories, will not only help reveal the connotation of the Other in the writing of Coetzee and the relationship between the author and the Other, but also help discover the significance of the images of the Other to the development of the postcolonial theories, the enrichment of the postmodernist theories and the revelation to the literary creation and criticism, and the contribution to world literature from theme to genre.

1. The Issue of the Other and Coetzee's Novels

The issue of the Other is closely connected with the binary opposition structure at the core of Western culture. From the binary opposition structures such as Being/Absence, Subject/Object, West/East, Self/Other, etc., we can see that the world has been divided artificially into two parts, in which one is in the position of subject and authoritativeness while the other in the position of object and subordination. The manifestation of the former's authority depends upon the subordination of the latter. The Other then refers to one different from the self, or the object different from the subject. Philosophically speaking, the Other is the object for the recognition of the self.

The issue of the Other can be traced back to Georg Hegel, the representative of the 18th century speculative philosophy, who, known to have found the philosophical value of the Other earlier than others, usually seeks totality and identity in solving philosophical problems. However, he does not repulse the importance of difference. The identity he pursues is that of difference in the world, thus resulting in the existence of the Other. Hegel begins his study from the master-slave relationship in *The Phenomenology of Mind* (1807) and stresses the importance of the Other for the establishment of the consciousness of the self, maintaining that the authentic self-consciousness lies in between one subject and the other, or between self (subject) and other (object), i. e. the product of so-called intersubjectivity.

The issue of the Other has developed further in the theory of Martin Heidegger, a 20th century German philosopher, who adopts the concept of "being-in-the-world" of Da-sein to interpret the basic connection between "Da-sein" and the world. He uses the unique concept "Being with" to show that the being in the world of Da-sein is that with the Other, claiming that "The world of Da-sein is a with-world" (Heidegger 112). The account of "with-world" relationship between the subject and the Other removes the possibility of solipsism by Edmund Husserl, the philosopher of phenomenology, who establishes the Other on the self through empathy, paving the way for the Other to become part of his philosophy.

Emmanuel Levinas, a French philosopher of Lithuanian Jewish origin, in opposing ontology, makes use of the Other to criticize Western ontological tradition with the intention to surpass it. Without denying the existence of the Other in traditional sense, he merely considers that Other as "relative other", one that can be transformed into identity or self. His philosophy emphasizes that a philosophy of "absolute otherness" is to be established if we want to break identity. He puts forward his concept of the Other, which is "irreversible, something else entirely, the absolutely other"(Levinas 35). He means that the Other should not be retrieved into the self or identity: it may meet with the self, but is totally different from the self. In his opinion, the single will of power the western colonialists, imperialists and capitalists show in their greedy pursuit of capital is the reflection of totality and identity in the real society, and its development to the extreme ends up with violence and war. He points out incisively that "Ontology, as first philosophy is a philosophy of power"(Levinas 46), holding that this is the fundamental cause of the crisis in Western culture.

Jacques Lacan, a French psychoanalyst and psychiatrist, develops Sigmund Freud's Structural Model of Personality (id, ego, superego) in his mirror image theory, holding that the Other and the self are of mutual consequence according to his psychoanalysis through three registers (the Imaginary, the Symbolic and the Real). However, his concept of the Other is quite complicated. In the light of his theory, one certain other may be of the same origin with the subject, or from the collective imagination of many other subjects, or even the certain variant in reality of the ideology. Relatively speaking, his idea of "the Other being non-self" is more practical, which has been widely employed in the interpretation of literary texts.

Karl Marx, a great German philosopher, does not discuss the issue of the Other in explicit terms, but his idea in discussing class consciousness by taking French petty farmers as an example has been popularly quoted in literary discussion.

> They are therefore incapable of asserting their class interest in their own name, whether through a parliament or a convention. They cannot represent themselves, they must be represented. The representation must be at the same time their dominators, the authorities high above them, and the governmental power without limit ("Selections" 677－678).

The word "representation", common in political practice by Elleke Boehmer's account, is at once concerned with the subject of action (self) and the object of action (the Other).

The issue of the Other in literature is closely connected with postmodernist and postcolonial studies. The concept of the Other in postcolonial theory appeared early in Edward Said's book *Orientalism* (1978). In his mind, the East is the Other of Europe and the deep European culture cannot be established without the participation of the East, for, in the binary opposition model of the West and the East, the imagination of the rational, advanced, human and high West needs to be supported by the irrational, backward, barbarous and low East, without which the Western culture can hardly be so brilliant. And the relationship between the West and the East is that of writing and being written. But he revises his opinion in his later book *Culture and Imperialism* (1994),

> What I left out of *Orientalism* was that response to Western dominance which culminated in the great movement of decolonization all across the Third World... Never was it the case that the imperial encounter pitted an active Western intruder against a supine or inert non-western native, there was always some

> form of active resistance, and in the overwhelming majority of cases, the resistance finally won out (Said xii).

This revision highlights the resistance of the Other, with the emphasis on the cultural resistance and the national identity.

Gayatri C. Spivak, the author of the famous essay "Can the Subaltern Speak", has devoted herself even before the publication of Said's *Culture and Imperialism* to the discussion of the voice of the subaltern under the colonial control, maintaining that it is suspicious for the main part of the subaltern to voice because it is difficult to define in accurate terms the oppressed class. And the Western academic background of the members in the Group of Subaltern Study can rarely convince people that they will be authentically on the side of the subaltern. So it is by no means easy to find the real voice of the colonial Other. In her mind, what the Western feminists need to speculate on is the question of the racial Other. In deconstructing the novel *Jane Eyre* by Charlotte Brontë from the perspective of postcolonialism, she holds that the brilliance of Jane Eyre is established upon the repression of Bertha, a sex Other from the colony in the Caribbean.

Homi Bhabha has found the problem of Said's standing, because even if the cultural interpreters feel dissatisfied with the Western authority of discourse, they may still turn a blind eye to the function of the Other if they comment on the issues unconsciously from the Western mono-entity and cultural perspective. As a result, they can hardly see the complexity of the colonial discourse and of course cannot see the possibilities of the anti-colonial discourse. He thinks that the subject of colonizers cannot be formed unilaterally without the colonized as the Other. The absence of the Other as reference will threaten the formation of the colonial subject.

Coetzee's novels are closely related to the issue of the Other, because the author has created group images of the marginalized Other. From the maiden work *Dusklands* (1974) which has allegedly started postmodernist writing in South Africa① to *Waiting for the Barbarians* (1980), "a political thriller in the tradition of Joseph Conrad, in which the idealist's naivety opens the gates to horror" (Engdahl, Press Release, October 2, 2003); from the Booker Prize winner *Life & Times of Michel K* (1983) which has highly developed the allegorical writing, to the novel *Foe* (1986) which Spivak has taken as a specific case for her study of marginalization theory; from *Age of Iron* (1990), a social political novel which improves the genre of dystopia developed by Franz Kafka and H. G. Wells, to *The Master of Petersburg* (1994) which "marks a turning point in Coetzee's career" (Head 72); from the second Booker Prize winner *Disgrace* (1999) which, according to Boehmer, "may well have paved the way for the 2003 award to the writer of the Nobel Prize in Literature" ("Sorry, Sorrier, Sorriest" 135) to *Elizabeth Costello: Eight Lessons* (2003) which has aroused quite a few controversies; from the unusual acceptance speech "He and His Men" at the Nobel Prize Awarding Ceremony to *Diary of a Bad Year* (2007) which gives readers visual impact by technical means, readers can see a mass of images of the Other, and the issue of the Other can hardly be separated from his novels.

Studies show that the Other in Coetzee's novels can be basically decided as the Other defined in postmodernist and postcolonial theories and the idea represented by Boehmer in her book *Colonial and Postcolonial Literature*

① Dominic Head declares that "It is sometimes said that postmodernism arrived in Africa with the publication, in 1974, of *Dusklands*, Coetzee's first novel (although he is frequently discussed as a 'late modernist')" (Head 2009: ix).

(1995) can evidently be taken as reference in interpreting the Other in Coetzee's work: "The concept of the Other, which is built on the thought of, inter allia, Hegal and Sartre, signifies that which is unfamiliar and extraneous to a dominant subjectivity, the opposite or negative against which an authority is defined" (21). Coetzee may purposely create the images of the Other or unconsciously depict the images of the marginalized Other, but one thing is clear: he has created more images of the Other than his contemporaries. What Georg Simmel, German philosopher and critic, states in the book *Georg Simmel on Individuality and Social Forms* (1971) may be more accurate in definition. In his mind, the Other in Coetzee's writings

> is the Stranger who is beyond being far and near. The *Stranger* is an element of the group itself, not unlike the poor and sundry 'inner enemy'— an element whose membership within the group involves both being outside it and confronting it. The West thus conceived of its superiority relative to the perceived lack of power, self-consciousness, or ability to think and rule, of colonized peoples (Simmel 144).

We know that human beings deliberately apply negative features to other groups or individuals and otherize the latter in order to establish their own status of dominant discourse power. People assume that the Other is less complex, advanced or civilized than the self. The activator of otherization often takes the Other as the humble and inferior to get psychological gratification and superiority. The presentation of group images of the Other displays the special feeling of the white intellectuals at the margin of the white South African mythology in the postmodernist context.

The Other in Coetzee's novels is concerned with differences in race, sex, identity, etc. For example, in the mind of the white, the Other is often the colored, and in the account of the male, the Other is generally the female. The Other in the narration of the people with discourse power is surely the one without discourse power. The Other in the speech of Empire's spokesman is always the colonized and the oppressed. Generally speaking, the life of the Other is connected with disorder, laziness, dirtiness, indulgence, folly, evilness, lack of moral responsibility, etc. This demonstrates from the opposite side the civilization, order, education, morality of the dominant subject, just as Frederic Jameson says in the book *The Political Unconscious: Narrative as a Socially Symbolic Act* (1981), "these are some of the archetypal figures of the Other, about whom the essential point to be made is not so much that he is feared because he is evil, rather he is evil because he is Other, alien, different, strange, uncertain and unfamiliar." (115)

Derek Attridge is correct in saying that Coetzee cannot evade politics, society and history ("Age of Bronze" 99), and the group images of the Other are inevitably associated with the real context of South Africa. Nadine Gordimer, another Nobel Prize laureate in South Africa, supports this viewpoint by saying in "Introduction" to the book *Critical Perspectives on J. M. Coetzee* (1996),

> J. M. Coetzee's critics almost all seem awed by his textual innovations which, as one puts it, traverse European literary and philosophical traditions... At the same time, the critics wrestle with whether or not Coetzee's fiction is part of the discourse of colonialism itself, avoiding its stark issues with elegant allegory or whether, indeed, his themes are distilled from that bloody

starkness(viii).

Professor Attridge expresses in unequivocal terms his interpretation of the writing attitude of Coetzee, the creator of group images of the Other.

> Nor should there ever have been any doubt about his strong opposition to the policies and practices of the Nationalist government in power between 1948 and 1994 and the older colonial traditions on which they were built, even though his fiction did not take the form of straightforward "resistance writing" ("Age of Bronze" 99).

The images of the Other in Coetzee's novels are rich in variety, similar in definition with the Other mentioned in Lacan's discourse theory of intersubjectivity, usually referring to the alien, strange, dangerous being present with the absence of discourse power. Coetzee's group images of the Other include the marginalized African colored people in the context of Eurocentrism and white supremacism, e.g. the Vietnamese in the project of Eugene Dawn the thinker and the Bushmen and the Hottentot in the mind of Jacobus Coetzee the actor in *Dusklands* which "was the first example of the capacity for empathy that has enabled Coetzee time and again to creep beneath the skin of the alien and the abhorrent"(Engdahl, Press Release, October 2, 2003), the barbarians in the mind of the military men of Empire in *Waiting for the Barbarians*, the otherized white in the postcolonial context as well, e.g. the old administrator in *Waiting for the Barbarians*, and the white with ideas different from the mainstream ideology, e.g. Elizabeth Costello in the novel *Elizabeth Costello: Eight Lessons*. The images of the

Other can be females who as the Christian Bible provides are in the position of the sex Other[①], e. g. Lucy in the novel *Disgrace* which displays the situation of the white "in the new circumstances that have arisen in South Africa after the collapse of white supremacy" (Engdahl, Press Release, October 2, 2003) and can also be the males who, with no longer the advantageous position to do what they will randomly after their loss of dominant discourse power, refuses to repent, e. g. Lurie the associate professor in *Disgrace*. And group images of the Other cover the displaced ones who, at the bottom of the society, keep moving about silently in the war-scarred South Africa, e. g. Michel K in the novel *Life and Times of Michel K*, and the otherized ones who have lost their discourse power by their determination not to be the accomplice of those with dominant discourse power in the era of colonial hegemony, e. g. the old administrator in *Waiting for the Barbarians*. Among group images of the Other, we can find marginalized human beings trampled down and maltreated, and the ill-fated animals even killed meaninglessly, only to cite a few. In consideration of Coetzee's oeuvres which have been accomplished in and after the notorious apartheid, or in the period of apartheid or post-apartheid era, the images of the Other can hardly be separated from the origin of history and social involvement, and can rarely be disconnected with the cruel reality in South Africa. The living condition and the irresistible fate of the group of the marginalized Other occupy an important position in Coetzee's novels.

2. Critical Review of the Other in Coetzee's Novels

As is mentioned above, the academia has not yet paid due attention to

① Genesis 2: 22 The Lord God fashioned into a woman the rib which He had taken from the man, and brought her to the man.

the group images of the Other, nor can we find systematic research or monographs on them, but, "Coetzee in the last decade and a half has attracted from critics more attention by far than any other author from this country, attention that predates his receiving the 2003 Nobel Prize in Literature" (Chapman 10). And critics have achieved a great deal from Coetzee's novels based on their academic researches. By adopting different strategies in interpreting Coetzee, critics can hardly avoid the interpretation of the marginalized characters on certain aspects. Their interpretations may reach different conclusions from different theoretical perspectives, but they have sure relations with the Other to varying degrees, providing beneficial reference to the study of the Other and the interpretation of the group images of the Other.

A study of the academic materials has shown that critics usually focus on the writing context, special identity and extraordinary experiences of the author[①]. For instance, Gayatri Spivak, the representative postcolonial theorist, has expressed her own concern about the experiences of the people in former colonies and the fate of the marginalized Other in her study of Coetzee's novel *Foe*. By combining the feature of intertextuality in Coetzee's novels into her study, Spivak has made a comparison between the marginalized male and female characters in the first 18th century images, concluding that both Friday and Susan Barton are typical marginalized

① Coetzee was born in South Africa of Dutch descent and educated in English in the conflict of the black and the white in South Africa. After his graduation from the University of Cape Town, he went to work as a computer processor in the United Kingdom of Great Britain before his PhD study in the University of Texas at Austin, USA. He worked as a literature teacher at the State University of New York at Buffalo and his application for permanent residence in the United States was denied due to his involvement in anti-Vietnam-war protest. He was obliged to return to South Africa where he taught literature at the University of Cape Town. His growth experiences have endowed him with feelings of marginalization and alienation.

characters. The former is marginalized because he is colored by race and his loss of tongue deprives him of the right to speak, while the latter is otherized because of her sex, losing her authority in discourse. This opinion in effect serves as a critical supplement to the idea of Derek Attridge demonstrated in his article "The Silence of the Canon: J. M. Coetzee's *Foe*, Cultural Narrative, and Political Oppression". Spivak feels that the intertexuality Coetzee adopts with Daniel Defoe's novel *The Adventures of Robinson Crusoe*(1719) shows that "He is involved in a historically implausible but politically provocative revision"(9). And this revision inevitably leaves traces of the time. Though she does not discuss specifically the issue of the Other, her study of the theory of marginalization and her discussion of the identity and fate of the characters in Coetzee's *Foe* broaden the horizon of readers, providing references for this research project in systematically studying the images of the Other. The opinion of Scott Bishop in discussing the issue of identity supports that of Spivak. He observes an overall progression of political commitment in Coetzee's writing: "The movement of the characters from their prototypes to their culmination in Susan and Friday shows that Coetzee's concern for political identity becomes increasingly evident throughout the course of the work."(Bishop 56) This concern for identity can hardly be commented as out of so-called identity complex, but it at least originates from the breakage of identification, which can be studied further by referring to W. E. B. Du Bois' cultural identity.

Professor Stephen Waston from the University of Cape Town, one of the major researchers on J. M. Coetzee, is also related to the issue of the marginalized, but his study is usually done from the perspective of postcolonialism. By placing Coetzee's work into postcolonial context, he explores the influence of colonialism upon his literary writing. Though he holds the idea in discussing the novel *Dusklands* that "Never before had a South African novel broken so obviously even self-consciously with the conventions of realism and so candidly announced its own artificiality, its own fictionality" (371), Waston realizes that Coetzee's work cannot be separated from the colonial reality in South Africa or the influence of Europe he knows from his own experiences, nor be free from his hybrid identity of Afrikaans. He has cited Coetzee's speech in an interview to support his own opinion: "I'm suspicious of lines of division between a European context and a South African context, because I think our experience remains largely colonial." (Waston 376) In this context, the Westerners treat the locals in South Africa in a superior way as colonizers, taking it for granted that the latter are the marginalized Other. Here, Waston maintains, "Just as Western people conquer nature in an effort to conquer their own self-division, so they cannot desist from enslaving other human beings who necessarily confront them as that Other, alien and forever threatening." (ibid) He intentionally cites the metaphorical discourse of gun in Coetzee's work for a further proof of his idea: "It is my life's work, my incessant proclamation of the otherness of the dead and therefore the otherness of life." (Waston 373) Such discourse of power politics, in defending the colonizers, exposes the author's emphatic concern for the hegemony of the colonizers, the power discourse and identity. And this concern may precisely provide references for this project to study the issue of the Other from a different perspective.

Elleke Boehmer①, "with a reputation as a commentator on experiences

① Elleke Boehmer, a female scholar and writer born in South Africa, is now a professor in Oxford University. Her important works include *Colonial and Postcolonial Literature: Migrant Metaphors* (1995), *J.M. Coetzee in Context and Theory* (2009) and *Empire Writing: An Anthology of Colonial Literature 1870 - 1918* (1998).

of social alienation and split belonging"("Australian Realism" 3), does not study specifically the issue of the Other either. Her major concern is "about paying for the past in South Africa, and so about the ethical status and epistemological limitations of secular confession"(Boehmer, "Sorry, Sorrier, Sorriest" 139). However, in her discussion, she naturally touches upon the present situation of the otherized, the former colonized people, and the relocation of the identity of different peoples in the post-apartheid era. Taking as background what the "South African Truth and Reconciliation Commission" has done in the 1990s to cure the historical trauma of the country, she explores the issue of whether the abusers repent and the abused forgive by employing as a case study the protagonist's refusal to apologize for his abuse of power. In her mind, "Coetzee has openly cast doubt on the possibility of achieving closure on a painful past, of ever adequately saying sorry."("Not Saying Sorry" 343) And she finds that "he proposes the far more painful process of enduring rather than transcending the degraded present."(ibid) Her study further shows that "the primary other in the alternative ethical schema explored in *Disgrace* is not human, not the historically degraded human, but the 'wholly other' or the extreme alterity of the stray dog" (Boehmer, "Sorry, Sorrier, Sorriest" 138). Although she herself feels this viewpoint controversial and even a little far-fetched, yet what is noteworthy is that she has categorized the Other into two distinct sorts: one is the above-mentioned racial Other and the other is "conventional other, the silenced woman: most obviously Lucy but also the abused Melanie"(ibid). Her thesis focuses on the trauma the white's evildoing and the black's tit-for-tat violence against violence have brought to the country in the apartheid, with only a touch on the issue of the Other without any further discussion, thus leaving a potential opportunity for an in-depth study.

David Attwell[①] also shows concern for the cultural identity and creative context in his research on Coetzee, but his study tends to discuss the relationship between the author and South Africa. In his study of South Africa and the politics of writing, he finds that

> Coetzee writes within a Western European tradition. This is a simple fact of his intellectual biography, a consequence not only of the global distribution of culture under colonialism but also of Coetzee's turning like thousands of other South Africans before and after him to the metropolis of Western culture for a better life and further education ... (Attwell, "J. M. Coetzee" 232).

This kind of writing has actually made Coetzee confronted with the dilemma of identity. "In South Africa ... Coetzee writes not as a citizen of the First World but of the Third or perhaps the First within the Third and therefore, like other white South African writers, he faces the problem of cultural authority." (ibid) He cannot represent the West because of his Afrikaans background, nor can he stand for South Africa due to his assimilation of Western culture. This objectively causes his marginalization in South Africa. In the thesis "Coetzee's Estrangements", Attwell continues to discuss the issue of relationship, holding that "Nearly all of Coetzee's fiction deals in one way or another with subjects who reluctantly find themselves forced to

① David Attwell is a professor of literature in the University of York, UK., long engaged in the study of South African literature. Important works include *J. M. Coetzee: South Africa and the Politics of Writing* (1993) and *Doubling the Point: Essays and Interviews* (1992), providing important and authoritative references from different perspectives for the study of J. M. Coetzee.

engage with a particular historical situation"(232). Thus, any estrangement from the society and history is in Attwell's mind an inevitable result, for he considers that experimental writing of modernism and postmodernism does not have to be subject to the issue of ethics today. However, Attwell does not continue to discuss whether the result of estrangement is caused by passive marginalization or by active otherization. This offers a space for further research in the study of the Other.

Michel Chapman① points out in his thesis "The Case of Coetzee: South African Literary Criticism, 1990 to Today" that "Coetzee's output escapes any overarching interpretative grid"(104), but he still tries to find out tactics which he thinks effective in decoding South African criticism through the case of Coetzee. He discusses the issue of the Other in his study, thinking that the Other in Coetzee's writing should be similar in meaning to the Other in Emmanuel Levinas' concept. "Unlike Memmi's 'colonizer who will' or the 'colonizer who won't', Coetzee subscribes to Levinasian ethics: the Same is obliged to acknowledge the singularity, the irreducibility, of the Other"(Chapman 105 - 106). He continues to interpret the "colonizer who will" as the apartheid racist who excludes the Other from the human community and the "colonizer who won't" as the liberal humanist who wishes to turn the Other into an image of the Self, or the Same. This interpretation has something similar with that of Mike Marais, who wrote a series of articles② to demonstrate the relationship between J. M. Coetzee and

---

① Michel Chapman is a professor of literature at the University of KwaZulu - Natal, Durban, South Africa. His important works include *Southern African Literatures* (2003), *Art Talk*, *Politics Talk* (2006), etc.

② "Who Clipped the Hollyhocks?": J.M. Coetzee's *Age of Iron* and the Politics of Representation. *English in Africa* 20. 2 (1993): 1 - 24; Writing with Eyes Shut: Ethics, Politics, and the Problem of the Other in the Fiction of J.M. Coetzee. *English in Africa* 25.1 (1998): 43 - 60; After the Death of a Certain God: A Case of Levinasian Ethics. *Scrutiny 2* 8. 1 (2003): 27 - 33; The Novel as Ethical Command: J.M. Coetzee's *Foe*. *Journal of Literary Studies* 16.2 (2006): 62 - 85.

Emmanuel Levinas. Nevertheless, Chapman does not agree with Marais' idea about Levinas, thinking that the adoption of the philosophical idea of Levinas to defend Coetzee's ethical responsibility "is not only misguided, but largely unnecessary. Misguided because Coetzee's novels, if not about the Same, are also not in any absolute sense about the Other"(Chapman 107). Of course, he does not illustrate it any further for his focus is not the issue of the Other, but a critical account of the literary criticism in South Africa after the abolition of the apartheid, and Coetzee's writing is taken only as a sample. Besides, when referring to Coetzee's fiction, he mainly cites examples from *Age of Iron*, and occasionally from *Disgrace*, thinking that "'alterity', or otherness [is] actually located in a social context" (ibid). In reality, Chapman has introduced the theory of sociology into Coetzee study.

It is observed from Chapman's comment that Mike Marais is a researcher greatly concerned with the Other in Coetzee's writing. In his thesis "Writing with Eyes Shut: Ethics, Politics, and the Problem of the Other in the Fiction of J.M. Coetzee", he studies the problem of the Other by making a comparison between the ethical ideas of Rosemary Jane Jolly and the political ideas of Sue Kossew. Marais maintains that Jolly develops her argument by "contending that Coetzee, in *Foe*, 'specifies' and 'embodies' the Other"(45), while Kossew insists that Coetzee's writing cannot be separated from politics. In effect, Marais takes it partial whether to emphasize ethics or to focus on politics. By adopting a middle-of-the-road approach to this issue, he synthesizes the opinions of the two scholars, suggesting that the academia should not illustrate Coetzee's fictional project in purely political terms, or interpret the author's writing as an attempt to give voice to the Other. The way of interpretation he proposes is to take his writing as a refusal in ethical terms. "Through this refusal... Coetzee attempts to establish a relation with the Other as other outside history." (Marais 45) The conclusion he reaches is that "For Coetzee, politics begins as ethics. Unlike postcolonial modes of writing which emphasize resistance, his fiction attempts to oppose without resisting"(ibid). Anyhow, such kind of eclectic idea leaves critics space for debate.

English scholar Derek Attridge seems to have different opinions with Marais on this issue and his understanding of the Other obviously bears political instead of ethical feature. In his mind, "Figures of alterity recur in these novels, usually as subordinate third-world individuals or groups perceived from the point of view of a dominant, first world culture..." (Attridge, "Literary Form" 249). To reinforce his idea, he lists the Vietnam enemy and the native South Africans in *Dusklands*, Friday in *Foe*, Vercueil in *Age of Iron* as instances of the figures of alterity. He does not make any specific discussion of the issue of the Other, but his idea of the figures of alterity can provide important references for the study in this research project.

The opinions of Sue Kossew, a female Australian scholar, as mentioned above, support effectively Derek Attridge's idea though they are not accepted by Mike Marais who points out that Kossew tends to study the political nature in literary work. By borrowing the concept of Bill Ashcroft about postcolonialism, Kossew uses the term "postcolonial" not to signify a time after colonialism, but rather "to cover all the culture affected by the imperial process from the moment of colonization to the present day"("Pen and Power" 1), exploring the contradictions and paradoxes hidden in colonial and postcolonial discourse and the politics of presentation. Her knowledge of the self and the Other is usually related to colonialism and she deems the feature of post-apartheid era as "the overturning of the old structures of repression and the release of hitherto often-silenced black voices"(ibid). In her mind, the Other is the colonized and the one who sympathizes with the colonized. After a comparative study between Coetzee's *Waiting for the Barbarians* and Brink's *A Dry White Season*, Kossew points out that Brink's novel arranges a narrator involved in the life of the Other (usu. represented by black South Africans), while

> Coetzee's novel explores the moral, political and personal dilemma facing a colonizer, the Magistrate, who himself becomes labeled as "other" and as "the enemy within" because of his resistance to the fixity of imperial discourse and practices, as shown in his crossing of the boundary (both literally and metaphorically) drawn between the Empire and the barbarian Others ("Pen and Power" 86).

The approaches Kossew uses in studying and interpreting the contradictions and paradoxes related to colonization and its representation are of great value in reference, however, her study of the Other is still limited and further efforts are expected.

Compared with the studies abroad, Coetzee study in China started a little late. The paper "The Cost of Cronus: An Interpretation of Coetzee's Booker Prize-winning Novel *Disgrace*"① is often taken as one of the valuable research achievements in the early Coetzee study. Zhejiang Literature and Art Press rapidly published a series of Coetzee's fiction after the Nobel Prize in Literature was officially declared in 2003. The Chinese versions are by no means perfect, but they set a solid foundation for the propagation and

① The paper was co-authored by Zhang Chong and Guo Zhengfeng and published in the fifth issue of *Foreign Literature* in 2001.

research of Coetzee's work. Internet statistics show that seven books have been published since *Foreigner Forever*①. The first book on Coetzee appeared in 2006 and three② of the books have been openly published. China National Knowledge Internet (CNKI) statistics show that from 2001 till now, more than 400 papers on Coetzee study have been published. The major journals which specialize in foreign literature study have made greater contributions to the study of Coetzee③. A critical survey of the papers in these journals indicates that the Coetzee study in China is still limited from theme discussion to text study and to the study of narrative approaches. Most theme discussions often focus on topics related to the postcolonial and the post-apartheid, including imperial ideals, free speech and writing on trauma, besides confession, forgiveness, reconciliation in the post-apartheid era; text study mainly concerns *Disgrace*, *Life and Times of Michel K*, etc. And discourse analysis usually takes *Diary of a Bad Year* and *Foe* as samples. The flaws of present study appear obvious: some apply mechanically relevant theories to the interpretation of Coetzee's fiction, some take Coetzee's fiction as cases to illustrate certain theories which are no longer new, some even parrot Westerners' research achievements. In demonstrating the theoretical cultivation of the authors, the research papers do not leave readers much impression of revelation, but an impression that any other case will help the authors of the papers to reach their purpose equally well.

Not many domestic scholars study the issue of the Other. Among the

① Wang Jinghui's PhD book at Beijing Languages University in 2006.

② Gao Wenhui's *Coetzee in the Postcolonial Cultural Context* (2008), Wang Jinghui's *Foreigner Forever* (2010) and Duan Feng's *Challenger to Historical Discourse* (2011).

③ Till June 2012, CNKI statistics show that *Foreign Literature* and *Contemporary Foreign Literature* publish 10 papers on Coetzee respectively, *Foreign Literature Study* publishes 8 papers of the kind and *Foreign Literature Criticism* publishes 6 papers on Coetzee.

limited research achievements, Gao Wenhui's paper "Colonizer's Self and Colonial Other: a Philosophical Reflection upon Master-slave Relationship", by cleverly making use of Kossew's topic "Colonizer/Colonized: Paradoxes of Self and Other", discusses the interdependence and inseparableness of the colonizer's self and the colonial Other in the South African cultural context. By discussing the replication of the colonizer's self and the imagined colonial Other, the author finds that Coetzee has analyzed the transformation of the subjectivity of the Other produced by the condescending colonizer from the one-way perspective, "revealing that the features of both the colonizer's self and the colonial Other are out of the control of power and the discourse construction, with its target against the philosophical foundation of colonial discourse" (Gao 85). The paper does not make enough "philosophical reflections" upon "master-slave" relation, while her discussion of the Other is evidently influenced by Kossew and her conclusion seems similar with that of Attridge. Zhou Li's thesis "On the Other under the Veil of Repetition in Coetzee's Work" appears to discuss mainly the issue of the Other from the topic, but in reality the author pays more attention to the discussion of "repetition", and the definition of the Other seems a little bit chaotic. Li Jing's English paper "Dogs, Women, and the Significant Otherness in J. M. Coetzee's *Disgrace*" takes dogs and women as the Other, maintaining that "Coetzee, ... [by] seemingly simple treatment of dogs and women as objects of subordination and abuse, exposes the complexity and multiplicity of existence for late-apartheid South Africa" (212). It is justified to say that this topic is of some significance, but the small space of the paper limits its further study.

It is seen from the materials presented above that the research achievements are rich and abundant abroad, but no systematic study of the issue of the Other has been found up to now, while the study in China seems to be in a starting period, without many achievements for display. It is safe to say that except the achievements of this project[①], no researchers have ever made a systematic analysis of Coetzee from the perspective of the Other. No one classifies the images of the Other in Coetzee's fiction, or studies the performance of the Other in different contexts, or explores how Coetzee reflects on civilization, justice, Empire, instrumental rationality, etc. by presenting the images of the Other. No scholar has systematically studied the intention of Coetzee in creating the images of the Other or made in-depth exploration of otherizing characters. No one has given a rational interpretation of his fiction of alterity, the otherization of characters or the self-otherization of the author.

3. Research Ideas and Framework of the Book

This book chooses for the research four important novels of J. M. Coetzee: *Waiting for the Barbarians*, *Life and Times of Michel K*, *Disgrace* and *Elizabeth Costello: Eight Lessons*. With the intention to make a panoramic study of the Other in Coetzee's novels, it will discuss the above novels from multiple dimensions. From colonial, post-Christian, post-apartheid and postmodernist dimensions respectively, the book will display the representation of the Other in Coetzee's literary texts, reveal the connotation of the Other and the implication of group images of the Other, explore the historical origin of the Other and its relationship with the reality,

① The achievements of this project have been partly published, including "J. M. Coetzee: A Spokesman of the Otherized Other" (2011), "The Other and Otherness: a Study of Coetzee" (2011), "*Diary of a Bad Year*: a Unique Postmodern Polyphonic Novel" (2012), "*Disgrace*: the Subverted Other in the Post-apartheid Era" (2012), etc.

probe into the reasons of Coetzee's preference for group images of the Other and study his philosophical reflections. The major theories involved in this research project include postcolonial theories and the theory of the Other by Jacques Lacan. And the theories involved in the process of demonstration are new historicism of Hayden White, power and discourse theory of Michel Foucault, trauma theory of Judith Lewis Herman, psychoanalytical theory of Sigmund Freud, feminist theory of Simone de Beauvoir, polyphonic novel theory of Mikhail Bakhtin and related theories of narratology.

This book maintains that the English education J. M. Coetzee received as Afrikaans, his experiences in seeking for his European roots in the UK, his estranged feeling in the "free" USA, his spiritual wandering after his compelled return to South Africa, and his reflections after his migration to Australia, have shaped his peculiarity of a writer otherized by the West. By revealing the themes of hegemony and violence, repression of human rights, negative influence of religious belief, Coetzee levels his criticism as the Other at the cruel rationalism and cosmetic morality of Western civilization. His allegorical presentation of the relationship between macro-history and micro-history, between human being and history, between reality and history shows the Other's deconstruction of historical authority and its ideological basis. The unconventional experiment in his work demonstrates a clear feature of otherness.

The book discusses the issue of the Other in four chapters:

The first chapter discusses from the dimension of colonial hegemony Coetzee's *Waiting for the Barbarians* with the application of the theories of postcolonialism and the Other. An examination of the story setting reveals that the author has adopted in the novel the virtual form of Empire, disclosing the nature of imperial civilization in the era of the colonial hegemony. Coetzee displays allegorically the hegemony of the Empire. Placed on the opposite are barbarians in the remote area, an imaginary enemy or the Other to the Empire. By arranging the racial Other for the dominant Empire and exhibiting the sufferings of the Other, Coetzee reveals the nature of the dominators of discourse power. By presenting the situation of the racial females, Coetzee illustrates the sex Other suffering from dual oppression in the patriarchal society in imperial civilization. What is more, Coetzee has arranged the marginalization or otherization of the narrator or the spokesman in the novel, endowing him with an identity of dual Other: a marginalized Other to Empire and a non-natural Other to “barbarians”.

Then with the application of new historicism by Hayden White, this chapter examines the qualification of the history recorder, finding that the narrator has an equivocal relation with Empire. He insists on resistance to imperial sense, acting as the alien or the Other to Empire, but at the same time cooperates and conspires reluctantly with Empire, behaving as the alien or the Other to nature. Coetzee, by making use of the query of the marginalized Magistrate, decodes the complicity of laws and imperial politics. The death of the old man as the Other after great tortures is used as a case for the exposure of the history which is unilaterally presented, distorted and fabricated by the dominant discourse power before it is endowed with historical legality. The author, taking the wooden slips unearthed as example, explains that the interpretation of history is an intellectual operation in specific historical discourse, usually ending up with different results from different interpreters.

This chapter goes on, according to the definition of John Lechte on justice with reference to the opinions of Thomas Hobbes and John Locke on the issue, to study the dispassionate observation and personal experiences of the narrator in Coetzee's writing, intending to find the nature of the imperial "justice". In order to maintain its order of government, the virtual Empire, making use of the "justice" institution in the control of the state, represses by brutal and inhuman means the Other in inconformity with imperial interests. Hegemonic domination and violent politics result in injustice and inhumanity. Coetzee, by exploiting the physical tortures the old Administrator suffers after being rudely taken as the alienated Other to Empire, challenges the authoritative imperial discourse while exposing the evildoings of the inhuman imperial victimizers.

The second chapter discusses Coetzee's novel *Life and Times of Michel K* from the dimension of post-Christian authoritarianism. In accordance with Friedrich Nietzsche's claim that God is dead, it first makes an observation of the situation in South Africa and the scenes of violent conflicts in so-called post-Christian era when Christianity declines and the Christian ideals have been attenuated, before a further study of the images of the Other in the violent society in Coetzee's novel. Here are Anna in unknown fear all day long, and Michel K, the otherized for his inborn harelip and mental deficiency.

This chapter then discusses by adopting Michel Foucault's theory of discourse power "silence", "a sign of disenfranchisement as well as resistance"(Head, "J.M. Coetzee" 98), the apparently passive but effective coping strategy the marginalized Other takes in his escape from the chaotic society where the policies of apartheid were formed and enforced in a rampant way. The chapter mainly explores the implication in discourse and mental activities of the Other's silence on different occasions, such as on Visagie farm, in police station and resettlement camps, and discusses the Other's refusal of discourse and his resistant physical response to food. These measures demonstrate the resistance of the humble Other to the dominant discourse power and display dumbly the ideal of freedom human beings persistently seek for.

With reference to theories of trauma and discourse power, the chapter discusses Coetzee's reflections on trauma, history, power, discipline, etc. The resistance of Michel K the humble Other to the dominant discourse power in his unique way of silence demonstrates that the author, in revealing the inhuman violence, ruthless separation, indelible hostility and self-deceiving ignorance in human society, discloses the nature of rational justice in Western civilization and criticizes its moral ethics. He speaks out of a sense of justice for the oppressed and down-trodden, the marginalized Other. His reflections on the trauma of the South Africans, the oppressive history of South Africa, discourse power, discipline and punishment show his great sympathy for the weak and his resistance to authoritarianism.

The third chapter studies Coetzee's second Booker Prize-winning novel *Disgrace* from the dimension of the post-apartheid power-shift. The black/white relationship, especially the changes between the black and the white in the post-apartheid era, reveals that the enforcement of democratic system does not eliminate the long existing contradictions and conflicts among different races in South Africa, and the annulment of apartheid does not remove the racial separation in people's mind. The black and the white have actually not realized the policy of diversity and tolerance, and the political domain in South Africa is clearly divided among the black and the white. The difference is that the white in new South Africa is marginalized or otherized.

With the support from the theory of discourse power and the theory of feminism, the chapter discusses the fate of the white minority represented by

Lurie, Lucy, etc. after their loss of protection by favorable policies and regulations. Lurie's persistence in behaving in the former ways after the white have lost their discourse power and his refusal to repent after the exposure of the scandal make him pay heavy price of constantly being otherized before his own final conscious marginalization and retreat from the city to the remote farm. And Lucy, the white woman of independence with a strong sense of self-domination, knowing that the advantageous position no longer exists for the white in the post-apartheid era, chooses after being gang-raped to face the reality and sensibly accept compromise, displaying Coetzee's idea of forgiveness or tolerance for the fusion of different races today.

The last section of this chapter, with reference to capitalist contract principle, Bataille's concept of "desirous body" and Friedrich Nietzsche's "will-to-power", investigates the inescapable fate of self-exile and self-otherization of the white once with dominant discourse power, for they have not realized the conflict between their instinctive sexual desire and the moral and sex ethics of human beings, nor have they adapted themselves to the new situation when the preferential laws and regulations in maintaining the white's hegemonic discourse have come to perpetual expiration. Coetzee reflects on the sex ethics and human morality by employing as example the experiences of Lurie who has been deprived of prerogatives in the post-apartheid era and become the Other in the changed era. He speculates on the price the Otherized white should pay and the responsibility they should take for the historical memory by using as a case study the event that Lucy was robbed and gang-raped. Coetzee, with the idea that the black and the white in South Africa should be in harmonious co-existence, suggests forgiveness and reconciliation among different races in order to live peacefully together, and conveys his idea of equal species and harmonious nature through the transformation of the white's perception of animals.

The fourth chapter discusses from the dimension of the postmodernist discourse the apparently disputable novel *Elizabeth Costello*: *Eight Lessons*. A brief comparison of modernism and postmodernism reveals the major features of literature in the postmodernist context — decentralization, subversion of the subject, play of meaning, negation of integrality, determinacy and standardability by taking as example Joseph Heller's *Catch-22*, Italo Calvino's *Cosmicomics*, and the writings of Gabriel Marquez, Donald Barthelme, etc.

Then the chapter examines how Coetzee becomes known with his differential otherness in the representation crisis of the postmodernist context. Deeply influenced by French structuralism, Samuel Beckett's theory of the absurd, Vladimir Propp's morphology of the folktale and inter-textual novel of Vladimir Nabokov, Coetzee has demonstrated in his novels individuality and otherness, which sometimes appears as a collage of irrelevant texts, showing the feature of metafiction, and sometimes as a fragmental soliloquy of the mind, constructing the psychological fantasy of a solitary Other. Sometimes he adopts the Kafkaesque way to show the disordered spiritual life, and sometimes he takes parody to hint obliquely at the Western classics. Sometimes he adopts the form of polyphonic novel, forming multiple relations of discourse with the author, and sometimes he decodes the mode of linear narration, displaying boundless openness, diversity and relativity.

The chapter focuses on the study of the heroine in the novel *Elizabeth Costello*: *Eight Lessons* published after his migration to Australia, intending to explore the concrete image of the differential Other based on the author's idea of the character, and to reveal the heroine's idea of literature, the significance of Coetzee's design of the heroine's performance before the dominant mainstream discourse. The chapter holds that the image of the heroine displays the true color of the differential Other in the process of gaze and being gazed at and in the different relationship of discourse. Grotesque and strange as her behavior and personality appear to be, she becomes the differential Other because of her inobservance of the established rules and regulations of the authoritative discourse, or her constant query on the traditional mainstream discourse. Never chiming in with the established concepts in different problems, she always declares her ideas independently. The author uses this kind of image of the Other in order to illustrate his knowledge of literature faith, literature pattern, nature of novel, literary reception, regional literature and literature language, etc. Coetzee demonstrates the differential otherness of Elizabeth through the comparative lectures of African writers in the novel, the argumentative dialogues between her and the professor of philosophy, and the silence of West, the novelist.

This book concludes that a study of the Other in Coetzee's fiction from multiple dimensions, in displaying different forms, different attributes and different connotation of group images of the Other, provides readers with a panoramic picture of the Other in his fiction and enlarges the dimensions of Coetzee study. The research achievements will not only enrich the postcolonial and postmodernist theories, but also provide references for the exploration of the development of global literature.

Chapter I

Waiting for the Barbarians: the Marginalized Other in the Era of Colonial Hegemony

J. M. Coetzee's *Waiting for the Barbarians* (1980) is an internationally acclaimed novel which wins James Tait Black Memorial Prize and Geoffrey Faber Memorial Prize. In the form of postmodern political allegory, Coetzee tells an "ahistorical" story with no determination of time and space or distinction between past and future, "often leave [leaving] open the possibility of different interpretations"(Canepari-Labib 15).

Critics have varied responses to Coetzee's unique and unparalleled allegorical writing. Gabriel Garcia Marquez, the author of *One Hundred Years of Solitude* (1967), read through the English, Italian and Spanish versions of the novel at one go and couldn't help calling the dramatist Michel Fitzgerald in excitement, commenting it as "one of the great achievements in fiction"(Fitzgerald 24). Some critics compare this novel with *Waiting for Godot* (1948) by Samuel Beckett; others link it to *The Tartar Steppe* (1940) by Italian novelist Dino Buzzati. Some Marxist-sympathetic critics accuse

Coetzee of "being politically evasive"(Chapman 58), while others argue that the novel has strong political implications, becoming a "historical epitome of racial and national conflicts" (Han 68). Some scholars, in probing into Coetzee's deliberately solitary lifestyle, contend that the allegorical writing style should be attributed to his reluctance to be involved in the social realities in South Africa.[①] Some critics point out that Coetzee aims at accomplishing "the deconstruction of realism" and his allegorical writing "is evidently intended ... as an act of decolonialization"(Watson, "Colonialism and the Novels" 18). Others, however, suggest "a nonallegorical reading" of the novel (Attridge, "Against Allegory" 67).

This chapter argues that Coetzee employs a virtual Empire to expose the nature of imperial civilization, and to display the wretched situation of the racial Other, sex Other and identity Other in the era of colonial hegemony. More importantly, the author makes use of the marginalized Other who used to represent the interests of Empire to observe and speculate on the grim reality as the first-person narrator from a different perspective with a different standpoint. The speculations, demonstrated sometimes through soliloquy, sometimes through seemingly objective comment and sometimes through subjective narration, focus upon the subjects of history, justice, civilization and humanity, reflecting the novelist's philosophical thinking about the above topics, exposing the masked truth in the era of colonial hegemony and revealing the author's yearning for equality, justice and freedom by means of the dreams of the protagonist.

---

① This can be observed in the following sources: 1) Whiteson, Leon. Bad Dream and Murky Motives, *Canadian Forum* 10 (1982): 26 - 27. 2) Howe, Irving. Waiting for the Barbarians. *New York Times Book Review* 18 April 1982: 36. 3) Gordimer, Nadine. The Idea of Gardening. *The New York Review of Books* 2 February 1984: 1 - 2.

1. Era of Colonial Hegemony

As is mentioned above, Coetzee employs in *Waiting for the Barbarians* a kind of writing style which Teresa Dovey calls as "allegory of allegories" ("Allegory of Allegories" 138). This kind of writing, which deliberately blurs the setting of the novel, is ascribed to the strict censorship in South Africa. Just as a South African writer says, "Censorship imposed itself on simply in the banning of books, but in the creation of a climate of fear, suspicion and insecurity"(Brink 46). Coetzee also mentioned personally that

> Having lived through the heyday of South African censorship, seen its consequences not only on the careers of fellow-writers but on the totality of public discourse, and felt within myself some of its more secret and shameful effects, I have every reason to suspect that whatever infected Arenas or Mangakis or Kis, whether real or delusional, has infected me too ("Giving Offense" 37).

The background for the events that occur in the novel is obscure, characterized with "timeless, spaceless, nameless, universal"(Levin 44), offering many a possibility of narrative implications for researchers to explore.

The time setting is of much importance for the interpretation of the story and different deciphering strategies taken by various researchers may result in different conclusions. In the course of decoding, some scholar defines the setting flatly as "the last years of the Empire — the old Empire" (Gao, "Discourse Analysis" 41). It is true that Coetzee mentions 43 times the word "empire", which proves unmistakably significant in his mind.

However, no evidence is found in the novel to support that the story happens definitely in the old Empire and the research fails to offer convincing evidences, either. Virtually, the only place where Coetzee mentions the old Empire is on page 150. Colonel Joll, spokesman of the virtual Empire, takes brutal measures to force the old Magistrate to confess his guilt of collaboration with barbarians and to admit that wooden slips are the tools through which they exchange messages. In deciphering the wooden slips, the old Magistrate mentions that "they can be ... read as a history of the last years of the Empire - the old Empire".① In effect, it is unmistakable that "the old Empire" here indicates the time when the wooden slips were made rather than the time when the story happens. Some scholar mentions the background of the novel's publication in decoding the intentions of Coetzee's allegorical writing, arguing that Coetzee employs this writing style to present his reflection upon imperial hegemony for the novel came out in the context of the publication of *Orientalism* (1978) which, "theoretically based upon the concepts such as 'cultural hegemony' by Antonio Gramsci and 'power' and 'discourse' by Michel Foucault," stimulates "a radical transformation in terms of the research in the world-wide academia (both the East and the West)" (J.H. Wang 153).

David Attwell, a prominent scholar in South African literature research, finds after some exploration into South Africa and the politics of writing that "Coetzee's Empire represents a continuation of the frontier hypothesis in colonial thinking since the eighteenth century, but specific features connect it to South Africa of the period when the novel was

① This is quoted from page 122 of J.M. Coetzee's *Waiting for the Barbarians* published by Vintage Books in London in 2004. Further references to this edition will be indicated by quoting page numbers in parenthesis.

written", concluding that "Coetzee's Empire is a parody of the apartheid regime, in its paranoia and attempted control of history"("J. M. Coetzee" 73). As a matter of fact, the novel was written and published in the period when the apartheid (1948 - 1994) was rampant before its decline and it is no surprise for Dominic Head to think that "it is impossible not to agree with David Attwell" ("Cambridge Introduction" 50). In an interview in 1978, Coetzee remarked that he was inclined "to see the South African situation [today] as only one manifestation of a wider historical situation to do with colonialism, late colonialism, neo-colonialism" (Watson, "Colonialism and the novels" 13). Stephen Watson explicitly expresses his ideas about the novel that "*Waiting for the Barbarians*, to my mind Coetzee's finest novel to date, is a novel of an imaginary empire, of an imperialism which is merely an extension of colonization"(ibid 14). This chapter tends to put aside the discussion of the highly disputable and obscure setting, and shed light on the real intention of Coetzee's application of allegorical writing from the dimension of colonial hegemony by referring to the grand historical context.

It is observed from the novel that Coetzee has taken the allegorical Empire as a symbol of dominant discourse and revealed the truth through dialogues among characters that colonialists invaded the land before gradually obtaining hegemony — the virtual Empire center is far away but incessantly expanding: "We have been here more than a hundred years, we have reclaimed land from the desert and built irrigation works and planted fields and built solid homes and put a wall around our town..." (55). This is a typical process of colonial expansion to obtain hegemony. According to the colonialists' logic, the occupied land has naturally become "part of our Empire" (ibid). How the land was violently and inexorably usurped is obliterated from historical memories. They overlook the deterioration of the environment: the sweet spring water becomes sour and bitter, the land is destroyed and everything around is worsening. Their concern is that these places should be "our outpost, our settlement, our market centre"(ibid), for that will guarantee the vested and potential interests of Empire. Thus, they establish an absolutely dominant discourse with the help of the seemingly invincible army, unprecedentedly powerful weaponry and immoral means. Here Empire is highly allegorical with great significance of its time.

For the convenience of discussion this chapter substitutes the era of colonial hegemony, an objective term in broad sense, for imperial era, post-imperial era or late imperial era. This reading will render the typical allegorical story with a universal significance in that, be it Roman Empire, Ottoman Empire, British Empire in history or superpowers in contemporary world, they are all characterized with hegemony.

As is known, "hegemony", derived from ancient Greece, originally indicates the domination of big city-states over other smaller ones. Later it refers to propositions, policies or actions aiming at acquiring the power to dominate the world affairs by sacrificing or offending other countries' sovereignty in the course of colonial and imperial practice. In the famous essay "Imperialism: the Highest Stage of Capitalism", Vladimir Lenin gives an incisive analysis of the nature, characteristic and basic conflicts of imperialism, and reveals the objective law of its birth, development and inevitable doom with the conclusion that "hegemony" is a "vital characteristic of imperialism"(653). In *Waiting for the Barbarians*, Coetzee employs a virtual Empire to demonstrate how it implements and maintains the dominant discourse, indicating the irreversible overall peak-to-trough decline of Empire significantly implied in imperial guards' failure to sustain hegemony by attempting to persecute and eradicate the "barbarians".

2. The Other in the Era of Colonial Hegemony

The era of colonial hegemony is featured with power politics, with an apparent distinction between center and margin, Subject and the Other. In the novel, Coetzee displays allegorically the degradation and degeneration of civilization with dominant mainstream discourse. Hegemony is embodied through the military force of the virtual Empire, with Colonel Joll as a typical representative who oppresses the locals brutally in maintaining the dominant discourse power. And his opposite is obviously the racial Other in remote areas. Hegemony is also observed in how a "barbarian" girl, the sex Other, is maltreated by this symbolic character with dominant discourse power. The most impressive is that Coetzee focuses on the relationship between the old Magistrate, Empire and the "barbarians", highlighting his status of identity Other.

Coetzee arranges first of all in the novel for Empire with dominant discourse power the racial Other, who, according to Boehmer, "is unfamiliar and extraneous to a dominant subjectivity, the opposite or negative against which an authority is defined" ("Colonial and Postcolonial Literature" 22). The Other here is the imaginary enemy of Empire, without whom Empire's authority would not have been established.

Readers may well realize that Coetzee has borrowed the title from Constantine Cavafy's poem "Waiting for the Barbarians" (1904) for his novel. This reference is by no means a coincidence though the novelist does not make any explanation to it. However, a comparison, or intertexual study might be necessary since both Cavafy and Coetzee employ the image of marginalized barbarians in their separate writings, with reference to the proposition that "all discourse is an intertextual play of signifiers" (qtd. in

Chen 216) deduced from Derrida's "differance". It is hoped that the knowledge of the marginalized Other in the two pieces published with a time interval of about 80 years by two different writers may help find out that Coetzee's so doing at least has the element of parody, which would further the theme of Cavafy's poem.

Cavafy points out in his poem that the highly civilized society has betrayed its degeneration because the society, losing its objective, becomes monotonous without anyone willing to make up for the civilization. People in the mainstream society, be it senators, emperors, magistrates or orators, lose faith in civilization, wasting their time in the fancy that the status quo would be transformed by external forces from the barbarians — the marginalized Other. The remark of Karl Marx may reinforce Cavafy's idea:

> [a] being which does not have its nature outside itself is not a *natural* being, and plays no part in the system of nature. A being which has no object outside itself is not an objective being. A being which is not itself an object for some third being has no being for its *object*; i.e., it is not objectively related. Its being is not objective ("Economic & Philosophic Manuscripts" 69).

Marx considers the being which has no object outside itself as "no being". The civilized society in Cavafy's writing just takes the barbarians as its outside object because the vigor of the barbarians forms a sharp contrast to the deterioration of the civilized. Coetzee is similar with Cavafy in this sense. The barbarians in his novel are not the force for the recuperation of the civilized society but the imaginative objects to be eliminated for the retention of the imperialistic authority. The imperialists will lose much of their weight without the foil of the otherized barbarians in rags, and in other words, the victimizers would not be so important without the existence of the victims. The existence of the barbarians is a perfect justification of Empire. Sue Kossew contends that "As Constantine Cavafy's poem 'Waiting for the Barbarians' suggests, the construction of borders between self and other and the invention of barbarians was itself 'a kind of solution' to the malaise of Empire"("Border Crossings" 63).

Coetzee parodies Cavafy in the novel *Waiting for the Barbarians*, where there is no eager civilized yearning for the barbarians or scene of the civilized ready to yield, but the suppression and exploitation of the people with dominant discourse power in the virtual Empire over the marginalized Other in disadvantageous position. In order to eradicate the barbarous Other in the virtual Empire, Colonel Joll, the representative of Empire, comes to the district where the old Magistrate is in charge. His work turns out to be quite "effective" since his soldiers capture successfully an old man and his grandson on their way to hospital and a group of fishermen, tribal people and natives within only four days. It is thus apparent that the military men with discourse power are subjective and arbitrary in determining the barbarians. From the narration of the old Magistrate, Coetzee unfolds the concept of the Other in the mind of the Empire guards and the otherization of the ordinary people. Virtually, Coetzee holds that the contempt of the civilized in dominant discourse for the barbarians who are defined as the Other "is founded on nothing" and the difference between the civilized and the barbarians lies merely in "table manners, variations in the structure of the eyelid" (55). He objectively displays the absurdity of the colonel in maintaining the imperial authority and serving so-called rational justice: they arrest the innocent as robbers and force the obedient to confess the fabricated crimes. The captured with both hands tied is accused of becoming "enraged" and "attack[ing] the investigating officer" (6) before he is tortured to death.

While displaying the wicked lies of the imperial discourse dominator with cold composure, Coetzee sternly exposes the nature of imperial civilization and rational justice in the era of hegemony. The otherized old man dies of brutal torture: "The grey beard is caked with blood. The lips are crushed and drawn back, the teeth are broken. One eye is rolled back, the other eye-socket is a bloody hole" (7). The objective presentation of the scene of the dead Other serves as a silent denunciation of the numerous crimes committed by the hegemonic discourse owners. Facing the tyranny, the Other deprived of the discourse power have to bear silently without any resistance or complaint till their death. However, Coetzee does not merely show the Other's agonies, but displays the imperial efforts to "push them [the barbarians] back from the frontier into the mountains" (53). In association with the author's allegorical writing, this practice is highly suggestive, for it shares similarity with colonizers' expelling aborigines to the remote area. The achievements of the imperial efforts in effect allude to their conquest of the marginalized Other.

The cruelty and moral degradation of the authoritative discourse owners are revealed in the torture of the innocent by the representatives of Empire according to their firm conviction that "Pain is truth; all else is subject to doubt"(5). However, the marginalized Other — the nomads, fishermen and aborigines, in short the non-white — are described to defend themselves subconsciously when threatened by the loss of security, even life. Coetzee purposely depicts the sufferings of the imperial army soldiers who have been misled by the locals into the desert and become the alienated Other to nature when they intend to exterminate the "barbarians". In addition, the outwardly strong and inwardly weak soldiers of Empire, running away in chaos from their imaginary dangers, rob unscrupulously the locals and slaughter mercilessly the innocent. The soldiers' crimes uncover a fact that they, the dominant discourse power, have nothing to do with civilization since they deliberately relegate different races to the Other and oppress them randomly. As a result, they are real barbarians — not only aliens to nature, but also the genuine Other to civilization in sharp contrast to the marginalized citizens.

The racial Other suppressed by hegemonic discourse live in misery; however, the sex Other — women or second sex — lead an even more misfortunate life. In the patriarchal society, the sex Other usually fail to decide their own life in the male-dominant discourse context. In *Waiting for the Barbarians*, the sex Other — the housekeepers, prostitutes, and female helpers in the kitchen — are all expected to work diligently and at the same time act as an object to meet the sexual desires of the imperial discourse owners. Generally speaking, man exists for his own sake and for his own will-power, while woman is quite different who becomes the insulted and abused Other, being controlled by exterior forces in the patriarchal society. Females do not have independent identity, being only symbols of the inferior. The author does not arrange any specific plot for them because they are classified as the typical Other. Nevertheless, this is normal for the author merely names the colonel and warrant officer of Empire with discourse power and all other characters including the old Magistrate are nameless, not to mention female characters, who are born the Other in the man-centered world.

The so-called "barbarian" girl, the character Coetzee focuses much of his attention on, has a dual identity though she is unnamed as well. First she is in the mind of the imperial guards a savage who is likely to threaten the safety of Empire. So it is justified for her to be labeled as the racial Other, and arrested and tortured both physically and spiritually. Second, she is a native girl, to be exact, a female maimed after the torture by the dominant discourse power, who looks sideways at people for her eyes are brutally burnt by hot iron, and keeps silent for the lack of discourse power. So she is categorized into a racial sex Other in silence, spending her time as a beggar aimlessly sometimes in the square and sometimes under the walnut trees.

Coetzee's presentation of such a special sex Other naturally suggests something particular. By the depiction of the narrator - the old Magistrate, "[She is] walking slowly and awkwardly with two sticks ... the same black hair cut in a fringe across the forehead, the same broad mouth" (37), Coetzee displays an image of homeless invalid Other. The narrator's further illustration of the girl, including the description of her lips, ears and deformed feet, her shabby appearance and eccentric body odor, makes prominent the figure of an enigmatic, pathetic but ugly victim.

However, Coetzee's exploration of this image of sex Other articulates his own profound reflections. J. G. Fichte, the 18th-century German philosopher, says, "Sense is the basic law of human life and also that of all spiritual life"(8). Through the sense and conscience that have remained in the old Magistrate as the narrator, by interpreting the traumatic body and the indifferent soul of the barbarian female and decoding her mystery and identity, Coetzee reveals her identity as a sex Other whose mind has been distorted in the process of otherization.

The old Magistrate's salvation of the crippled barbarian female who has almost lost her sight after the brutal torture by the imperial soldiers can be taken as Coetzee's deliberate design and the subsequent plot betrays the author's intention. From the old Magistrate's condescending posture to his habitual threatening tone, Coetzee displays at the beginning of the novel an image of a complacent white with dominant discourse power, while his epiphany at the female's astonishment after his unconscious touch provides a best proof of the female's identity of the sex Other. It is undoubtedly true in his epiphany that "The difference between myself and her torturers, I realize, is negligible"(29). His previous self-claimed charity reveals its own nature.

Professor Jennifer Wenzel of Michigan University once put it frankly when talking about this barbarian girl, "Torture has transformed her into a text to be read" (65). By constructing this girl into a text, Coeztee eventually finds a way to connect the individual experience with the discourse and power in a broad sense. However, the decoding of this text requires first of all the recognition of the code. But, just as Lacan says, "Code is called so simply because it is a lost language"(442). Searching for a lost language demands the explorer's perseverance and wisdom. Through the close contact between the Magistrate and the girl, Coetzee interprets this text gradually more profoundly, just like the Magistrate undoing the dirty foot-binding cloth before washing the girl's ugly feet harmed by the torturers.

The process of demystifying the scars is one to cognize the barbarian girl and confirm her identity as the racial sex Other. The Magistrate's help in cleaning up the barbarian girl is highly symbolic. Though the recipient "neither helps nor hinders" (29), the gradual relaxation of the victim's stiff body suggests not only the correctness in decoding the riddle-like female, but also in bridging the seemingly insurmountable gap between them. Coetzee not only demonstrates the swollen scars in the victim's feet and eyes, but also gets the essential answers to "what and why". This answer obviously is both within and out of the explorer's expectations. The crimes and sins the imperial soldiers committed against the otherized girl in her recovered memories are far beyond the imagination of the explorer.

The harms done to the girl by the imperial soldiers are only due to her being recognized as a racial sex Other under the criterion set by the "civilized" victimizers. Coetzee intentionally arranges the scene of the barbarian girl's return to nature. In this event, all the others in the group suffer from diarrhea and nausea, but the otherized girl appears perfectly normal in natural environment. "She eats well, she does not get sick, she sleeps soundly all night ... her face as peaceful as a boy's"(65). The unique performance of the girl in nature, totally different from that in the white-dominant town, shows that this so-called barbarian girl labeled as the sex Other in the imperial civilization proves to be the subject in nature and the real alien to nature should be the victimizers.

The above discussion shows that the racial Other and the sex Other in the novel are without exception so-called barbarians in opposition to the virtual Empire, and more significant is that the central figure — the narrator or the spokesman of the author is also designed as the marginalized Other, highlighting the author's intention.

Similar to every marginalized Other, the central character or the narrator in the novel is not given a name but only a highly suggestive title, who is just one among the "lonely and isolated figures [who] try to find the true meaning of their lives"(D'Hoker 36). He lives far away from the center of the virtual Empire together with the natives for 30 years. "I have not seen the capital since I was a young man"(2). The influence of the virtual Empire on him is continuously receding. As a representative of Empire with dominant discourse power, he should have been considered in opposition to the natives for he is supposed to preserve the interests of Empire. However, his alliance with Empire seems to end up gradually for he has obtained a fresh understanding of "humanity", "value of existence" and a new perception of history and justice since his long stay with the natives in the local environment. As a result, he distances himself on his own initiative from the center of Empire, becoming a self-alienated Other to Empire and involving himself in his mind in the life of the natives.

In sequence, Coetzee juxtaposes the old Magistrate with Colonel Joll and warrant officer Mandel, forming a sharp contrast. All the three are representatives of the virtual Empire in name, but Joll and Mandel are in the genuine service of Empire, while the old Magistrate has been otherized since he, sympathetic with the abused natives, begins to query the validity of the soldiers' practice. Coetzee arranges his return to his humanitarian self when he reflects on the imperial civilization in a way that fits in with human ethics and morality.

His humanity is displayed in multiple dimensions: regardless of his involvement with the barbarian girl which might impair his relationship with Empire, he adheres to sending the girl home. When imprisoned by the warrant officer for his sympathy with the barbarian girl he does not feel frustrated or complain about anyone or anything. Instead, he comes to have a sense of elation because "my alliance with the guardians of the Empire is over, I have set myself in opposition, the bond is broken, I am a free man. Who would not smile? But what a dangerous joy!"(85)

However, Coetzee's arrangement of the old Magistrate's break with Empire does not necessarily mean that he thus becomes a real member of the natives. Though with a clean conscience, he is after all closely linked to

Empire; though sympathetic with the barbarians, he can hardly develop an intimate relationship with them; though with pity for the nomads, fishermen and aborigines, he acts as a conspirator unconsciously. Confronted with the brutal crime of Colonel Joll, he bravely shouts out "No" and feels no regret for his impulse though he is maltreated after that. All in all, he is a symbol of Empire but disapproves of its practice. He follows routinely the instructions from Empire, acting as an unconscious conspirator, but with a sense of resistance to Empire. For Empire, he is a marginalized and alienated Other; and for the natives, he is after all a representative of Empire though he sympathizes with the wretched and reprimands the brutal practice of Empire in his mind. In certain sense, the old Magistrate is in a dilemma for he is the Other to both Empire and the natives, just as he ridicules himself as "a go-between, a jackal of Empire in sheep's clothing!" (79) Thus, the old Magistrate has a status of dual Other or to some extent, his identity is unstable since he is neither in the center nor at the margin, neither a subject nor an object.

Coetzee has made through the old Magistrate much philosophical speculation, which is embodied sometimes in monologue, sometimes through objective narration, and sometimes via subjective comment. In this way, Coetzee explores and comments on the issues of Empire, history, justice, civilization, humanity, etc. Meanwhile, the speculation signifies the unusual identity of the narrator and the author's pondering on the Other through this character.

3. Speculations of the Marginalized Other

As a Magistrate of Empire at a frontier town the protagonist of the novel is supposed to be an active pioneer and a firm maintainer of imperial benefits. But his dual Other identity leads to his sense of resistance to Empire, making it possible for the writer to have his speculations. In discussing the spring attack with the aggressive officer, the Magistrate expresses his understanding of Empire as well as of the barbarians, saying that Empire has in fact become the master of the land after several hundred years' colonization. However, the "barbarians" reject this kind of proposition since they always regard the colonizers as intruders and visitors, and expect that these people would "pack [their] carts and depart to wherever it was [they] came from"(55). Why do they think so? Coetzee concludes by referring to the Magistrate's unique dual identity of the Other and the related experiences that "What has made it impossible for us to live in time like fish in water, like birds in air, like children? It is the fault of Empire"(146). Coetzee thus uses large space for his reflection on and inquiry into Empire by making use of the otherized Magistrate.

In his idea, "Empire has located its existence not in the smooth recurrent spinning time of the cycle of the seasons but in the jagged time of rise and fall, of beginning and end, of catastrophe"(146). A general survey of the world history shows that the formation of empires is always accompanied with plunder and conquest. The modern history of South Africa is evidently a history of conquest from European powers. The successive occupation of the country by Netherlands, the British Empire, France, and the British Empire again in sequence, the large-scale migrations of Boers and two Anglo-Boer Wars are evidences of the rampant power politics and hegemony. The empire thus established is the consequence of unnatural alienation and racial power suppression. As the Other with sense of resistance to Empire, Coetzee realizes that the highlands of sterility and drought in South Africa, the displaced migrations and numerous brutal fights and slaughters among the natives, shape and cultivate the character of South Africans. They advocate a simple life, resort to forces in solving problems and refuse to be dominated by outside forces, with a strong sense of pride in their racial character. This is generally the character of the people away from the centre of imperial civilization. With independence in mind, spirit of tenacious resistance and perseverance, they are destined to be the Other to the civilized, never to be obedient under the regime of Empire. Coetzee, by making use of the case in which the old Magistrate suffers from brutal torture and repeated insult, speculates on the existence of Empire, thinking that "Empire dooms itself to live in history and plot against history"(146), due to the nature of Empire. However, the idea "how not to end, how not to die, how to prolong its era"(ibid) keeps haunting in the loyal guards of Empire. This is why they imagine and diffuse the rumor about the arrival of barbarians, the otherized natives.

From the stance of the Other, the old Magistrate speculates on the mechanism of Empire. To prolong its life, Empire depends upon its vicious guards, who, despising laws and moral principles, wretchedly suppress resistance of the "enemies", actually the otherized natives: "By day it pursues its enemies. ... By night it feeds on images of disaster: the sack of cities, the rape of populations, pyramids of bones, acres of desolation" (146). Colonel Joll and warrant officer Mandel, who track "the enemies of Empire through the boundless desert, sword unsheathed to cut down barbarian after barbarian"(ibid), are representatives devoted to Empire. They are extremely cunning, brutal and inhuman, who employ all the means possible to torment the captured. Showing his indignation, the old Magistrate claims bluntly that "I wish that these barbarians would rise up and teach us a lesson, so that we would learn to respect them"(55). The so-called barbarians, in effect the insulted and downtrodden Other, with "nothing more substantial than differences in table manners, variations in the structure of the eyelid"(ibid) do not submit to the abuses or tortures from the soldiers. Pure violent suppression merely leads to hatred and resistance and the failure of Empire is doomed. The development of the story provides evidences for the idea of the otherized Magistrate.

The old Magistrate's speculation on Empire is more than demonstrating the consequences of the expansion of imperial civilization. He questions closely the performance of different people in the process of conquest and anti-conquest, probing into Empire as well as himself. Limited by the space, this chapter intends to take only the narrator of the novel as an example. As is known, the narrator is a frontier town Magistrate. If Coetzee had solely focused on the description of the Magistrate's resistance to Empire, it would have impaired the credibility of the character, or diminished the effect of the narration and even impacted the depth of the allegorical writing. Anyhow, a study shows that the speculation of the narrator — the otherized Magistrate — does not impair the effect of the novel at all, instead it discloses the historical reason for the existence of Empire from another dimension.

As is discussed above, the old Magistrate in Coetzee's writing is a dual character, a reluctant accomplice with Empire. His sense of justice, different from the concept of Empire, makes him alien or the Other to Empire, but the duty as a local Magistrate makes him help the dispatched soldiers to fulfill their mission. He intentionally exonerates the captives — the old man and his grandson by saying that "This so-called banditry does not amount to much... No one would have brought an old man and a sick boy along on a raiding party"(4). He knows clearly what has happened in the granary, but finds himself powerless to do anything. He has objection to the death of the old man, and is furious about the boy's compulsory company with the dead grandpa, thinking it inhuman, especially to a child, but he says to the boy,

> Listen: you must tell the officer the truth. That is all he wants to hear from you — the truth. Once he is sure you are telling the truth he will not hurt you. But you must tell him everything you know. You must answer every question he asks you truthfully. If there is pain, do not lose heart(7).

The apparent contradiction arranged by Coetzee does signify an undeniable fact that he involuntarily performs his duty to Empire, aware that "I cannot pretend to be any better than a mother comforting a child between his father's spells of wrath. It has not escaped me that an interrogator can wear two masks, speak with two voices, one harsh, one seductive"(8). Willing or not, the narrator plays double roles: mellifluous inducer and wicked accomplice and he knows that well: "I was the lie that Empire tells itself when times are easy, he [Colonel Joll] the truth that Empire tells when harsh winds blow. Two sides of imperial rule, no more, no less"(148-149).

As the Other to Empire, the Magistrate's reflection is thought-provoking. Looking at the barbarians who "stand in a hopeless little knot in the corner of the yard, nomads and fisherfolk together, sick, famished, damaged, terrified"(26), he is choked up with emotions, obviously with sympathy with the captured and despise of the imperial guards. However, he cannot do anything for them, lamenting:

> It would be best if this obscure chapter in the history of the world were terminated at once, if these ugly people were obliterated from the face of the earth and we swore to make a new start, to run an empire in which there would be no more injustice, no more pain (ibid).

He offers specific suggestions plausibly to obliterate the ugly races by letting the latter disappear themselves: "to have them dig, with their last strength, a pit large enough for all of them to lie in (or even to dig it for them!), and, leaving them buried there forever and forever" (26). However, people of good sense will immediately find that his words have strong sense of irony, because first of all, he regards the present situation as "obscure chapter in the history of the world" (34), which betrays Coetzee's sympathy with the victims and fury about the injustice on them. Second, the narrator expects an empire without injustice or pain, suggesting that injustice and pain do exist in Empire now. Third, the narrator's remark leads straightway to the responsibility for the injustice and pain, which will not be eradicated if the source is not found. One thing is clear that it is the so-called ugly races who suffer from the injustice and pain. The eradication of the sufferers won't do any good to the clearance of injustice and pain. Up to now, the author's intention is distinct: only when the source is found can injustice and pain be really removed. Coetzee discloses the truth in black humor.

The old Magistrate's questioning of and reflection on Empire from the viewpoint of a marginalized Other, revealing his spiritual journey as a dual identity with sense of justice, reflect the author's unique writing style to "uncover the nature and laws of imperial power mechanism" (Shi 97) through a meticulously designed character. Coetzee, with incisive realization of the nature of imperial invasion, predicts the doom of Empire by means of allegories and dreams, because of his hostility toward the inhumanity of Empire in the course of its conservation and expansion.

Coetzee's prediction of Empire's doom is made through the recurring dreams and illusions of the marginalized Other. The word "dream" appears 44 times in the novel, indicating the significance of dreams in the allegorical writing. Dominic Head summarizes that "the dream sequence is non-linear (unlike a memoir or a confession), and non-circular (unlike literary pastoral)" ("Cambridge Introduction" 54). The recurring dream in fact displays the same scene: with the background of endless white snow, a child is

> building a fort of snow, a walled town ... the battlements with the four watchtowers, the gate with the porter's hut beside it, the streets and houses, the great square with the barracks compound in one corner. ... But the square is empty, the whole town is white and mute and empty(57).

The scene in the dream is much similar to that of the frontier town. But the question is, why is it mute and empty? Head firmly believes that "The empty model of the town is both a forewarning of the town's demise, the flight of its inhabitants, and a figurative demonstration of the vacant human center of the outpost of Empire"("J.M. Coetzee" 91). The development of the story reaffirms the recurring image in the novel. The town is abandoned at the end of the novel when the traces of Empire have been removed almost completely except the existence of the Other or the alienated narrator, for Empire, instead of eliminating the barbarians, has been conquered by the latter. It is an irresistible trend and the inviolable law of history. In the consciousness of the Magistrate, there will be no real ideal country unless with real equality, justice, comfort and freedom.

When revealing the nature and the fate of Empire, Coetzee speculates on the truth and fabrication of imperial history. He purposely endows the old Magistrate with an identity of amateur archaeologist besides his political identity of the marginalized Other. The dual identity of the Magistrate in the context of uncertain past and present functions as a bridge in between, providing evidences for him to know and interpret history. The 256 pieces of enigmatically-inscribed wooden slips in different times, collected in an archaeological excavation, are highly symbolic or allegorical. How to decode these wooden slips? The speech by Hayden White the prominent philosopher at the symposium "21st century Chinese History and Comparative History" in Fudan University is of significant reference.

> Historical discourse in the West is motivated by a desire to discover form in a past which, by the clutter of remains left to us, we know to have once existed but which now presents itself as ruins, fragments, and clutter. We want to know what these cluttered remains can tell us about a past form of life, but in order to elicit from them a comprehendible message, we must first impose some order on these remains, give them form, endow them with pattern, establish their coherence as indicators of parts of a whole now disintegrated ("Metaphysics of Western Historiography" 50).

Decoding the historical remains is concerned with a scheme provided by the decoder and this scheme actually is a kind of subjective discourse of power.

Would the way of assembling the wooden slips affect the decoding? For instance, would the shape of 16×16 or 8×8 of wooden slips transform the historical information? What realistic meanings are conveyed by the symbols on the wooden slips? Does the ring stand for sun or simply a circle? Does the triangle indicate a woman or just a triangle? Does the ripple signify lake water or merely ripple? What is the difference if the pieces are read from the obverse side and the reverse side? Enigmatic wooden slips are the historical text kept by the ancestors for late-comers to know the past. White argues that "the principal task of historians is to uncover these stories and to retell them in a narrative, the truth of which would reside in the correspondence of the story told to the story lived by real people in the past"("Content of the Form" ix-x). History in his mind is, just like literature, a kind of narrative. Frederic Jameson, with different interpretation of history, also holds that "as an absent cause, it [history] is inaccessible to us except in textual form, and that our approach to it and to the Real itself necessarily passes through its prior textualization, its narrativization in the political unconscious"(35). Louis Montrose supports the idea that history and text should be interrelated and his concept of "textuality of history" (Greenblatt 410) has been universally accepted.

Historians and literary critics all agree that history has textuality and texts can hardly be separated from fabrication. History texts thus can rarely reflect the reality objectively, because the subject of narration tends to construct history texts by preserving and erasing what he/she wants to keep or remove, and the interpreters of history also selectively decode the history texts in accordance with their own need. This procedure is not arbitrary but definitely restrained by discourse of power and ideologies.

Coetzee, based on his understanding that historical narration inevitably involves the participation of the narrative subject's ideology and of the history interpreter's ideology, reflects on and inquires into history by making use of the Magistrate's retrospection at the end of the novel. His meditative discourse, in contrast and mutual complement with his dialogue with Colonel Joll when forced to decode the wooden slips, demonstrates the idea of history of the marginalized Other to Empire.

The old Magistrate should have been a qualified subject to record the history of Empire, but otherized as he is, he says blatantly, "I wanted to live outside history" (169). He realizes that he has equivocal relations with Empire: his resistance to Empire and sympathy with the barbarians have made him the alien and the Other to Empire, but his political identity as the representative of Empire and his reluctant conspiracy with Empire have made him the alien and the Other to nature. His dual identity of the Other makes him vigilant at and suspicious of the authoritativeness of his narration. The process of the Magistrate's self-query is actually the process of decoding his accessory relation with imperial politics. He knows well that he can comment history from multiple dimensions but he cannot write history.

Collateral evidence can be found in the words of the colonel, who feels it funny for the Magistrate to complain, rage at the action of the imperial soldiers and insist on freedom, democracy and social justice. The noble silence the Magistrate keeps when otherized and imprisoned after his company with the barbarian girl to her tribe infuriates the colonel who appears to see through the intention of the old man. He says, "You want to go down in history as a martyr, I suspect. But who is going to put you in the history books? ... People are not interested in the history of the back of beyond"(125). So far as the essence is concerned, history is an objective existence, but the objective representation of history is subject to the recorders of history since history exists in the form of texts. However, facing the imperial violence, individuals are helpless because history writers can erase any period of history with any excuse.

Besides, historical truth might be distorted and changed arbitrarily and the altered records may be accepted and legalized by the dominant power of discourse. The treatment of the official transcripts of the interrogation is a good example. It is common sense that the transcripts of the interrogation are the original material for historical records. Coetzee intentionally designs the plot of the dual Other's treatment of the transcripts. In the report submitted to him, the old Magistrate finds out,

> During the course of the interrogation contradictions became apparent in the prisoner's testimony. Confronted with these contradictions, the prisoner became enraged and attacked the investigating officer. A scuffle ensued during which the prisoner fell heavily against the wall. Efforts to revive him were unsuccessful (6).

Is the report a faithful record of the real situation at the scene? The old Magistrate's deliberate question to the guard is unusually suggestive: "Did the officer tell you what to say to me?" The guard's reply proves that the prisoner is bound when interrogated, impossible to attack others, and the report turns out to be a counterfeited document. But, as the Magistrate, he has to sign his name in haste and end the case since the innocent old man is dead, unable to protest. Though the old man's tortured body indicts the crimes and injustice of Empire, the single-sided record becomes a fabricated true one and legalized to be authoritative. The Magistrate is well aware of his ignominious role as an accomplice though reluctantly. But, later generations won't pose the slightest doubt at the legalized fabrication.

Historical interpretation is a knowledge operation concerning the interpreter's political stance and the interpretation of the symbols in wooden slips mentioned above is the perfect evidence. Since Colonel Joll has taken the old Magistrate as the Other, and the interpretation of the wooden slips is of great significance to the representative of Empire for the latter needs to create an imaginary enemy. The interpretation in the context under great pressure can be anything but objective. In the mind of Colonel Joll, the wooden slips are the tools of communication between the Magistrate and the barbarians: "A reasonable inference is that the wooden slips contain messages passed between yourself and other parties, we do not know when" (120 - 121). However, the old Magistrate's interpretation is subject to the historical context and his identity. His reading in an order from the right to the left greatly mystifies the wooden slip while reinforcing his credibility because Arabian, Hebrew and Urdu are all written in this sequence. In reading one piece of wooden slip, he interprets the symbols on it as "war, revenge and justice". And his penetrating interpretation indicates that Coetzee's understanding of history coincides with that of postmodernism: history is formed through different understandings of the world by human beings in applying rationality. Historical truth is like the man-made wooden slip, inscribed with unrecognized symbols. According to the discourse theory of Foucault, the essence of the wooden slips as objects does not reside in what is written but implied. Just as he tends to "present important remains essentially"(Foucault, "Preface" 134), Coetzee suggests putting aside the interior meaning of the objects and focusing instead on the discourse as object and the exterior meaning formed by the relationship among different discourses.

Coetzee, in making the old Magistrate interpret the wooden slips in the novel, avoids the literal meaning of the discourse, focusing upon the actual existence of objects. From the narration of the novel, the wooden slips were discovered by the old Magistrate the previous year. An unknown past is disclosed through "corner-posts stand [ing] out here and there in the desolation... faded carvings of dolphins and waves"(10). As a decoder, the otherized Magistrate is not occupied with the literal meaning of the symbols on the wooden slips, but with the meaning of their objective existence. Undoubtedly, these unearthed pieces are relics left by the ancient and their reappearance testifies the existence of the past producers of the wooden slips now absent. "I look at the lines of characters written by a stranger long since dead" (121). So relics justify the existence of objective substance. The otherized Magistrate even suggests proving his idea by evacuating any site: "Graveyards are another good place to look in ... you simply dig at random: perhaps at the very spot where you stand you will come upon scraps, shards, reminders of the dead" (123). Coetzee means to say that the so-called barbarians, in effect the otherized non-white locals, are the objective existence on this land and no one can change this reality no matter what stance the interpreter of history takes, what ideology he/she has or whatever strategy, language or writing symbols he adopts.

Coetzee reinforces this idea by a luxuriant imagination in which the otherized Magistrate describes his own death: dead and air-dried there, he would "not be found until in some distant era of peace the children of the oasis come back to their playground and find the skeleton, uncovered by the wind, of an archaic desert-dweller clad in unidentifiable rags"(110). This imagination predicts the future situation in which the remaining bones of the old Magistrate mean nothing but his ever existence, just as the symbols inscribed in the wooden slips which testify only the existence of the writer who has long been dead.

Coetzee's reflection upon the historical narration of Empire is also of great significance to the understanding of the nature of Empire. As has been mentioned, the history of Empire is that of brutal aggression and frantic conquest. One hundred years of colonization makes the colonizers fancy that they have become the masters of the colony. In order to expand its authority and consolidate its ruling position, Empire makes laws to legalize its invasion, and at the same time skillfully reaches its purpose by means of narration or writing of the civilized society. They spare no efforts to distort the images of the natives by their dominant discourse power, marginalizing and otherizing the natives as "lazy, immoral, filthy, stupid"(41). However, though the one-sided narration of Empire sounds plausible and the arbitrary assertion of Empire greatly baffles people, the objective reality can never be covered up. It is of course futile for Empire to create imaginary enemies or otherize the locals, making the latter marginalized barbarians, for that will only betray its own barbarianism and injustice.

Following this train of thought, Coetzee goes on to speculate in the novel upon barbarianism and civilization, injustice and justice dialectically. It is universally acknowledged that the so-called lawful acts of Empire such as civilization expansion, maintenance of imperial benefits, adherence to justice etc. are in effect disguises for its ruthless exploitation, depriving people of their basic rights regardless of human justice and equality. The imperial guards in the cloak of civilization in the novel are actually the real barbarians and the alien force to nature, on the contrary, the otherized natives signify the force of primitive civilization in harmony with nature.

Coetzee poses doubts in the novel about civilization, humanity and justice. Since the issue of civilization and barbarianism has been much discussed, the following part will focus on justice and humanity.

Justice, in Australian sociologist John Lechte's definition, is "habitually linked to the law and equality" (129). Justice is a principle, criterion or yardstick to establish social relation, order and organize the system of social rights and obligations. John Rawls, American political philosopher, taking "justice as fairness", states briefly that "Justice is the first virtue of social institutions, as truth is of systems of thought" (3). Compared with justice, humanity is a broad and controversial term. The Westerners tend to investigate and discuss human nature from the perspectives such as primitive desires, metaphysical pursuit and rational appeals. British philosophers Thomas Hobbes and John Locke contend that the fundamental motive of humans is the pursuit of pleasure and avoidance of pains. However, this book holds that "yeaning for life, freedom, equality, dignity and happiness" should be the essence of humanity, while benevolence and difference from beastliness are universally accepted features of humanity.

In the novel *Waiting for the Barbarians* Coetzee reveals with coolness the rigorousness of imperial domination and the nature of so-called imperial justice through the sober perception and humiliating experiences of the otherized Magistrate. In the novel, Empire with power politics, by selectively forgetting history and highlighting social order of domination and state will, takes brutal, inhumane, immoral measures to suppress the elements affecting imperial interests, fully utilizing the "institution of justice" under the control of Empire, without paying any attention to freedom, basic rights, dignity and happiness of individuals. In displaying the painful and despairing experiences of the otherized "barbarians" — the insulted and downtrodden natives, Coetzee questions in plain language the justice and humanity of the imperial practice.

Great Greek philosophers almost all make comments on justice and humanity, e.g. Plato ever said,

> ... in establishing our city, we are not looking to make any one group in it outstandingly happy, but to make the whole city so as far as possible. For we thought that we would be most likely to find justice in such a city, and injustice, by contrast, in the one that is governed worst (103).

Aristotle highlighted the importance of justice by arguing that "justice is the bond of men in states, for the administration of justice, which is the determination of what is just, is the principle of order in political society" (6). In both philosophers' mind, justice is a social order based on the happiness of all citizens, embodying the harmony of the country. They advocate that an individual should be subordinated to a collective. In the book *The Social Contract*, Jean-Jacques Rousseau presents the idea of popular sovereignty, claiming that "In vulgar usage, a tyrant is a king who governs violently and without regard for justice and law"(129). However, Empire in Coetzee's *Waiting for the Barbarians* unscrupulously carries out hegemonic government and violent power politics, which are in severe conflicts with ideals of Plato's *Republic*, let alone the idea of popular sovereignty.

Coetzee presents two kinds of representatives of Empire in the novel — the old Magistrate on one side and Colonel Joll and warrant officer Mandel on the other, discussing the issue of justice implicitly. It can be observed from the idling about of the old Magistrate that Coetzee designs him solely as a symbol, an otherized alien to Empire. However, Colonel Joll and warrant officer Mandel are quite different, whose speeches and behaviors reflect the power politics and hegemony of Empire.

Coetzee's exposure of the plausible justice of Empire is made from two aspects. Based on the sober-minded observation of the old Magistrate, he illustrates how Empire employs discourse power to suppress the otherized aborigines ruthlessly, and at the same time, he makes use of his own feelings to reinforce the intolerability of the brutal conduct in such a system. Empire does not approve of the idea that justice represents the happiness of all citizens. For the sake of the considerable happiness of some groups, Empire conjures that barbarians would beset the civilized society and therefore dispatches army soldiers commanded by Colonel Joll to suppress them in order to preserve the degraded civilization and maintain the social stability. Taking no account of justice and humanity, Empire relentlessly represses the otherized natives, attempting to eliminate them, resulting inevitably in injustice and inhumanity.

Such kind of injustice and inhumanity can be easily derived from the observations of the otherized narrator. The administration of Empire is tyranny in Rousseau's term, without any sense of justice or humanity. The objective presentation of the old man's death scene is practically appalling: "The grey beard is caked with blood. The lips are crushed and drawn back, the teeth are broken. One eye is rolled back, the other eye-socket is a bloody hole"(7). And unbearable to witness is another scene: the guard of Empire even spins a knife in the body of a boy to "obtain truth", causing "hundred little stabs"(11) in him. In the name of maintaining justice and social order, Empire launches mopping-up operations to imaginary enemies who virtually do not exist at all. What is extremely absurd is that the soldiers give the natives a name "barbarians" and capture them arbitrarily, without caring if they are fishermen, nomads or aborigines. The tortures the captured suffer remind distinctly of the atrocities of Hitler in concentration camps. For instance, they use hot forks with two teeth to burn the eye of the otherized female, they make the grievous woman take the dead child in arms, only to mention a few. An American philosopher said, "It [justice] does not allow that the sacrifices imposed on a few are outweighed by the large sum of advantages enjoyed by many" (Rawls 4). The above-mentioned people cannot be proved to be the dangerous "barbarians" who will damage the security of Empire. The individuals have their own rights of existence and freedom. The imperial soldiers capture and torture them willfully out of fabricated names of crime, arousing great suspicion of the legitimacy of the soldiers' actions in the name of maintaining social order and stability. Coetzee's speculation upon "justice" through an allegorical writing serves as an exposure of the immoral practice of Empire under the guise of justice. Apparently the exposure aims at all tyrannies in the hegemonic era, instead of a specific empire or regime.

What the otherized Magistrate displays through his observation of the sufferings of the racial Other and sex Other indicates the injustice of the imperial tyranny. However, Coetzee, apparently unsatisfied with the present exposure, goes one step further on the way of disclosing the nature of the justice and humanity of Empire by making an exploration into the issue through the old Magistrate's own fate of being otherized and abused both physically and spiritually.

The Magistrate's company with the otherized female — the barbarian girl to her homeland establishes his identity of the Other and the alien to

Empire and wins him spiritual freedom, for the decision itself suggests the resolved break away from the ally and bond with the imperial guards. Some critic says, "... the Magistrate, wants to serve the interests of justice even if it means he is the 'One Just Man' who opposes Empire, ..."(Urquhart 5 - 6). For this he is otherized and injured: "The wound on my cheek, never washed or dressed, is swollen and inflamed. A crust like a fat caterpillar has formed on it. My left eye is a mere slit, my nose a shapeless throbbing lump. I must breathe through my mouth"(125). He suffers from physical pains but holds on to his own belief, never thinking of falling back to the track of accomplice with Empire again. Personal experiences of suffering from inhuman tortures make him understand better the nature of Empire and its so-called justice. He realizes that justice can only be guaranteed on the basis of human treatment and equality, otherwise everything else is in vain. His truthful feeling when tortured by his former partners of Empire serves as a best illustration of his idea:

> A body which can entertain notions of justice only as long as it is whole and well, which very soon forgets them when its head is gripped and a pipe is pushed down its gullet and pints of salt water are poured into it till it coughs and retches and flails and voids itself. (126)

The savage torture of Empire destroys the victims physically and spiritually, fully demonstrating the tyrannical nature of the imperial dominators. Human cruelty has been exaggerated to the full and humanity here has been replaced by beastliness, let alone the word "justice".

In displaying the horrible physical tortures and the outrageous spiritual insult of Empire on the barbarianized or otherized groups, Coetzee meticulously designs another scene, disclosing with full evidences and abundant reflections the injustice of Empire and the absence of humanity under its institution.

The belief of Colonel Joll that "all else [except pain] is subject to doubt" (5) reflects the true relation among humans in the era of colonial hegemony, conforming to the argument that the normal human relation has been completely ruined and "It is one between two abstractions, two living machines, who use each other"(Fromm 135). Empire imposes its will upon the subjects, without considering the individual will at all. The imperial soldiers randomly capture the otherized natives and torture them at will for they believe that "Pain is truth"(5). The Magistrate's shout "No" at Colonel Joll's bestial maltreatment of the otherized victim expressly manifests his unquenchable anger, embodying the presence of his humanity as the Other or the alien to Empire. He protests against Empire by shouting that "we are the great miracles of creation", insisting that humans should not lose humanity. He unremittingly reminds the imperial soldiers that the tortured are in fact men — their own species though they are otherized or barbarianized by Empire with wicked intention, admonishing them: "You would not use a hammer on a beast, not on a beast!" (117) It is clear here that the truly alienated or dehumanized are not the otherized old Magistrate or the barbarianized natives but the representatives of the virtual Empire, the so-called messengers of justice and civilization.

One more plot Coetzee designs illustrates in a more convincing way the loss of humanity in the hegemonic system of Empire. The innocent and curious girl's flogging of the victim instigated by the victimizers demonstrates pathetic indifference, apathy and degeneration of humanity among the masses of the onlookers. Coetzee's reflection through the old Magistrate is stimulating. In his mind, the scene of atrocity in Empire has contaminated the pure souls, and humanity would be distorted and the society corrupted if no measures were taken to stop the tendency. However, he questions himself whether he "dared to face the crowd to demand justice for these ridiculous barbarian prisoners" (118). He knows clearly that justice can hardly be reached because it is easy to say "no" to the victimizer but it is extremely difficult to defend justice for people. As a matter of fact, he has bravely protested against the brutal torture and suffered from otherization and imprisonment after a brutal beating, but still it seems impossible to get justice for the otherized, because the justice for the otherized means without any doubt the damage to the fundamental interests of Empire. His monologue betrays his mind: "Easier to lay my head on a block than to defend the cause of justice for the barbarians: for where can that argument lead but to laying down our arms and opening the gates of the town to the people whose land we have raped?"(118) It is undeniable that the present situation is caused by the imperial invasion and plunder, but Empire won't tolerate any form of challenge to the status quo because it is crucial for Empire to obtain interests through aggressive expansion. Empire can make at its will beneficial laws, carry out the joint policy of obscurantism and violence to retain the present order. The justice here does not have any sense of equality since it is subject to the interests-maintenance mechanism and power politics which confuse the natives. Empire would not consider whether the justice affects the citizens' rights of freedom and equality, or whether humanity is ruined. It is no wonder that the old Magistrate bemoans that this is "time for the black flower of civilization to bloom"(86).

In *Waiting for the Barbarians*, Coetzee, in an unusual allegorical writing style, poses forceful challenges at the discourse power of Empire and speculates upon the issues such as the imperial consciousness, concepts of history, justice, humanity and civilization and barbarianism by exposing, on the ground of resistance to the imperial civilization, the violence Empire takes in suppressing the imaginary barbarians — the otherized natives. The thought-provoking speculation Coetzee makes by an allegorical novel owes to some extent to Coetzee's long-term meditation on the apartheid in South Africa originating from *The Natives' Land Act*. Though featured with otherization, the speculation is illuminating with philosophical sagacity.

Chapter II

Life & Times of Michel K: The Silent Other in Post-Christian Era

J. M. Coetzee's *Life & Times of Michel K* (1983) is a prominent novel which wins the Booker Prize and the French Prix Femina Étranger. By adopting the form of allegory which naturally conceals the historical context, Coetzee demonstrates a typical postmodern Kafkaesque picture through the anti-hero plot of Michel K, a riddle-like insignificant character who is the solitary and taciturn Other with a hare lip and lower intelligence. Without mentioning the skin color of the characters, the novel, commented as a "post-Christian myth" (Marijke 94), tells a story about Michel K's flight "from growing disorder and impending war to a state of indifference to all needs and speechlessness that negates the logic of power" (Engdahl, Press Release, October 2, 2003). By exposing various brutal performances of humans in the society of modern civilization, and displaying the extreme solitude and desperation of the marginalized Other in alienation, and the resistance of the Other to the dominant discourse power by means of active silence for the human freedom, the novel reveals the absurdity of the reality in the modern society and the sense of doomsday in the vast land of South Africa, resulting in a thought-provoking effect among readers.

Life & Times of Michel K arouses a fair amount of controversy on publication. A review entitled "Much Ado about Nobody" appears in *African Communist* shortly after the official announcement of the Booker Prize. The reviewer argues that

> The absence of any meaningful relationship between Michel K and anybody else... means that in fact we are dealing not with a human spirit but an amoeba, from whose life we can draw neither example nor warning because it is too far removed from the norm, unnatural, almost inhuman. Certainly those interested in understanding or transforming South African society can learn little from the life and times of Michel K (Z. N. 103).

Many critics think that the transformation of Michel K in the novel cannot be separated from the complicated relations between domination and interests.① Derek Wright takes Michel K as in fact less a man than a spirit of ecological endurance, "a Gaian ideograph, it remains to ask wherein lies his relevance, whether to the contemporary political situation of South Africa or to the ecological one of the African continent at large"(D. Wright 439). The leftists in South Africa criticize Coetzee for giving prominence in his allegorical writing to "a state of agonised consciousness" and subordinate

① Dovey, Teresa. *The Novels of J. M. Coetzee: Lacanian Allegories*. Craighall: Ad. Donker, 1988; Stephenson, Glennis. Escaping the Camps: The Idea of Freedom in J.M. Coetzee's *Life and Times of Michel K*. *Commonwealth Novel in English* 4. 1 (1991): 77 - 88; Attwell, David. *South Africa and the Politics of Writing*. Berkeley Cape Town: University of California Press, 1993.

attention to "material factors of oppression and struggle in contemporary South Africa"(Vaughan 137). Similarly, Nadine Gordimer, recipient of the 1991 Nobel Prize in Literature, argues that "organicism that George Lukács defines as the integral relation between private and social destiny is distorted here more than is allowed for by the subjectivity that is in every writer" (Gordimer, "Idea of Gardening" 6). English critic Jane Poyner finds that "What unites all these critics is the need to extract the novel's allegorical meaning"(71). However, the mainstream critics throughout the world still render Coetzee high acclaim, agreeing with the idea Per Wastberg gives as Presentation Speech for the Swedish Academy:

> Coetzee sees through the obscene poses and false pomp of history, lending voice to the silenced and the despised. Restrained but stubborn, he defends the ethical value of poetry, literature and imagination. Without them, we blinker ourselves and become bureaucrats of the soul (18).

The research finding shows that J.M. Coetzee, in the novel *Life & Times of Michel K*, touches with the imaginative fiction, concise line-drawing technique and stern language upon the down-trodden with no discourse power in the low-class society and displays the life of ordinary being represented by the protagonist Michel K, a marginalized Other who, numb in appearance but sensitive and adamant within, never quits his belief in freedom in times of adversity or distress when the policy of apartheid comes into being and gradually becomes rampant in South Africa.

The novel depicts through the allegorical presentation of the Kafkaesque subjects such as loneliness, escape, alienation and absurdity etc. the experiences of

Michel K, a typical marginalized Other, and his unremarkable pursuit of leading a dignified life in the context of impending war. Graphically presented are Michel K's alien thought of having nothing to do with wars and conflicts in the troublous society, his resistance to the dominant discourse power by means of silence and his persistence in returning to nature even when he is extremely weak physically. They demonstrate that Coetzee, by disclosing the wickedness of human society such as brutal violence, mutual estrangement and hatred and stupid self-deceit, revealing the nature of "rational justice" in Western civilization and criticizing the concept of the Western morality and ethics, speaks for the marginalized Other – the disadvantageous who are outrageously oppressed and exploited and reflects on the issues such as the trauma of South Africans in history, the suffocating history in South Africa, power of discourse, discipline and punishment in South Africa. Moreover, the author poses the questions such as whether an individual can get divorced from social reality in silence and whether a marginalized Other can fulfill his own pursuit in conflict with his surroundings, etc.

1. The Other in the Post-Christian Society of Violence

The astounding declaration that "God is dead" (109) by Friedrich Nietzsche, the founder of modern Western philosophy, has a relentless lash on God, indicating that Christianity is doomed to decline hopelessly. The development of modern science and technology has made even the pious theologians admit that God in Christianity is demystified and deprived of the supernatural power. Modern sciences prevail over Christianity and humans realize that the secular world is basically irrelevant with God. The world has entered a post-Christian era when God still functions with beliefs partially accepted and partially rejected, but one thing is clear that God can hardly become the moral norm or the ultimate aim for human society, and people's values and world outlook are no longer subject to Christian tenets.

South Africa in the 1980s is situated in the era of transition when the old gives way to the new, still a post-Christian era when Christian beliefs linger and at the same time an era of violence and horror when the country is clouded with constant wars due to the policies of the apartheid. Coetzee cites in the preface of the novel the lines of Heraclitus, a Greek philosopher in the 6th century B.C. that "War is the father of all and king of all. Some he shows as gods, others as men. Some he makes slaves, and others free."① The citation, virtually preparation for the development of the story, obviously attaches great importance to the word "war". In effect, war, in the term of Carl von Clausewitz, a Prussian military theorist and historian, "is nothing but a duel on an extensive scale... an act of violence intended to compel our opponent to fulfill our will"(13). Elizabeth Frazer in the Department of Politics and International Relations in the University of Oxford argues that modern states are very special because "they successfully monopolize the legitimate (that is to say, justified) use of violence"(91). Coetzee's novel *Life & Times of Michel K*, replete with scenes of violence, touches upon the performances of different people in the context of the apartheid, especially that of the marginalized Other.

Violence is an inexhaustible issue especially in South Africa. People use violence to destroy the existing social order, intending to subvert the old and construct the new. Objectively speaking, violence theoretically catalyzes and motivates the development of civilization but endangers the existence of

① This is quoted from page 1 of J.M. Coetzee's *Life & Times of Michel K* published by The Viking Press in New York in 1984. Further references to this edition will be indicated by quoting page numbers in parenthesis.

human being all the time. The history of South Africa is a history of colonizers' violent invasion, a history of rivalry of different colonizers for hegemony, a history of violent suppression over people by dominant power and a history of people's resistance to the outside force and pursuit for rights of liberty and justice by means of violence.

Karl Marx said that "competing nations also permitted themselves all sorts of acts of violence when the opportunity arose"("The Capital" 1489). Violence is the only means colonizers took from East Indian Company's occupation of Cape Peninsula in 1652, to the first Boers' seizure of the land of Khoi, the oldest people in South Africa in 1657, and then to Boers' unscrupulous colonial expansion in the 1770s. According to Marx's dialectical materialism, this is due to the antagonistic economic interests. To defend their own land, South Africans resisted fiercely to Dutch colonizers for more than one century. At the turn of the 18th to 19th centuries, the British occupied Cape colony twice and the South Africans launched 6 wars against aggression within more than half a century. In the 1860s and 1880s, the discovery of mines rich in diamond and gold attracted more and more European migrants to South Africa, intensifying the rivalry by violence among different colonizers. All events of violence such as Two Boer Wars, World Wars and Soweto Massacre are without exception concerned with the suppression by violence of the rivals for the interests of certain sides. Consequently, the innocent people, forced to be involved into lasting calamity, suffer from chaos, homelessness and desperation.

The protagonist in the novel is a menial life of the marginalized Other. Though the midwife, finding the hare lip the moment he was born, said to his mother, "You should be happy, they bring luck to the household"(3), it is impossible for Michel K with disfigurement to be happy or bring any luck to the household. In an era when the normal non-violence does not lead to compromise or stability and wars are prevalent, even the healthy and vigorous colored people are doomed to lead a tragic life in South Africa where the black and the white are still in enmity and severe collision, and apartheid reinforces hostility between the black and the white instead of removing violence, let alone the retarded Michel K with hare lip. In the turbulent South Africa where a desperate profit-driven struggle of plunder and anti-plunder, oppression and anti-oppression, hegemony and anti-hegemony keeps going on, no one can expect to escape the fate of being involved. Michel K with features distinctly different from normal people is predestinated to be a marginalized Other the moment he was born with defects. The violence in South Africa stimulates his status of marginalization.

Coetzee deliberately manifests the scene of violent conflicts in Cape Town in the first chapter: galloping military jeep, fierce street fights, smashed cars, a hail of stones, revolver shots, broken windows and lights, woman stripped naked in street, police van with a flashing blue light, cracks, screams, shouts, wounded people lying on the ground everywhere... Among all the roars, screams, shoots and cracks, Michel K and his mother "huddled quiet as mice in their room beneath the stairs, not stirring even when they smelled the smoke, even when heavy boots stamped past and a hand rattled the locked door" (12). An unnamed hatred exists among the people in the chaotic world and anything negligible might serve as a sparkle, leading to a riot of unimaginable scale. This is a truthful portrayal of the situation in South Africa and the frequent brutal violence brings only horror and bad luck to the obscure character who stands aloof from the world of trouble, resulting in his further marginalization.

Coetzee's presentation of the shocking living environment paves the way for Michel K's vagrancy. "Vagrancy", as Paul Franssen says, "is usually associated with marginalization and lack of power" (453). As the marginalized Other, Michel K has no other choice but to flee away from the rampant violence together with his sick mother, Anna. They want to leave the chaotic, horrible Cape Town to the birthplace of Anna, hoping to have a peaceful life in the countryside. Coetzee's arrangement of the plot is rational and logical for human needs to have a basically reliable environment to live in. And his design for Michel K's ideal life is to own "a whitewashed cottage in the broad veld with smoke curling from its chimney, and standing at the front door his mother, smiling and well, ready to welcome him home at the end of a long day" (9). However, the insignificant but reasonable requirement and the dream of the agrarian age can hardly break through the shackles of machinery in the apartheid South Africa. The marginalized Other without any political power can only comfort themselves by building castles in the air, for the political power, in the term of John Locke the English philosopher, is "the power of life and death"(308). Overcrowded is Cape Town where people at the bottom of the society are mostly homeless and jobless, but it is extremely difficult for people to leave the city without an authorized permit by dominant discourse power. The permit application procedures are fairly complicated and concerned with bureaucratic authoritarianism. The process is actually a deplorable story in which the marginalized Other at the bottom of the society suffers grievously before compulsively leaving Cape Town "illegally" without any official permit when in despair and collapse.

The miserable situation and painful repression of South Africans with no power of discourse are expressly shown in Anna's provocative statement that "I feel like a toad under a stone living here"(9). Her bitter life experiences serve as a mirror of the downtrodden in Cape Town: rough life with frequent frustrations including the absence of husband, the company of a retarded son, bad health, constant fear of being sacked, intolerable accommodation, etc. The humiliating experience in the hospital Coetzee arranges specially for Anna is only an epitome of the sufferings of the people in South Africa. Totally neglected in the hospital where too many injured people from violence need urgent treatment, Anna is deprived not only of medical treatment, but also of the dignity as a human being. Here the author demonstrates the extremely painful life the otherized Anna leads in a society of brutal violence and sternly depicts the living condition of the Other at the bottom of the society.

If Coetzee's design of Anna's pains attracts readers' attention to the pains of South Africans in general, then Michel K's depression and agony can be said as special cases of the typical Other in which people suffer more. His difference in appearance with other children always arouses smiles and whispers from others, which hurt him as much as his mother. He feels alienated at a very young age and his mother, a charwoman, decides to keep him away from other children, telling him to keep silent on the carpet when she is working. So he has to be accustomed to the solitary life. And at school age, he is expelled from school after a short trial "because of his disfigurement and because his mind was not quick"(4). He has to attend a school especially set up for the "unfortunate children learning the elements of reading, writing, counting, sweeping, scrubbing, bed-making, dishwashing, basket-weaving, woodwork and digging"(ibid). Humiliation and frustration accompany him all the time, and his early work as a gardener or a night watchman virtually does not provide him any opportunity to get in touch with humans. Otherized as he is, he lives silently in the world for 16 years without any friend or intimate, without any chance of social life. Long time of such existence makes him unsociable and eccentric in character. He is gradually accustomed to others' indifference and to his status as the inferior Other. Silence becomes often the first choice for him before others.

However, what stimulates him to have the life-long vagrancy is his sick mother's dream of leaving Cape Town which she thinks is a place full of bloody violence, arrogant shop owners, alarm sound, curfew, dampness and coldness. Her dream of leaving for her birthplace makes Michel K for the first time feel life significant because he has his life objective ever since, that is "to look after his mother"(7). Nevertheless, for the marginalized Other at the bottom of the society, the difficulty of leaving Cape Town is beyond his imagination, and so is his further vagrancy. In the troublesome journey his mother dies in hatred and Michel K continues trudging on his way with ashes of his mother. Violence accompanies him everywhere even when he is out of the city. Thus, more significance is attached to his vagrancy as the Other. On his journey, he is confronted with robbery by soldiers as well as robbers. Michel K's question to the robber-like soldiers "What do you think the war is for? ... For taking other people's money?"(37) to some extent represents the author's indignation and protest. However, the soldiers' rude and threatening answer reveals a cruel but unchangeable reality. "You could be lying in the bushes with flies all over you. Don't you tell me about war"(37). Violent answer often goes together with violent force. Michel K the marginalized Other is doomed to be accompanied by violence. Under the threat of violence, he is forced to do hard labor; and intimidated physically by violence, he loses his identity and freedom, driven to resettlement camps or relocation camps time and again. But his yearning for freedom never vanishes. Michel K, weak in body but adamant in mind, makes constant attempts to flee away from the camps and violence. He gets away from crowds and retreats to an isolated place where he, by planting pumpkins and watermelons, lives a primitive animal life but obtains some kind of freedom, though the peaceful life is transient in the harsh reality.

2. Silence of the Other in the Troublous Era

In *Life & Times of Michel K*, Coetzee chooses Michel K the alienated Other as the protagonist rather than the middle-class Buhrmanns who discard their home or a distorted warder in Transformation Camp or Detention Camp to trace "Noël's journey of the heart"(Zhai 70). Though wars bring incurable trauma to each individual and this kind of trauma can be better demonstrated from the perspective of a middle class protagonist who has to give up his home, though warders can also be a good choice in reflecting the rigorousness in the chaotic South Africa, for they, similar to prisoners, become "a prisoner to this war"(157) with almost endless bondage in the process of supervising prisoners and their personality is vulnerably twisted in the circle of supervision and anti-supervision, yet Coetzee chooses resolutely and determinedly as protagonist Michel K who gets away from Cape Town with great difficulty but is plunged into unexpected troubles. In displaying Michel K's perseverance in holding his slim hope and his retreat into dead silence, Coetzee represents the situation of the marginalized Other in South Africa and his tenacious resistance to the miserable fate, by means of taking as symbol the silence of the subject.

Some critic argues that the novel "paints a chilling picture of the helplessness of the innocent individual against the minions of power and greed"(Kratz 462). Surely, Coetzee's description of the life and times of Michel K is very impressive and mournful. The author does not unfold the grand historical background of the era directly but all the scenes such as the running military vehicles, the frontier passes guarded by soldiers, the fast-moving and noisy jet-fighters in the sky, the detention camps and the hospitals overcrowded with the wounded, constantly remind readers of a chaotic and dangerous place where bloodshed may happen at any moment and life is not safe at all. Therefore, fleeing from danger becomes a normal theme in the life of South Africans and chaos is the basic setting of the novel.

Generally speaking, dominance and negation are always closely connected with discourse, but Coetzee does not employ the speech of the Other to resist the dominant discourse power. Instead, he demonstrates frostily the silence — the absence of speech in communication — an apparently passive but virtually effective coping strategy for the marginalized Other to take in fleeing from the society during the chaos. Silence with its innate obscurity and discourse space it creates stimulates readers' imagination. Head's comment of silence in the novel is of significant reference: "Another aspect of K's elusiveness is his silence, a sign of disenfranchisement as well as resistance" ("J. M. Coetzee" 98). Michel K's silence is full of unspeakable stories. Coetzee describes the silence of Michel K from multiple perspectives. Without presenting the character in an unconventional way, he depicts step by step the formation of his silent temperament, basically following the chronological order. His childhood witnesses other children's despise and ridicule because of his hare lip and gaped nostril. Long-term depression makes him generally silent. The jobs he takes (gardener → night watcher → gardener again) objectively deprive him of opportunities to communicate with others. When he is in the Touws River camp, his active preparation for the escape needs all the more silence. So, it is justified that "Silence is not the end of speech, but another way of expressing meaning, in contrast with speech" (Foucault, "History of Sexuality" 27). In many cases, silence signifies the depth and diversity rather than the void of meanings.

Michel K's silence on different occasions not only contains discourse meaning conveying linguistic message but truly reflects the psychological process of the marginalized Other. According to the research of psychological linguistics, "all the different significances attributed must have their sources in the structural expectations engendered by the surrounding talk" (Levinson 329). K's silence has distinctive features: at the Visagie farm, virtually an unpopulated land, K works from sunrise to sunset and does not have to prove his existence with language since he is detached from the outside world and from the chaotic time. Language has lost its function of communication here. But it does not mean that K stops thinking, or that K ceases thinking in language though he is gradually forgetting Cape Town, wars and the process of his arrival at this farm.

The appearance of Visagie's grandson makes linguistic communication possible but K tactfully acts as a mute to confuse and fool him. Silence here indicates a kind of conscious self-control, implying K's unwillingness to speak and covering the truth. When the grandson attempts to relegate him as a servant he leaves speechlessly. Apparently K cherishes his freedom and tries to resist the dominating discourse with the power of silence. He would rather retreat into mountains for the enjoyment of his freedom than stay in the Visagie's house with shelter but without liberty.

The shortage of food in the cave forces the extremely feeble K back to the human crowd. The moment he arrives at Prince Albert he is arrested and taken into the police station. People with dominant discourse power charge arbitrarily him with “leaving his magisterial district without authorization, not being in possession of an identification document”, and even charge him incredibly with “infringing the curfew, and being drunk and disorderly” (70). Coetzee does adopt some strategies to rescue K from the control of power discourse and to realize the discourse redemption of the subject: “The most effective of these strategies of resistance is silence”(Marais 73). As has been mentioned above, silence is not the end of thinking but the extension of consciousness. The externalization of K’s consciousness after his hospitalization is a good example: “a hospital, it seemed, was a place for bodies, where bodies asserted their rights”(71). How does an otherized body with low status assert its rights in such a wicked context?

K’s performance in Jakkalsdrif Camp gives proof of the opinion. He does not know why he is sent to this place or how long he will stay there. Though he arranges some short dialogues of K with other characters and reveals his deep psychological insights straightforwardly, Coetzee basically makes K innately silent. Michel K knows very well that he must take some effective measures if he doesn’t want to be controlled and subordinated by dominant mainstream discourse. He is well aware that he is not a prisoner and should not be deprived of his freedom. But it is regulated in the camp that “No one leaves the camp except on labour calls. No visits, no outings, no picnics. Roll-calls morning and evening, with everyone present to answer”(92). He is dying for free life, but when he lies down squinting into the sun in the warm grey sand finding all the colors of the rainbow, he begins to realize that he is “like an ant that doesn’t know where its hole is”(83), which foreshadows his invisible life.

K’s return to Visagie after fleeing away from Jakkalsdrif Camp is an important event in the novel. K here and now naturally retreats to his own world of silence again, and lives on the farm by transcending human language. He does not use human language nor does he need it for his life is primitive without any communication with human beings. Objectively, the absence of language makes him free from exterior oppression. To preserve the precious freedom K abandons Visagie shelter and lives in a cave he digs beside the embankment where he plants pumpkins and watermelons for a prosperous future. He often catches insects, lizards, ants and grasshoppers for his own survival and constantly fights against goats to protect melon vines, the hope of his future life. Leaving no sign to keep time and making no efforts to record the moon's waxing or waning as Robinson Crusoe does, K behaves completely like an alien in no man's land. In avoiding the possibility of being found, he learns to be accustomed to acting at dawn or dusk and allows some leisure for himself. His speculation about children and meditation on the relation between children and their parents provide footnotes for his silent life in this place without any conventions. He believes that he is neither a prisoner nor a tramp and his life beside the embankment has nothing to do with term of imprisonment a criminal has to serve, though in effect he has to be a vagrant, for vagrancy, as is indicated above, is usually associated with marginalization and lack of power. The present situation is a best proof..

K realizes that he is divorced from human society and probably becomes as timid as a mouse. However, he knows that even this situation is much better than his loss of freedom: "Would it not be better to hide — day and night, would it not be better to bury myself in the bowels of the earth than become a creature of theirs? (And would the idea of turning me into a servant even cross their minds?)"(106) He compares himself to one "Like a parasite dozing in the gut... like a lizard under a stone"(116). The author's metaphor reveals the ruthlessness of the tyrannical society as well as the perseverance of the miserable otherized beings. K's pondering on "master" and "parasite" is of great significance for it further castigates the authoritarian society. The exclamation "What a pity that to live in times like these a man must be ready to live like a beast" (99) reinforces the castigation.

The objective presentation of Michel K's life as a marginalized Other seems not enough to Coetzee in denouncing the evils of the authoritarian society in South Africa. He alters the perspective from the omniscient third-person narration in the first part to the limited first-person narration in the second part. Hiding himself invisibly behind the medical officer of the camp, he observes closely the life and silence of Michel K, involving himself straightway as medical officer or implied author so that he can make direct remarks on whatever he feels like to comment.

Coetzee tactfully adds the letter "s" to Michel at the beginning of the second part so that Noël the camp administrator always calls him Michels, so do the medical officer and the implied author. Naming, as we know, is concerned with an important issue of identity. Being aware that these people are talking to him, the protagonist attempts to correct the mistake of the discourse, which should be taken as his efforts to restore his identity as an independent subject. But the fact proves that all the efforts of the marginalized Other end up in vain. Under such circumstances, Michel K's identity as an independent subject has been objectively deprived of and this has become an unavoidable reality, which is of course beyond K's limit of acceptance. He can do nothing but show his resistance by means of silence.

Michel K does not resist everything in the camp by refusing speech and his resistance by silence is selective. To the medical officer's questions about his mother and food, he does not refuse communication though he is often taciturn. Coetzee purposely offers a description of K's physical situation when he arrives at the camp. "There is every evidence of prolonged malnutrition: cracks in his skin, sores on his hands and feet, bleeding gums. His joints protrude, he weighs less than forty kilos" (129). Ironically, for such a weak being of skin and bones, the relevant official document records: "Michels is an arsonist. He is also an escapee from a labor camp. He was running a flourishing garden on an abandoned farm and feeding the local guerrilla population"(131). The record actually betrays that the camp picks him up not out of charitable purpose and the camp is by no means an institution of philanthropy. In effect, the administrator of the camp is the one with dominant discourse power, and represents the interests of the government. The plot that Coetzee intentionally adds a letter "s" to Michel's name, as is discussed above, the action that otherizes Michel K by depriving him of his identity of the subject, objectively paves the way for the exposure of the attempt of Noël. The camp administrator keeps K for the possible information about the local guerrillas so that government army may suppress them with the help of the information.

K in Coetzee's writing can hardly be said to resist deliberately the authorities because he sees through the nature or attempt of the camp. As readers with more information than the characters in the novel, we know that he has nothing to do with the guerrillas and does not have any valuable information about them. His silence is in some sense a kind of instinct resistance. No matter how elaborately Noël the camp administrator accounts in high-flown phraseology or how earnestly and patiently the medical officer tries to convince him, K keeps silent all the time and "the silence lengthened"(138). Judging by appearance, long silence makes the alienated

Other seem weak before the dominant discourse, but this strategy plays the role of keeping his independence as the Other virtually due to his abandonment of orthodox discourse. Whenever he is reluctant to speak he closes his mouth sternly and gazes furiously and sometimes indifferently at Noël or the medical officer. Just as a British dramatist says, silence implies "the mutual hostility among characters and creates conflicts" (V. Herman 93), demonstrating indifference, rejection and resistance, as well as "a huge threatening" (ibid 99). Michel K shows his resistance with his strength though feeble and "intuits that to become an object of charity would be to relinquish his claim to dignity and autonomy, and declare himself helpless and utterly dependent on others" (Dragunoiu 70). His words "I am not in the war" (138) at last greatly irritate and infuriate Noël, making the latter lose all patience. But what should not be neglected is that his silence to resist the dominant discourse produces an unexpected effect. Invisible behind the medical officer, Coetzee comments that "He is not of your world. He lives in a world of his own" (142).

In *Life & Times of Michel K*, Coetzee not only focuses on the transformation of characters' psychology but emphasizes the description of the developing implications of images. And more importantly, he skillfully integrates them into an artistic whole. In depicting the process of the characters' psychological transformation, the author always takes an attitude of generous narration with moderation. His dexterous use of the strategy of silence perfectly demonstrates the power of discourse and silence.

Coetzee's control of the strategy of silence, besides the resistance to speech discussed above, is shown in his design of Michel's silence of the physical body, i.e. K's body shows a resistant physical reaction to the food in the final resettlement camp. The transition from resisting speech to resisting food symbolizes a qualitative leap in terms of Coetzee's using the art of silence and shows his free rein of the strategy of silence. Generally speaking, keeping silent is the rational choice of the subject. Even if we say that K's silence before Noël the camp administrator is out of instinct due to the unbalanced information, the rationality of his resistance still overweighs instinct. However, Coetzee appears to think that such kind of resistance cannot fully show the power of resistance. His design of K's physical reaction — body's silence, is an instinctive resistance, purely out of natural force, with nothing to do with human consciousness. This reaction, just like his exceptionally different pursuit of freedom which is not a rational one, is out of instinctive need. It is just because of this natural instinct that produces overwhelming and thrilling power. Now Coetzee has reached the supreme state in using the strategy of silence. The marginalized Other he depicts allegorically gets sublimated and K's pursuit is no longer anything absurd but adorable ideal of human beings. To further reinforce the theme, Coetzee arranges purposely the stream of consciousness of the warder in the camp, which clearly shows the overwhelming power of the instinct. Even the warder feels regret for failing to flee away with Michel K. Freedom, the sublime ideal that humans are in constant pursuit of, is elevated in silence.

3. Reflections from the Silent Other

Coetzee, in showing the character's resistance to the dominant discourse by means of silence in *Life & Times of Michel K*, has made a profound reflection on the issues of trauma, history, power, discipline, etc. He reaches his purpose sometimes by combining traditional omniscient and omnipotent narration with the use of the character's stream-of-consciousness, sometimes by direct narration, or hiding behind the otherized protagonist invisibly in silence, making use of the latter's experiences and extending the meaning accordingly.

The long history of the apartheid South Africa has left upon people unforgettable traumatic memories, including individual and collective trauma, physical and spiritual trauma, direct and indirect trauma. "Trauma is from modern violence ... signifies the violence nature of modern civilization"(Tao 117). David Attwell, a prominent scholar in the study of Coetzee, argues,

> *Life and Times of Michel K* was written partly — with the emphasis on partly — in response to a particular political and constitutional debate in South Africa in the early 1980s, when the nation seemed to enter a cycle of insurrection and repression whose outcome threatened to be bloody ("South Africa" 88).

The rampant violence in endless circulation brings about catastrophe and huge trauma to the innocent people in South Africa. Coetzee prefers an allegorical narration of the realistic story disclosing traumas for that is "both a medium to demonstrate traumatic pressure and a way to release the great pressure or a method to grasp and control the event"(Macarthur 11).

Coetzee, with unique intention, conceals the historical background with no mentioning of the skin color of characters but employs the figure featured with a hare lip as the protagonist. One thing is clear that since the novel has adopted an allegorical form, the hare lip is more than a physical defect in general sense. Though a legend is popular on South American Continent that the hare lip signifies God's kiss, and the midwife's saying that it will bring luck to the family is related to this legend, yet the great amount of researches on myths show that the implication of hare lip just goes to the opposite direction. Levi-Strauss claims that hare lip is closely connected with twinning, the former results in the partial splitting of an embryo while the latter is completely split within the womb. In some tribes, the baby with hare lip, similar to the twins, regarded as freak, beast or human-beast reincarnation, or related to evil spirit or devil, should be "killed at birth" (Levi-Strauss 42), otherwise it will definitely turn into disaster. In the description made according to the power relation through Lacanian gaze, "the hare lip" becomes another name for defects, a symbol of indifferently marginalized Other.

As is well-known, Coetzee is deeply influenced by postmodernist thinking of anti-hegemony, anti-centeredness, highlighting the marginalized and advocating dialogues. Choosing after much thought a deformed character as the protagonist, he actually chooses the marginalized Other as an object. Statistics in 2010 show, the white only account for 9.1% of the population in South Africa, but they represent the mainstream in the country and the colored are in great majority, but in most cases they are marginalized or otherized. Therefore, it is not difficult to know why Coetzee chooses the marginalized Michel K as the protagonist in the novel. Nadine Gordimer the Nobel Prize winner for literature argues that,

> *Life and Times of Michel K* are the life and times of the millions of black South Africans who were removed, dumped, set wandering, hiding from Endorsement Out under *the Group Areas Act*. Michel K was one of them, all of them. Whether by making him "all of them", allegorically, Coetzee evaded the demands of his time and place or whether he enhanced commitment to these, ... ("Preface" xi).

Though it sounds a little arbitrary to conclude that Michel K represents the black and other subalterns since Coetzee deliberately overlooks the skin color of this character, undisputable is the point that K's trauma is virtually that of the marginalized, also of the inferior whose subsistence is threatened due to the invasion of colonizers.

As we know, Coetzee has made it clear at the very beginning of the novel that K is branded as the marginalized Other at birth for hare lip is as much despised as the skin color of the black. His mother, a low-class labourer, severs his communication with other children due to their ridicule and gossip. It is often the case that Michel K is asked to sit quietly on a blanket watching his mother working monotonously and endlessly. The control or deprivation of one's free expression usually means the loss or limitation of the individual autonomy and freedom. Judith Herman, an expert in the traumatic theory, contends that "The core experiences of psychological trauma are disempowerment and disconnection from others" (133). K's rights of basic discourse and communication with others are deprived at childhood and his later experiences as a gardener and night watchman further reinforce this kind of deprivation. This reminds people of the apartheid in South Africa, which causes the segregation of the white and the non-white (including the black, Indians, Malaysian and other mixed races) and the discriminative treatment in politics and economy. The experiences of Anna, Michel K's mother, attest the above idea. The humiliation and injustice she suffers in Somerset Hospital, Cape Town, the inhumane treatment she shares with her son after she feels lucky to "escape this purgatory"(5) and her final death in a cold bed of a hospital on the way to her homeland, epitomize the traumatic life of the down-trodden women at the bottom of the society and of the marginalized Other in the context of apartheid in South Africa.

Coetzee, by displaying the experiences of Anna and K in the hospital, implicitly criticizes the *Reservation of Separate Amenities Act* which distinguishes the white from the non-white. By referring to the experience of K's return with his mother to the latter's hometown, Coetzee quietly exposes the absurdity of *the Group Areas Act* which segregates the habitants of different races. The trauma that South Africans are afflicted with can be traced in the novel *Life and Times of Michel K*. Nevertheless, Coetzee does not indulge himself in complaints full of remorse after the exposure of the trauma, instead he adopts an allegorical writing to display the trauma of Michel K. In placing K in predicament where his menial life suffers from physical and spiritual torture of being chased and imprisoned, Coetzee shows one fact that K does not bow down his noble head even when he feels hard to survive. Being frustrated, K does not lose his strong power of endurance, nor does he give up what he wishes to accomplish as his ideal. Thus, vividly presented is an image of thin but tenacious life which persistently seeks its living space in the spiritual purgatory. Coetzee's practice indicates clearly for readers the bottom line in spirit of being a man, disclosing the nature of human existence and demonstrating the significance of humanitarianism he adheres to.

Coetzee's repeated representation in the novel of historical trauma, reminiscence of and reflection upon the history of South African turbulence, exploration and restoration of the truth of history, reveal his profound humanistic concern for South Africans. History, in terms of new historicism, is an extended text, and text is a compressed history. "History and text, constituting a political metaphor in reality, is an existing body with the unification of diachrony and synchrony" (Y. C. Wang 158). In the literary text with a strong sense of political allegory, Coetzee has a profound and penetrating reflection on the history of South Africa. In his 1987 Jerusalem Prize Acceptance Speech, he summarizes South Africa as a master-slave society where "no one is free" and "The slave is not free, because he is not his own master; the master is not free, because he cannot do without the slave" (Coetzee, "Doubling the Point" 96). In such kind of society, the typical feature is that nobody is actually free. This naturally reminds readers of the interrelation between the rigorous social reality resulting from the apartheid and the miserable experiences of the people in the history of South Africa. South Africans, especially the ordinary people at the bottom of the society, are discriminated in many aspects such as politics, economy and social life. Their living state is deplorable. They live a painful life without freedom physically or spiritually, and their personality is always distorted since they cannot get rid of their loneliness or give vent to their suppressed feelings. They are often brutally suppressed by the governmental army when they protest against the social injustices. It is an era full of blood thirst, atrocity and callousness, which forms special historical and cultural context of South Africa.

Born and raised in South Africa, Coetzee, with a fair knowledge of the history of the country, has a cordial abhorrence of the evil apartheid. And he understands that it entails dominant discourse to record and comment historical events. He conveys the proposition explicitly in the novel: the objectivity and legality of historical events are decided by narrative behavior which is subject to ideology and the subjective tendency of individuals, so fabrication based on particular ideology is inevitable. At the same time, the individuals in the society, especially the marginalized weak, are subject to the restraints of fictional history.

Michel K's experiences Coetzee demonstrates in the novel show that the history of the marginalized Other is not the reality created through words but the fabrication invented by the people with dominant discourse. K is only an inconspicuous figure living silently in the jungle-like society. He is simply "a toad under a stone"(9), not caring the conflicts in the chaotic society, nor having any information about the conflicts. Ironically, he is arrested and imprisoned as an insurgent. What's lamentable is that "he barely knows there is a war on"(130). His personal history is recorded as "an arsonist", "an escapee from a labour camp" and food provider for "the local guerrilla population"(131). It is crystal clear that this history is not the record of facts, but it shows an undeniable fact that the history of the weak individuals in inferiority is subject to the fabrication of the dominators. This apparently plain and simple scene in effect brings forth ever-lasting influence and motivates readers to subvert the fabricated history.

Coetzee's comment made invisibly behind the medical officer strengthens the idea of historical restraint. The medical officer is said to be the only person who understands the silence of Michel K. He has an objective cognition of K, thinking that the latter is accustomed to simple life, completely unaware of the events in the society, for he is "too absorbed to listen to the wheels of history"(159). Can such an otherized man escape from the restraint of the fabricated history? In effect, Coetzee uses larger space to praise K's effort to get away from history, contending that

> We ought to value you and celebrate you, we ought to put your clothes on a maquette in a museum, your clothes and your packet of pumpkin seeds too, with a label; there ought to be a plaque nailed to the racetrack wall commemorating your stay here(152).

However, well aware of the insignificance of the Other's efforts in the authoritarian society in South Africa, he still points out the futility of human effort in history:

> But that is not the way it is going to be. The truth is that you are going to perish in obscurity and be buried in a nameless hole in a corner of the racecourse, transport to the acres of Woltemade being out of the question nowadays, and no one is going to remember you but me, unless you yield and at last open your mouth (ibid).

His eventual appeal "Michels, yield!" (152) explicitly shows that human being, the marginalized Other without discourse power in particular, is insignificant and powerless when confronted with the artificial history.

Coetzee's meditation on "power" in some sense reinforces the idea above. The word "power" usually reminds readers of Michel Foucault's theory of discourse power. In his mind, "power is not an institution, and not a structure; neither is it a certain strength we are endowed with; it is the name that one attributes to a complex strategical situation in a particular society"(Foucault, "History of Sexuality" 93). This situation is vested with the power to control and dominate people's thinking and behaviors and will change in different historical or cultural periods. Foucault analyzes power from the mechanism, taking power as a suppressive force, which, of course, will suppress nature, instinct, the collective as well as the individual.

The suppressive power is observed everywhere in the novel, e.g. South Africans are strictly not allowed to leave their original administrative district without permit; they are prohibited from stopping alongside motorways; they might be shot to death if they sleep on others' grassland. Many other weird things have become normal in the daily life of South Africa, such as curfew, barricades and gangster-like policemen. All this indicates the control and domination of the horrendous administration of South African authorities in the apartheid era. In examining the authoritarianism permeated in South Africa, Coetzee mainly adopts allegorical writing, using many metaphors such as the big stone above the toad, etc. besides exposing the suppression mechanism mentioned above. However, the most apparent demonstration of the suppression mechanism is the existence of the large number of resettlement camps and detention camp, manifesting the completion or maturity of the suppression institution and segregation mechanism in the country.

Coetzee illustrates the operation mechanism of the authoritarianism in South Africa by deliberately depicting Jakkalsdrif Camp, a camp for both resettlement and transformation. "It might be one of the resettlement camps, that the tents and unpainted wood-and-iron buildings might house people, that its perimeter might be a three-metre fence surmounted with a strand of barbed wire"(73). And the camp is preserved by fully-armed devil-like guards. However, Coetzee evidently does not want to make readers mistake the camp for a prison because the people taken in as camp members "work for food"(77). People here have limited freedom, for they can walk at will within the camp, looking at the free motion of the clouds in the sky, but leaving the camp has become a luxurious fancy. K's talk with a guard shows this point clearly:

> "... So can you open the gate?" said K.
>
> "The only way to leave is with the work party," said the guard.

> “And if I climb the fence? What will you do if I climb the fence?”
>
> “You climb the fence and I’ll shoot you, I swear to God I won’t think twice, so don’t try.”(85)

The situation here is a mirror of the segregated living area of the colored because it has the feature of a big labour camp and it is very much similar to the core idea advocated by the Race Association of South Africa: “all the citizens in *Bantustans* have fixed home and land within the preservation area.... Out of the area, they have neither land nor political rights” (Jaenecke 153). Just because of this theory, the black outside the preservation area become the aliens in their own country and the South African authorities attempt to drive all the black into the preservation areas, hoping to force the 70% of the population to survive in the area which only accounts for 13.7% of the country. Here suppression from the authoritarianism is normal. People are deprived of their basic rights and the only right they have is to do physical labour. Coetzee’s description of the camp reveals the mechanism of power or discipline in South Africa. In meditating on the power, he ponders on the discipline mechanism of the South African authorities and its relevant consequences.

The power mechanism of the South African authorities, illustrated by the life of K in the camp, is also displayed typically through the experiences of Robert’s entry into the camp. Before his entry into the camp, Robert used to work on a farm and the sluggish wool market makes him jobless and homeless. Forced to go wandering, he is arrested by the police and shut up “here in Jakkalsdrif behind the wire”(80). The authorities won’t endure the dislocation of citizens because the moving people are hard to control or dominate. Bell Hooks, a famous American social activist, points out bluntly that power "equals to the reign and control of men and things"(83). To preserve the interests of the rulers involves the forceful resettlement of the objects out of control. Once in the camp, people naturally lose their subjectivity and freedom, and they are always under authoritative supervision as potential suspects. The medical officer's speech betrays the nature of the labour camp: "This is a camp, not a holiday resort, not a convalescent home: it is a camp where we rehabilitate people like you and make you work! You are going to learn to fill sandbags and dig holes, my friend, till your back breaks!"(138) Mandatory labour exhausts the camp members, making the latter unable to think otherwise. And the people with dominant discourse power hold that this is exactly the effect the discipline should reach.

Foucault's idea of power is often significant in understanding the nature of power: "Power ... was essentially a right of seizure: of things, time, bodies, and ultimately life itself; it culminated in the privilege to seize hold of life in order to suppress it"("History of Sexuality" 136). Only when the authoritarian is satisfied can camp members stay peacefully in the segregated "home", otherwise, they will suffer a worse fate, even lose their life. The following remark is a proof:

> And if you don't co-operate you will go to a place that is a lot worse than this! You will go to a place where you stand baking in the sun all day and eat potato-peels and mealie-cobs, and if you don't survive, tough luck, they cross your number off the list and that is the end of you! (138)

This is not a mere threat but an undeniable reality for the otherized and displaced in the apartheid South Africa.

The clergyman's preach Coetzee designs for this purpose strengthens the power and the legality of the discipline of the authorities. The clergyman requires the pious Christians to "Let peace enter our hearts again, O Lord, and grant it to us to return to our homes cherishing bitterness against no man, resolved to live together in fellowship in Thy name, obeying Thy commandments" (83). The sermon is imbued with the sense of subtle persuasion admonishing people to be obedient. They should endure everything unbearable, they should learn to yield when facing the dominant discourse power and they should believe in predestination that freedom makes no sense to them. Thus, South African authorities can smoothly control the thoughts of the members in camps, making all the activities in the camp confined by this special discourse power. However, the plot of K's success in fleeing away from the camp and returning to the free world through his shocking resistance from his physical instinct to the limitation of the dominant discourse power, especially the plot of the camp administrator's admiration for K's fight for freedom and his final success in obtaining his freedom after breaking away from the rigid control, totally subvert the original discipline of the medical officer and the idea of justification of the oppression by the dominant discourse power.

Coetzee's meditation on trauma, history, power and domination reflects his profound thinking of the status quo of the apartheid South Africa. Colonization and apartheid leave nothing beneficial for South Africans but a history full of traumas. The rulers' abuse of power and discipline ruins the life of the marginalized Other and what's worse, the authorities attempt to conceal the truth. In the essay "Into the Dark Chamber: The Writer and the

South African State", Coetzee writes in an ironical tone that

> If people are starving, let them starve far away in the bush, where their thin bodies will not be a reproach. It they have no work, if they migrate to the cities, let there be roadblocks, let there be curfews, let there be laws against vagrancy, begging, and squatting, and let offenders be locked away so that no one has to hear or see them("Doubling the Point" 36).

Coetzee's exposure and criticism of the absurd social reality and his presentation of the sense of doomsday on the vast land of South Africa offer precious references for the people today to know the place and the living state of the people there. In the third part, he allegorically tells readers that the marginalized Other can resort to their own ideals by keeping "silence" as a means of resistance, for freedom is so precious that it deserves human perseverance and constant pursuit.

Coetzee, by making allegorical use of the experiences of Michel K the marginalized Other, who lacks meaningful relationship with others in the novel *Life & Times of Michel K*, depicts metaphorically the living state of the down-trodden populace with the images of amoebas, stick insects and ants. He moves readers with the story of the insignificant character's fight with his fate and perseverance with his faith of freedom, criticizing the stereotyped thought of the apartheid South Africa in the postcolonial context. The silent Other in Coetzee's novel has overwhelming power. The optimism demonstrated in the description "the mountains purple and pink in the distance, the great still blue empty sky, ... you suddenly saw a tip of vivid green, pumpkin leaf or carrot-brush"(183) and K's thought "as long as there is water, one can live", leave people endless hope of freedom. This hope cannot be smothered by the evil apartheid in South Africa; instead, it gives courage and confidence to the silent Other to survive in their predicament. Contrary to the opinion expressed in *the African Communist* at the beginning of the chapter, those who are interested in knowing and improving South Africa will definitely get revelation from the life and times of Michel K.

Chapter III

Disgrace: the Subverted Other in the Post-apartheid Era

With an almost outline-drawing style and startling tone *Disgrace* by Coetzee tells a story about how David Lurie, a white professor in literature and communication who excelled in sensible calculation, paid a heavy price for his misconduct and was transformed from a dominant subject to a discourse-deprived object in the era when colonial entity no longer exists and the apartheid officially ends in South Africa. Once published, the novel won much critical acclaim. It was awarded Man Booker Prize and Commonwealth Writers' Prize, nominated for National Book Critics Circle Awards, and selected as the best book by *New York Times Book Review* in the year. Boehmer claims that "it may well have paved the way for the 2003 award to the writer of the Nobel Prize in literature" ("Not Saying Sorry" 342). Cornwell illustrates that the novel "already generated a voluminous and various critical response... it is likely to continue to do so" (43). Attridge argues that "Few novels in recent decades have generated as much serious debate (in addition to media attention) as J. M. Coetzee's *Disgrace*" ("Coetzee's *Disgrace*" 315).

Some critics contend that "J. M. Coetzee's novel *Disgrace*... can be read as a political text, post-apartheid work that deals with the difficulties confronting the white community in South Africa and with some of the choices available to them" (Sanvan 26). "J. M. Coetzee's *Disgrace* draws an anxious, comfortless picture of postapartheid South Africa" (Cooper 22). Shashi Deshpande, chair of the panel of the Commonwealth Writers Prize, described it as "a complex story" that "embraces with remarkable skill the politics of a new nation" (McDonald 321), adding that the "unflinching honesty with which [it] confronts complicated moral issues makes it a work of great significance for our times" (ibid 322). Wood maintains that "*Disgrace*, which is a kind of South African version of Turgenev's *Fathers and Sons* — an issue novel about the generation wars — is a novel with which it is impossible to find fault" ("Parables and Prizes" 43). However, others don't attach much importance to the novel. *Disgrace* has been treated harshly by some critics who feel that the novel "contributed nothing positive to representations of the post-apartheid status of the 'new' South Africa" (L. Wright 99). Thabo Mbeki, former president of South Africa, felt unhappy with the novel *Disgrace*, saying even indignantly that "South Africa is not only a place of rape" (Pienaar, "Brilliant yet aloof" October 3, 2003). And his idea has been endorsed by researchers, who argue that "The situating of a white South African female as the victim of post-apartheid violence unsurprisingly caused great offence to the black community who felt this undermined the on-going struggle for democracy and equality" (Tran 1).

This chapter studies the novel *Disgrace* from the dimension of the post-apartheid power-shift and shows that Coetzee gives his concern with and takes a dialectical attitude towards the white-black relationship in the post-apartheid era in South Africa. More specifically, the novel displays how

Lurie, a representative of the middle-class white man, became the subverted "Other", demonstrating the writer's philosophical reflection on themes such as the manipulating discourse among the white and the colored, the status quo of the relationship between the white and the colored, the historical burdens and individual responsibility, and rational principles and ethical questions, etc. Coetzee explored the cruel Western rationalism and shallow moral outlook by embodying the otherization of Lurie, a white man advocating freedom, as well as employing animals as "the essential third term in the reconciliation of human self and human other"(Boehmer, "Not Saying Sorry" 346).

1. White/black Relationship in the Post-apartheid Era

The establishment of the new coalition government consisting of the African National Congress, National Party and Inkatha Freedom Party in 1994 indicates the abolition of the apartheid, one of the most brutal racial segregations in history, due to the joint efforts of the substantial pressure of the colored peoples in South Africa as well as the severe denouncement and sanction of the international communities. Some scholars put a premium on the abolition:

> The birth of the New South Africa, characterized with democracy, unity and racial equality, is a historical landmark in the cause of peoples' fight against racism and colonialism, marking the end of the most inhumane racial segregation system and the huge victory of the national liberation movement on African continent (Xu and Liang 567).

In 1996, the constitution of South Africa solemnly announced:

> Human dignity, the achievement of equality and the advancement of human rights and freedoms/non-racialism and non-sexism/supremacy of the constitution and the rule of law/universal adult suffrage, a national common voters roll, regular elections and a multi-party system of democratic government, to ensure accountability, responsiveness and openness. ①

However, the abolition of racial segregation and the practice of democratic system do not mean the complete disappearance of the racial conflicts in South Africa.

The democratic revolution symbolizes the expiration of the white/black conflicts which have lasted for more than 300 years, but the long-lived social problems are not resolved once and for all because of the sudden transformation of systems. The black resistance culture accumulated and formed in the course of the white/black conflicts still exerts a profound influence due to people's stereotyped ideology and shows its existence stubbornly in diverse social movements. Most importantly, the termination of the apartheid will not eliminate the deep-rooted spiritual racial segregation.

New South Africa fails to eliminate the astonishing gap between the rich and the poor within a short time after the abolition of the apartheid. It is very hard to change the fact that white people who merely account for 10% of the population own 95% of the wealth of the country, and the majority of

---

① Statutes of the Republic of South Africa-Constitutional Law (Issue No 38) Constitution of thc Republic of South Africa Act, No. 108 of 1996. 1243.

the black people are in extreme poverty and sustain themselves with less than one dollar a day. The unshakably high ratio of unemployment, the vulnerability of the black and other colored peoples to the fluctuation of economic situation are ascribed to the factors that the black have a poor education and do not have professional knowledge or skills. Besides, the black and other colored have to live in Bantustan, an area isolated from the downtown. But in effect, the black have to swarm into the city to survive, and stay there "illegally", thus forming slums. The situation in these slums is hard to change immediately after the abolition of the apartheid, and peoples' health and education can rarely be guaranteed.

Distinct inequalities still exist after the abolition of the apartheid, and at the same time the black resistance culture formed in the apartheid has stood the test of cruel struggle and the street protest, demonstrating that their dissatisfaction has become a unique landscape of the black people's life. This culture has been universally accepted by the black people, playing a crucial role in abolishing apartheid and claiming democratic rights. The black people take pride in this culture and refuse to give it up with the development of democratic revolution. However, for the new South Africa, the culture suggests latent crises, for the protest involved with the issue of racial estrangement may lead to the disorder of the society. Different from the principle of nonviolence and non-cooperation advocated by Nelson Mandela, some extremists, including the black, have begun to take violent actions in their protest. In addition, the abolition of apartheid does not make revolutionary influence upon people's ideology. In effect, the white have never in their mind admitted the human equality among different races, nor changed their idea of taking the black as inferior citizens. And similarly the black have never in their mind considered the white as their brothers or sisters nor has their hatred against the white faded away because of the expiration of the apartheid. Their deep-rooted hatred inevitably leads to new forms of racial oppression.

Objectively speaking, the black authorities do not take any large-scaled revenge against the self-assured "superior" white people, instead, they take initiative measures to protect the interests of the white when the latter have lost the protection of political power. However, the measures, compared with the policies of the white government, obviously fail to satisfy the white people since it was impossible for them to continue enjoying some privileges or priorities. In a sense, the privileges of small proportion of the white mean the deprivation of the rights of the black, the overwhelming majority. To accomplish the coexistence of different races based on equality and justice, the black government has taken corresponding measures, for instance, a plan called "Growth, Employment and Redistribution" was put forward in 1995 to eliminate the gap between the rich and the poor, and 11 languages such as English, Afrikaans, Southern Sotho, Zulu, etc. are stipulated by the new constitution as official languages in 1996. Furthermore, it is affirmed that South African cultures, regardless of races or sexes, should be inherited. However, in the eyes of the white accustomed to enjoying priorities, these policies mean the subversion of their former status. They feel oppressed by the black and marginalized under the rein of the black government.

In reality, the white's feeling of marginalization does not come out of thin air and this can be observed in multiple aspects of the political life in South Africa. For instance, despite of the establishment of the coalition government of the white and the black at the abolition of the apartheid, more and more white officials are expelled from vital positions when the black leaders from national parties such as African National Congress and

Inkatha Freedom Party have won more and more support from the masses of black people. Consequently, what have been left for the white are only the positions entailing professional qualifications. In the political domain of South Africa, the contrast between the white and the black is an apparent feature and the gradual otherization and marginalization of the white have become an undeniable fact.

The accomplishment of democratic transformation in 1994 is the mere change of the institution, but the inequality caused by the long-term apartheid has continuously aroused social problems among the African people. As has been analyzed, the income discrepancy does not vanish with the abolition of the apartheid. With the black in control of the government, some blacks begin to believe that the wealth of the white has mostly been grabbed in crooked ways by means of suppressing and exploiting the black and should be justifiably returned to the black. The government, approving of this opinion in a sense, gives tacit consent to it and supports it with specific actions. They withdraw mineral resources formerly monopolized by the white and adopt a kind of "active discrimination" policy, regulating compulsorily that 25% to 40% shares should be possessed by the black once a company dominated by the white has got any project involved with the government. These policies characterized with distinct nature of forceful exploitation make the white realize deeply how the black was ever maltreated in history when the latter was marginalized. In the post-apartheid South Africa, everything changes completely. Black resistance culture evolves into various social movements but the spiritual racial segregation is hard to eliminate among different races. The crime rate keeps rising irresistibly and the wealthy white become the main victims of the robbery. The tension between the black and the white has never been relieved and the marginalized white people have lost the sense of security. Some choose to leave South Africa in hopelessness and others take radical measures to deal with the violence of the black, thus intensifying the already tense relationship. In South Africa in the post-apartheid era, people are confronted with some crucial and imminent problems: how to solve social and economic problems, how to realize the coexistence and fusion of different races or nationalities, how to maintain the social stability, and how to implement the policy of freedom and equality, diversity and toleration virtually with action.

2. The subverted Other in *Disgrace*

Coetzee's novel *Disgrace*, published five years after the abolition of apartheid in 1994, "offers a dark depiction of South Africa's transitional tremors, for the legacy of apartheid does not dissipate overnight" (Segall 40).

With two threads the novel exposes various problems among different races resulting from the evil apartheid and its impacts, demonstrating that the social status of the white is completely subverted and the white become the marginalized Other after their power of discourse is deprived. A thought-provoking conversation has been arranged between Lurie and Lucy at the end of Chapter 22, embodying the experience of the white in the context of post-apartheid South Africa and the harsh reality they have to confront.

> "How humiliating," he says finally. "Such high hopes, and to end like this."
>
> "Yes, I agree, it is humiliating. But perhaps that is a good point to start from again. Perhaps that is what I must learn to

accept. To start at ground level. With nothing. Not with nothing but. With nothing. No cards, no weapons, no property, no rights, no dignity."

"Like a dog."

"Yes, like a dog."①

The two participants of the conversation are both white with rich and varied experiences. Their stories illustrate the process of otherization of the white when the white's priority has been overnight deprived of, their central status substituted and their dominating discourse power subverted.

As the protagonist of the novel, Lurie is initially a respectable professor specializing in linguistics in Cape Town University College. However, he is turned into an associate professor since "Classics and Modern Languages were closed down as part of the great rationalization"(3). He is transferred from modern languages to communications and enjoys a special policy "irrespective of enrolment"(ibid). But, he is not popular among students since communications is not within his research area and, in addition, he is not good at teaching. Virtually, the platform does not offer him much pleasure in embodying the discourse power. However, he feels that it is just an occupation sustaining his life. Although passionless, he still devotes himself to his work. Coetzee does not focus on the description of the work of Lurie. He mentions the occupation of Lurie only to elicit Melanie Isaacs, another important character whose relation with Lurie completely changes the orbit of his later life.

The white professor of Dutch descent is over fifty, but his passion with

① This is quoted from page 205 of J. M. Coetzee's *Disgrace* published by Vintage Books in London in 1999. Further references to this edition will be indicated by quoting page numbers in parenthesis.

females is by no means lessened. His sex relation with Melanie enrages her jealous boyfriend and her conventional father, causing their complaint to the university authority and a protest from a campus female association against the abuse of professor's rights. *Argus*, a campus newspaper, publicizes this under the title "Professor on Sex Charge" and the university organizes a disciplinary board on the charge of sex harassment. But he stubbornly refuses to admit his fault, let alone apologizing for what he has done to the victim, resulting in his being dismissed from his position. He insists that Western democracy should include sexual freedom and the instinctive gratification — a matter of privacy in his eyes should not be intervened by the public. "A dog will accept the justice of that: a beating for a chewing. But desire is another story. No animal will accept the justice of being punished for following its instincts" (90). However, he neglects that a great Greek philosopher announced clearly two thousand years ago: "it is clear that the rule of the soul over the body, and of the mind and the rational element over the passionate, is natural and expedient; whereas the equality of the two or the rule of the inferior is always hurtful"(Aristotle 9). Man is not an inferior animal. If man is degraded to the status of a dog and acts in consistence with the "pleasure principle" (Freud 1), satisfying his sexual desire and acting completely manipulated by his instinct regardless of any moral principles, his dignity and sacredness of being a man are in reality impaired. A harsh reality Lurie must confront is that he lives no longer in a society where the white plays a dominant role. His sense of superiority of the white — "*We Westerners*"(202) — is obsolete and everyone is now equal according to the new constitution. Human dignity, the achievement of equality and the advancement of human rights and freedom affirmed in the constitution refer to the dignity, equality, human rights and freedom of all peoples regardless of their races or colors. Therefore, it is inevitable that Lurie should be deprived of the discourse power as a university professor and become a marginalized Other, unwillingly leaving his university and position to find his daughter on a remote farm.

Lucy's experiences display in a more typical way the process of the subversion of the white's dominant status and the otherizaton of the white, while Lurie's position as a marginalized Other is further affirmed on the farm and more evidences indicate that his helplessness after the subversion is undoubtedly irreversible.

A famous French writer and philosopher says, "A woman feels inferior because female requirement virtually degrades her. She instinctively chooses to be a sound being, a subject and free being facing the world and the future" (De Beauboir 467). Lucy, another important figure in Coetzee's writing, is unique with independent thinking as modern females often do. As an acknowledged lesbian, she has a strong sense of domination, leaving the city life for Grahamstown six years ago "as a member of a commune"(60) and living a simple life with her partner Helen. Coetzee's arrangement of time is significant if coincidence is removed. The fact that Lucy the white woman breaks away from city life for the remote country is more symbolic than the event itself. Lucy's six years of country experiences are exactly the years after the abolition of the apartheid. White women in the area where the great majority of population is black are objectively in the position of minority. In addition to the expiration of the policies favorable to the white, the priority of the white no longer exists. The social structure established according to the concepts of rights or subject rights derived from West Europe is now evidently sided with the black in South Africa. The relationship between the two social entities, intense in opposition and cooperative in exploitation, pushes forward the social development of new South Africa in the process of conflict and compromise in accordance with the old principle of contract.

Coetzee arranges Lurie to experience personally the robbery and to witness the gang-rape to his daughter. The two events that take place simultaneously show that the tension between the black and the white in new South Africa has not been alleviated, nor has the resistance culture of the black been changed although the new democratic system has raised the status of the black and subverted the discourse power of the white. Coetzee demonstrates the confusion of Lucy via a conversation between her and her father: "But why did they hate me so? I had never set eyes on them"(156). However, what is noteworthy is the report from the *Herald*:

> Three unknown assailants have attacked Ms Lucy Lourie and her elderly father on their smallholding outside Salem, making off with clothes, electronic goods and a firearm. In a bizarre twist, the robbers also shot and killed six watchdogs before escaping in a 1993 Toyota Corolla. (115 - 116)

Here, robbing property and killing dogs are reported in details but no single word is mentioned about the rape. Of course, it is not due to the carelessness of the reporter, nor does the newspaper want to hide anything, but because of Lucy's silence in the matter. Lurie fails to understand it, but he can do nothing though furious. A reasonable explanation is that the deep-rooted principle of rationality in the mind of the white has been internalized as a kind of collective unconsciousness which will demonstrate itself consciously or unconsciously in different ways. The instinctive response of Lurie who has been subverted recently from the position of university professorship is to appeal to laws for the truth and the punishment of the rapists. He knows well how the accident has hurt his lesbian daughter: "Raping a lesbian worse than raping a virgin: more of a blow"(157). However, being immersed longer in the black-dominant environment, Lucy has to make a choice within a limited time when confronted with the sudden insult though she feels painful and unbearable. She decides to face the harsh reality rationally because she knows clearly that she is "in their territory" and a white woman means "nothing to them"(ibid). It is futile not to admit that the black are in power and the white have lost their priorities. In the government dominated by the black it is impossible to ask for the rights of the white and to punish the black. When the white/black relationship is in great tension, would the black police protect the white at the risk of offending the black? Everything is in suspense. "How to think and talk about a new South Africa in the light of its fragmented past and its complex and violent present is exactly the subject which J. M. Coetzee investigates in his novel *Disgrace*" (Buikema 188). What Coetzee chooses is indeed the typical event in South Africa. He pushes his characters into the whirl of contradiction and conflict, testifying the characters' wisdom, and reveals the conflicts in post-apartheid South Africa after the choice of the characters, commenting on the effects of their choices.

Lucy prevents her father from revenging and chooses endurance and slavery which have been the life of the black people for more than 300 years. She is ready to accept the protection of Petrus, her former employee and "co-proprietor since March" (62), with great tolerance, perseverance and magnanimity. She is willing to become the mistress of Petrus, transferring her land and making the unborn baby the child of Petrus. She shows no concern with anything and almost gives up everything with one condition: "the house remained mine"(204). Lucy's choice is a shrewd one since the white have lost their privileges. The choice implies that the white have to face the reality, compromise themselves and accept their fate in new South Africa. It might be the prerequisite for them to realize the fusion with the white in real sense, though in the innermost recesses of her mind, she still wishes to have her own independent status for the house suggests independence or identity.

Lucy's choice infuriates Lurie, but his own choice is similarly lamentable. After being expelled from the university he has been gradually marginalized: moving out from Cape Town to a country farm. He turns from a professor to a helper, feeling himself "as obscure and growing obscurer. A figure from the margins of history"(167). In his great agony when he feels powerless at his daughter's being insulted, his sense of superiority vanishes completely with the words of his daughter at his contemplation of revenge: "Wake up, David. This is the country. This is Africa"(124). This is what the character says but it epitomizes the thinking of Coetzee. How can the white master their own fate in new South Africa where they have lost their discourse power? In a sense, the author implies that the racial conflicts or revenging conducts will not melt the ice among different races and the only solution to this issue should be racial mix and tolerance.

3. Reflections on the Subversion of Dominant Discourse

As is discussed above, J.M. Coetzee in the novel *Disgrace* demonstrates the situation of the white subverted from their discourse power, in an attempt to arouse readers' attention to the issues popular in today's South Africa. "If J. M. Coetzee's novels often leave the reader with uncomfortable, unanswerable questions, it is because Coetzee addresses uncomfortable, unanswerable questions to himself" (Barnard 199). Barnard comes to the point in his remark and such kind of questions can be found almost in all Coetzee's writings including the novel *Disgrace*, just as Sue Kossew points out that "*Disgrace* is a complex exploration of the collision between private and public worlds; intellect and body; desire and love; and public disgrace or shame and the idea of individual grace or salvation" ("Politics of Shame and Redemption" 155). Referring to the phenomena of sexual violence and sexual inundation in South Africa, Coetzee has made reflections on reasoning principles, ethics, historical burdens and individual responsibilities while embodying the otherization of the white, whose former central status and dominant discourse are subverted.

First and foremost, Coetzee makes his reflection on **reasoning principles** and **moral principles** by presenting an old theme "sex" which has obtained new significance in his novel *Disgrace*. Confronted with a similar problem, Lurie the hero in the first part of the novel and Lucy the heroine in the second part are in effect both symbols of the white who have been otherized in the period of discourse power shift with the expiration of the apartheid. Coetzee explores different responses of the white and the black in the context of the complex and complicated post-apartheid South Africa in transition. Choosing the white professor of over fifty years old as a sample, Coetzee has intentionally deployed the sex experiences and contract principles of Lurie the associate professor to ponder on moral principles and ethical tendency, for "All human actions... will be returned to the ambit of moral judgment" ("Into the Dark Chamber" 5) according to the understanding of Coetzee.

Coetzee puts forward the issue of sex bluntly at the very beginning of the novel, claiming that Lurie, fifty-two, divorced, solved his sex problem well. His solution is actually a typical money-sex transaction instead of one via legal remarriage or in cohabitation. This fits in seemingly well with the reasoning principle in the capitalist West. As a university professor, Lurie adheres to the contract principle of capitalism: paying 400 rupee per week (of which half goes to Discreet Escorts) for a 90-minute sexual life. From the description "honey-brown, unmarked by the sun"(1) by Coetzee, the other side of the transaction is obviously a colored woman called Soraya. Lurie now feels complacent for he enjoys his sense of superiority as a master over the woman in inferior position in his mind as the Other. Unfortunately, "Man was born free, and everywhere he is in chains. Many a one believes himself the master of others, and yet he is a greater slave than they" (Rousseau 156). Arrogant as he is, Lurie assumes that he has followed the rational exchange principle, enjoying his sense of master and his performance within 90 minutes reinforces this illusion. However, an accidental meeting and eye-contact with the woman in public disillusions him. The evident indifference and coldness she displays shocks him into a stupor, realizing that he is by no means a master to anyone and his former life is so false and hollow that his self-display of sex experiences is really ridiculous. His so-called sex freedom is nothing but the satisfaction of "animal desire"(Bataille 47). He fails to be his own master but becomes the slave of his desires instead. In an attempt to resume relation with the woman, he feels once again chilled. "You are harassing me in my own house. I demand you will never phone me here again, never"(10). The shrillness of the woman's voice demonstrates that Lurie, who "lives... within his temperament, within his emotional means"(2) and always supposes with self-approbation that he can control others freely based on the compact principle, has lost his privilege as a white and become the Other in the new government of the black.

If the relation between Lurie and Soraya or another "unpractised, to his mind coarse"(8) "Soraya" from Discreet Escorts is a legal transaction on compact principle, Lurie's relation with his secretary Dawn a casual behavior expelling his dullness, then his relation with Melanie Isaacs cannot be justified by contract or rational principle, but by Bataille's concept of "desirous body" (Cheng 808) which witnesses the conflict between humanity and barbarity, and Nietzsche's "will-to-power"(333).

Melanie is a student from an optional course Lurie gives on Romantic poets. Their relation is apparently that of teacher and student, thus forming an ethical relation, because both sides, as a special moral community, are obliged to undertake a certain moral responsibility and obligation. The supreme personality and correct moral thinking of teachers often transform positively students unconsciously and work as a guide in their life. Just as Mr. Isaacs, Melanie's father, says, "We put our children in the hands of you people because we think we can trust you." However, he was proved to be wrong since he sent his daughter "into a nest of vipers"(38). As a professor, Lurie is so audacious that he has taken advantage of his position to seduce Melanie into sexual intercourse with him, violating the ethical principle in teacher-student relation and the voluntary principle in sexual relation. If their first sexual intercourse on Lurie's floor can be justifiably taken as seduction for the girl passively accepts it out of Lurie's fancy title, the second in the apartment of Melanie obviously violates directly the principles of sex ethics — principle of the fusion of soul and body, principle of freedom but self-discipline, and principle of self respect without harm to any side. Apparently Melanie feels disgusted at the forced sexual intercourse. And sex under such circumstances will never make both sides happy spiritually, emotionally or psychologically, on the contrary, it hurts the girl enormously. Melanie does not resist, but she shows her unwillingness in unequivocal term, foregrounding the gang rape Lucy suffers in the latter part of the novel.

With one whole paragraph Coetzee depicts and comments on Lurie's behavior:

> Not rape, not quite that, but undesired nevertheless, undesired to the core. As though she had decided to go slack, die within herself for the duration, like a rabbit when the jaws of the fox close on its neck. So that everything done to her might be done, as it were, far away(25).

If this situation can be interpreted with "sex philosophy" which always takes "sexual enjoyment" and "sexual consumption" as human rights, then it is likely to have over-emphasized the rights of the white professor in superior position and neglected the rights of a colored student in disadvantageous situation. The performance of Lurie is the embodiment of the "will to power", i. e. "as an insatiable desire to manifest power, or as an employment or exercise of power, as a creative drive, etc."(Nietzsche 333). Lurie's exercise of power upon the girl student demonstrates his natural quality which goes against the sexual moral principle in human society.

A well-known neurologist once said that "The racism inherent in whites labeling themselves as 'civilized' in comparison to the savage Others maintains power by protecting white interests and privileges through law" (Traber 23). The white professor in this case is irrational because he fails to realize that the new South Africans have woken up and the laws maintaining the interests and priority of the white have been abolished, resulting in the fact that the former savage others have become their equals. Coetzee's depiction of the responses to the scandal seems incidental, but the denouncement of the brute professor, the support to the victim and the report in mass media obviously show that the white no longer enjoy the priority in this event. With more scandals exposed by the committee of inquiry, Lurie realizes clearly that his reserve as a white in his unconsciousness cannot help him avoid the fate of notoriety, just as his ex-wife Rosalind predicts that "No sympathy, no mercy, not in this day and age. Everyone's hand will be against you, and why not?" (44) Desmond Swarts confirms this point by saying

> Ideally we would all have preferred to resolve this case out of the glare of the media. But that has not been possible. It has received a lot of attention, it has acquired overtones that are beyond our control. All eyes are on the university to see how we handle it (53 - 54).

Lurie has made apologies but refused to repent, without admitting that his sexual gratification by instinct has severely violated the moral principles. However, Coetzee conveys an unmistakable message that Lurie's tragedy is irreversible and he cannot evade his fate of self exile and self-otherization.

"Critical commentary has devoted attention to David Lurie's ethical status, with some of it sympathetic towards his lonely defiance of society's and the university's strictures..."(Kissack 51). However, Coetzee shows no mercy or sympathy with Lurie at all. His trenchant exposure of the white's disgrace is featured with apparent critical insights. His objective depiction of the shameful conduct of the white propels readers to realize that after the white has lost the discourse power and become otherized, Lurie has not kept pace with the situation in South Africa, being still indulged in the former days when the white enjoyed priorities.

If Lurie's experiences in Cape Town have been used by Coetzee to reflect upon sex ethics and human morality, then, the farm scene in *Disgrace* with Lucy's being robbed and gang-raped obviously reveals Coetzee's reconsideration of **historical burdens** and **individual responsibilities**. In explicit terms, Coetzee ponders over what price the white should pay in the post-apartheid era and what responsibilities the white individuals should take for historical memories after their fall from the dominant discourse position to the marginalized position of the Other.

What Lurie the Other witnesses and experiences on his daughter's farm after his loss of teaching post in a university in Cape Town provides sufficient evidences for Coetzee's reflection. As is mentioned above, Lucy the white lesbian is robbed and relentlessly gang-raped by three black men. Unfortunately, such events have been popular in the post-apartheid South Africa. A history of white oppression of over three centuries within which the savage apartheid lasts for half a century, and at the same time a history of black resistance of similar length which has become a cultural tradition, have made the contradictions and conflicts between the black and the white intense and irreconcilable. The problems Coetzee presents are by no means fictitious, but the truthful demonstration of the reality in South Africa. Since the Parliament of South Africa declared from February to June 1991 to revoke over 80 racialist laws like the *Native Land Act*, *Group Areas and Segregation Act*, *Population Registration Act*, the Reservation System has actually been called to an end. However, the residual of racial history does not vanish with the legal disappearance of the apartheid, instead it runs rampant in today's South Africa. So far as land reform is concerned, the black government has carried out policies inspiring to the black, bringing about the change in land ownership, but the government-dominated reform can hardly meet the needs of all the black due to the complexity of balancing the interests of different sides. As a result, the black begin to complain that the slow governmental reform renders the poor black at the bottom of the society little chance to get land or property quickly. Besides, their appeal, apparently like the winners of skin color revolution settling old scores with the white, causes numerous cases of the black robbing or killing white farmers in South Africa.

Lucy's confusion "Why they hate me so much?" after being robbed and raped reflects Coetzee's meditation over the heavy historical burdens in front of the black government in their reconstruction of the country. He proposes his opinion explicitly by Lurie's answer: "It was history speaking through them. ... A history of wrong. ... It may have seemed personal, but it wasn't. It came down from the ancestors"(156). Indeed, South Africans have suffered from white colonization and oppression endlessly in modern history, and the crimes the European white committed against the black are too numerous to record in South Africa.

> In the course of colonial conquest over South Africa, the white colonizers appealed to direct violence for the deprivation of the black of their land. After the establishment of the federal government, the deprivation of the land went on mainly by means of racial segregation (Ning 33).

The execution of racial segregation is "based upon the severest violence"

(Marx, “The Capital” 819). The pain inscribed in the depth of black racial memory cannot be removed overnight, nor can their enmity for the white and desire to revenge be easily relieved. Although the new black government's *Black Economic Empowerment* has injured the whites' vested interests and meant to protect the black's interests, it does nothing to make the black gain actual benefits, only driving the white with high academic degrees or technology abroad. Therefore, the white out of their discourse power become the marginalized Other, the object of the black's animosity. The great wealth the white possess is one of the causes that make the black angry, for they consider it the property of the South Africans, which should be returned to the black after being grabbed relentlessly from the white. Objectively speaking, the new black government doesn't promulgate any policy concerning the white's properties, and it is the black that initiatively rob the white at their own will. Consequently, the high crime rate in new South Africa leads to the lack of sense of security among the black and the white alike. So the black government decides on a racial reconciliation policy. In 1995, black archbishop Tutu established “South African Truth and Reconciliation Commission” to alleviate the great tension between the black and the white. However, unavoidable are the pains and sufferings in the process of social reformation, and intense conflicts between the old and the new concepts in the social integration.

The response of Lucy, one more marginalized Other, to the robbery and gang-rape reveals Coetzee's hope for racial reconciliation in South Africa. “... forgiveness, rebirth, and restitution constitute complex engagements with the themes currently dominating the South African situation” (McGonegal 1). Whether the black revenge upon the white out of historical animosity should be “righteously” crusaded against and punished, or tolerated and forgiven, is essential to whether the South Africans can successfully unload the historical burdens and rebuild a harmonious South Africa, leading normally a democratic and free life. A French philosopher's idea may be of significant revelation, "Forgiveness is a sort of healing of the memory, the completion of its mourning period. Delivered from the weight of debt, memory is liberated for great projects. Forgiveness gives memory a future"(Ricoeur 144). How to remit crimes and compensate for the harms of the legion terrors and crimes the white once committed, and to get the forgiveness from the black people after the apartheid is the lingering theme in this novel. Coetzee doesn't pinpoint the relationship between the novel and historical reality, which is confusing and ambiguous, but his meditation upon potential forgiveness, regeneracy and compensation proves to be beneficial.

Lurie's difficulty in understanding Lucy's tolerance without insisting on the investigation into the robbery and gang-rape reveals the confusion of the most otherized white in new South Africa: should the modern white in new South Africa take the responsibility by definition for the crimes of their ancestors — Boers' colonization of South Africa or former white oppression and exploitation upon the black? Should the white today experience once again all the sufferings and pains the black experienced in the past since the white have been otherized and marginalized in the same situation as the black before? Coetzee doesn't give any answer in the novel, but "charity" and "forgiveness" are two key words in his discussion about the South African racial relationship. When interviewed by Derek Attridge, he remarked, "What saves me from a merely stupid stupidity, I would hope, is a measure of charity, which is, I suppose, the way in which grace allegorized itself in the world"(Coetzee, "Doubling the Point" 246).

A comparison between the after-treatment of Lurie's sexual harassment of Melanie in the first part of the novel and that of Lucy's experience of being gang-raped in the second part may clearly show Coetzee's idea about the otherized white and about his suggested solution to the conflicts between the black and the white, or between the dominant subject and the marginalized Other. With no statement of repentance after the exposure of his scandal, Lurie admits his crime and accepts the due punishment. What's more, he later comes to the Essex's for the forgiveness from the victim.

> I am being punished for what happened between myself and your daughter. I am sunk into a state of disgrace from which it will not be easy to lift myself. It is not a punishment I have refused. I do not murder against it. On the contrary, I am living it out from day to day, trying to accept disgrace as my state of being. Is it enough for God, do you think, that I live in disgrace without term? (172)

Though the victim is absent and his supplication is more about what he has paid for his disgrace than consideration of the contempt and shame Melanie bears, the Essex family finally forgives him without attaching any prerequisites.

Different from Lurie, the toppled white from his vantage position, Lucy, the marginalized Other after the expiration of the apartheid, immediately clears the crime scene, refusing to admit the fact of being sexually harassed after the gang-rape. Instead of thinking about "just" and "righteous" revenge, she keeps meditating on why the black hate the white so much, and on the harms her victimizers had during the apartheid. Her shocking decision made after her painful reflections is actually that of the author. Jacques Derrida believes "if anyone has the right to forgive, it is only the victim"(qtd. in McGonegal 135). Though Coetzee doesn't arrange the possibility of forgiveness and reconciliation between Lurie the Other and Petrus the symbol of the black who has newly gained discourse power, Lucy's decision in the novel effectively reaches the reconciliation between the white and the black. In the writer's mind, the otherized white should not indulge themselves in their past glory or in their ideology of white dominance at present when the black have the discourse power in South Africa, instead they should accept the fact that they have been marginalized and become the Other. They cannot treat with sense of superiority the black who used to be inferior in their eyes, and instead they should treat them with sense of equality. Only in this way can the racial mix be accomplished.

Racial reconciliation in the post-apartheid era has been a focus in *Disgrace* and this is interestingly associated with the **concern with animals**. As is discussed above, Coetzee has transformed Lurie from an arrogant professor with a strong sense of superiority into a farm helper with great sympathy with animals. This transformation is highly symbolic with great significance, for Coetzee the allegorist has displayed his dexterity in reinforcing his theme through his creative imagination.

Before Lurie's transformation, Coetzee has demonstrated with minute details the inversion of social status of the white and their situation in the post-apartheid South Africa. Toppled down from the dominant position and marginalized as the Other, the white of European descent have to adapt themselves to the changed roles. Ettinger, a typical European "who speaks English with a marked German accent"(100), has installed "bars, security gates, a perimeter fence," in short, turned his home "into a fortress"(113) for security, but unfortunately as Lucy predicts, "It is just a matter of time before Ettinger is found with a bullet in his back"(204). Lucy, a lesbian with romantic temperament, has to be the mistress of her former helper Petrus after being intolerably gang-raped by three blacks. Coetzee even makes use of the change of languages in the inversion of human positions. Western languages — vehicle of the powerful discourse of the European colonizers — become no longer effective, they are "like a dinosaur expiring and settling in the mud" (117). On the contrary, local languages like Sotho and Xhosa become vigorous, conveying conveniently the true feelings of the people who regain their discourse power. Under such circumstances, the former colonizers and their descendants cannot be arrogant any longer and their transformation has become necessary in the postcolonial and post-apartheid era.

In this context, the conflict between the black in power and the otherized white can hardly be alleviated. In order to suggest a solution to the issue, Coetzee attaches great importance to forgiveness among people with the hope that different races compromise with each other, but he does not preach that point directly. Though he uses the character Lucy to tell readers bluntly that time is changed and South Africa is not what it was when the white controlled the discourse power, yet he turns to the way of forgiveness and compromise, an "allegorical way" in his own term. And the way he suggests is demonstrated in the text mainly through Lurie's transformation in terms of his attitude towards animals besides the allegorical plot of Lucy's decision to become Petrus' mistress.

Coetzee's arrangement of Lurie's transformation is an important touch in his accomplishment of his theme. Displaced, the otherized Lurie shows no interest in animals when he first comes to the Animal Welfare clinic. When asked whether he fancies animals, Lurie answers, "Do I like animals? I eat them, so I suppose I must like them, some parts of them"(81). The remark truthfully reflects the mind of Lurie who merely takes animals as potential food for human beings. In effect, Coetzee displays quite a few scenes related to animals, but no scene is pleasant with animals well treated. For instance, the gang-rape scene is accompanied with the cruel shooting of dogs by the black. The most impressive that precipitates Lurie's transformation includes the scenes of twin Persian sheep and the dead dogs. The former scene concerns Lurie's change of attitude towards the sheep to be killed while the latter involves his decision to keep the dead dogs' dignity before they are incinerated. Humans show no sympathy or humanitarianism with either state of animals, which are regarded not as a member of nature but as inferior species, deserving no respect from human beings. Consequently, the sheep are tethered for butcher's knife, exposed to the scorching sun with no water or grass, while in handling the dead dogs, "the workmen began to beat the bags with the backs of their shovels before loading them, to break the rigid limbs"(144 - 145). Human beings are so accustomed or comfortably numb to such scenes that almost no protest will be staged against the above-mentioned practice. Nevertheless, different is Lurie whose experiences of being decentralized and otherized have made him normalized as human being who becomes humanly sympathetic and empathetic with animals. Lurie's transformation of attitude towards animals is highly symbolic, in effect demonstrating Coetzee's idea of nature.

Coetzee purposely juxtaposes the "superior" man with "inferior" animals such as sheep and dogs in traditional concept for the exploration of their relationship. In explicit terms he conveys his idea through the heroine in the novel *Elizabeth Costello: Eight Lessons*, "Respect for everyone's world-view, the cow's world-view, the squirrel's world-view, etc."(91 - 92). It is known that species in nature are all equal with the right of harmonious coexistence. Human beings should take animals as equals in their mind and respect the life of animals and keep their dignity. Coetzee's allegorical use of animals provides readers with great revelation: it is because of human division of species into different orders that endows evil Hitler with excuses for his establishment of death camps and for his atrocious slaughter of the Jews. In Coetzee's mind, "it was from the Chicago stockyards that the Nazis learned how to process bodies" (*Elizabeth Costello: Eight Lessons* 97). It is high time for humans to end their practice of labeling animals and prisoners as aliens.

When human beings begin to consider the welfare of animals, treating them as equals in the natural world, people are justified to believe that human beings will no longer maltreat each other. This might be Coetzee's hope for the South Africans in the post-apartheid era, for people indeed need to reconsider the value of life and identity of the individual. Gone forever are the stereotyped ideas like Eurocentrism and white supremacism, which should be kept in the historical memory. Coetzee's allegorical writing, with superb metaphors, expresses the author's wish of equal and free life for the black and the white alike, and of racial reconciliation without being hamstrung by historical burdens. Via the character Elizabeth Costello, Coetzee expresses his idea by saying, "In history, embracing the status of man has entailed slaughtering and enslaving a race of divine or else divinely created beings and bringing down on ourselves a curse thereby" (*Elizabeth Costello: Eight Lessons* 103). This tragedy should not be repeated, and the right way is to stop human imposition of their own will upon animals or their own species.

Coetzee displays in the novel the true relationship between the black and the white in an allegorical way in the new historical context in which the white have been otherized after the power-shift with the black gaining their discourse power in the post-apartheid South Africa. By revealing graphically the great agony of the Other represented by the white professor Lurie who has committed "moral disgrace" and Lucy who pays back allegorically for the disgraceful history of colonization and torture of the black by their white ancestors, by displaying the contradictions and conflict between Lurie and Lucy who represent different groups of the white with different feelings, Coetzee discloses the absurdity and hypocrisy of the rational society in paradoxes, interrogating emphatically the problems of historical memories and individual responsibilities, the rational principles and moral principles.

European white ancestors have committed in history severe crimes on African blacks, leaving a variety of disgraceful memories, and the white continue habitually to leave disgraceful records after the expiration of the apartheid. How to understand the humiliating memories and histories and how to deal with the historical burdens, are important questions raised before the black and the white alike. It entails the wisdom of different races, especially the power of humanity. In a metaphorical way, Coetzee, with great love of South Africa, has made through the discourse and performance of the characters a plea for forgiveness, reconciliation and coexistence between the black and the white, believing that two races should live in harmony. He does not hope to see the black revenge the marginalized white by misusing their discourse power, nor does he want to see the constant occurrence of bloody scenes from the otherized white's tit-for-tat or eye-for-eye violence. He does not hope to see the white who have been deprived of discourse power bear in mind constantly the "glorious" past when they enjoyed the priorities, nor does he hope to see that the otherized white stick to their inherent and stereotyped ideology. He suggests that the white learn to know the present context and to get accustomed to the new South Africa in the post-apartheid era. With the metaphorical plot of the transformation of Lurie's attitude to animals Coetzee conveys the ideas of the equality and harmonious coexistence among species.

Chapter IV

Elizabeth Costello Eight Lessons: the Differential Other in Postmodernist Context

Coetzee, a prolific writer with constant innovation, has endlessly carried on his differential writing experiment in his 38 years of literary career, and published 21 books of different styles including fiction, biography and essay collections, showing inexhaustible vigor in literary writing. From his maiden work *Dusklands* (1974) to the latest work *Summertime* (2009), Coetzee brings readers happy surprises every time when a book is published, often leaving readers a feeling of uniqueness. He rejects "realistic device such as linear plot, well-rounded characters, clear settings and close endings" (Canepari-Labid 15), makes innovations on plot arrangement, characterization, environment design and narration forms, and innovations on form, including reference to different genres, intertextualization, etc. He has a penetrating cognition of the white writing in South Africa and writes seven essays discussing the history of South African white writing from "the burgeoning white travel literature of the seventeenth century to the farm novels of the mid-twentieth" (Kissack 11) and published them in a book entitled "White Writing". He deliberately makes innovations in writing, "No two books ever follow the same recipe" (Engdahl, Press Release, October 2, 2003). Though Canepari-Labid says "In Coetzee's case, ... none of the usual critical labels apply" (15), yet postmodernity is obviously observed in his works and thus critics often call him postmodernist writer or metafiction writer. Victoria Glendinning, famous English biographer and critic, feels it hard to convey just what Coetzee's special quality is, commenting in *The Sunday Times* that "His writing gives off whiffs of Conrad, of Nabokov, of Golding, of the Paul Theroux of *The Mosquito Coast*. But he is none of these, he is a harsh, compelling voice" (qtd. in Coetzee, "In the Heart of the Country" back cover). Nadine Gordimer the Nobel laureate says, "J. M. Coetzee's critics almost all seem awed by his textual innovations which, as one puts it, traverse European literary and philosophical tradition" ("Preface" viii).

Coetzee's writing starts originally in the postmodernist context or his literary writing career begins synchronically with the development of postmodernist theory. His computer stylistic analysis of Samuel Beckett in the University of Texas at Austin for his doctoral book, makes him imbued with knowledge of the literature of the absurd; his study and subsequent teaching in American universities at the rise of postmodernism in the 1960s and 1970s endow him with unique understanding of postmodernism and his literary writing is inevitably marked with postmodernism. This chapter attempts first of all to begin with an analysis of the features of literary writing in the context of postmodernism, then review Coetzee's writing for revealing the differential otherness in his works. The focus of this chapter is the study from the dimension of the postmodernist discourse of the novel

Elizabeth Costello: *Eight Lessons*, a 21st century literary text published after Coetzee's migration to Adelaide, Australia. By exploring Elizabeth Costello, the differential Other in the fiction, this chapter intends to discuss how Coetzee makes use of this image to show the differential Otherness in his fiction writing, hoping to find the real connotation of the fiction's differential otherness and the author's contributions to and influence on the postmodernist theory and literary writing.

1. Coetzee's Differential Writing in Postmodernist Context

Modernism with rationality and humanism as its core idea develops to its extreme in the 20th century with the evolution of the spirit in European enlightenment, science and technology, and rationality itself. Due to the development of science and technology, rationality becomes no longer noble and admirable for it has fallen down into instrumental rationality, turning from the instrument of liberation to that of domination over nature and human being. Humanism has lost its brilliance of humanity and become the slave of instrumental rationality, making humans lose their rational subjectivity and the object of human service.

Modernism, with the feature of subjective introversion, skillful use of symbolic metaphors, pursuit of the profundity of art, expression of beauty and sublimity of humanity by exposure of ugliness and self-negation, and zeal for artistic innovation and experiment, produces new literary schools of all sorts under the influence of existentialism. These schools, based on irrationalism and often known as postmodernist, negate historical discourse without believing any longer heroes or heroines and prefer no longer grand narrative, showing a tendency of violent anti-tradition. Negating the integrality, determinacy, standardability and purposiveness, they advocate openness, multiplicity and relativity without limit, and oppose all forms of limitation to literary creation, including the conventional concept of regulation, model, centre, etc.

Typical examples can be found in quite a few writers. For instance, Joseph Heller purposely adopts a disheveled structure to show the absurdity and disorder of the reality in his novel *Catch*-22 (1961). He subverts the continuity of the plot, discards the conventional characterization, filling the novel with an atmosphere of disorder, noise and madness. "... in an age of ultimacies and 'final solutions'," Samuel Beckett's work in his own way "reflects and deals with ultimacy, both technically and thematically"(Barth 313). Italo Calvino, in pursuit of the self-revelation of the text in the novel *Cosmicomics* (1965), combines wisely the allegory of the Space Age with contemporary life in Italy by employing the form of the ancient theology, making a perfect postmodern work by the fusion of the colorful dream and the hopeless life in reality. Gabriel Garcia Marquez goes even further by putting together in disorder the elements of literature and non-literature, such as art, theology, politics, reality, magic, cartoon-like satire, terror, etc. He juxtaposes the past, the future and the present in a playful way, resulting in the work filled with philosophical ideas in the satirical appearance. Donald Barthelme's writing witnesses some extreme experiments for he pays special attention to contingency and fragmentality. He inserts with seemingly optional way his non-word expression in the novel, e.g. some elusive pictures or unintelligible monotonous color lumps, and tirelessly employs stereotypes, parodies of the society, historical events and the self, showing the author's query of the official discourse and the mockery at the conventional writing. The appearance of these works and more reinforces John Barth's famous claim of "the literature of exhausted possibility — or more chicly, the literature of exhaustion"(310).

In the representation crisis of the postmodernist context, Coetzee, the celebrated experimental writer, becomes better known with his differential otherness in the world literature. He won twice the Booker Prize but refused to go to London for the prize for the second time in 1999, let alone making an acceptance speech in normal sense. When everyone was guessing if he would refuse to accept the Nobel Prize in 2003, he appeared unexpectedly at the Royal Swedish Academy of Sciences, and read at the solemn ceremony a short story "He and His Man" instead of making an acceptance speech, surprising everyone at present. As a professor on the Committee on Social Thought at the University of Chicago, Coetzee has delivered quite a few lectures internationally at invitation, but "For some time now, he has been in the habit, when invited to deliver a lecture, of employing a richly deflective device: he reads out a story about a writer asked to give a lecture" (Wood, "A Frog's Life" 15). And his newly gained habit subverts the practice of conventional lectures of developing ideas, verifying arguments or conveying information through formal, orderly and usually extended expression with special terms, specific rhetoric, etc. Influenced by French structuralism[①], Samuel Beckett's literature of the absurd[②], Vladimir Propp's theological analysis[③], Vladimir Nabokov's intertextual novel[④], Coetzee's literary writing displays a striking feature of differential otherness.

① Coetee admits that "it [French structuralism] certainly broadened the horizons of someone who had grown up in a European enclave in Africa, who disliked travel, who preferred books to life"("Doubling the Point: Essays and Interviews" 24).

② Coetee says "Beckett has meant a great deal to me in my own writing — that must be obvious" (ibid. 25).

③ Interviewed by Attwell, Coetee declares openly that "the line that intrigued me most was Vladimir Propp's analysis ..." (ibid. 23)

④ According to David Attwell, "*Dusklands* is structurally indebted to *Pale Fire*" (ibid. 28).

Coetzee says, "I believe one has a duty (an ethical duty? — perhaps) not to submit to powers of discourse without question" ("Doubling the Point" 200). His first CNA prize winning novel *Dusklands* (1974), not limited by any regulations or patterns of novel writing, juxtaposes the 20th century Vietnam War① and the 18th century Boers' exploration in Africa, displaying "Two forms of misanthropy, one of them intellectual and megalomaniac, the other vital and barbaric, [which] reflect each other" (Engdahl, Press Release, October 2, 2003). The first text follows the narrator's account of his participation in Coetzee's project but it constantly hints at the process of revision and even provides readers with the original "preface" to the project, showing a distinct feature of metafiction, while the second text is even more unique for its differential otherness. The author creatively arranges before the original novella a brief "Translator's Preface", saying that the language used for the original text is Dutch with the preface in Afrikaans. In this way, the writer of this novel immediately becomes the translator, hence distancing the text and the reality. The responsibility which should be taken by the veritable author is thus transferred to the professor at the University of Stellenbosch mentioned in the "Translator's Preface". At the same time, the author's suggestive discourse invisibly connects the two texts, creating a new text of differential otherness. The novel *In the Heart of the Country* published three years later does not care at all about the integrity, determinacy and standardability. Instead it is structured in fragments numbered 1 - 266 to convey a seeming sense of linearity, conveying the episodic monologues of an unmarried white woman on an isolated farm in South Africa, in which her father dies in different forms and her identity has

① In his stay in the United States of America, Coetzee was involved in anti-Vietnam-War protests and later was denied when he sought permanent residence in the United States.

been endowed with different interpretations. By the demonstration of her self-mockery, her passion for her father, patricide, desire for the male and endless existentialist speculations, the author constructs the rhapsody of a pure lonely woman and provides readers with a new genre of novel of irresistible power with otherness.

In his literary writing in 1980s, Coetzee shows more innovative spirit in his literary experiment. His novel *Waiting for the Barbarians* (1980) which first won him world recognition often reminds readers of Samuel Beckett's *Waiting for Godot*. He denies historical discourse by adopting the postmodernist form of political allegory and tells an anti-history story by using the first person singular narration of endless monologue, examining the issue of grand history of civilization. However, his first Booker Prize winning novel *Life and Times of Michel K* (1983) takes no longer heroes as protagonists, and shows no more interest in grand narrative, but exhibits by Kafkaesque approach① human spiritual life in the disordered situation and the relationship between human beings and the outside world.

In the next novel *Foe* (1986), Coetzee cleverly removes the prefix "de" from Daniel Defoe, the founder of realist novel in the English Enlightenment, suggesting his inseparable tie with Defoe. By using Susan's three kinds of first person variant form of narration — reminiscence of the past, exchange of letters, experience of events, Coetzee gives an account of the process that Susan as a female narrator wants to get discourse power through manipulation of the text. His application of postmodernist

① In answering David Attwell, Coetzee says, "You ask about the impact of Kafka on my own fiction. I acknowledge it, and acknowledge it with what I hope is a proper humility." And he also discusses the relationship between Kafka's Joseph K and his Michel K. (Coetzee, J.M. *Doubling the Point: Essays and Interviews*. ed. David Attwell. Cambridge, Massachusetts: Harvard University Press, 1992. 199.)

intertextuality not only serves as a parody, but expresses his concern for postcolonial issues by hinting obliquely at Western classics. After a brief turn to realist writing in *The Age of Iron* (1990), a brief episode in the process of his innovation, he begins once again his experiment of innovative writing in *The Master of Petersburg* (1994), which, in present continuous tense, introduces into the story Dostoyevsky and the figures in his life and novels, forming multiple dialogic relations of equality with the author by multi-layer intertextuality. This novel is thus commented as the polyphonic of the polyphonic novels.

Coetzee's first fiction after his migration to Australia *Elizabeth Costello*: *Eight Lessons* (2003) enters the long list of the Booker Prize but arouses great disputes among readers for it consists of eight chapters and a postscript, though the chapters are called "Lessons". It is actually "a series of philosophical dialogues bound into rather fitful fiction"(Wood, "A Frog's Life" 15), in which most stories begin with academic lectures, and six out of the eight stories have been published or made public at lectures. For instance, "Realism" was originally presented as a keynote lecture at Bennington College in Vermont in 1996, and subsequently published as "What is Realism" in the journal *Salmagund* in 1997. "The Novel in Africa", a lecture Coetzee delivered at University of California, Berkeley in 1998, was printed as "Occasional Papers Series" of the university in 1999. "The Lives of Animals", which occupies almost one third of the book, is a script for the 1997 – 1998 Tanner Lectures at Princeton University. The script including "The philosophers and the Animals" and "The Poets and the Animals" was published by Princeton University Press in 1999. "The Humanities in Africa", written in German and English, was printed by Siemens Foundation, Munich in 2001. "The Problem of Evil" is a script for a lecture on the problem of evil at a conference in the Netherlands in 2002.

Exactly speaking, the eight co-related pieces are theses about modern life and writing career; however, with the connection of Elizabeth Costello, the differential Other in the meticulous design of the author, they become an organic whole, a unique text in the postmodernist context. English novelist and critic Adam Mars-Jones holds that "it [*Elizabeth Costello*: *Eight Lessons*] is very novel", but at the same time she questions "but is it actually a novel?"① David Lodge's comment is brief but of typical significance, "It is a book which begins like a cross between a campus novel and a Platonic dialogue, segues into introspective memoir and fanciful musing, and ends with a Kafkaesque bad dream of the afterlife."② Anyhow, the novel deconstructs the pattern of linear narration in conventional novels, manifesting itself with openness, multiplicity and relativity without limitation. Differential as it is, the novel has obviously become an experimental metafiction with speculations, contributing a great deal to the Australian literature and world literature.

Diary of a Bad Year is J. M. Coetzee's one more ingenious attempt of changing readers' concept of novel, leaving behind a genre of differential otherness. The novel adopts in an unprecedented way horizontal lines in the book, making innovations in structure of book pages. Coetzee makes first of all two sections on one page by one horizontal line and then three sections by two horizontal lines after an intentional blank page, resulting in a strong visual impact upon readers. The upper section is arranged with 31 disputable

① Mars-Jones, Adam. It's very novel, but is it actually a novel? *The Observer* 14 September 2003.

② Lodge, David. Disturbing the Peace. *The New York Review of Books*, November 20, 2003. Accessed on June 30, 2012. HTTP: //WWW. NYBOOKS. COM/ARTICLES/ARCHIVES/2003/NOV/20/DISTURBING-THE-PEACE/? PAGINATIO N=FALSE.

"strong opinions" and 24 metaphorical "diaries", the middle section with the experiences and musings of Señor C, an aging South African writer in Sydney, while the lower section with stories narrated by a young lady named Anya and Alan's depreciation and disproval of Señor C. With these three voices simultaneously presented, Coetzee has created a differential novel

> in his violation of that organic unity of material required by the usual canon, his joining together of the most varied and incompatible elements in the unity of novelistic construction, and in his destruction of the unified and integral fabric of narration (Bakhtin 40).

Someone even holds that "*Diary* is Coetzee's most extended meditation on the genre of the novel and his most thorough retooling of the dynamics of literary creation" (Ogden 466). The novel's complex narrative structure masterfully weaves multiple voices and viewpoints into a beautifully textured literary counterpoint. With incompatible elements of different nature put incredibly together on the same page, the novel leaves readers an impression of wonderful originality.

When critics wonder if Coetzee has exhausted his ingenuity in his constant pursuit of novelty, *Summertime* with definitely differential otherness challenges once again the queries. "Coetzee draws on fragments from his own journals to tell the story of a writer" (Carrigan 94). He purposely adopts different modes of narration, constructing the whole framework of the novel from different perspectives. The book is divided into three parts, with notes at the beginning and the end, and interviews in the middle. Objectively, the structure becomes a sandwich for the record of the consciousness of the objectified subject wraps up the statements of other people. "To this book, readers will ask: is it a fiction or a memoir?"① Generally, this book is considered as one of the autobiographical trilogy together with *Boyhood* (1997) and *Youth* (2002), for the author has placed under these titles the words "Scenes from Provincial life". However, does this book fit in with the canon that "Autobiographies are personal histories and stories of one's life, which tend to lay claim to objective truth"(Vambe 81)? Although he adopts the third person singular narrative to replace the first person singular narrative, Coetzee has changed the conventional model of autobiography writing in *Summertime*, turning it into a differential "autrebiography". In the book, the author assumes that others write a biography for him after his death and his image is restored from the comments and criticisms of the characters related to him from different perspectives. Coetzee arranges his own notes, the interviews from the biographers, the discourse of the interviewees etc. for this purpose, but he simply stands outside the scenes, observing the performances of different character with complacent speech that autobiography is an "autre-biography [or] an account of another self"(Coullie 1).

The differential otherness Coetzee shows in his literary writing provides literature with innovative models. In his writing of original forms, he dexterously displays his image of the differential Other.

2. The Differential Other in *Elizabeth Costello: Eight Lessons*

Critics find after research that Elizabeth Costello, a fictitious character in different speeches of J. M. Coetzee has quite a few similarities with the

① This was first published as a review on *Daily Telegraph* and was later printed on the cover of the book *Summertime*.

author himself. However, David Lodge, the famous English novelist and literary critic, thinks otherwise, holding that the title character in the book *Elizabeth Costello*: *Eight Lessons* is not the author himself①. Coetzee observes the world, gives speeches and experiences events through this outstanding writer. His profound thinking, incisive reflections on the world and criticism of the instrumental rationality are articulated through this female writer. In the dialogical relationship the author meticulously designs with different characters — audience of the lectures, experts at lectures, professors with different opinions, fellow travelers, etc., in different voices — praises, objections, criticisms, even silence with multiple meanings. And in different situations — warm welcome, tepid reception, embarrassment, etc., Elizabeth has accomplished the task Coetzee has designed for her in gazing at the world and being gazed at by the world, manifesting the image of the differential Other and showing Coetzee's differential otherness while realizing Coetzee's textual experiment.

The identity Coetzee designs for Elizabeth Costello the heroine is a senior female Australian writer who becomes well-known because of a novel related with James Joyce's masterpiece *Ulysses*. To reinforce the status of the female writer, he provides readers not only with information about her age, her work of prominence, etc., but particularly with the information that "in the past decade there has grown up a small critical industry, there is even an Elizabeth Costello Society, ... which puts out a quarterly *Elizabeth Costello Newsletter*"(1 - 2). Indeed, such a successful writer with relation to James

① David Lodge published "Disturbing the Peace" in *The New York Review of Books* (November 20, 2003), making a detailed comparative analysis of Elizabeth Costello and J. M. Coetzee, listing the similarities such as both being major world writers and by no means a comforting writer, and differences such as the gender, birth place, growing environment, etc.

Joyce must have her peculiarity in writing and Coetzee's design in effect paves the way for the differential otherness of Elizabeth Costello from the very beginning. One of the differentials of this character is first demonstrated in her close connection as a key role with the eight lectures. Coetzee's presentation of the peculiar character is done in the name of making keynote speeches at invitation, but he does not follow the stereotyped way of objectively introducing the female writer to a lecture. Instead, he adopts a standard way of novel writing, and compares Elizabeth first to "an old tired circus seal" and then to a feline, "one of those large cats that pause as they eviscerate their victim and, across the torn-open belly, give you a cold yellow stare" (5). The application of symbolic writing immediately turns the lecture narration into novel narration. In displaying the exhaustion of the female writer in drifting along with the world, Coetzee reveals her features of constant exploration and clear-headed observation.

As a female novelist giving lectures on different occasions, her peculiarity lies also in her idea about the important propositions of literature. At the moment when scholars at present call for the establishment of consensual and terminal belief in literature, an examination of the viewpoints of the female novelist in Coetzee's writing will surface her identity of the differential Other. As to the belief in literature, Harold Bloom the American literary critic has a remarkable statement in his book *The Western Canon: the Books and School of the Ages*, "Believing is being, because something in deepest being cannot be destroyed"(455). However, Coetzee arranges Elizabeth Costello to put forward questions when confronted with the final judgment, "What if I do not believe? What if I am not a believer?" (194) This discourse seems to mean on the surface that Coetzee has tried to show the female writer's loss of literary belief, but actually not. Elizabeth Costello, with her particularly keen sense, realizes that the tragedy of commending one literary belief and depreciating another has become popular in the present era when ideology plays an overwhelming role. The female writer expresses strong opposition to the issue of the compulsory identification existing in the field of literary writing, saying "That in my line of work one has to suspend belief. That belief is an indulgence, a luxury. That it gets in the way" (213). Taking belief as something that "gets in the way" actually reveals the female writer's idea of literary writing. She thinks that it is absurd to force the writer to accept certain literary belief by this compulsory means.

Elizabeth Costello's speech does not mean that she gives up her necessary belief in her practical writing, nor does that mean that she forgets the ethical belief and basic mission as a public intellectual. It expresses such kind of idea: literary writers testify their own existence by their differences in their writing, especially by the originality in literary writing instead of proving their own value through the mainstream beliefs, or affirming their own existence by the identification with the mainstream discourse. The essence of literature is creation, with nothing to do with mainstream discourse. Confronted with reality, literature sometimes can be a direct and forceful intervention, and sometimes can be a secret expression of individuals. The two forms are in fact complementary, without the artificial distinction of which is better. Suspense of the mainstream belief with great concentration on literary creation may make the writing covered temporarily for the failure to be commonly accepted by the whole society. Such writings may temporarily or in a relatively long period fall into oblivion for their incompatibility with the time, anyhow, this kind of writing filled with vigor will not be forgotten in the long history. Harold Bloom's remark supports to some extent Elizabeth Costello's idea: "But belief is a redundancy, because a personal god is only a metaphor for one's sense of indestructibility, a sense that unifies us despite ourselves" (Bloom 455). However, if we observe it from another perspective, we will find that in front of mainstream literature with dominant discourse power, Costello's speech naturally becomes otherized.

This is because the mainstream discourse with dominant power will always resort to extreme measures in coercing the writers without mainstream beliefs to submit. The monotonous interrogations and the brainwashing tortures in spirit in the lesson "At the Gate" are enough to show the hegemonic power of the dominant discourse and the determination of the power holders to change the interrogated. But, Costello is not so easy to be conquered and she knows clearly what the mainstream discourse owners wish her to say and at the same time she is also familiar with the high-sounding tirades. Coetzee reveals by a monologue her inner world after the continuous interrogations by the judge:

> *I believe in the irrepressible human spirit*. That is what she should have told her judges. ... *I believe all humankind is one*. Everyone else seems to believe it, believe in it. ... why can she not, just for once, pretend? (207)

Nevertheless, Coetzee does not need Costello to disguise against her will, nor can he tolerate that such kind of character won't adhere to her own voice. He can never bear the obsequious characters who always echo others' voices. That is why Elizabeth Costello can be independent from the interrogators as the differential Other.

If we say that Elizabeth Costello has insisted on suspending literary beliefs and concentrating on literary creation, then the story she tells about the life cycle of the little frogs when she once again faces the judge, clearly shows her cognition of beliefs and existence. "... the Dulgannon and its mudflats are real. ... the frogs are real. They exist whether or not I tell you about them, whether or not I believe in them"(217). The belief shown through allegory but without being acknowledged by the judge appears weird to the authorities with discourse power for its difference with the popular discourse, but in fact, faith indeed does not affect the existence of things. The relationship between literature and reality, between literature and human existence is not fixed without any alterations. This naturally shows that literature should be interpreted differently for only in this way can literature be colorful. The expression of the writer's thought should not be intervened by presupposed faith, nor be enslaved by such faith, otherwise, it will be "Too literary... A curse on literature"(225). The literary works enslaved by faith might in a short period of time satisfy the mundane wishes, but will stimulate the instant gratification culture. The differential otherness Costello displays on the issue of faith shows actually Coetzee's idea of literary creation in the form of allegory, demonstrating the author's unique aesthetic pursuit.

The different characters that form dialogic relations with Elizabeth Costello prove the latter's differential otherness from different perspectives. Among them, the first should be his son John, an associate professor of physics and astronomy[①] in a university. He accompanies his mother with

① The title associate professor of physics and astronomy stands for rationality to some extent, in sharp contrast with the passionate writer Elizabeth Costello. Adam Mars-Jones thinks that Coetzee does so "to dramatise the divide between arts and sciences" (Mars-Jones 2003: 17).

care and comes to rescue whenever she is in trouble, often arguing with others for the protection of his mother. His discourse with his mother, filled with worry and concern, provides not only some kind of a buffer for his mother's aggressive speech, but some theoretical interpretations for the latter's passionate speeches, and at the same time arouses in question form readers' interest in his mother with differential otherness, e.g. "But which is she, the fish or the fowl? Which is her medium, water or air?"(10)

Another character that serves as a foil is Susan Moebius, the interviewer from a radio station, whose witty remarks and sometimes sharp-tongued and sometimes mild questions constantly inspire Costello's thought and will to fight, stimulating the female writer to show her differential otherness, making readers enjoy more in expanding their mind and strengthening the philosophical ideas. The third person worth mentioning is Teresa, a blind worshipper called by John as "Flecks of gold circling the dying whale, waiting their chance to dart in and take a quick mouthful"(6). Her fan-like questions in the dialogue appear obviously without any sense of propriety, but often help develop the issues into their depth, broadening the horizon for readers. And of course they give readers hints about the differential otherness of the female writer.

The African writer Emmanuel Egudu Coetzee arranges to give a lecture together with Elizabeth Costello forms in effect a striking contrast with the latter. On one side, Egudu follows the standard routine of a lecture by raising a question, verifying it from different aspects with appropriate extensions, proposing the argument with adequate evidences before reaching the conclusion and answering questions from the audience. He skillfully meets the expectation of the mainstream discourse and the audience. As a result, his lecture filled with passion and strength causes long and warm applauses from the enthusiastic audience. On the other side, Elizabeth Costello proposes in an unconventional way some incredible ideas and of course modest applause comes from the audience though obviously without enthusiasm. This reflects the inevitable outcome of non-mainstream idea delivered in unconventional ways.

Coetzee also designs the argumentative dialogue between Thomas O'Hearne the professor of philosophy and Elizabeth Costello, concerning the rights of animal, animal life and its nature, etc. In debate, the former challenges the latter on behalf of the mainstream discourse and the convention, e. g. O'Hearne insists on the issue of the rights of animals, saying emphatically that animals cannot enjoy legitimate rights,

> because they are not persons, even not potential persons, as fetuses are? [.] In working out rules for our dealings with animals, does it not make more sense for such rules apply to us and to our treatment to them, as at present, rather than being predicated upon rights which animals can claim or enforce or even understand? (107)

Elizabeth Costello gives in a rational way her straightforward objection to such typical anthropocentrism, refuting the arbitrary conclusion of human beings that animals are imbecile. Evidently, her argument is actually contrary to the mainstream idea, thus seeming quite differential or alien to the audience. Coetzee, by means of this argumentative dialogue, illustrates his own philosophical ideas, considering that the conclusion is reached on the basis of scientific experiments, while "scientific experiment ... is profoundly anthropocentric. ... the standards by which animals are being measured in these experiments are human standards"(108). His idea in effect touches the essence of the problem. Thus in the shoes of Elizabeth Costello the differential Other who holds the position of anti-anthropocentrism, what is imbecile is indeed not the animal, but the animal experiment, or the standards human beings set for animals. These ideas which seem alienated to the authorities of the mainstream discourse make people think deeply.

What is especially worth mentioning is that Coetzee employs another novelist named West as a referential contrast in order to show Elizabeth Costello's differential otherness. The person named West once wrote a novel about Adolf Hitler, in which "Certain pages burned with the fires of hell" (171). Compared with Thomas O'Hearne who prefers violent debate, West, the novelist who always holds an attitude of rejection towards the female writer, has a very special performance at Elizabeth Costello's speech about "evil". Facing her question or discussion, "He clears his throat, but then says nothing, continuing to gaze ahead... Again, tenaciously, the man holds his silence" (ibid). Obviously, he does not agree with the female writer's idea, but his rejection is nothing but silence, or lengthened silence. This kind of silence is actually a discourse, a resistant discourse, or a symbolic presence of discourse, without leaving far way from discourse. This repellent discourse appears in the absence of language, making Elizabeth Costello's discourse work all by herself, suggesting apparently that the West keep silent collectively towards the female writer's opinions. The evidences provided by Coetzee from the perspectives of psychology, philosophy and logic, otherize all the more the female writer who despises the mainstream discourse.

3. Reflections on the Differential Other and Otherness

The above discussion shows that Elizabeth Costello is the Other with the feature of differential otherness. It is found that differential otherness does not necessarily suggest grotesqueness, while the novelist with differential otherness can by no means be called an eccentric. No doubt, the female writer Elizabeth Costello in Coetzee's writing can be defined as the differential Other, not because that she is weird in action or absurd in character, but because that she does not follow the established rules and regulations of the dominant discourse power and constantly questions the canon of the traditional mainstream discourse. Never parroting the mainstream discourse in different issues, she airs out her own opinion independently.

Coetzee uses the identity of Elizabeth Costello to discuss in a unique way the issues such as the present situation of regional fiction, fiction language and reader cultivation, etc. And her earnest discussion is conspicuously of individual feature, contradictory with the mainstream discourse, but full of penetrating judgment and deep insight expressly with independent thinking. She might be called the differential Other, but her conclusion can hardly be denied. For instance, in discussing the issue of African novel, Elizabeth Costello first raises a thought-provoking question, "Why are there so many African novelists around and yet no African novel worth speaking of?" (50) Coetzee knows clearly that there exists a tremendous difference between the traditions in Africa and Europe. The long history of European writing and the reading group inspired by the European Renaissance and Enlightenment have formed a fixed model of taking reading as an entertainment, while different is Africa which is known as a "shared" continent, where Africans like to sing and dance together. They do not appreciate self-separation, and their history, culture and conventions are usually passed down from mouth to mouth, resulting in a very small reading group. Thus, fiction writing in native language will, objectively speaking, come across the question of lacking readership in Africa. This issue is not confined in African continent only and can be taken as of universal significance. Avoidance of this issue is practically in vain, and differential as she is, Costello comes bravely to the point.

Rational and convincing is Coetzee's analysis via the character Costello, who says, "The English novel... is written in the first place by English people for English people. That is what makes it the English novel. The Russian novel is written by Russians for Russians"(51). However, in his mind, African literature is different, "South African literature is a literature in bandage"(Coetzee, "Doubling the Point" 98). And the basic cause is that "the African novel is not written by Africans for Africans"(51). Neither the subject (writers of African fiction) nor the object (readers of African fiction) is African, and even if the novelist is an African, the novel is not necessarily written for Africans. African writers have fallen into a dilemma of writing in native language or non-native language. The writing in native language usually suffers from the limitation of a very small readership and can hardly reach readers outside the country, or even outside certain region, let alone the recognition in the world. At the same time, the writing in non-native language suffers from the similar trouble for such writing, though accepted outside the country, has little readership in its own country. As a matter of fact, many famed writers tend to write for readers outside their native land. However, since they choose to write for foreign readers, they have to give up their writing in native languages. Furthermore, they have to cater to the need of the foreign readers who are usually curious and novelty-seeking. Sometimes, the African writers in English need to intentionally keep or even exaggerate the features of South Africa, so

> African novelists ... seem ... to be glancing over their shoulder all the time they write, at the foreigners who will read them. Whether they like it or not, they have accepted the role of interpreter, interpreting Africa to their readers... Having to perform your Africanness at the same time as you write. (51)

African writers' novels of this kind often have a cold reception from the readers in the native country due to the problems of language barrier or the wrongly intended readers, though they can be pretty popular in foreign countries.

Coetzee supports firmly from another perspective Elizabeth Costello's tenacious insistence as the differential Other by the typical case of Nigerian writer Tutuola's novel writing in non-standard English and at the same time discusses the position and future of the regional literature in the present world literature. Tutuola, a man with no more than elementary schooling, critically borrows the discourse from the Western mainstream but insists on his own habit of discourse, adopting a special way of literary creation, i.e. writing his novels by non-standard English. Editors in English speaking countries do not spend much time in modifying his writing style when reading Tutuola's works. Instead, they simply correct the mistakes which look obviously awkward or in total discordance with the regulations of writing or speech, but purposely keep "what seemed authentically Nigerian, that is to say, what to their ears sounded picturesque, exotic and folkloric" (47). However, Tutuola's writing itself has an incurably fatal defect, i.e. if he wishes to be successful, he must accept the decoration of the editors, while the editors' decoration of the regional writers will inevitably cater to the interest of Western readership. So Tutuola must appear in the West as an image of an exotic novelist with typical African sentiment, and he has to make some compromise in his literary writing and sacrifice some subjectivity in literary creation. Tutuola thus appears as a different writer or the otherized writer before both Western readers and Africans. The case of Tutuola's writing is of typical representational significance to the development of regional literature, fully showing the reflection of Coetzee on this issue, who is firm in his belief, holding that if African writers follow this train of thought, "the novel has no future in Africa"(50).

One more fact Coetzee presents to show that Elizabeth Costello is the differential Other only to the mainstream discourse is Costello's concern for the development of regional novels. As is known to all, Coetzee migrated to Australia in 2002, one year before the publication of the novel *Elizabeth Costello: Eight Lessons*. Though he feels that novel has no future in Africa, yet he does not give up hope himself. By using effectively the character of the differential Other (Elizabeth Costello) as a spokesman, he takes Australian literature as an example to illustrate his idea on the development of regional literature①. "We finally got out of the habit of writing for strangers when a proper Australian readership grew to maturity, something that happened in that 1960s"(51). The maturity of readership in Australia is the basis for the development of Australian literature, and the hope and future of Australian literature. The readership on this basis is totally different from that before. "When our market, our Australian market, decided that it could support a home-grown literature"(52), the Australian writers begin to write to meet the expectation of the native readers. Such

---

① Coetzee's adoption of Australian literature as an example in effect has its natural limitation, for according to the statistics of Internet in 2006, 60% of residents in Australia are the descendants of European migrants, and what's more, the official language in Australia is English.

practice provides writers in Australia with an opportunity for the pursuit of a new writing tradition and the reconstruction of national culture and subjectivity. On the land of free literary creation, Australian writers gradually become stronger in literary writing and produce extensive influence over the world. In the end, they subvert the conventional canon imposed upon them and reconstruct the classics of Australian literature. Elizabeth Costello speaks a little proudly that, "We finally got out of the habit of writing for strangers... That is the lesson we can offer. That is what Africans can learn from us" (51 - 52). Her sense of pride, established upon the basis of sense of autonomy and original writing free from bondages, demonstrates at once the so-called differential otherness of Elizabeth Costello and the ideal situation of literary creation in the author's mind. It is therefore discovered that the differential otherness of Elizabeth Costello is in reality the representation of the author Coetzee's uniqueness or otherness in literary creation and this uniqueness or otherness does not simply show in the individualized performance of the differential Other, but also in many aspects of novel writing.

The contradiction Coetzee designs on purpose in the novel is one of the aspects that show the differential otherness, and the conflict between Elizabeth Costello's speech and the narration of the novel is a good example. Almost immediately after the unfolding of the plot, Coetzee makes use of the character Costello to say in discussing the normal state of literary narration,

> It's not a good idea to interrupt the narrative too often, since storytelling works by lulling the reader or listener into a dreamlike state in which the time and space of the real world fade away, superseded by the time and space of the fiction(16).

This is obviously the conventional way of narration which requires the absence of the author's intervening comment and summarized judgment of value, and the substitution of a mouthpiece in narration, i.e. the reader and the author should communicate with each other through the fictitious reader and the fictitious writer. Nevertheless, Coetzee does not follow the normal narration, instead, he runs the risk of destroying the fancy of the reader by forcefully breaking into their dream and calling their attention to the innate construction of the story in the novel regardless of Elizabeth Costello's warning. Consequently, he subverts the traditional way of intentionally concealing the existence of the narrator and narration, and eradicates the illusion the traditional novel deliberately creates that the story goes on by itself. By adopting painstakingly the form of dialogue between the omniscient and omnipotent narrator and the imaginative reader, Coetzee exposes the existence of the narrator on purpose and blatantly introduces the voice of the narrator. For instance, in the first lesson "Realism", Coetzee, by employing the narrator to tell the story and give comments, often inserts into the story obvious reminders to display the sense of story and textuality, e.g.

> We skip (2).... We skip to the evening, to the main event (15).... The presentation scene itself we skip (16).... The skips are not part of the text, they are part of the performance (16).... We skip ahead (17).... We skip the rest of the foyer scene, move to the hotel (22)...

Such kind of insertion always reminds readers not to fall into the trap of traditional novels. This self-contradiction often makes Elizabeth Costello appear alienated and differential, and sometimes seem ridiculous, but at the same time reveals clearly the features of otherness in Coetzee's novel writing.

Of course, the differential otherness also appears in Coetzee's speculation on literature demonstrated in Elizabeth Costello's ideas presented at different lectures. On the issue of the nature of fiction, i.e. the literary fictionality, Coetzee insists on his own assertion. He holds that so far as art is concerned, fiction is more truthful than memoir, because the artistic truth reflects more effectively the nature of life or even humanity than the real events in life. Wolfgang Iser, the important German theorist of receptive aesthetics, says,

> Literary texts are the mixture of fiction and reality and the result of the inter-entanglement and inter-penetration of the established and the imagined. It might be said that the idiosyncrasy of interfusion of reality and fiction far surpasses that of their opposition ("Act of Reading" 104).

Coetzee shows his agreement with Iser's idea in an interview, saying by referring to Friedrich Nietzsche that "We have art, said Nietzsche, so that we shall not die of the truth"("Doubling the Point" 99). For this purpose, he speaks via the differential Other Elizabeth Costello, "Making up someone other than yourself. Making up a world for him to move in"(12). In the fictitious world, literary writers have a fictitious identity. They indulge freely in their rich imaginative world, and let the fictitious characters perform freely at will.

"Fiction transcodes the known world, transforming the unknown world into the imagined, and the reset world by imagination and reality is the new world presented to readers"(Iser, "Fiktive und Imaginare" 016). Coetzee tries in his fiction in the new century to "Make up an Australia..."(12) and discusses the identity of Australian writers and the comment on Australia by the dialogue between Elizabeth Costello and the interviewer from the radio. In talking about Australia, Coetzee expresses his ideas directly via the differential female writer and resists explicitly Eurocentrism or the centralism of Europe and America, thinking that "You won't find many Australians nowadays prepared to accept it [margin]." He does not think that Australia is far away at the margin, and asks in an evidently confident way, "*Far from where*?" (15) Coetzee emphasizes it by italicizing the question, for there is no centre in this world, how can we find the margin? Elizabeth Costello's anti-centre opinion is indeed contrary to the mainstream discourse, though it is the tendency in the postmodernist context. And this differential otherness is in reality the effusion of the author's consciousness.

What is more, the differential otherness is again revealed in the model Coetzee designs for the demonstration of literary works. By combining the lecture and story into an organic whole, the novel *Elizabeth Costello: Eight Lessons* develops smoothly in the form of a story and always conveys ideas in an allegorical way. The philosophic contemplation, academic ideas and relativity with the subject often lie not only in the discourse in quotation which Coetzee labels with a sign "lecture", but also indirectly, subtly and implicitly in the process of the whole narration of the story. And the story becomes natural and appropriate for it displays philosophical speculation and academic thinking itself. For instance, under the title "Realism", the author puts forward from the perspective of the omniscient and omnipotent narrator the issue of "how to get us from where we are, as yet, nowhere, to the far bank"(1), that is, how to bridge the present with the future, simply before the presence of Elizabeth the differential Other. The design indicates immediately the theme of the lecture and at the same time paves the ground for the development of the novel. In the lesson "The Novel in Africa", Coetzee does not arrange Elizabeth Costello to give the title-related lecture "the Novel in Africa", but let her instead give a lecture entitled "the Future of the Novel" with the content merely occupying a very small space (less than a page, to be exact), which seems pretty strange to ordinary readers. Of course, in manifesting the differential otherness of the protagonist, the author obviously does not want to weaken the theme of the novel with digressions. But, the issues concerning the position of the African novel and the identity of African writers appear in the lecture of the Nigerian writer and the argumentative discussion of Elizabeth Costello with him. This discussion or debate is not the best means to reveal the otherness of the latter, but at least readers can reach their epiphany after they realize the intention of the novelist that the novel with a mixture of story and lecture is totally different from the model of novels at present. "The Humanities in Africa" is even a better example, in which Elizabeth Costello appears at her sister Blanche's graduation ceremony. The discussion about Hellenism, humanities in Africa, etc. related with the theme of the fifth lesson is permeated in the argument of Elizabeth Costello with Blanche, and in the former's letter to the latter. Coetzee seems to narrate a story of two sisters in discordance, but his philosophical speculation upon the theme through the plot of the story betrays itself without the consciousness of readers. The epiphany after reading is often so shocking to readers that they suddenly find that such an unprecedented demonstration model does show its differential otherness of the author, instead of the protagonist only.

The most striking performance of the differential otherness of Coetzee lies in the last lecture and the postscript. Coetzee changes his almost fixed pattern in the lecture at the end of the novel. Here is definitely no more invitation for academic exchange and Elizabeth Costello has no longer company at side and of course no more lectures or debates are observed. As is discussed above, this is a lecture which has never been published openly. Compared with the lectures before, this one is filled with mystery and more symbolic meanings. The author, in metaphorical language on purpose, conveys complicated and abstract ideas through plain, ordinary and concrete images, making readers feel all the more the allegorical significance and profound philosophical meaning. In front of the "Gate" with more allegorical meaning, before the repeatedly appearing judge, the applicant for the entrance to the gate has been interrogated time and again for her belief, and the meditation of the interrogated over the belief and the insistence of the differential Other as a professional writer, reflect the author's profound thought of literary writing and his persistent pursuit for the writing model. The framework of Coetzee's novel here is similar with that of Franz Kafka's *Before the Law*. Facing the special gate with rich connotation and great allegorical significance, Kafka, who always pursues dream world and grotesque style, and advocates strong passion, deliberately describes the person who tries to enter the gate as a country man. However, Coetzee here substitutes the country man with Elizabeth Costello, an exhausted professional female writer who has had abundant experiences of challenging the mainstream discourse. The Kafkaesque protagonist has spent his whole life "for permission to enter the Law by a door intended specifically for him, and dies with only a glimpse of the object of his desire"(Robertson xxv). And Elizabeth Costello the differential Other in Coetzee's writing has constantly modified and repeatedly stated her belief for the purpose of entering the gate, but also ends up in vain. In such kind of strongly allegorical text, readers feel keenly that Elizabeth Costello the differential Other can never enter the gate for her insistence on her ideal in the innermost recesses of her mind. Her idea of never willing to submit to the mainstream discourse seems incredible to the door keeper and the judge.

The novel's ending is brief but coherent with the style of the whole book, contributing to the differential Otherness of the novel. In the novel entitled eight lessons, how the author brings the lecture-like novel or novel-like lecture to a perfect ending after eight lectures is a challenging issue to Coetzee, because this ending should meet the requirements of both lecture and novel, and at the same time ensure the differential otherness of the novel, guaranteeing the continuance of the content and the consistence of the style. Coetzee here shows his surprisingly rich imagination by quoting a paragraph of "Letter of Lord Chandos to Lord Bacon"(1902), a famous piece from Hugo von Hofmannsthal, an important Austrian writer of Romanticism and Symbolism. It is known that the letter itself is in truth the fictitious work of Hofmannsthal, concerning the language crisis of the fictitious character Lord Chandos or the crisis of language in expressing human experiences. Coetzee here quotes only three sentences about being and significance, clearly displaying the modern anxiety of Hofmannsthal. And we naturally connect this kind of anxiety with the sense of exhaustion of Elizabeth Costello, the protagonist in the book who constantly resists to the dominant discourse power, especially when she has just had the experience of being repeatedly interrogated. If the study goes one step further, Coetzee may be found to hint at the anxiety of Elizabeth Costello over her failure to express human experiences in language for her writing simply adds a female voice (Molly Bloom) to the typical modernist novel *Ulysses*.

Coetzee's last design appears to confirm the authenticity of Lady Chandos' letter to Francis Bacon, but virtually reinforces the anxiety that language can hardly convey the experiences. The postscript "Letter of Elizabeth, Lady Chandos, to Francis Bacon" is purely a text Coetzee fabricates. In the postscript, Elizabeth pledges to Sir Bacon that her husband is not mad at all, earnestly requesting the rational Bacon to save him from his pains, for the latter finds that "Not Latin,... nor English nor Spanish nor Italian will bear the words of my revelation"(230). Careful readers soon find that the author of the letter is "Elizabeth", the same with that of the protagonist in the novel. Such kind of coincidence in Coetzee's novel actually betrays the author's intention. Can we take the "pains" Elizabeth repeatedly describes in her letter (including her pains and her husband's), and the last appeal "Save us"(ibid) as the strong common feelings of the implied author and the protagonist? Or does the author mean to express her turn of literary creation by the postscript? Due to the limited space, these issues remain unsolved, which might be explored in further studies. Anyhow, one thing is clear, the last part full of creative ideas displays the pattern of Coetzee's novel writing, fitting exactly in with the style of the whole book.

In *Elizabeth Costello*: *Eight Lessons*, Coetzee, adopts the differential model of lecture-like novel or novel-like lecture, interprets with the aid of an image of the differential Other his cognition over literary beliefs, literary model, nature of fiction, literary reception, regional literature, literary language, etc. He demonstrates the differential otherness of Elizabeth Costello by means of different dialogic relationship among different characters, e. g. comparative lectures of African writers, Costello's argumentative dialogue with a philosophical professor, the novelist West's highly suggestive silence, etc. Through the performance of Costello the differential Other, through the conflict of her speech with the narration of this book, through Costello's ideas published at different lectures, through the model of narration including the model of ending, etc. Coetzee displays undoubtedly the differential otherness in his novel. The efforts of Coetzee provide a new genre for the fiction writing and at the same time offer a sample for reference in enriching the connotation of fiction. Although his fiction is labeled as metafiction or anti-fiction, yet the present labels can never epitomize the model and connotation of this novel and its significance will deeply influence literary writing and criticism.

Conclusion

J.M. Coetzee, a contemporary South African writer and Nobel laureate in literature worth our research, is well known for his constant writing experiment in literary creation. Each of his new works always stirs up world literature with his new attempt, new genre and new surprise, and at the same time he is known for the image series of the Other in his fiction writing. Every image of the Other is graphic and interesting with its different representation, behind which is the author's differential but rational speculation, involving his macro-thinking over the essential issues in the apartheid and post-apartheid South Africa, and the profundity of the author on these issues.

This book has made in four chapters a systematic study of the Other in Coetzee's representative novels — *Waiting for the Barbarians*, *Life and Times of Michel K*, *Disgrace*, *Elizabeth Costello*: *Eight Lessons*. With the application of the related theories of modern literature, philosophy and psychology, it gives a critical presentation of the images of the Other in Coetzee's novels from the colonial, post-Christian, post-apartheid and postmodernist dimensions. By displaying the different facets of the Other in different forms Coetzee contributes to the world literature, it discusses the connotation of the Other in Coetzee's important novels. The discussion concerns the representation of the Other, tension between denotation and connotation of the Other, and allegorical significance of the Other. Furthermore, the book discusses Coetzee's speculation as a writer over the fundamental issues of human concern based on the experiences of the Other in his novels, and finds out the relationship between the writer and the Other in the fiction after a study of the writer's allegorical writing and the expression of the idea of the Other.

The discussion is based on the fact that Coetzee's fiction writing and publication are actually done within a time space of about 40 years from 1970s till present, which well witnesses the occurrence and development of many literary theories including postmodernism and postcolonialism, and the prosperity, decline and expiration of the evil apartheid. Referring to the facts that South Africa only broke away from the bondage of colonialism in 1960s, and abolished the apartheid in 1990s, and the South Africans have experienced the weakening process of religious belief from the blind faith to the gradual skepticism, this book mainly discusses Coetzee's novels from different dimensions with the application of the theory of the Other in the post-modernist context. In discussion, it focuses on the intention of the author's allegorical presentation of the Other, exploring the connotation of the Other in his fiction and finding the revelation of Coetzee's fiction to the literary creation in the world and his contribution to enriching the literary theory, especially after a comparative study on the relationship between the author and the time.

This book finds after an emphatic study of the above-mentioned four novels that Coetzee, in the novel *Waiting for the Barbarians*, purposely adopts the allegorical writing style to display the representation of the racial

Other, sex Other and identity Other in South African society in the era of colonial hegemony. By making full use of the different experiences of the Other in different forms, he has made a series of speculative query over the issues of colonialism, civilization, justice, etc., demonstrating a modern novelist's concern for the social reality and objectively providing the world with a brand new interpretation of the author's image as a recluse avoiding world affairs.

In the novel *Life and Times of Michel K*, Coetzee exhibits metaphorically the life of the longanimous Other in silence at the bottom of the South African society in the era when people have lost their faith in Christianity and the brutal violence is rampant everywhere in South Africa. The novel, by presenting vividly the miserable experiences of Michel K and his unique way of resistance, interprets that the silent endurance of the South Africans is not equal to the acknowledgment of the present situation or to the submission of the people to the authorities, but to the resistance in silence. This shows clearly the author's profound understanding of and his attitude towards the reality in South Africa.

In the novel *Disgrace*, Coetzee, by presenting the situation of the otherized white who have lost their superior position after the expiration of the evil apartheid in South Africa, reveals from another perspective the injuries of the man-made inequitable and unfair system to the ordinary South Africans. He exposes the absurdity and hypocrisy of the so-called rational society with different paradoxes, and questions the issues such as historical memory and individual responsibility, rational and moral principles, etc. through his description of the experiences of the white who have been subverted from their privileged position under the rule of the coalition government with the black at dominant position. Hereby, the author gives in a metaphorical way his hope that the black and the white in South Africa should advocate forgiveness, compromise and reconciliation, so as to reach a perfect kind of symbiosis. This once again shows distinctly the author's strong sense of social responsibility against the superficial impression of reclusiveness people have upon Coetzee.

Coetzee has developed the allegorical writing and the spirit of speculation to the utmost in the novel *Elizabeth Costello*: *Eight Lessons*, which finds its expression of the genuine cause of the people's otherization in postmodernist context in an image of the differential Other. Here, Coetzee intentionally chooses an Australian female writer as the protagonist — the differential Other, and the major plot he designs for the novel is the lectures at invitation in different contexts. This provides the author with an adequate space for his speculation over different issues, endowing him with abundant opportunities to oppose with consummate ease the mainstream discourse from content to form, demonstrating the author's unique thought and authentic self before the mainstream literature.

The achievements of this project "a study of the Other in Coetzee's novels" are of the following significance.

First of all, this project takes the lead in the literary criticism of J. M Coetzee via a systematic study of the Other in Coetzee's novels backed by postcolonial and postmodernist theories. Through sketching the contours of group images of the Other in Coetzee's novels in postmodernist context, this book first outlines patterns of characters of the Other and presents them as a whole by induction according to the features of marginalization, taciturnity, being subverted and specificity. At the same time, it selects the representative images of the Other in Coetzee's novels for an in-depth analysis, making an exploration of the Other from the dimensions of race, sex and identity. This study has provided the academia with a rational interpretation of group images of the Other in Coetzee's novels, breaking a new path with beneficial references for the further study of Coetzee's works.

The different perspectives of theories the book takes for the systematic research of Coetzee's novels are of great referential value. Guided by postmodernist and postcolonial theories at dominant place, the book applies the theory of the Other into the whole process of the research, resulting in an organic whole with four relatively independent chapters. Each chapter explores in a separate way the representations, connotation and denotation of the Other and the author's speculation over the essential issues, but they are closely connected by the main theme of the Other in the research. In the process of argumentation, the book employs important views from different theories such as traumatic theory, theory of justice, theory of discourse and power, theory of psychoanalysis, theory of feminism, etc. for the subsidiary discussion in separate chapters besides the application of the dominant theory of the Other throughout the discussion, highlighting the intention of the author in presenting image series of the Other in his novels. The support from different theories has made the book more persuasive and the way of argumentation offers a useful reference to the literary study.

Furthermore, the project has focally clarified in discussion the origin of the dominant theory of the Other and the foothold of different literary and critical theories. It has determined the literary definition of the Other used in this book, based on the summary of the philosophical foundation of the theory of the Other, and the reference to the Lacanian concept of "the Other being non-self" and Elleke Boehmer's concept of "the Other [being] the opposite or negative". Such definition has fixed its theoretical foothold in the application of the theory of the Other into the study of Coetzee, virtually avoiding the ambiguity or contradiction of the theoretical stances often seen in the discussion of the issue of the Other at present, and contributing to the correct interpretation of the connotation and denotation of the Other in Coetzee's novels. The application of the distinctive and unambiguous definition of the Other and the discussion of the relationship among the characters of the Other, provide an explicit theoretical support for the construction of the unique patterns of characters in Coetzee's novels.

In the process of argumentation, the book always focuses on the kernel element "the Other" throughout Coetzee's novels. By an association analysis of the Other in Coetzee's novels and the allegorical writing, it explores the causality of the power discourse and allegorical writing with reference to Coetzee's personal views in interviews, present research achievements and the particularities of the South African society. Comments on the basis of these efforts are of realistic significance to the comprehensive evaluation of the Other in Coetzee's novels.

In the process of research, the book has also explored the relationship between the author and the group images of the Other in Coetzee's novels. It is found that the author's unique European descent, complicated education background, his suzerain experiences in England, his eventful stay in the United States of America, his compulsory return to South Africa and his migration to and naturalization in Australia, etc. have played a key role in the formation of his sense of the Other. And the critical study of the above events and the related materials has helped illustrate the positive influence of the passive and active otherization in Coetzee's novels.

This book has discovered that the image of the Other in Coetzee's novels is diversified, and the great diversity is closely connected with the postcolonial and postmodernist theories. And the achievements of this book not only provide Coetzee study with valuable references, but also make contributions to enriching the postcolonial and postmodernist theories.

Due to the limited time, space and my personal ability, the book inevitably has much to be desired, e. g. the choice of the four important novels for the sample analysis is of course convenient for the study of the image of the Other in Coetzee's novels, especially for the establishment of the research system and the framework of the research, but do these novels exhaust all the types of the image of the Other, or are Coetzee's novels all involved in the presentation of the Other? Although the book has made a general account of this issue, yet a study of each novel for the issue of the Other remains necessary in the future study, so that the patterns of the Other in Coetzee's novels will be more colorful and give readers more revelation.

In addition, it is observed that this book has employed different theories with the theory of the Other as a dominant one in postcolonial and postmodernist context. Does the Other discussed in different chapters refer to the same in concept? The Other in Coetzee's novels is of course the key link to different chapters, what about the similarities and the differences among the marginalized Other, the silent Other, the subverted Other and the differential Other? The key to the above questions can only be found in the conclusive part of the book without any special chapter for the further discussion, thus leaving a space for further study.

The research of this book on the Other in the novels of J. M. Coetzee has made obvious achievements which can be found in the explicit presentation of group images of the Other in Coetzee's novels, the accurate definition of the Other in fiction, rational exploration of the connotation and denotation of the Other, dexterous employment of the literary theories and adequate argumentation. In the postmodernist context, the achievement in this research project is of general significance, providing a new research orientation for Coetzee study and new revelation for literary study as a whole.

Works Cited

Aristotle. *Politics*. tr. Benjamin Jowett. Kitchener: Batoche Books, 1999.

Attridge, Derek. Literary Form and the Demands of Politics: Otherness in *The Age of Iron*. *Aesthetics and Ideology*. ed. George Levine. New Brunswick: Rutgers University Press, 1994. 243 - 263.

——. Age of Bronze, State of Grace: Music and Dogs in J. M. Coetzee's *Disgrace*. *Novel* 34. 1 (2000): 98 - 121.

——. J. M. Coetzee's *Disgrace*. *Interventions* 4.3 (2002): 315 - 320.

——. Against Allegory. *J. M. Coetzee and the Idea of the Public Intellectual*. ed. Jane Poyner. Athens: Ohio University Press, 2006. 63 - 82.

Attwell, David. Editor's Introduction. *Doubling the Point: Essays and Interviews*. Cambridge, Massachusetts; London, England: Harvard University Press, 1992.

——. *J. M. Coetzee: South Africa and the Politics of Writing*. Los Angeles, California: University of California Press, 1993.

——. Coetzee's Estrangements. *Novel* 41.2 (2008): 229 - 243.

Bakhtin, Mikhail. *Problems of Dostoyevsky's Art*. Minneapolis: The University of Minnesota Press, 2003.

Barnard, Rita. J. M. Coetzee's *Disgrace* and the South African Pastoral. *Contemporary Literature* 2(2003): 199 - 224.

Barth, John. The Literature of Exhaustion. *Postmodern Literary Theory: an Anthology*. ed. Niall Lucy. Oxford: Blackwell Publishers Ltd., 2000.

Bataille, Georges. *L'histoire de L'erotisme*. tr. Liu Hui. Beijing: Commercial Press, 2003. [巴塔耶,乔治. 色情史. 刘辉,译. 北京:商务印书馆,2003.]

Bishop, Scott G. J. M. Coetzee's *Foe*: A Culmination and a Solution to a Problem of White Identity. *World Literature Today* 64.1(1990): 54-56.

Bloom, Harold. *The Western Canon: the Books and School of the Ages*. London: Harcourt Brace and Company, 1994.

Boehmer, Elleke. *Colonial and Postcolonial Literature*. New York: Oxford University Press Inc., 1995.

——. Not Saying Sorry, Not Speaking Pain: Gender Implications in *Disgrace*. *Interventions* 4.3 (2002): 342-51.

——. Sorry, Sorrier, Sorriest: The Gendering of Contrition in J. M. Coetzee's *Disgrace*. *J. M. Coetzee and the Idea of the Public Intellectual*. ed. Jane Poyner. Athens: Ohio University Press, 2006: 135-147.

——. J. M. Coetzee's Australian Realism. *Coetzee Study and Post-colonial Literature Research*. ed. Cai Shengqin and Xie Yanming. Wuhan: Wuhan University Press, 2011: 3-17.

Brink, Andrew. Literature and Control in a Future South Africa. *Freedom to Read: Papers presented at a Seminar on the Future of Publications Control and the Free Flow of Information in South Africa on* 11 *June* 1993. ed. Dieter E. Westra. Cape Town: South African Library, 1994.

Buikema, Rosemarie. Literature and the Production of Ambiguous Memory. *European Journal of English Studies* 10. 2 (2006): 187-197.

Canepari-Labib, Michela. *Old Myth — Modern Empires: Power, Language and Identity in J. M. Coetzee's Work*. Oxford, Bern, Berlin: Peter Lang, 2005.

Carrigan, Henry L. Coetzee, J.M.: *Summertime*. *Library Journal* December 2009. 94.

Chapman, Michel. Coetzee, Gordimer and the Nobel Prize. *Scrutiny 2* 14.1(2009): 57-65.

——. The Case of Coetzee: South African Literary Criticism, 1990 to Today. *Journal of Literary Studies* 26: 2 (2010): 103-117.

Chen, Yongguo. Intertexuality. *Key Words of Western Literary Criticism* ed. Zhao Yifan, etc. Beijing: Foreign Language Teaching and Research Press, 2006: 211-221. [陈永国. 互文

性//赵一凡.西方文论关键词.北京：外语教学研究出版社，2006. 211－221.]

Cheng, Danggen. Desire. *Key Words from Western Literary Criticism*. ed. Zhao Yifan. Beijing: Foreign Languages Teaching and Research Press, 2006. 806－816. [程党根.欲望//赵一凡.西方文论关键词.北京：外语教学研究出版社，2006. 806－816.]

Clausewitz, Carl von. *On War*. New York: Oxford University Press, 2007.

Coetzee, J.M. *In the Heart of the Country*. London: the Penguin Group, 1977.

——. *Life and Times of Michel K*. London: Viking Penguin Inc., 1985.

——. Into the Dark Chamber: The Novelist and South Africa. *The New York Times Book Review* December 1, 1986: 1－5.

——. *Doubling the Point: Essays and Interviews*. ed. David Attwell. Cambridge, Massachusetts: Harvard University Press, 1992.

——. *Giving Offense: Essays on Censorship*. Chicago and London: The University of Chicago Press, 1996.

——. *Disgrace*. London: Vintage, 1999.

——. *Elizabeth Costello: Eight Lessons*. London: Secker and Warburg, 2003.

——. *Waiting for the Barbarians*. London: Vintage, 2004.

——. *White Writing: On the Culture of Letters in South Africa*. Braamfontein: Pentz Publishers, 2007.

Cooper, Pamela. Metamorphosis and Sexuality: Reading the Strange Passions of *Disgrace*. *Research in African Literatures* 36. 4 (2005): 22－39.

Cornwell, Gareth. Disgraceland: History and the Humanities in Frontier Country. *English in Africa* 30. 2 (2003): 43－68.

Coullie, J.L., S. Meyer, T.H. Ngwenya and T. Olver. *Selves in Question: Interviews on Southern African Autobiography: Writing Past Colonialism*. Honolulu: University of Hawaii Press. 2006.

D'Hoker, Elke. Confession and Atonement in Contemporary Fiction: J.M. Coetzee, John Banville, and Ian McEwan. *Critique* 48. 1 (2006): 31－43.

De Beauboir, Simone. *Le Deuxieme Sexe*. tr. Tao Tiezhu. Beijing: China Book Press, 2004. [波伏娃，西蒙. 第二性. 陶铁柱，译. 北京：中国书籍出版社 2004.]

Dovey, Teresa. Coetzee and His Critics: The Case of *Dusklands*. *English in Africa* 14 (1987):

15 - 30.

——. *The Novels of J. M. Coetzee: Lacanian Allegories*. Craighall: Ad. Donker, 1988.

——. *Waiting for the Barbarians*: Allegory of Allegories. *Critical Perspectives on J. M. Coetzee*. ed. Graham Huggan and Stephen Waston. London: Macmillan Press Limited, 1996.

Dragunoiu, Dana. J. M. Coetzee's Life & Times of Michel K and the Thin Theory of the Good. *The Journal of Commonwealth Literature* 4.1 (2006): 69 - 92.

Engdahl, Horace Oscar Axel. Press Release. 2 October 2003. <http: //nobelprize. org /nobel _prizes /literature / laureates /2003 /press. html>

Fichte, J.G. *The Essential Characteristics of Current Age*. tr. Shen Zhen and Liang Zhixue. Shenyang: Liaoning Education Press, 1998. [现时代的根本特点. 沈真,梁志学,译. 沈阳：辽宁教育出版社,1998.]

Fitzgerald, Michel. Serendipity. *World Literature Today* January-April 2004: 24 - 25.

Foucault, Michel. *The History of Sexuality*. translated from the French by Robert Hurley. New York: Pantheon Books, 1978.

——. *Preface to L'Archeologie du Savoir*. ed. Du Xiaozhen. Shanghai: Shanghai Far East Press. 2002. [福柯集. 杜小真,编. 上海：上海远东出版社,2002.]

Franssen, Paul. Fleeing from the Burning City: Michel K, Vagrancy and Empire. *English Studies* 5 (2003): 453 - 463.

Frazer, Elizabeth and Kimberly Hutchings. On Politics and Violence: Arendt Contra Fanon. *Contemporary Political Theory* 7 (2008): 90 - 108.

Freud, Sigmund. *Beyond the Pleasure Principle*. tr. James Strachey. New York and London: W.W. Norton and Company. 1961.

Fromm, Eric. *The Sane Society*. London and New York: Routledge Classics, 2002.

Gao Wenhui. Discourse Analysis of the Later Empire. *Journal of Zaozhuang Institute* 6 (2006): 41 - 45. [高文惠.晚期帝国叙述的话语分析. 枣庄学院学报 6 (2006): 41 - 45.]

——. Colonizer's Self and Colonial Other: a Philosophical Reflection upon Master-slave Relationship. *Journal of Suihua Institute* 1 (2008): 85 - 89. [高文惠.殖民者的自我与殖民地的他者：主奴关系的哲学反思.绥化学院学报, 1 (2008). 85 - 89.]

Gordimer, Nadine. The Idea of Gardening. *New York Review of Books* February 2, 1984:

3 - 6.

——. Preface. *Critical Perspectives on J. M. Coetzee*. ed. Graham Huggan and Stephen Waston. London: Macmillan Press Limited, 1996. i-xii.

Greenblatt, S. and G. Gunn. *Redrawing the Boundaries*. New York: The Modern Language Association of America. 1992.

Holliday, Adrian, John Kullman and Martin Hyde. *Intercultural Communication: An Advanced Resource Book*. London; New York: Routledge, 2004.

Han, Ruihui. On the Process and Significance of Otherization. *Journal of Zhejiang Normal University (Edition of Social Sciences)* 4 (2007): 68 - 71. [韩瑞辉. 论小说《等待野蛮人》中的他者化过程及其意义.浙江师范大学学报：社会科学版,4 (2007): 68 - 71.]

Head, Dominic. *J. M. Coetzee*. Cambridge: Cambridge University Press, 1997.

——. *The Cambridge Introduction to J. M. Coetzee*. Cambridge: Cambridge University Press, 2009.

Heidegger, Martin. *Being and Time*. Oxford: Basil Blackwell Publisher Ltd., 1962.

Herman, Judith. *Trauma and Recovery*. New York: Basic Books, 1997.

Herman, Vimala. *Dramatic Discourse: Dialogue as Interaction in Plays*. London: Routeledge, 1995.

Hooks, Bell. *Feminist Theory: From Margin to Center*. Boston, USA: South End Press, 1984.

Huggan, Graham and Stephen Waston. Introduction. *Critical Perspectives on J. M. Coetzee*. ed. Graham Huggan and Stephen Waston. London: Macmillan Press Limited, 1996.

Iser, Wolfgang. *The Act of Reading, A Theory of Aesthetic Response*. London: Routledge & Kegan Paul Ltd., 1978.

——. Das Fiktive und das Imaginare: Perspektiven Literarischer Anthropologie. tr. Chen Dingjia. Changchun: Jilin People's Press, 2003. [虚构与想 象——文学人类学疆界. 陈定家,等,译.长春：吉林人民出版社,2003.]

Jaenecke. H. *Die Weissen Herren 300 Jahre Krieg und Gewalt in Südafrika*. tr. Zhao Zhenquan. Beijing: World Knowledge Press, 1981. [白人老爷.赵振权,等,译. 北京：世界知识出版社,1981.]

Jameson, Frederic. *The Political Unconscious Narrative as a Socially Symbolic Act*. New York: Cornell University Press, 1981.

Kissack, Mike and Michel Titlestad. The Dynamics of Discontent: Containing Desire and Aggression in Coetzee's *Disgrace*. *African Identity* 3. 1 (2005): 51 - 67.

——. Forward: Reflections on an "unsettled habitation". *White Writing: On the Culture of Letters in South Africa* by J. M. Coetzee. Braamfontein: Pentz Publishers, 2007.

Kossew, Sue. *Pen and Power: A Postcolonial Reading of J. M. Coetzee and André Brink*. Amsterdam: Atlanta, GA. 1996.

——. The Politics of Shame and Redemption in J. M. Coetzee's *Disgrace*. *Research in African Literatures* 34.2 (2003): 155 - 162.

——. Border Crossings: Self and Text. *J. M. Coetzee in Context and Theory*. ed. Elleke Boehmer, Robert Eaglestone and Katy Iddiols. New York: Continuum International Publishing Group, 2009.

Kratz, Henry. Review of *Life and Times of Michel K*. *World Literature Today* 58: 3 (1984): 461 - 462.

Lacan, Jacques. *A Selection of Lacan's Works*. tr. Chu Xiaoquan. Shanghai: Shanghai Joint Publishing Company, 2001. [拉康选集. 楮孝泉,译.上海: 上海三联书店. 2001.]

Lechte, John. *Key Contemporary Concepts*. London: SAGE Publications Ltd., 2003.

Lenin, Vladimir I. *A Selection from Lenin's Works, Volume II*. Beijing: People's Press, 1995. [列宁. 列宁选集. 第二卷. 北京: 人民出版社,1995.]

Levin, Bernard. On the Edge of the Empire. *Sunday Times* 23 November 1980: 44.

Levinas, Emmanuel. *Totality and Infinity*. Pittsburg: Duquesne University Press, 1969.

Levinson, Stephen C. *Pragmatics*. Cambridge: Cambridge University Press, 1983.

Levi-Strauss, Claude. *Myth and Meaning*. tr. Wang Weilan. Taibei: China Times Publishing Company, 1980. [神话与意义. 王维兰,译. 台北: 时报文化出版企业公司, 1980.]

Li, Jing. Dogs, Women, and the Significant Otherness in J. M. Coetzee's *Disgrace*. *Coetzee Study and Postcolonial Literature*. ed. Cai Shenqin and Xie Yanming. Wuhan: Wuhan University Press, 2011. 201 - 212. [库切研究与后殖民文学. 蔡圣勤,谢艳明,编. 武汉: 武汉大学出版社,2011.201 - 212.]

Locke, John. *Two Treatises of Government*. Cambridge: Cambridge University Press, 1960.

Lodge, David. Disturbing the Peace. *The New York Review of Books*, November 20, 2003. ＜HTTP: //WWW. NYBOOKS. COM/ARTICLES/ARCHIVES/2003/NOV/ 20/

DISTURBINGTHE-PEACE/? PAGINATION=FALSE>

Macarthur, Kathleen Laura. *The Things We Carried: Trauma and Aesthetic in Contemporary American Fiction*. Diss. Columbia College of Arts and Sciences of the George Washington University, 2005.

Marais, Mike. Writing with Eyes Shut: Ethics, Politics, and the Problem of the Other in the Fiction of J.M. Coetzee. *English in Africa* 25. 1 (1998): 43 - 60.

Marais, Michel. The Hermeneutics of Empire: Coetzee's Postcolonial Metafiction. *Critical Perspectives on J. M. Coetzee*. ed. Graham Huggan and Stephen Watson. London: Macmillan, 1996, 66 - 81.

Marijke, Van Vuuren. Beyond Words: Silence in William Golding's *Darkness Visible* and J. M. Coetzee's *Life and Times of Michel K*. *English Studies in Africa* 48: 1 (2005): 93 - 106.

Mars-Jones, Adam. It's very novel, but is it actually a novel? *The Observer* 14 September 2003.

Marx, Karl. *Economic & Philosophic Manuscripts of* 1844. tr. Martin Milligan. Moscow: Progress Publishers, 1959.

——. The Capital. *Karl Marx and Frederick Engels, Vol*. 23. Beijing: People's Press. [马克思.资本论.马克思恩格斯全集. 第23卷.北京：人民出版社,1972.]

——. *Selections of Marx and Engels, Volume One*. Beijing: People's Press, 1995. [马克思,卡尔. 马克思恩格斯选集. 第1卷. 北京：人民出版社,1995.]

McDonald, Peter D. Disgrace Effects. *Interventions* 4. 3 (2002): 321 - 330.

McGonegal, Julie. *Imagining Justice: The Politics of Postcolonial Forgiveness and Reconciliation*. Library and Archives Canada, 2004.

Nietzsche, Friedrich. *The Will to Power*. tr. Walter Kaufmann and R. J. Hollingdale. ed. Walter Kaufmann. New York: Random House, 1967.

——. *The Gay Science*. ed. Bernard Williams. Cambridge: Cambridge University Press, 2001.

Ning, Sao. On the Apartheid in South Africa and Its Colonial Plunder from the Black. *World History* 6(1979): 31 - 40. [宁骚.论南非种族隔离制及其对黑人的殖民掠夺.世界历史 6 (1979): 31 - 40.]

Ogden, Benjamin H. How J. M. Coetzee's *Diary of a Bad Year* Thinks Through the Novel. *Novel: A Forum on Fiction* 43.3 (2010): 466-482.

Pienaar, Hans. Brilliant yet Aloof, Coetzee at Last Wins Nobel Prize for Literature. *The Independent*. 3 October 2003. <http://www.independent.co.uk/arts-entertain ment/books/news/brilliant-yet-aloof-coetzee-at-last-wins-nobel-prize-for-literature-581951.html.>

Plato. *Republic*. Cambridge: Hackett Publishing Company, Inc., 2004.

Poyner, Jane. Introduction. *J. M. Coetzee and the Idea of the Public Intellectual*. ed. Jane Poyner. Athens: Ohio University Press, 2006.

——. *J. M. Coetzee and the Paradox of Postcolonial Authorship*. Surrey: Ashgate Publishing Limited, 2009.

Rawls, John. *A Theory of Justice*. Cambridge, MA: The Belknap Press of Harvard University, 1971.

Ricoeur, Paul. *The Just*. tr. David Pellauer. Chicago and London: The University of Chicago Press, 2000.

Robertson, Ritchie. Introduction. *Trial* by Franz Kafka. Oxford: Oxford University Press, 2009. xi-xxv.

Rousseau, Jean-Jacques. *The Social Contract*. tr. He Zhaowu. Beijing: Commercial Press, 1983. [社会契约论. 何兆武,译. 商务印书馆, 1983.]

——. *The Discourse on the Sciences and Arts and The Social Contract*. tr. Susan Dunn. New Haven and London: Yale University Press, 2002.

Said, Edward. Introduction. *Culture and Imperialism*. New York: Vintage Books, 1994.

Sanvan, Charles. Disgrace: a Path to Grace. *World Literature Today* January-April 2004. 26-29.

Segall, Kimberly Wedeven. Pursuing Ghosts: The Traumatic Sublime in J. M. Coetzee's *Disgrace*. *Research in African Literatures* 36.4 (2005): 40-54.

Shi, Yunlong. The Other and Otherness: A Study of Coetzee. *Foreign Languages Research* 2 (2011): 95-100. [石云龙 他者·他性——库切研究. 外语研究, 2 (2011): 95-100.]

Simmel, Georg. *Georg Simmel on Individuality and Social Forms*. Chicago: University of Chicago Press. 1971.

Spivak, Gayatri C. Theory in the Margin: Coetzee's *Foe* — Reading Defoe's "Crusoe/Roxana". *English in Africa* 17.2 (1990): 1-23.

Statutes of the Republic of South Africa — Constitutional Law (Issue No 38) Constitution of the Republic of South Africa Act, No. 108 of 1996.

Stephenson, Glennis. Escaping the Camps: The Idea of Freedom in J.M. Coetzee's *Life and Times of Michel K*. *Commonwealth Novel in English* 4.1 (1991): 77-88.

Tao Jiajun. Trauma. *Foreign Literature* 4 (2011): 117-125. [陶家俊.创伤.外国文学，4 (2011): 117-125.]

Traber, Daniels S. *Whiteness, Otherness, and the Individualism Paradox from Huck to Punk*. New York: Palgrave MacMillan, 2007.

Tran, Danielle. "Swine! The Word Still Rings in the Air": David's Reaction and the Perpetuation of Racial Conflict in J.M. Coetzee's *Disgrace*. *Postamble* 7.1 (2011): 1-6.

Urquhart, Troy. Truth, Reconciliation, and the Restoration of the State: Coetzee's *Waiting for the Barbarians*. *Twentieth-Century Literature* 52.1 (2006): 1-21.

Vambe, Maurice Taonezvi. Fictions of Autobiographical Representations. *Journal of Literary Studies* 25.1 (2009): 80-97.

Vaughan, Michel. Literature and Politics: Currents in South African Writing in the Seventies. *Journal of Southern African Studies* 9.1 (1982): 118-138.

Wang, Jinghui. *Foreigner Forever*. Diss. Beijing Languages University, 2006.

——. Contrast of Two Empires: Reading Coetzee's Allegorical *Waiting for the Barbarians*. *Foreign Literature Studies* 6 (2006): 153-158. [王敬慧. 两种帝国理念的对照：论库切寓言体小说《等待野蛮人》. 外国文学研究,6 (2006): 153-158.]

Wang, Yuechuan. *Literary Theory of Postcolonialism and New Historicism*. Jinan: Shandong Education Press, 1999. [王岳川.后殖民主义与新历史主义文论.济南：山东教育出版社,1999.]

Wastberg, Per. Award Ceremony Speech, December 10, 2003. <http://nobelprize.org/nobel_prizes/literature/laureates/2003/presentation-speech.html>

——. Speech for the Swedish Academy quoted in "He and His Man the 2003 Nobel Lecture." *World Literature Today* May-August 2004. 16-20.

Waston, Stephen. Colonialism and the Novels of J. M. Coetzee. *Research in African*

Literatures 17.3 (1986): 370 - 392.

——. Colonialism and the Novels of J. M. Coetzee. *Critical Perspectives on J. M. Coetzee*. ed. Graham Huggan and Stephen Watson. London: Macmillan Press Ltd., 1996.

Wenzel, Jennifer. Keys to the Labyrinth: Writing, Torture, and Coetzee's Barbarian Girl. *Tulsa Studies in Women's Literature* 15.1 (1996): 61 - 71.

White, Hayden. *The Content of the Form: Narrative Discourse and Historical Representation*. Baltimore & London: Johns Hopkins University Press, 1987.

——. The Metaphysics of Western Historiography. *World Philosophy* 4 (2004): 50 - 58. [怀特,海登. 西方历史编纂的形而上学. 陈新,译. 世界哲学 4(2004): 50 - 58.]

Wood, James. Parables and Prizes. *The New Republic* December 20, 1999. 42 - 46.

——. A Frog's Life. *London Review of Books* 25.20(2003): 15 - 16.

Wright, Derek. Black Earth, White Myth: Coetzee's Michel K. *Modern Fiction Studies* 38.2 (1992): 435 - 443.

Wright, Laura. "*Writing Out of all the Camps*": *J. M. Coetzee's Narratives of Displacement*. New York & London: Routledge, 2006.

Xu, Tianxin and Liang Zhiming. *A World History: Contemporary Volume*. Beijing: People's Press, 1997. [徐天新,梁志明. 世界通史・当代卷. 北京: 人民出版社,1997.]

Z. N. Much Ado about Nobody. *African Communist* 97 (1984): 101 - 103.

Zhai, Yejun and Liu Yongchang. On J. M. Coetzee's *Life and Times of Michel K*. *Foreign Literature* 2 (2006): 70 - 72.[翟业军,刘永昶. 无神时代的约伯—— 论库切的《迈克尔・K的生活和时代》. 外国文学, 2(2006): 70 - 72.]

【附录】

1. 石云龙库切研究系列论文

他者·他性——库切研究

摘要：诺贝尔文学奖得主库切在文学创作中，表现出非凡的探索创新精神，荷兰白人后裔在种族隔离制度盛衰之地南非以及英美澳的独特经历，决定了他的文学创作的丰富性，他的数重身份及其后种族隔离时代对身份的追寻、对人性的拷问、对弱者的关注，决定了他为边缘化的他者代言；他对哲学伦理的探究、对西方文明中缺乏人性的理性主义和肤浅道德准则的批判、对文学表现样式的不懈探索，使其作品中透出一种强烈的异于南非文学传统的他性，为文学发展提供了新路径。

关键词：库切；种族；他者；他者化；他性

图分类号：1109.9　**文献标识码**：A　**文章编号**：1005－7242(2011)02－0095－06

旅居澳大利亚阿德莱德的南非英语作家、2003年诺贝尔文学奖得主约翰·马科斯韦尔·库切(J. M. Coetzee)以其特立独行的风格，写出大量"篇幅有限而范围无限"的作品，被称为是能够"想象出无法想象的东西"的"后现代寓言家"；诺贝尔奖评选委员会认为，这位此前曾两获英联邦布克奖(1983，1999)的作家是"一位审慎的怀疑者(scrupulous doubter)"，他"以无数姿态表现了局外人令人诧异的牵连"，"无情地批判了西方文明中残酷的理性主义和肤浅的道德观"(以上见 Engdahl 2003：1)。

库切的特殊经历、作品的独特背景与别样风格，使评论界对其产生了广泛兴趣。

近年来的研究成果中不乏对库切作品的后现代主义研究(Hutcheon 1988;Colleran 1994)、后殖民主义研究(Durrant 2005;Spivak 1991;Jolly 1996;Diala 2001;卫岭 2006)和历史研究(Meskell & Weiss 2006;Easton 2006),也有大量语境研究(Barnett 1999;Barnard 2002)、叙事研究(MacLeod 2006;Wright 2006)等。

人们在库切研究中,无论是较多关注作家的后殖民流散经历,还是研究作品的后现代特征;不管是探讨殖民者欠下的历史旧账,还是研究文本的存在语境,都认为不能割裂其作品与现代南非小说创作语境的联系。他的复杂身份及其在后种族隔离时代对身份的追寻、对人性的拷问、对弱者的关注,决定了他为被边缘化的他者代言;他对哲学伦理的探究、对西方文明中缺乏人性的理性主义和肤浅道德准则的批判、对文学表现样式的不懈探索,使其作品中透出一种强烈的异于南非文学传统的他性,为文学发展提供了新路径。

他者问题是社会科学研究的核心课题之一,发现"他者"哲学价值的是黑格尔,这位思辨哲学的代表人物虽然是在追求"总体"、"同一"的维度上努力解决哲学问题,但他认识到差异的重要性,力图在世界的"差异"中求"同一",这为"他者"的出现开辟了空间。海德格尔对于"此在"在世的论述是一大创新,他用独有的"共在"概念来表达"此在"在世是与"他人"同在。"'在之中'就是与他人共同存在。"(Heidegger 1962: 155)这种主体与他人的"共在"关系论述,消除了现象学家胡塞尔通过"移情作用"将他人建立在自我基础之上的唯我论嫌疑,为"他者"成为其哲学一部分铺平了道路。而莱维纳斯反对本体论,借助"他者"批判西方本体论传统并企图超越,但他并不否认传统意义上"他者"的存在,只不过认为那是"相对他者",是可以转化成同一或自我的他者,而他的哲学强调,要打破"同一性",必须建立一种"绝对他性"哲学,提出一种无法还原为自我或同一的"他者"(irreversible, something else entirely, the absolutely OTHER),与"我""相遇"而完全不同于"我"的"彻底他者"或"绝对他者"。(Levinas 1969: 35)在莱维纳斯看来,西方殖民主义、帝国主义、资本主义在对资本的贪婪与追求过程中所体现的那种单一权力意志,正是"总体"、"同一"理念在现实社会中的投射,而其发展到极致便是暴力和战争。他一针见血地指出,"作为第一哲学的本体论是一种权力哲学,"(Ontology, as first philosophy is a philosophy of power) (ibid.: 46)认为,这是西方文化危机的根本所在。

对他者的研究以及对文学作品中他性的研究，在后现代后殖民研究风起之后，渐成当下研究热点，给他者定义者往往是主导性主体，如德国著名哲学家、评论家西摩尔认为，他者“是超越远近距离的‘局外人’。这种人是群体本身的一部分，形似各色各样的‘内部敌人’，是群体既与其保持距离又要直面正视的成分”(Simmel 1971：144)。而著名英国学者、后殖民批评家艾勒克·博埃默则指出，“‘他者’这个概念，……指主导性主体以外的一个不熟悉的对立面或否定因素，因为它的存在，主体的权威才得以界定”(博埃默 1998：22)。由他者衍生出来的“他者化”，则指人们通过将负面特点加诸他者(其他群体或其他个人)而获得自我身份认同的过程。人们假设“他者”不如“自我”复杂深奥，“他者化”的施动者常把“他者”视为卑微劣等的对方，从而获得心理上的满足和优越感。(Holliday，et al. 2004：191)这里的他者研究通常涉及种族、性别、身份等差异，如白人叙述者眼里的“他者”往往是有色人种，“他者”的生活总是与混乱、懒惰、肮脏、放纵、愚蠢、邪恶、道德责任感匮乏等联系在一起，这就从反面证明了主导性本体的文明、秩序、修养、道德。正如弗雷德里克·杰姆逊所说，“人们对他产生恐惧并不因为他邪恶，而是因为他是‘他者’——异己、不同、奇怪、肮脏、陌生”(Jameson 1981：115)。对于与理论相关联的他性的各种不同阐释，是后殖民文化研究的历史前提。

被诺贝尔评奖委员会称为“后现代寓言家”的库切，在其文学创作中以典型的库氏寓言、迥异于南非文学传统的他性书写方式，多元化多层次再现强权政治语境下主导霸权话语形成的规律，展示后种族隔离时代权威话语者对被殖民者他者化的过程及其结果，以冷峻的笔触叙述话语权缺失的他者的生存与心理状态。

库切笔下的他者，与拉康主体间话语理论中的他者(L'Autre)极为相似，指异己、陌生、危险的“在者”和权力话语上的“不在场者”。这些他者缺乏辩解机会，通常只有沉默的形象。从“深入异己者与憎恶者内心”的南非最高文学奖(CAN)获奖小说《幽暗之地》(Coetzee 1974)到“承继康拉德手法的政治恐怖小说”《等待野蛮人》(Coetzee 1980/1999)，从“根植于笛福、卡夫卡和贝克特”文学的作品《迈克尔·K的生活与时代》(Coetzee 1983)到“阐释陀思妥耶夫斯基生活和小说世界”的《彼得堡的大师》(Coetzee 1994/1995)，从展示“白人至上观念瓦解之后南非新形势”下人们际遇的《耻》(Coetzee 1999/2009)到表现“作者与邪恶争斗”的著作《伊丽莎白·科斯特洛》(Coetzee 2003)，从文体与视角各异的三栏式小说《凶年纪事》(Coetzee 2007)到探究真相的自嘲式自我重估小说《夏日》(Coetzee 2009)，库切推出的他者形象不仅包括异族部落有色人种(如"思想者"尤金·唐恩计划中的越南人、"行动者"雅各·库切心目中的布须曼人和霍屯督人、帝国少壮派军人眼中的"蛮族"人等),包括"逃离动荡不安和战争迫近局势"的像迈克尔·K一样的沉默无语、苦苦挣扎的卑微残缺的生命,包括在自然界任人宰割、受人虐待、毫无意义地牺牲的动物,也包括在后帝国后殖民后种族隔离语境中不再享有特权、丧失主导话语的白人以及似与时代环境格格不入的人。

库切循着主流话语叙述者的惯常定义,通过白描手段再现处于边缘化境地的他者,冷静地检视帝国主义、殖民主义、种族隔离制度不复存在后的南非社会变迁,表现后帝国后殖民后种族隔离时代主体与他者文化嬗变中的位移与冲突,揭示出在颠覆了"白人至上"观念的南非社会里人性的扭曲和道德伦理的严重错位。

无论是《幽暗之地》中自称"我是个思想者"(Coetzee 1974: 1)的唐恩,被陆建德(2007: 7)称为"行动者"的雅各·库切,还是《等待野蛮人》中远离帝国中心的边境地区老行政长官,都在叙事话语中涉及被边缘化的他者形象。作者通过叙述者超然冷静的陈述,展现后帝国后殖民后种族隔离时代他者的际遇,让读者清楚地看到权力话语者心目中预设的他者以及他者化过程。

《幽暗之地》中参与越南战争升级计划设计的"思想者"、主张种族隔离崇拜暴力的"行动者"、《等待野蛮人》中来自国防部三局、戴着有色眼镜的军队上校等是权力话语主控者;关在笼子里"形容枯槁……目光呆滞"的"赤色分子"、经受酷刑坚贞不屈却在药物作用下精神崩溃、终日"躲在角落里以泪洗面,沿网栏踱步、念念有词"的"鬼魂或缺失自我的幽灵"(16 - 17)、被割去脑袋的越南人,《等待野蛮人》中被半路拦截严刑拷打的爷孙、被威权主体妖魔化的野蛮人(边境地区的土著人)等则成了为"界定主体权威"而存在的"不熟悉的对立面或否定因素"。

《幽暗之地》中的"思想者"用一组血腥浓重的越战照片不动声色地为读者解读他者意蕴,而在"开拓闭塞之处给黑暗带来光明"(Coetzee 106)的"行动者"则以赤裸裸的行为诠释其"征服蛮荒者的人生"(ibid.: 77)。图片中,美军特种部队军士威尔逊"手提一颗割下的人头放在面前地上",另一位军士贝利"抓头发拎着两颗脑袋"。叙述者未加评论地说明征服者的强权本质上要以血腥镇压他者来维持,那些"如石头般僵硬的"(ibid.: 15)头颅在无言地叙述着强权者的暴行;而作者采用第一人称复数进行的直白叙述,印证了强权者的兽行:"我们把他们的肉体切开……我们强暴他们的女人……女人身体像石头一样冰冷。"(ibid.：18)强权者令人发指的暴行，在"行动者"口中成了漫不经心的描述，如"美丽的死亡"(ibid.：100)、生擒布须曼人后将其"绑在火上烤，甚至用烤出的脂肪抹在其身体上烤炙"(ibid.：60)等事件。

《等待野蛮人》通过老行政长官的陈述，揭示了帝国卫士们心中预设的他者以及他者化的过程。其实，库切认为操控话语权的"文明人"对被界定为他者的"野蛮人"的蔑视"植根于子虚乌有的基础"。两者之间的差异只不过在于"用餐规矩不同、眼皮长得不一样什么的"(Coetzee 1999：51)。他客观地再现了那位为维护帝国威权、伸张所谓理性正义而崇尚程式化"执法"的上校那些欲加之罪何患无辞的行径：明明是路上正常行走的爷孙，却被帝国卫士当成抢劫案嫌犯；明明是见到威权者就战战兢兢的守法平民，却被迫根据乔尔上校预设的标准交代真相；明明双手被缚，却被控"情绪失控"、意欲"攻击调查人"(ibid.：10)。作者没有展示刑讯室内酷刑伺候的场景，也没有刻意为当时并不在场的叙事者展开想象，而是客观冷静地呈现了老行政长官亲眼目睹的事实：老人"灰色胡须被血併在一起。双唇变形凹陷，牙齿碎了。一眼凹在里面，另一眼成了血洞"(ibid.：12)，轻而易举地颠覆了帝国权威话语者的谎言，让读者明白，西方文明中所谓理性正义的实质是威权话语者的残酷无情和道德人性的丧失殆尽。

作为具有全球视野的知名作家，库切关注特定时代南非的人与事，在文本中揭秘帝国权力系统的本质特点与运行规律，客观展示强势话语的语境，凸显他者的生存状态，解构和颠覆强势话语的权威。

库切作品中再现的他者层次丰富、意义多元。在首获布克奖的小说《迈克尔·K的生活与时代》中，库切采用冷峻的语言、近乎白描的表现方式，震撼人心地展示了在南非种族隔离政策逐渐成形继而猖獗的年代普通人的生存状态。这里通过一系列诸如孤独、逃逸、异化、荒诞等卡夫卡式寓言主题呈现的边缘化他者已经超越了肤色和种族，作者将笔触伸入无话语权的下层社会，包括有色人种与白人。作品不仅表现了有色人种游击队为争取权利而针对主导话语持有者所进行的斗争，更展示了在战争即将迫近时南非下层白人迈克尔·K这个典型的卑贱他者的经历及其近乎卑微的诉求——过上有人格尊严的生活。这一人物的命运在某种程度上代表了所有无话语权者的共同命运，他默默无闻的抗争，包括执着地帮助母亲实现落叶归根、魂归故里的愿望、为实现自己的自由理想而反复坚持以羸弱的生命主体回归自然的举措，认为自己与战乱频仍、社会动荡无涉的"异类"思想，无不表现出作者在揭示人类社会的残忍暴力、相互隔绝、彼此仇恨、愚昧自欺，检视西方文明理性正义本质、批判其道德伦理的同时，为遭受压迫和蹂躏的边缘化弱势群体仗义言说，提出人能否在历史社会中沉默隐身，他者在与环境的冲突中能否有自己的诉求等问题。

如果说库切在《迈克尔·K的生活与时代》中开始转向从社会、历史、精神等层面探讨主体和他者的关系，那么，在其重要小说《耻》中，作者转换视角，将目光投到殖民主体不再存续、种族隔离制度已经消亡的时代主体文化与他者文化嬗变中的位移与冲突。

小说通过寓意深刻的主题“耻”，表现被消解了昔日中心地位、主导话语权被颠覆的白人殖民者后裔在当下南非社会所陷入的“耻辱”地位。这里，同性恋白人女子露西经受双重侮辱——被有色人种强暴后委曲求全，沦为原雇工黑人佩特鲁斯的小老婆和佃农；大学传播学副教授卢里在特权丧失后因昔日看上去微不足道的性丑闻而失去教职，不得不与等级低下的黑人共事，而且失去话语权，沦为默默无语的传递工具的帮手。作者在剥离了附在白人身上所有光环、去除所有人为优势之后，再将其言行暴露在光天化日之下，使读者轻而易举地发现崇尚自由的白人所秉持的自由观念实质是什么，他们所奉行的伦理道德观究竟能否经得起理性推敲。卢里之耻，是其从“白人至上”地位跌落下来不能自由自在、为所欲为而感受到的耻辱，是种族隔离制度消亡后不得不与昔日卑贱者平等相处、甚至遭受白眼而感到的耻辱，是他对女儿露西遭遇暴力事件后的“软弱”表现而感到的愤愤不平，是殖民者后裔不得不为其先辈的殖民侵略暴行付出代价而感到的耻辱。从本着西方文明的契约原则付费召妓，到利用教授地位引诱有夫之妇，到违背人伦道德观念去性侵大学女生，到无可奈何地与乡村黑女人贝芙·肖的性爱关系，卢里的白人形象处处闪现着道德缺失的“耻”的辉光；从表现出的无性别特征外貌，到违背常态的同性恋倾向，到被施暴后的委曲求全，露西的白人女性形象既有女性主义的印记，更有白人在当代社会丧失了主体地位、被他者化后的生态变化痕迹。库切展示的南非白人与黑人、特权与无权、男性与女性等几组二元对立的位移或颠覆，表明了他对不同人种主导话语权地位、关系现状等问题进行的深层次反思，拷问他者化过程中人性扭曲、伦理道德错位的根本原因。他在这里所关注的，已经超越了多维所说的“到底是站在压迫者一边还是被压迫者一边”(Dovey 1993: 18)的问题，而是人类如何清除障碍、消除文化冲突、排除种族、性别歧视等去实现自由平等、和谐相处的问题。

库切对他者的呈现与探讨并不局限于被边缘化了的人,他还从哲学与诗学两个角度讨论被人类视作他者的动物。在《动物的生命》(Coetzee 1999)中,他分析了野生动物、圈养动物、宠物的生存现状,借科斯特洛夫人之口,将听众的注意力引向动物生存与死亡问题,对哲学家笛卡尔"动物存在,就像一台机器存在一样"的说法提出挑战,对其公认的名言"我思故我在"进行调侃:"如果一个生物不进行我们[人类]所谓的思考,从某种程度上来说,就成了二等动物。"(ibid.:33)理性通常是区别生物高低贵贱的标准,人类沾沾自喜,认为自己具有理性,因而比动物高贵,但是,这种理性的标准恰恰是人类制定的。"理性既不是上帝的存在也不是宇宙的存在。它像是人类思想的存在……理性像是人类思想的某种倾向的存在。"(ibid.:23)同理,人类认为动物低能,依据的是科学实验,而科学实验则完全是以人为中心进行的,用来衡量动物的标准原本是用于人的。库切认为,在人类掌握枪支征服动物后,就使其成为任人摆布的他者。更有甚者,人类还假借神明之口说,"凡活着的动物都可以作你们的食物"(Genesis 9.3)。这就为自己大肆杀戮动物的行为找到了借口,而且在这些行动里自然可以不去顾忌处于他者地位的动物的感受。人类可以因为需要肉食、因动物毛、骨等的实用价值而猎杀动物,也可以因娱乐、消遣,甚至泄愤等种种原因而猎杀动物。《等待野蛮人》开篇出现的场面——成百上千的鹿、猪和熊被杀死,漫山遍野都是动物尸体,多得没法收拾,只好让它们去烂掉"(Coetzee 1999:1)——便是人类毫无节制的贪婪的缩影。《耻》中采用较大篇幅呈现的人类对动物的残酷行径,更进一步表明库切对人类理性的质疑。他通过卢里为待宰的羊喂食、为濒死的猫狗安排有尊严的死亡等善待动物的行为,在从反面衬托动物他者地位的同时,表达了他渴望人与自然建立良性和谐关系的愿望。

库切在作品中为被边缘化的他者代言,与其自身经历及其文学创作语境密切相关。英国后殖民研究专家波因纳曾经说过,"库切的社会文化遗传、他游离于阿弗利堪社区外围的立场、他对政治语言风格的深刻疑惧,使他在南非产生了边缘感"(Poyner 1996:3)。库切于1940年出生在开普敦荷兰人后裔说英语家庭,这种家庭历史渊源决定了他从一开始就具有不同于当地人的复杂的身份特征,他所使用的家庭内外有别的语言,使他本能地与南非阿弗利堪社会产生疏离感;他作为虔诚的基督教教徒而被安排上了天主教高中的经历,使他从思想上无法与所处群体和谐共处,因而使这一疏离感加深;他在英国做了5年计算机程序员工作,在美国研究荒诞派作家贝克特,参与反越战示威游行，申请移民被拒，被迫回南非后又离开赴澳洲定居，这些经历在拓宽其视野、丰富其阅历的同时也无可否认地使其产生游离、另类的感觉。他的文学书写在主题发掘上充满了对后殖民他者身份的探究，在风格上富于后现代他性的探索。

库切在文学书写伊始，便踏上富于他性的创新之路。他的《幽暗之地》被称为结构新奇、形式实验的"先锋"之作(陆建德 2007：1)。作者将两个表面似乎毫不相干的故事纳入同一意识形态构架中进行多层次考察，深入异己者与憎恶者内心，取后者作恶而不自知的立场言说，谴责越战和南非种族歧视，表现出超小说的特质。《等待野蛮人》以主人公绵延不绝的独白，将种族和文化问题引向超越道德层面的深层反省，用谁也捉摸不透的"蛮族"姑娘以"他者"的存在形式来检视文明世界的价值荒谬，挑战文明与野蛮的定义，展示历史轮回交替的文明轨迹。根植于笛福、卡夫卡和贝克特文学的作品《迈克尔·K的生活与时代》采用第三人称加营地医生第一人称叙述视角，以不带任何感情色彩的语言，冷峻地推出卡夫卡式寓言，表现了意识到无力反抗命运只能以他者身份默然旁观的主人公在种族隔离时代的可悲命运。阐释陀思妥耶夫斯基生活和小说世界的《彼得堡的大师》采用现在进行时方式，表现出情节的共时性，以鲜活开放的他人意识和人物独立自主的声音，参与作者的平等对话，形成巴赫金的所谓复调，在众声喧哗的对话和错综复杂的文本中完成作者的意图。此后，库切似乎对小说叙事策略的实验兴趣更浓，《伊丽莎白·科斯特洛》的出版仿佛为小说增添了新的样式。作者利用女小说家的演讲就不同议题与不同人物对话，使作品主人公陷入看世界与被世界看的双重境地，将自己对理性的批判通过她那通常较为极端的方式推出，在后者历经驳诘、冷落或尴尬而不改立场的偏执中显现出作者观察世界的智慧。《凶年纪事》在叙事策略上走得更远，全书前 23 页加水平线分上下两栏、第 25 页开始加两条水平线分上中下三栏，作者通过这一独特的做法，将C先生为某图书公司撰写的 31 篇涉及不同主题的言论和 24 篇札记与这些材料写作、定稿过程中发生在C先生、协助C先生整理手稿并进行电脑输入的少妇安雅及其同居男友、新自由主义代言人艾伦之间的故事分层次排版，在每页都似碎片拼贴画、间离效果鲜明的文本中，奉献给读者一个天灾人祸施虐的凶年时代。在被认为是自传三部曲最后一部的《夏日》中，库切也表现出独辟蹊径的他性风格。他采用别具一格的"他传"(autre-biography)手法，由一位名叫文森特的英国传记作家将 8 个标明日期的笔记片段、5 个不同人物的访谈录和 5 个标有"未标明日期"字样的笔记片段不加处理地聚合在一起，通过受访对象对约翰阐释的矛盾性而产生的复杂声部，展示了事实与虚构的关系、知性文化、道德伦理与种族隔离制度下南非生活现实的冲突。在后现代的碎片拼贴、嬉戏性中实现了作者的寓意。

库切的文学实验是成功的。他采用大量后现代文学创作手法，刻意模糊小说与非小说的界限，在别出机杼的异样文体中，以超然淡定的他者姿态，为后现代后殖民后种族隔离时代被边缘化的弱势他者言说，以笔下主人公自身不可避免的命运不断与主流社会的权力意志相抗衡，批评锋芒直指权威话语权拥有者的意识形态、文明世界的道德伦理准则、理性原则，在呈现他者化的他者命运过程中表现出鲜明的他性。

参考文献：

[1] Bernard, Rita. Coetzee's country ways[J]. *Interventions* 4.3 (2002): 386 - 394.

[2] Barnett, Clive. Construction of apartheid in the international reception of the novels of J. M. Coetzee[J]. *Journal of Southern African Studies* 25.2 (1999): 287 - 30.

[3] Coetzee, J. M. *Dusklands*[M]. Harmondsworth, Middlesex, England: Penguin Books, 1974.

[4] Coetzee, J. M. *Waiting for the Barbarians*[M]. New York: Penguin Books, 1980/1999.

[5] Coetzee, J. M. *Life and Times of Michel K*[M]. Johannesberg: Raven Press, 1983.

[6] Coetzee, J. M. *The Master of Petersburg*[M]. London: Minerva Paperback, 1994/1995.

[7] Coetzee, J. M. *The Lives of Animals* [M]. Princeton, New Jersey: Princeton University Press, 1999.

[8] Coetzee, J. M. *Disgrace*[M]. London: Vintage Books, 1999/2009.

[9] Coetzee, J. M. *Elizabeth Costello*[M]. London: Secker & Warburg, 2003.

[10] Coetzee, J. M. *Diary of a Bad Year*[M]. London: Harvill Secker, 2007.

[11] Coetzee, J. M. *Summertime*[M]. London: Harvill Secker, 2009.

[12] Colleran, Jeanne. Position papers: Reading J. M. Coetzee's fiction and criticism [J]. *Contemporary Literature* 35.3 (1994): 578 - 592.

[13] Diala, Isidore. Nadine Gordimer, J. M. Coetzee, and Andre Brink: Guilt, expiation, and the reconciliation process in post-apartheid South Africa [J]. *Journal of Modern Literature* 25.2 (2001): 50 - 68.

[14] Dovey, Teresa. J. M. Coetzee: Writing in the middle voice[C]// Sue Kossew. *Critical*

Essays on J.M. Coetzee. New York: G. K. Hall, 1993. 18 - 29.

[15] Durrant, Sam. Postcolonial narrative and the work of mourning: J. M. Coetzee, Wilson Harris, and Toni Morrison [J]. *Modern Fiction Studies* 51. 3 (2005): 714 - 717.

[16] Easton, Kai. Coetzee, the Cape and the question of history [J]. *Scrutiny* 11. 1 (2006): 5 - 21.

[17] Engdahl, Horace Oscar Axel. *Press Release*. [EB/OL]. 2 October 2003. [2011 - 03 - 30]

[18] Heidegger, Martin. *Being and Time* [M]. Oxford: Basil Blackwell, 1962.

[19] Holliday, A. et al. *Intercultural Communication: An Advanced Resource Book* [M]. London: Routledge, 2004.

[20] Hutcheon, Linda. *A Poetics of Post-modernism: History, Theory, Fiction* [M]. London: Routledge, 1988.

[21] Jameson, Fredric. *The Political Unconscious: Narrative as a Socially Symbolic Act* [M]. New York: Cornell UP, 1981.

[22] Jolly, Rosemary Jane. *Colonization, Violence, and Narration in White South African Writing: Andre Brink, Breyten Breytenbach, and J. M. Coetzee* [M]. Athens: Ohio UP, 1996.

[23] Levinas, Emmanuel. *Totality and Infinity* [M]. Pittsburg: Duquesne University Press, 1969.

[24] MacLeod, Lewis. "Do we of necessity become puppets in a story?" or narrating the world: On speech, silence and discourse in J. M. Coetzee's *Foe* [J]. *Modern Fiction Studies* 52. 1 (2006): 1 - 18.

[25] Meskell, Lynn & Lindsay Weiss. Coetzee on South Africa's past: Remembering in the time of forgetting [J]. *Anthropologist* 108. 1 (2006): 88 - 99.

[26] Poyner, Jane. Introduction [C] // Graham Huggan & Stephen Watson. *Critical Perspectives on J. M. Coetzee*. Houndmills, Basingstoke, Hampshire: Macmillan Press Limited, 1996.

[27] Simmel, Georg. "*The Stranger*" *Georg Simmel on Individuality and Social Forms* [M]. Chicago: University of Chicago Press, 1971. 144.

[28] Spivak, Gayatri Chakravorty. Theory in the margin: Coetzee's *Foe* — Reading Defoe's *Crusoe/Roxana*[J]. *English in Africa* 17. 2 (1991): 1 - 23.

[29] Wright, Laura. "Does he have it in him to be the woman?" The performance of displacement in J. M. Coetzee's *Disgrace* [J]. *Ariel* 37.4 (2006): 83 - 102.

[30] 博埃默，艾勒克. 殖民与后殖民文学[M]. 盛宁，等，译. 沈阳：辽宁教育出版社，1998.

[31] 陆建德. 序[C]//幽暗之地. 杭州：浙江文艺出版社，2007. 1 - 21.

[32] 卫岭. 论库切小说《耻》的后殖民主义话语特征[J]. 四川外国语学院学报 2 (2006): 29 - 33.

（原载《外语研究》2011 年第 2 期）

约·麦·库切——为他者化的他者代言

内容提要：库切基于对南非历史和当下的深刻认识，在寻找自身话语位置时大胆质疑并解构前殖民者话语霸权，用白描手法展现前殖民地上他者的边缘地位，考察他者沉默的内涵，再现他者的他者化过程，对西方契约原则指导下的道德观和残酷的理性主义给予无情的批判。

关键词：库切；小说；再现；他者；他者化

Abstract: Based on his in-depth understanding of the history and present situation of South Africa, John Maxwell Coetzee bravely challenges and deconstructs the discourse hegemony of the former colonizers in seeking for his own right of discourse. In objectively presenting the marginalized position of the other in the former colony, he studies the silence of the other, represents the otherization of the other, and relentlessly criticizes the moral concepts in the western contractual free principle and cruel rationalism.

Key Words: Coetzee; novels; representation; other; otherized

约翰·麦克斯韦尔·库切(John Maxwell Coetzee)是一位极具个性特点的作家，其作品在南非和国际文坛的遭遇可谓冰火两重天：南非"有政治头脑的人"认为库切作品"不合时宜……丑化了黑人、丑化了黑人政权下的南非社会"(邹海仑 226)，因而对其大加鞭挞，甚至连获得国际盛誉的小说《耻》(*Disgrace*)在出版后也"直接遭到了南非[前]总统姆贝基的批评"(段枫 141),就连许多曾把库切视为同志、战友的自由思想知识分子也对其横加指责。库切在南非一度成为众矢之的,这导致他最终选择自我流放的道路,离开祖国远赴澳大利亚定居。然而,库切作品在西方却获得一片喝彩,在国际上连续获得重要奖项。[①] 诺贝尔奖评选委员会认为库切是"一位审慎的怀疑者(scrupulous doubter)",其作品"无情地批判了西方文明中残酷的理性主义和肤浅的道德观"(Engdahl 1)。根据不完全资料,中国学界对库切的评介始于《当代外国文学》刊发的论文《一曲殖民主义的哀歌——评1999年布克奖获奖小说〈耻辱〉》,该文"对南非当代著名作家寇兹[库切]的获奖小说《耻辱》的内容和思想意义进行了论述"(王丽丽132)。然而,真正激发起人们对这个在非洲、欧洲、美洲有着典型流动经历并最终定居澳洲的"离散"作家产生起浓厚研究兴趣的是他2003年获得了诺贝尔文学奖。中国期刊网搜索结果表明,从2003年至今,各类刊物发表的与库切有关的论文已逾百篇,其中多数重要刊物论文集中研究库切小说《耻》。[②] 虽然学者们从后殖民、后现代、新历史主义、自由主义、人道主义、心理分析等角度对库切进行颇有成效的研究,但"与国外的相关研究在深度和广度上都相差甚远"(段枫 139)。

确实,作为后殖民时代摆脱了殖民枷锁的土地上成长起来的白人后裔作家,库切出生的荷兰裔家庭、接受的传统英国式教育、在美国得克萨斯大学从事的贝克特文体学研究、纽约州立大学的教职、南非开普敦大学任教、澳大利亚定居等独特非凡的经历从一开始就为他的文学创作注入了命定的特殊性。库切是南非第一个将后现代主义的思考书写成文学作品的小说家,而且他的创作题材丰富,体裁多样,大有包罗万象之嫌,所以,库切受到的关注是世界范围的,对库切的研究也几乎涵盖现代文学批评的所

---

① 库切于1980年获英国詹姆斯·泰特·布莱克纪念奖,1984、1999年两次获得英国布克奖,1985年获法国费米娜奖,1987年获以色列耶路撒冷奖,1994年获爱尔兰时报国际小说奖,2003年获诺贝尔文学奖。

② 周长才. 风月所以惊世界——对库切小说的一种解释. 外国文学,2004,1;卫岭. 论库切小说《耻》的后殖民主义话语特征. 四川外语学院学报,2006,2;蔡云,脱剑鸣. 析 J. M. 库切小说《耻》中超越种族的生存困惑. 兰州大学学报:社会科学版,2006,1;蔡圣勤,李丽娟. 库切小说《耻》中人物的文化身份与生民视角. 湖北社会科学,2006,9;杨铭瑀. 解读《耻》中的歌剧与狗. 外国文学研究,2007,1;李茂增. 宽恕与和解的寓言. 外国文学,2006,1;王珺鹏. 耐人寻味的态度大转变——对库切小说《耻》中梅拉妮指控行为的解读. 当代小说,2009,1.

有理论路径①。不过，人们在库切研究中有一共识，即研究库切作品不能背离南非现代小说创作语境，不能忽略南非特殊的历史条件和库切本人的学术背景和流散作家身份，不能忽略西方在社会契约原则下的所谓理性道德观，而库切在寻找自身话语位置时对权威和理性的质疑、对前殖民者话语霸权的解构、对被殖民他者边缘地位的探讨、对他者沉默的思考，无疑应该是诠释其文学作品、探索其创作思想的有益导引。

美国当代南非文学研究专家科勒伦教授对库切的评价十分贴切，认为其小说"代表了现代文学的一个独特时刻，在那里后现代和后殖民因素在特定领域和地点相会……"(Colleran 578)。在后现代、后殖民语境下，库切的笔触十分自然地涉及经历独特的南非人（包括黑人和白人）的命运，尤其是被前殖民者他者化了的南非人的命运。

---

① 后现代主义研究：Hutcheon，Linda. *A Poetics of Post-modernism*：*History*，*Theory*，*Fiction*. London：Routledge，1988；Colleran，Jeanne. Position Papers：Reading J. M. Coetzee's Fiction and Criticism. *Contemporary Literature* 35. 3(1994)：578 – 592；后殖民主义研究：Durrant，Sam. Postcolonial Narrative and the Work of Mourning：J. M. Coetzee，Wilson Harris，and Toni Morrison. *Modern Fiction Studies* 51. 3(2005)：714 – 717；Spivak，Gayatri Chakravorty. Theory in the Margin：Coetzee's *Foe* Reading Defoe's *Crusoe /Roxana*. *The Consequences of Theory*，eds. Jonathan Arac and Barbara Johnson，Baltimore：The Johns Hopkins UP，1991；Jolly，Rosemary Jane. *Colonization*，*Violence*，*and Narration in White South African Writing*：*Andre Brink*，*Breyten Breytenbach*，*and J. M. Coetzee*. Athens：Ohio UP，1996；Diala，Isidore. Nadine Gordimer，J. M. Coetzee，and Andre Brink：Guilt，Expiation，and the Reconciliation Process in Post-Apartheid South Africa. *Journal of Modern Literature* 25. 2 (2001)：50 – 68；历史研究：Meskell，Lynn & Lindsay Weiss. Coetzee on South Africa's Past：Remembering in the Time of Forgetting. *Anthropologist* 108. 1 (2006)：88 – 99；Easton，Kai. Coetzee，the Cape and the Question of History. *Scrutiny* 11. 1 (2006)：5 – 21；对比研究：Hayes，Patrick. An Author I Have Not Read：Coetzee's *Foe*，Dostoevsky's *Crime and Punishment*，and the Problem of the Novel. *Review of English Studies* 230. 57 (2006)：273 – 290；Martin，Richard G. Narrative，History，Ideology：A Study of *Waiting for the Barbarians* and *Burger's Daughter*. *Ariel*：*A Review of International English Literature* 17. 3 (1986)：3 – 21；Hewson，Kelly. Making the Revolutionary Gesture：Nadine Gordimer，J. M. Coetzee and Some Variations on the Writer's Responsibility. *Ariel*：*A Review of International English Literature* 19. 4(1988)：55 – 72；语境研究：Barnett，Clive. Construction of Apartheid in the International Reception of the Novels of J. M. Coetzee. *Journal of Southern African Studies* 25.2 (1999)：287 – 30；Barnard，Rita. Coetzee's Country Ways. *Interventions* 4. 3 (2002)：386 – 394 and Dream Topographies：J. M. Coetzee and the South African Pastoral. *South Atlantic Quarterly* 93. 1(1994)：33 – 58；心理分析：Poyner，Jane. *J. M. Coetzee and the Idea of the Public Intellectual*. Athens，Ohio：Ohio University Press. 2006；Hayes，Grahame. Psychoanalysis in the Shadow of Post-Apartheid Reconstruction. *Theory & Psychology* 18. 2(2008)：209 – 222；叙事研究：MacLeod，Lewis. "Do We of Necessity Become Puppets in a Story?" or Narrating the World：On Speech，Silence and Discourse in J. M. Coetzee's *Foe*. *Modern Fiction Studies* 52. 1 (2006)：1 – 18；Wright，Laura. "Does He Have It in Him to Be the Woman?"：The Performance of Displacement in J. M. Coetzee's *Disgrace*. *Ariel* 37. 4 (2006)：83 – 102.

他在《动物的生命》(*The Lives of Animals*)中借用伊丽莎白·科斯特洛的口说,"古时候,人类声音因理性而提升,但会遭遇狮子的咆哮、公牛的吼叫。人类与狮子、公牛开战,经过许多年代之后,赢得确定性的胜利。如今,这些动物失去力量,剩下沉默,只能用沉默与我们对抗"(Coetzee 25)。这里,他用典型的库切式寓言说明了一种世间常态,一种主导霸权话语形成的规律,一种将一类生物他者化的过程以及他者化后的结果,这不仅适用于人类与动物间的关系描述,而且更加适用于人类之间话语现状的呈现。在南非大地上,欧洲人自17世纪以来长期统治着原住民,他们利用手中的强势力量反客为主地掌握了权威话语,使有色人种原住民从土地的主人进入地位卑微的无话语沉默状态。而在南非共和国成立的1961年后,白人当局由于在国内推行臭名昭著的种族隔离政策,大行种族歧视,更加恶化了被他者化了的有色人种的生存环境,进一步降低了他们的权力话语地位。库切在小说中以艺术手法再现了这些话语权缺失的他者们的生存状态、心理状态,包括对主流话语拥有者敢怒不敢言的现状。

在诺贝尔文学奖授奖词中,库切的小说《等待野蛮人》(*Waiting for the Barbarians*)被认为是"一部承继约瑟夫·康拉德的政治恐怖小说(political thriller in the tradition of Joseph Conrad)"(Engdahl 2)。众所周知,康拉德式小说中,白人叙述者往往将有色人种形象基本定位为原始落后、懒惰放纵、道德责任感匮乏的"他者"。人们在谈到他者时,话语中总是充满着疑惑、猜忌和敌意,而这个想象中的他者只是抽象的概念,而非具象的实体,他没有自我辩解的机会,而只是沉默的形象,一如《黑暗的心》(*Heart of Darkness*)中白人叙述者马洛口中那些在黑母鸡事件中被迫杀死丹麦人弗雷斯莱温的非洲原住民、深入内陆船上饥饿难忍以河马腐尸果腹的水手、科兹"电闪雷鸣"淫威下默默无语的黑人。库切继承了康拉德小说创作的架构、寓言式手法,同时还以生动形象的人物为载体,为后殖民时代依然处于边缘地位的他者代言,并且以缜密的手法、隐喻化语言,论证了他者的他者化过程。

库切笔下的他者,并非指拉康镜像理论中指向自我的他人(l'autre),而是指主体间话语理论中的他者(L'Autre),即那个异己的、陌生的、危险的"在者"和权力话语上的"不在场者"。这里不仅指通常意义上的被殖民者异族部落有色人种,如帝国少壮派军人乔尔上校眼中的"蛮族"人,指在充满战争、军队、种族隔离的社会中像迈克尔·K一样的沉默无语、苦苦挣扎的卑微残缺生命,指在自然界任人宰割、受人虐待、毫无意义地牺牲的动物,也指在后现代语境中不再享有特权、丧失主导话语的白人。库切通过再现他者化的他者，为他者代言，检视殖民主义已经消退的南非后种族隔离时期的社会环境和后殖民文化冲突，特别是在白人特权消失后的社会里，人性的扭曲和道德伦理的严重错位。

由此看来，库切再现的他者层次丰富、意义多元。库切带着"审慎怀疑者"的目光，循着主流话语叙述者的惯常定义，去展示后种族隔离时期权威话语者指涉的他者以及他者的待遇，在其冷峻叙述中，读者体验到其中寓意蕴涵。《等待野蛮人》中的叙事者"我"——长期远离帝国中心、生活在边界地区并谙熟当地习俗的年老的行政长官，通过不动声色地讲述自己的经历，读者清楚地看到权力话语者心目中预设的他者和他者化的他者形成的过程。小说伊始，赫然出现的是帝国权力话语的代表——来自国防部三局、戴着两片圆圆的暗色玻璃、甚至在屋内也不肯摘下的乔尔上校，一副典型的"戴有色眼镜者"形象。库切让此人以此形象出场，不仅说明代表着帝国话语权的上校高深莫测，而且表明帝国话语存在着明显的预设立场。作为帝国军人，他必须站在西方契约原则指导下的所谓"权利本位"立场。为了维护帝国的权力本位、声张所谓理性正义，上校崇尚程式化"执法"，即采取"强制手段……施压，崩溃，再施压，然后才是真话"(5)。他的理念落实到个案上，就是在路上拦住根据预设标准有问题的一对爷孙，经过那一套程序后，老人便"经抢救无效死亡"。帝国官方的记录表明："据说"囚犯情绪失控，意欲"攻击来调查的长官"(6)。库切并没有展示刑讯室内的酷刑和真实的拷打场景，也没有为当时并不在场者的叙事者展开想象的翅膀，而是为他设计了恍若漫不经心的对话，代替那个已经永远沉默的他者给出了客观真相。叙事者轻描淡写地问那位向他汇报情况的卫兵："是那个长官要你这样对我说的吧?""那个囚犯的手[当时]是被绑着的吗?"(6)这样，库切以意味深长的能指向权威话语权拥有者鼓吹的"真相"和"正当性"提出了质疑：一个双手被缚的战战兢兢的老者是如何攻击威风凛凛的壮汉长官的呢？在强调维护帝国权利本位时，有没有必要维护人的权利本位？而紧接其后的情景客观呈现，则更进一步证实了库切质疑的合理性：老人"灰色胡须上沾满了血。压破的嘴唇瘪了进来，牙齿都碎了。一只眼睛凹在里面，另一只眼睛成了一个血洞"(7)。作者并非刻意渲染血腥，而是在颠覆帝国权威话语者赤裸裸的谎言，是对以此残酷手段达到所谓理性正义所做的无声抗议。

库切对南非的历史和当下的情境有着深刻的认识，在《双重视角：散文和访谈集》(*Doubling the Point*：*Essays and Interviews*)中，他旗帜鲜明地说，"几个世纪以来，南非是一个主奴社会,现在它是一个受压迫者公开反叛、主人处于混乱中的大地”。他尖锐地指出,“在主奴社会里,没有人自由。奴隶不自由,因为他不是自己的主人;主人不自由,因为没有奴隶他不能做主人”(Coetzee 96)。库切清楚地意识到,欧洲殖民与南非独立后的种族隔离制度给人民带来的伤害有多么深重,主奴意识已经深深地植入了这块土地。权威话语者为了维护其主子的地位、理性道德秩序,需要有顺民来屈从。一旦受压迫者意识到自己的受压迫地位并且开始反抗,主人的镇压是毫不留情的,否则他们做不成主人。

如果说《等待野蛮人》中这些经夹在权威话语者与话语权缺失者之间的过渡阐释者叙述的他者是一种预设的他者的话,那么,首次获得英国布克奖的《迈克尔·K的生活与时代》(*Life & Times of Michel K*)中采用全知全能加第一人称(医生)双重叙事方式展示的主人公迈克尔·K就是在南非种族隔离政策逐渐成形继而猖獗的年代丧失主体性、沦为物质性的客体存在的他者典型。后者因自身缺陷(豁嘴且智力不如别人)自出生那天起就注定被人当作异类,他纯朴善良却沉默寡语,寓言般地代表了南非隔离制度下的他者形象,他的生活与时代是南非独立后实行的罪恶制度下他者生存现状的真实写照。大城市开普敦的生活充满着暴力、枪击、抢劫、警报声、宵禁……迈克尔虽然与母亲安娜像老鼠一样蜷缩在寒气逼人的楼梯底下的小屋里,但常常被隔街的喧嚣声、尖叫声、射击声和打破玻璃的声音惊得无法入眠。他们处于社会的底层,没有任何言说的自由,甚至连其存在都不为人所见。不过,他们作为即便是物质性的客体存在,也需要有基本的存在条件。为了这基本的生存条件,迈克尔开始了梦魇般的历程。他颠沛流离,归乡途中丧母;遭受政府军抢劫,全部家当尽失;被警察逮住,旋即被派义务苦工;寄身荒芜农场,却遭逃兵排斥;露宿街头,被抓进难民营;逃入山中,差点没饿死;重返农场,却被当作奸细抓进监狱;越狱逃跑,遇到一群流浪者;他渴望过上有人格尊严的生活,哪怕生活原始落后也在所不惜。

库切在诺贝尔文学奖授奖大会上曾以“他和他的人”为题发表演讲,以寓言体书写探讨了作家和生活、作家与想象的关系。他在《迈克尔·K的生活与时代》中,以追求普遍的人道主义为旨归,展示了迈克尔·K的遭遇及其近乎卑微的要求——过上有人格尊严的生活,大力为受压迫者受蹂躏者言说,让种族隔离制度下不可见的他者重见天日。虽然库切的白人移民者身份使他意识到,他只能根据“他的人”的信息和“他”的想象来还原非洲原住民的苦难,但是他依然采用近乎白描的方式,震撼人心地展示了南非种族隔离制度下的普通人生存状态，展示了他对这种普遍存在的问题所作出的严肃思考。迈克尔・K的经历是当时当地那个罪恶制度下卑微他者的典型遭遇，而他在强权面前表现出的沉默已成惯性，但也发人深省，因为沉默并非总是一般意义上的顺从和默认，它还昭示着冷漠、拒绝和抵抗，"沉默也可以是巨大威胁"(Herman 99)。它可以是一种拒斥之力，默默表达他者拒绝屈服于权力话语体系的态度。

库切在作品中展现后殖民时代话语缺失的他者采用的方式是多层次的，既讨论被边缘化了的人，也将触角伸入被人视作他者的动物。他在《动物的生命》中，就曾谈到动物们在生时和死时所面临的种种恐怖情形，但几乎与此同时他又将杀戮动物与第三帝国集中营的屠杀进行了类比，其用意应该不证自明。在讨论生命的意义时，库切引用阿尔贝・加缪童年记忆后提出，"如果有人说生命之于动物不如之于我们人类那样重要，那么，他肯定不曾看见动物在自己的手中挣扎求生的情景"(Coetzee 65)。库切考察了后隔离制度时代的动物生存状态，并在其作品中展示动物的他者地位。在《等待野蛮人》里开篇，他通过乔尔上校引以为豪的狩猎成果来揭示处于弱势地位的动物在人类毫无节制的贪婪下所经受的磨难："成百上千的鹿、猪和熊被杀死，漫山遍野都是动物尸体，多得没法收拾，只好让它们去烂掉。"(1)在《耻》中，库切将目光投入救治狗、山羊、鱼鹰等的动物福利会，用较大篇幅呈现了人类对动物的残酷行径，后又以卢里善待动物、为待宰的小羊喂食、为濒死的猫儿、狗儿安排有尊严的死亡等事例从反面衬托动物他者的地位；而在《迈克尔・K的生活与时代》里，库切为展示迈克尔・K在这个强调理性的现代社会里的他者地位，常将其比作原生状态的动物，让他咀嚼植物的根、吞食昆虫来维持生命，并通过K说出"生活在这样的时代里，一个人必须准备像畜生一样地活着"(135)，以此来揭露种族隔离制度时代的可恶。在《动物的生命》中，库切分析了食用动物、圈养动物、宠物的生存现状，通过科斯特洛的口告诉读者，"在监禁中，生存的完整性无法实现"(33)。自然界的动物受到人类凶残的猎杀，为屠杀目的而养殖的动物受到了人类虐待，这都是人类自恃高于动物的表征。库切渴望人与自然建立良性和谐的关系，而这种关系建立的基础应该是平等自由的相互关系，是脱离了库切所说的那种主奴范式的新型关系。然而，这种建立平等的相互关系的努力最终都以失败而告终，库切明白，主奴关系的打破并非一日之功，主导话语者与话语缺失的他者从根本上来说是无法建立起真正自由平等的关系的。

库切的作品是精致的，给南非文学带来了清新空气。正如托尼・莫费特在谈论其早期作品《幽暗之地》(*Dusklands*)时所说的那样,库切的小说标志着“一种新的叙述形式、一种新的想像方式,一种新的行文方法已经进入了南非文学”(Morphet 14)。他对世界文学的贡献不仅在于他在作品中通过凸显他者的现状来引起人们的关注,从而设法消解殖民主义和种族隔离制度的神话合法性,他还悉心设计了“那个时代、那个地方”是如何将预设的他者他者化的过程。

《等待野蛮人》中主导话语的帝国卫士们眼中的野蛮人,其实就是游牧部落的人。库切认为文明人对“野蛮人”的蔑视“是植根于子虚乌有的基础上的”。其实,权力话语者与“野蛮人”之间的差异只不过在于“餐桌上的规矩不同、眼皮长得不一样什么的”(51)。现代文明给这“蛮荒大地”带去了什么呢?库切旗帜鲜明地指出,文明的侵蚀使“湖水正在逐年变咸”(51)。“文明”的远征军为了讨伐野蛮人而大肆焚烧灌木,“他们才不在乎一旦土地如此收拾,风就会剥蚀土壤,沙漠就会向前推进”(82)。他们“打劫那些手无寸铁的牧羊人,强奸他们的女人,掠夺他们的家财,把他们的牲畜撵得四下逃散”(90)。他们在对付被设定的“野蛮人”时,“把叉子放到煤火上烤灼,然后用它烫你、烙你”(41)。库切在展示主导话语者张扬的兽性、残忍与贪婪的同时,诠释了作为非洲大地的主人是如何被一步步逼上失却话语权的他者境地的。库切还利用老行政长官的亲身经历及其尖锐的评论,来进一步阐释他者化过程。后者因同情话语权缺失的他者而被上校关进了牢房,受尽了折磨,亲身体会到那“是文明的黑暗之花开放的时候了”(79)。监禁的生活使他“日渐一日地变成一头野兽或是一架简单的机器”(84)。

有人认为,“库切的文学本质上是一种个人的文学……如果说库切的文学创作中有对种族隔离或种族歧视的批判的话,那也是出于对自由主义的个人主义和人道主义的捍卫”(王旭峰 108)。此种说法倒与托尼·莫费特有关库切等南非小说家和自由人文主义传统联系密切的观点有些雷同(Morphet 53 - 59)。然而,我们在考察了库切作品后发现,情况并不完全如此。从 1974 年发表的第一部作品《幽暗之地》到 2007 年的《凶年纪事》(*Diary of a Bad Year*),库切无时无刻不在关注着这个特殊的时代在南非这块特殊的土地上发生的故事,关注着那里的人民对自由平等的渴望。他通过在文本中展示帝国权力系统的运行过程揭示叙述背后的霸权话语,凸显他者的生存状态,从而来解构和颠覆强势话语的权威。这恐怕很难用“个人的文学”来解释。

库切清楚地知道,“南非文学是奴役中的文学……充满了无家可归的感情和一种无名的自由的渴望”(qtd. 王家湘 189)。这种感情和渴望确实与时代相关,与地域相关。他的文学具备较大的阐释空间,因为,作为世界知名的作家,库切不仅拥有广博的文学、历史知识,而且还具备全球性视野。他所关注的不仅是如多维博士说的"他到底是站在压迫者一边还是被压迫者一边"的问题(Dovey 18),而是人类甚至是生物如何清除障碍、消除异质文化冲突、排除种族和物种歧视等去实现自由平等、和谐相处的问题。

在后期小说《耻》中,库切转换视角,将目光投到殖民主体不再存续、种族隔离制度已经消亡的时代人们的生存状态。他采取一种思辨性姿态,对白人与有色人种主导话语权地位问题、对白人与有色人种的关系现状问题进行深刻反思,利用崇尚自由的白人的他者化过程来继续拷问当下西方文明中残酷的理性主义和肤浅的道德观。

工于理性计算的白人大学副教授卢里道德感消失、人性扭曲。他按照西方文明的契约原则,为满足自己的私欲,堂而皇之地去找妓女,甚至沾沾自喜,后来竟发展到将人类伦理置于脑后,性侵自己所教女学生。然而,他已不再享受昔日殖民统治和种族隔离时期白人男性的特权,在遭受指控后被迫离开学校。张冲等曾将小说内涵归纳为道德、个人和历史之耻,认为这种种耻辱是"篡越"造成的,所以"耻"是殖民主义付出的代价(张冲 87 - 89)。

我们清楚地知道,库切在《耻》中为我们提供了一幅后种族隔离时代南非社会白人与有色人种之间微妙的关系变化全景图。有关殖民、种族隔离制度对人性的扭曲、道德的沦丧话题可以另文进行深度探讨。在此,我们不妨也反思一下,作品中主人公是怎样从一个主导话语者演变成话语缺失者的,库切通过主人公的他者化过程试图说明什么?而小说中,原话语缺失者是如何从被动沉默地位发展到开始拒斥、反抗、甚至报复的?英语、西班牙语、意大利语等作为强势话语权的载体在突发事件面前处于怎样的毫无用处的尴尬地位?

库切展示了主人公卢里怎样利用强势话语者地位(白人、传播学副教授、阅历丰富)"越界"性侵无话语地位的弱者(有色人种、青年学生、阅历简单)的图景。这种在崇尚自由的幌子下进行的罪恶,并不能让深受西方文明浸染的卢里产生任何道德负疚感,随后发生的种种陋行皆偏离了道德规范,然而,为什么他会这样做而且死不悔改,甚至认为"好色可敬,好色和感伤一样可敬"(66),这就值得大家冷静思索。我们认为,这是因为根深蒂固的殖民主义意识残存、白人蔑视有色人种社会道德标准、自恃白人种族优越而产生的情感体验和行为,也是库切对西方肤浅的自由观念、道德伦理观的冷峻嘲讽。然而，在殖民主义、隔离制度等已经消亡的当下，库切没有让卢里因其特殊的身份而免于惩罚，而是让他在主流话语中失去了声音，被迫自我流放到乡村。这是时代发展的必然，因篇幅原因不在此赘述。而弱势话语者的变化也是特定时代的产物：从索拉娅、梅拉尼等原先受契约原则下的"理性"支配而沉默被动地承受难忍之事，到她们公开拒斥、反抗她们无法忍受的一切；从卢里怀着白人的优越感、大学教授的高傲，对卑贱者的蔑视与乡下人相处，到遭受抢劫后脱胎换骨的变化——为先前自己不齿者当下手，开始同情弱势动物等。曾几何时，耀武扬威的殖民者便失去了过去的辉煌：说英语带着明显德国口音的白人老头爱丁杰得随身佩枪，住所防护设施周密，但依然无法确保性命无虞；卢里的女儿露西遭到黑人轮奸，而且被施暴者所表现出的仇恨所吓倒，为保障人身安全，她忍辱沦为原帮工佩特鲁斯的情妇，完全丧失自尊；欧洲殖民者的强势话语载体——西方文明语言竟然"像头陷在泥潭里垂死的恐龙，变得僵硬起来"(117)，倒是索托语、科萨语等当地语言活力四射，恰如其分地表达着当时当地人民的真情实感。库切通过这一系列的倒置安排，使原先白人眼中的他者在自己的土地上恢复了应有的话语地位，而原先的白人话语权拥有者在当时当地的他者化衬托了后殖民、后种族隔离时期的乾坤颠倒状态。

库切对南非大地怀有深深的情感，对这块土地上的人民，尤其是原住民的生存状态、话语权现状表示出深切的关注。他在作品中表现他者际遇时，在展现他者化过程时，在白描其后果时，无不表示出自己对殖民主义、种族隔离制度的愤怒谴责，表示出自己对自由、对平等的渴望。他对西方文明以契约原则为基础的所谓理性道德、理性正义采取了批判态度，主张追求高尚情操和道德境界，保持人格的尊严和价值，倡导种族之间、物种之间保持和谐关系，表达了对美好共生的自然环境的向往。

参考文献：

Coetzee, J. M. *Doubling the Point*: *Essays and Interviews*. ed. David Attwell. Cambridge, MA: Harvard University Press, 1992.

——. *Disgrace*. London: Vintage, 2000.

——. He and His Man. Nobel Lecture. Swedish Academy, Stockholm. Sweden. 7 Dec. 2003. <http://novelprize.org/novel-prizes/literature/laureates/2003/coetzee-lecture-e.html>.

——. *The Lives of Animals*. Princeton, New Jersey: Princeton University Press, 1999.

——. *Life & Times of Michel K*. London: Secker & Warburg, 1983.

——. *Waiting for the Barbarians*. Harmondsworth, Middlesex, England, New York: Penguin Books, 1982.

Colleran, Jeanne. Position Papers: Reading J. M. Coetzee's Fiction and Criticism. *Contemporary Literature* 35.3 (1994): 578 - 592.

Dovey, Teresa. J. M. Coetzee: Writing in the Middle Voice. ed. Sue Kossew, *Critical Essays on J. M. Coetzee*. New York: G. K. Hall, 1993. 18 - 29.

Engdahl, Horace Oscar Axel. Press Release. 2 October 2003. Accessed 17 September, 2010. <http://nobelprize.org/nobel_prizes/literature/laureates/2003/press.html>

Herman, Vimala. *Dramatic Discourse: Dialogue as Interaction in Plays*. London: Routledge, 1995.

Morphet, Tony. Reading Coetzee in South Africa. *World Literature Today* 78.1 (2004): 14 - 16.

——. Stranger Fictions: Trajectories in the Liberal Novel. *World Literature Today* 70.1(1996): 53 - 59.

段枫. 库切研究的走向及展望. 外国文学评论，2007，4：139 - 145.

王家湘.《青春》译后记//库切. 青春. 王家湘，译. 杭州：浙江文艺出版社，2004.

王丽丽. 一曲殖民主义的哀歌——评1999年布克奖获奖小说《耻辱》. 当代外国文学，2000，3：162 - 165.

王旭峰. 库切与自由主义. 外国文学评论，2009，2：105 - 115.

张冲，郭整风. 越界的代价——解读库切的布克奖小说《耻》. 外国文学，2001，5：86 - 89.

邹海仑.《迈克尔·K的生活和时代》译后记//库切. 迈克尔·K的生活和时代. 邹海仑，译. 杭州：浙江文艺出版社，2004.

（原载《英美文学研究论丛》2012年总15期）

《凶年纪事》：独特的后现代复调小说

摘要：诺贝尔文学奖获奖小说家J. M. 库切在移居澳大利亚后发表的重要小说《凶年纪事》，以在书页中加平行线构成两栏继而在刻意空页后加双平行线建构三栏的独特手法，强烈地冲击着读者的视觉。作者以政论和随感来表现具有独立价值的意识、以平等对话关系来表现各意识主体之间的关系，在表面奇特的形态掩盖下，展示出众多独立意识主体以不同方式发出的不同声音，为小说提供了新样式，同时增强了小说的厚重感。

关键词：库切；《凶年纪事》；后现代；复调

中图分类号：1106.4　**文献标示码**：A　**文章编号**：1005－7247(2012)04－0093－04

1. 小说样式：三栏共鸣

巴赫金在评论俄国文学的卓越代表陀思妥耶夫斯基(F. M. Dostoyevsky)时指出，"面对这个新的世界，这个由众多各自平等主体、而非客体形成的世界，无论叙述、描绘或说明，都应采取一种新的角度"(Bakhtin 2003：7－8)。2002年移居澳大利亚的库切在《伊丽莎白·科斯特洛：八堂课》(2003)之后推出的《凶年纪事》(Coetzee 2007)是一次别出机杼的尝试，因为他又一次采取全新视角，实验崭新模式，再次成功地颠覆了读者头脑中固有的小说概念。该小说开天辟地地采用在书页中加平行线构成两栏继而在刻意空页后加双平行线建构三栏的手法，首先以强烈的视觉冲击造成琴瑟钟鼓齐奏共鸣局面。全书以31段饱含争议的政论加24段隐喻极强的随感为上栏，以垂暮之年移居澳大利亚的南非著名作家C先生视角讲述见闻感受为中栏，以少妇安雅随意使用俗字俚语讲述的故事外加其同居男友艾伦刻意贬斥、任意反驳C先生的文字为下栏，在众声喧哗中平行推进，以各自为政而又藕断丝连的话语方式发展着小说。这种做法显然"打破了一般小说成法所要求的材料的有机统一……把不同性质、互不相容的因素结合在一部小说的整体结构中……打破了传统而完整的叙述格调"(Bakhtin 2003：40)。有人认为，"《凶年纪事》是库切在小说样式上在文学创作上进行的最彻底的重组"(Ogden 2010：466)。

这种三栏式小说的政论/随感、见闻感受与讲述评论等不同性质、互不相容的因素不可思议地同时出现在一页纸的不同栏目里，自然打破了传统独白式小说的成法，如整体推进式阅读则有关联性不强的印象，如分栏阅读则给读者各栏特立独行的感受。然而，它们之间其实并非截然分开毫无瓜葛，这就给读者带来阅读麻烦的同时带来了无比奇妙的新奇感受。无论是横向还是纵向阅读，不管共时还是历时品味，文本都表现为若即若离、藕断丝连：上栏政论/随感表面上自成一体，但实际上是中栏C先生内心感受和下栏安雅述说和艾伦评论的依据；中栏虽然文字相对较少却在独白式或自问自答式的文字中展现了上栏文字作者C先生的意识流动，帮助读者了解上栏文字作者书写时的思想动态；而下栏的述说与评论，既有对上栏文字的感悟、对上栏文字作者的评说，也有不同意识的主体所表达的思想。这里有帮助说明上栏文字的内容，如政论缘起、文类定性之类，也有安雅对上栏作者的"有点凭主观想象，有点不切实际"(Coetzee 2007：73，下文中本书引文只注页码)之类评价性文字、安雅与艾伦对上栏作者本人及其政论的讨论。下栏文字拓展补充了上两栏文字，使得三栏文字在众声喧哗中得以贯通。这种陌生化手法所达到的间离化效果使小说特异他性显现无遗。

2. 独立的意识主体

除去视觉效果的三栏他性特征之外，读者接触到文本实质后就会发现，库切在小说中没有把主人公看成是被描绘的客体，或者说没有把主人公当作与自然界或周围环境同处一个层面的客体，而是把主人公看作"活生生的"主体，赋予主人公以相对独立的意识，给予他自由的声音和独立的个性。有学者认为，"如果说主人公的思想独立于那个被我们称之为'陀思妥耶夫斯基'或者'狄更斯'的、表达着诸多声音的思想着的个体，在逻辑上不免荒谬"(黄梅 1989：11)。虽然这种评论从本质上来说是正确的，主人公的思想无法独立于创造该主人公的思想，不过，这并不妨碍我们沿着巴赫金的复调小说思路去讨论库切小说在呈现主人公意识时所表现出的特异之处。《凶年纪事》的主人公C先生形象和定位与传统小说主人公不同之处在于，作者扩大了他的视野和自我意识范围，不再如独白式小说那样在其背后论定与评判，这就使他成为自主表现自我意识的主体。从C先生定位来看，他是上栏政论的撰写者与随感的记录者，是与安雅交集的感受者，也是安雅与艾伦评论的对象，因而具有较为充分的主体意识和完全的独立人格。虽然对小说人物C先生的定位确实出于作者的构思，但是，作者始终没有对C先生进行"独白"式的论断，C先生在文本的不同对话关系中一直保持相对独立的自主性，他深受自己的思索所折磨、为自己的情感而纠结，这种独立性是不受库切意识支配的表现，并且恰恰符合逻辑的意识呈现，安雅与艾伦这对同居恋人实际上也具有完全的主体意识，他们对C先生的议论与评价符合自身的身份和关系特征，而且没有证据证明这些评论是作者的意思，因而可以说，小说中三个主要人物在价值判断上保持了相对的独立性。

上栏前半部的政论，根据C先生向安雅所做的解释，是一位德国出版商策划的名为《危言》之书的约稿，因为"该计划由6个来自不同国家的撰稿人任选话题发表言论，争议越大越好"(21)。这应该是作家库切为主人公搭建的一个平台，或者说为主人公设计的撰写政论、发表言论的缘起(尽管一般复调小说不提供缘起，只提供相互作用的空间)，当然，他还通过C先生与安雅的对话关系为主人公涉足政论设计了框架与前提，即当下这个世界出了问题，需要有识之士不避风险、无所顾忌地提出问题、直抒胸臆，引发广泛讨论，引起充分重视，这样才能拯救这个世界。这个前提应该是当今世界的共识，并不涉及作者的任何倾向性、评价性设计，也没有纵向的思考和排列。在这种前提与框架中，主人公的哲学思索、意识流动过程并未受到作者"统一意识"的控制，而且其思索结果也没有得到作者的评价。作者只是把各种矛盾对立的思想意识集中于同一平面上来展示，这就确保了C先生在与作者、与安雅的对话关系中保持主体意识，并自由地表达有独立价值的意识，这或许符合巴赫金心目中的共时性艺术特征。

用政论和随感来表现有独立价值的意识，如同《伊丽莎白·科斯特洛：八堂课》中的同名主人公采用讲座表达观念一样，应该说是库切的拿手好戏。对于国际社会生活中的热点话题——从国家起源到无政府主义，从民主到马基雅维利，从恐怖主义到制导系统、基地组织，从关塔那摩到国家的耻辱，C先生都发表了议论。这些政论观点犀利，未必代表着作家库切的意见，没有证据证明C先生是作者的传声筒。不过，这些政论明显充满着未定论，充斥着对现存观念的质疑，表现出巴赫金所坚持的未完成性。

以国家话题为例，主人公C先生引用日本导演黑泽明的电影《七武士》透视的国家起源理论，引申出有关“扩张的民主”。他以美国在中东的实践为例，对“扩张的民主”进行了阐释，指出这意味着“拓展民主的治理”。这种拓展民主实质上就是将美国式的民主不由分说地强加给中东地区，让人们“自由地在甲或者乙之间进行选择”(9)，说穿了就是强权政治的集中体现，其结果必然是，“为争取有关政治的超政治系统话语是徒劳无益的”(9)。C先生在“论恐怖主义”中揭示了这种扩张的民主在当代国际社会中的存在现状：“不仅原来赤裸裸的不加掩饰的对自由言论的限制死灰复燃——美国、英国已完成立法，现在是澳大利亚——而且还加上在全球范围对电话和电子媒介的监控(通过特务机构)。”(22)这并非人物的臆想，而是客观存在。C先生清楚地知道自由言论的虚伪性，他在“论民主”中不无讽刺地说，“在每一个人都声称自己打心眼里就是具有民主精神的人的时代里，对民主提出异议，你就有与现实疏离的危险”(15)。他对屡屡打着民主大旗进行权力变更的做法更是不屑一顾。于是，他极尽冷嘲热讽之能事，认为只要不使国家陷入内战，权力继承方式如何运作关系不大。作为一个经历丰富的老作家，他竟有点愤世嫉俗地提出“长子继承、民主选举与抛掷硬币决定”孰优孰劣的问题，不能不说是对西方国家热衷民主选举的一种公开大不敬。不过，研究发现，这些言辞激烈的政论中抱怨成分多于定论。而且，人们无法简单地断定这些是库切本人的思想，无法断定主人公C先生是作者思想观念的直接表现者。因为，无论是在中栏显示的C先生与自我的对话关系，还是下栏安雅与C先生的对话关系、安雅与艾伦的对话关系中，都找不到作者甚至隐含作者的影子。库切不再如在《伊丽莎白·科斯特洛：八堂课》里那样直接跳出来发表看法、评价主人公，他竭尽全力展示的只是不同视角的意识，而且即便不是主要人物，无论是安雅还是艾伦，都具有独立的意识和自主的声音。作者在这里只是要展示一种独立的思想意识，至于这种意识正确与否，作者任由人物之间对话评价。C先生在陈述自己的思路、推出自己的政论和感想时，充分显示出他的自我思考、固执的自尊和不屈的反抗意识，他“对自己、对世界的议论，同一般的作者议论，具有同样的分量与价值”(Bakhtin 2003：7)。他在这里恰似现实生活中的真人那样，无所顾忌、不无尖刻地评价这个世界，又在坦诚地进行着自我剖析。他对客观世界做出的反应自然而真切，对自己和周围的环境的认知清醒而准确，对世间的人和事有着不受别人干扰的看法。这充分证明,“主人公在思想观点上自成权威,卓然独立,他被看作是有着自己充实而独到的思想观点的作者……已然不再是作者言论所表现的客体,而是具有自己言论的充实完整、当之无愧的主体”(ibid.:5)。库切在评论菲利普·罗斯的小说《与美国相悖的情节》的文章《菲利普知道什么》中曾这样说过,“小说家知道,我们写的故事有时开始书写自身,其后,故事的真伪脱离了我们的掌控,作者的意图之说已失去意义”(Coetzee 2004:4)。他的坦诚或许是主人公独立意识的最好证明。

3. 对话关系

平等对话关系是库切《凶年纪事》的另一大他性特色。作品中主人公与自己、主人公与人物、人物之间进行着积极平等的对话。在对话中,众多意识得以并存互动,在不同的声音和意识之中,作品的巧妙构思、混成音响等交响乐效果得以显现。平等对话关系在《凶年纪事》中大致可以被认定为两大层次:一是作者设计的小说内部结构之间的对话关系,大概可以归结为巴赫金提出的“大型对话”关系;二是小说人物自身内心的对话(包括C先生内心矛盾的冲突和把他人意识作为内心一个对立的话语进行对话)以及人物之间的对话关系,相当于巴赫金所说的“双声语对话”或“微型对话”关系。

根据巴赫金的理论,“复调小说整个渗透着对话性。小说结构的所有成分之间,都存在着对话关系”(Bakhtin 2003:55)。库切设计的三栏式小说,如上文所述,在形式上具备非同凡响的效果,充分显示出作者独特的创新意识,不过,这三栏之间实际上存在的对话关系倒为巴赫金的复调理论提供了富有说服力的证据。从安排上来看,作者在前23页只设计了上下两栏,上栏为主人公撰写的政论,下栏以第一人称单数叙述主人公与安雅邂逅后遭遇的“形而上之痛”(7)、再次偶遇“欣喜并痛苦”的经历和感受,在作者醒目地留白一页后,才开始真正的三栏模式。这种设计从逻辑上来说极为合理,因为只有在经历了上下两栏的基本对话、主人公开始了部分政论撰写后,才需要并且有可能开始第三栏的议论与评论。事实上,前23页的结构对话性关系为后面的小说发展做出了铺垫,提供了定位。主人公在第23页为上栏政论与札记做出了定性式说明:这是“一个公开发牢骚的机会,一个对不愿迎合我想象的世界施展魔力报复的机会,我怎么会拒绝”(23)。上中下分栏的这种结构性对话关系既具有高屋建瓴、宏观设计的

"大型对话"特点，又具备回溯性自省式（主要在中下栏）的"微型对话"特点。

库切设计的在复调理论家看来是所谓"双声语对话"的复杂的对话关系，应该是从25页开始。他的特异之处在于，除了上栏的政论/随想以外，中、下栏的对话关系都是以第一人称单数展开的，而这两种第一人称却代表了完全不同的意识主体（中栏为C先生，下栏为安雅）。"它[双声语对话]立刻为两个说话人服务，同时表现两种不同的意向……在这种话语中有两个声音、两个意思、两个情态。"（巴赫金 1989：110）这在两栏文本中往往表现为隐蔽的对话体或带辩论色彩的自由体等，例证俯拾皆是。

> 我看到那上面写道，据丹尼尔·笛福说，地道的英国人讨厌"纸和纸张那类东西"。勃列日涅夫的将军们"呆在小便池那里"。
>
> 我一边听录音一边打字，然后拿去做检查，她这么跟我解释。或许拼写检查有时会出错，但还是比我想象的要好一些。
>
> 拼写检查不需要自己动脑子，我说。如果你打算用拼写检查这活儿来消磨人生，你等于是在玩骰子。
>
> 我们不必扯什么人生。我们说的是打字。我们说的是拼写。（25－28）

这段文字非常典型地展示了库切的隐蔽对话体风格，它可以被认为是主人公C先生在写作之余内心意识的自然流动，他在将自己对安雅的不满与爱怜等心迹袒露于人前时，明显地采用了带有辩论色彩的对话形式，或者说让对话关系隐含在流动着的意识之中。这是主人公看到安雅错误百出的打字稿后的一段文字。他原本通过话筒录音说的是"地道的英国人讨厌辣椒及辣椒之类"、"勃列日涅夫的将军们坐在乌拉尔山上"，可是，被安雅输入打字成文稿后却错成现在这个样子。面对打印稿，主人公没有询问，更没有指责，他或许在思考自己原来说的是什么。至此的一切都可以被认定仅仅是内心意识的流动而已，接下来依然是他的意识，却明显是另一种声音，这是安雅回应他的声音。故而，这里显然出现了两种声音，两种意思。两人之间的话语交集既是"我"的记忆与陈述，也隐含着两人意识的交锋，两种情态的表达。作为雇主和垂垂老者的C先生与年轻貌美的雇员安雅小姐之间的意识流动反映出两者思维方式、行为方式的迥然不同。老者心中对安雅有种说不清道不明的感觉，这在此前洗衣房的邂逅中就有意识流露："我打量着她时，一种痛楚——一种形而上的痛楚爬上我的心头，我无法抵挡……这是冲着她而来的羡慕之情,冲着她的美貌、青春以及短短的连衣裙。”(7) C先生对安雅只是一个过气的老者对年轻美貌姑娘的自然本能反应,虽然没有明确地表现出有所企图,但是,他对后者精神上的依赖与渴望暴露无遗;相反,安雅最初对待这份差事的心态与C先生大相径庭,她或许对这位老作家心存好奇,但并不需要C先生的关爱与人生教诲,明白自己只是对方雇用的打字员而已。两个具有独立意识的主体的对话是通过C先生的意识流淌而表现出来的,库切没有将自己的意志情感和思想观念强加于人物,而是在这里展示了一种平等的对话精神。这种暗暗地在叙事话语中展开对话,使叙事的辩论性、对话性和丰富性大为增强的做法,应该就是巴赫金复调理论中双声语的作用吧。

库切在下栏采用安雅的视角来展示意识的流动,其中当然包括她与艾伦和她与C先生的双声语对话关系。通过安雅时而自主意识流动、时而与不同意识碰撞,读者觉察到了此栏不可或缺的重要性。作者在这里使用的双声语对话存在着双重指向:一重指向话语的内容,一重指向话语主体的态度。下栏双声语对话涉及内容颇为广泛,其中既有对上栏政论的评价,也有对撰写政论的C先生的议论。当然,议论C先生也同时包括议论其观点与为人。库切通过话语主体安雅仿佛呢喃的叙述、她与同居男友艾伦对C先生的频繁议论、对其书稿的尖刻评价以及她与C先生的对话关系,不仅展示了独立意识主体之间的关系,而且还让读者看到一个立体多面的C先生形象:他一方面抓住机遇慷慨激昂地向社会发表着有些过激的言论,发泄着自己心中的愤懑情绪,在有着独特阅历的文人撰写政论过程中表现出严谨的态度与严密的逻辑;另一方面,他与安雅邂逅后生命爱欲开始觉醒,在绅士外表下掩盖了与一个纯物质化的女性交往时的微妙心理和隐秘心曲。当然,作为意识主体的安雅,在这些或意识流动或隐含对话或意识交集过程中,也充分地展示了自己的心路历程,展示了话语主体从不屑到同情的态度变化。

4. 复调的众声喧哗

《凶年纪事》是独特的,它的独特性不仅体现在破天荒的三栏式小说表象,更在于它那奇特表面形态掩盖下众多独立意识主体以不同方式发出的不同声音。库切为各种意识主体提供了自主表演平台,“主人公的意识在这里被当作另一个人的意识,即他人的意识;可同时它并不对象化,不囿于自身,不变成作者意识的单纯客体"(Bakhtin 2003: 7)。作者不再利用创作便利去干预意识主体的表现,"主人公的议论在这里也不是作者本人的思想立场的表现"(ibid. : 7)。激烈言辞的政论与札记置于上栏,可以解释成库切为避免审查制度可能带来的麻烦而进行的特别设计。不过,这些政论与札记在阐发主人公作为知识分子评论家的意识形态的同时,实际上为中下栏不同的主体意识发展提供了机遇。中下栏代表不同意识主体的第一人称单数,在意识流动中完成叙事,在隐含对话的双声话语中表现出未定论、未完成和开放性等特点,形成独特的复调小说特征,同时也展示了库切的特异他性。正如评论家莫拉尔斯在评论《凶年纪事》时所说,"我们在这本书中发现,J. M. 库切是……一位综合的多面人"(Morales 2009: 43)。库切在《凶年纪事》创作中的特异他性不仅表现在独特的复调形式上,而且表现在众声喧哗的各种意识形态本身,这就在小说提供新样式的同时,增强了小说的厚重感。

参考文献:

[1] Bakhtin, M. M. *Problems of Dostoyevsky's Art* [M]. Minneapolis: the University of Minnesota Press, 2003.

[2] Coetzee, J. M. What Philip knew [N]. *The New York Review of Books* 18 November 2004.

[3] Coetzee, J. M. *Diary of a Bad Year* [M]. London: Harvill Secker, 2007.

[4] Morales, Dolors Collellmir. J. M. Coetzee's *Diary of a Bad Year* [J]. *A Journal of English and American Studies* 40 (2009): 43 - 52.

[5] Ogden, Benjamin H. How J. M. Coetzee's *Diary of a Bad Year* thinks through the novel [J]. *Novel: A Forum on Fiction* 43.3 (2010): 466 - 482.

[6] 巴赫金. 巴赫金全集. 第三卷[M]. 白春仁,等,译. 石家庄:河北教育出版社,1998.

[7] 黄梅. 也谈巴赫金[J]. 外国文学评论,1989 (1): 10 - 25.

(原载《外语研究》2012 年第 4 期)

后种族隔离时代的颠覆他者——对库切《耻》的研究

内容提要：库切在小说《耻》中关注后种族隔离时代黑白之间的关系，采取思辨姿态，展示以卢里为代表的中产阶层白人成为颠覆他者的经历，对白人与有色人种主导话语权地位、关系现状问题，对历史重负与个体责任、理性原则与道德伦理等问题进行反思，利用崇尚自由的白人的他者化过程来继续拷问当下西方文明中残酷的理性主义和肤浅的道德观，并且利用动物作为"人类自身与他人之间和解的基本第三方条件"。

关键词：库切；《耻》；后种族隔离；颠覆他者

Abstract: In the novel *Disgrace*, Coetzee, with concern over the relationship between the black and the white, demonstrates the experiences of the subversion of the middle-class white represented by Lurie, speculates on the issues like dominating discourse power, historical burden and individual responsibility, rational principle and moral ethics, queries the cruel rationalism and cosmic morality of contemporary western civilization by the otherization of the white, and "proposes animals as the essential third term in the reconciliation of human self and human other".

Key Words: Coetzee; *Disgrace*; post-Apartheid; subverted other

导 言

库切的小说《耻》(*Disgrace*, 1999)以近乎白描却令人心怵的笔调，讲述了戴维·

卢里，一位工于理性计算的文学与传播学白人副教授的故事，他在殖民主体不再存续、种族隔离制度已经消亡的时代为自己的行为付出沉重代价、由主导话语者演变成话语缺失的他者。小说发表后，获得英国文学最高奖曼布克奖、英联邦作家奖和美国全国书评家协会奖小说奖提名，被《纽约时报书评》评为年度最佳图书，引起学界高度重视，博埃默认为"它很可能为作者获得 2003 年诺贝尔文学奖铺平了道路"(Boehmer 2006：135)。该小说在出版后"已经产生大量各式各样的批评反应……很可能会继续反应下去"(Cornwell 43)。"最近几十年来很少会有小说能像 J. M. 库切的《耻》产生这么多严肃的争论。"(Attridge 315)

有评论家认为，"J. M. 库切的小说《耻》可以读作政治文本、后种族隔离时代作品，涉及南非白人团体遭遇的困境以及对他们来说可利用的机会"(Sanvan 26)。"J. M. 库切的《耻》描写了一幅后种族隔离时代南非令人担忧的图景。"(Cooper 22) 英联邦作家奖评审委员会主席沙希·德希潘德(Shashi Deshpande)认为《耻》"采用非凡技巧描述了一个新民族的政治"(McDonald 321)。"[它]在遭遇错综复杂的道德问题时坚定不移的诚实，使它成为当下具有伟大意义的作品。"(ibid.：322)伍德认为"《耻》是一种南非版屠格涅夫的《父与子》"，并称其为"一部无可挑剔的小说"(Wood 43)。然而，有人认为库切作品丑化了黑人、丑化了黑人政权下的南非社会，甚至连南非前总统姆贝基(Thabo Mbeki)也对《耻》大为不悦，颇为愤慨地说"南非不仅仅是一个充满强奸的地方"(Pienaar 1)。有研究者附和说，"将一个南非白人女性置于后种族隔离时代暴力受害者地位的做法，引起黑人社团的极大愤慨，"他们觉得，"这种做法破坏了正在进行中的民主和平等的斗争。"(Tran 1)

研究认为，库切在小说《耻》中将关注的目光投向后种族隔离时代黑白之间的关系，采取一种思辨性姿态，展示以卢里为代表的中产阶层白人成为颠覆他者的经历，对白人与有色人种主导话语权地位问题、对白人与有色人种的关系现状问题、对历史重负与个体责任问题、对理性原则与道德伦理问题等进行深刻反思，利用崇尚自由的白人的他者化过程来继续拷问当下西方文明中残酷的理性主义和肤浅的道德观，并且利用动物作为"人类自身与他人之间和解的基本第三方条件"(Boehmer 2002：346)。

一、小说《耻》中颠覆的他者

种族隔离制度废除 5 年后问世的库切小说《耻》"刻画了一幅南非转型震颤时期的

黑暗图景，因为种族隔离时代的遗产不会一夜之间消亡”(Segall 40)。小说通过卢里与露西两条线索揭露了种族隔离制度消亡后南非种族之间所发生的种种问题，用艺术手法讲述了白人少数族裔在失去偏袒性制度规则保护后，权力话语被颠覆、沦落为边缘化他者的故事。库切在小说的第22章结尾安排了主人公卢里与露西间的一场对话，真实地反映了后种族隔离时代白人的遭遇以及他们在新南非必须直面的现实。

> “这多让人丢脸，”他开口说道。“那么高的心气，到头来落到这个地步。”
>
> “不错，我同意。是很丢脸。但这也许是新的起点。也许这就是我该学着接受的东西。从起点开始。从一无所有开始。不是从‘一无所有，但是……’开始，而是真正的一无所有。没有办法，没有武器，没有财产，没有权利，没有尊严。”
>
> “像狗一样。”
>
> “对，像狗一样。”(Coetzee 2009：205)①

这段对话的参与双方是一对经历丰富的白人父女，他们的故事诠释了白人在种族隔离制度消亡的时代优势地位被颠覆，中心地位被取代，从主导话语地位沦为话语缺失的边缘地位的他者化过程。

作为小说的男主人公，卢里最初是受人尊敬的开普敦科技大学语言学教授，“因经典和现代语言学学科停办”(3)而无奈成了传播学副教授。主人公从语言学专业转到传播学专业，因教非所学，教学效果差，讲台没有让他感受到掌控话语权的快乐。库切并未在卢里的教职上花费笔墨，提及职业生涯，意图是导出与其将会发生关系并影响他后半生的人物——选修课班上的学生梅拉尼·艾萨克斯。

这位祖籍荷兰的白人大学教授虽已逾知天命的年龄，但追逐异性热情不减，他与梅拉尼的关系最终引来了一系列麻烦，最终因卢里的固执而导致校方将其解职。虽然他坚持认为，西方人的自由民主应该包括满足个体性欲的自由，而个体本能的满足纯属私人性质，公众不能干涉。然而，他显然忽略了一个问题：西方哲人早就对此作出

① 以下文中未标明出处的引文均出自《耻》(Coetzee，J. M. *Disgrace*. London：Vintage Books，2009)，译文均自译。

论断：“身体的从属于灵魂和灵魂的情欲部分的受制于理性及其理性部分，总是合乎自然而有益的；要是两者平行，或者倒转了相互的关系，就常常是有害的。”（Aristotle 9）人非低等动物，如果仅遵循所谓“快乐原则”（Freud 1），按照本能行事，则在客观上降低了人格的神圣与尊严。而且，卢里面临的一个严峻事实是，他身处的不再是一个白人政权主导下的社会，他意识中或下意识中的那些白人——“我们西方人”（202）——优越的观念已经过时，南非宪法规定，“尊重人的尊严与平等，促进人权与自由”，不容忍对人权和自由践踏和破坏。因此，无可避免的是，大学教授卢里丧失话语权，成为被边缘化的他者，从城市中心逃离，去了位于偏远地带的女儿的农场。

女主人公露西的经历更加典型地表现了白人地位被颠覆、白人被边缘化他者化的过程，而在露西的农场，卢里的边缘化他者地位更进一步呈现出来，文本中更多的证据表现出他的地位在被颠覆后无奈的境况。

波伏娃曾经说过，“女人之所以感到劣等，实际上是因为女性的要求确实贬低了她。她本能地选择了做一个健全的人，一个面向世界和未来的主体和自由人”（波伏娃 467）。库切笔下呈现的露西实际上就是这样一位特立独行的女性，她崇尚独立自主，是一个同性恋者，一个自我支配意识强烈的女人。她6年前离开城市生活，“以公社成员的身份”（60）来到格雷汉姆镇，后与女友海伦留在农场生活。如果这不是机缘巧合，库切的时间安排应该颇具深意。白人女子露西脱离处于中心地位的城市，来到偏僻边缘的乡村这个事实象征意义大于事件本身。而这6年时间正是种族隔离制度废止的6年，作为白人女性，身处绝大多数人口为黑人的区域，客观上处于少数地位，加之偏袒白人的政策已经废除，白人的优势地位已不复存在。曾经来自西欧的围绕主体权利观念而建构的社会结构，在南非大地上已经明显倾向了黑人。二元社会主体之间既紧张、对立又合作、利用的关系，在新时代的南非循着古老的“契约性”原则在冲突、消解、再冲突、再消解的过程推动着社会向前发展。

库切安排卢里来到农场以后，亲身经历黑人抢劫事件和女儿被人轮奸。这两个同时发生的事件由此可以看出：黑白二元对立关系在新南非没有得到缓解——新的民主制度建立在提高了黑人话语地位的同时，颠覆了白人原本拥有的话语地位，而黑人暴力抵抗文化传统并没有得到丝毫改变。库切通过卢里与露西的对话，表现出露西的困惑，“他们为什么那么恨我？我可连见都没见过他们”（156）。然而，意味深长的是，《先驱报》在报道中罗列抢劫财物、枪杀寄养狗等细节，却只字未提露西被轮奸之事。

这不是记者的疏忽或报纸粉饰太平,而是露西在接受采访时刻意掩盖了被黑人轮奸的事实。为此,卢里苦思冥想而不得其解,愤愤不平却无计可施。较为合理的解释是,深深浸透于白人思想意识中的理性原则,已经内化为一种集体无意识,自觉不自觉地以不同的方式表现出来。刚刚失去大学教授位置的卢里本能地表现出来的方式是诉诸法律,通过查清真相来惩罚罪恶,因为他明白这场祸害对同性恋的女儿造成的伤害有多深。然而,对于在黑人主导的环境中生存时间更久的露西来说,面对这突如其来的侮辱,她虽异常痛苦,却不得不在较短时间内做出抉择,决定理智地直视现实,因为她清楚“自己身处他们的领地”。“在他们眼里,我什么都不是,一文不值。”(157)白人在新南非的优势地位已经被颠覆,不承认被边缘化的现状也是于事无补,在黑人新掌握政权、百废待兴的政府里,要求主张白人的权益、惩治黑人是否有可能?在黑白二元冲突一触即发的环境里,黑人警察是否会为了给白人伸张正义而甘冒激怒黑人大众的风险?一切都是未知数。“如何根据南非片断性的过去和暴力复杂的当下来思考和讨论新南非正是库切在小说《耻》中探讨的主题。”(Buikema 2006: 188)库切选取的确实是南非经典性事件,他将小说人物推入矛盾冲突的漩涡之中,考察人物的智慧,在人物面对事件作出的选择中,来揭示南非当下客观存在的矛盾,评说抉择所带来的影响。

露西制止了父亲的复仇冲动,选择过去黑人民族逆来顺受的隐忍方式,以坚忍的毅力、豁达的胸襟,准备接受过去的黑人雇工佩鲁斯的保护,自己可以不计身份(愿意当后者的第三个老婆、甚至情妇)、可以转让土地,可以让被强奸后怀孕尚未出世的孩子成为后者的孩子,唯一的条件是标志着独立自由身份的“这房子还归我所有”(204)。露西的选择是抛弃白人优越想法后明智的选择,是白人在新南非不得不接受的妥协、不得不面对的现实、无法逃脱的命运,甚至可能是黑白最终能够达到真正平等、融合的必要条件。

虽然露西的选择令其父卢里感到愤慨,但是,后者的选择又何尝不同样令人唏嘘呢?在大学的话语权被颠覆、教职被解除后,卢里步步趋向边缘,从开普敦到农场、从教授到雇工的帮手、到动物保护站助手,连自己都觉得“身份卑微,而且越来越卑微”,成了“历史边缘的孤单身影”(167)。在女儿遭到侵害、自己作为父亲却无能为力,心情痛苦之时,他那残存的白人优越意识、设法报复黑人的想法也随着女儿的断喝而消失:“醒醒吧,戴维。这是在乡下。这是在非洲。”(124)这是人物的话语,更是库切的思想。在这样的语境下,失去主导话语权被他者化了的白人,应该怎样认识自己的境遇,怎样主导自己的行为？作者在某种程度上警示人们，种族之间的对抗性、报复性行为无法化解根深蒂固的种族矛盾，只有倡导多元宽容的思想才能实现种族融合。

二、主导话语颠覆引发的反思

"如果库切小说常常给读者留下不安、难解的话题的话，那是因为库切给自己提出了令人不安和难解的话题。"(Barnard 199)库切在小说《耻》开头就提出了这样的话题，正如库切研究专家科休所指出的那样，"《耻》采用较为复杂的方式探讨个人与公众世界之间、智力与身体之间、欲望与爱情之间、公开耻辱与个人荣誉观或救赎之间的冲突"(Kossew 155)。他以南非常见的性泛滥、性犯罪现象作为切入点，在表现曾经处于中心强势地位的白人被边缘化，在其原有地位被颠覆后成为话语权缺失的他者的同时，对理性原则与道德伦理、历史重负与个体责任等问题进行了反思。

(一) 理性原则与道德伦理

"性"这个古老的话题在小说《耻》中焕发了青春，成为中心话题，实际上前半部卢里的问题和后部分露西的问题基本上属于同一类型话题。库切将这个敏感话题置于后殖民后种族隔离时代，讨论南非在社会转型时期，白人与有色人种在错综复杂的新形势下的反应。库切选取年逾半百的白人教授为样本，以卢里的性经历与契约原则观念来反思新南非的道德原则和伦理取向，因为依据作者本人的想法，"人类所有行为……都会转向伦理道德评判的范围"(Coetzee 1986：5)。

库切在小说《耻》伊始开宗明义地提出性话题，称 52 岁且离过婚的卢里"性需求的问题解决得相当不错"(1)。而这种解决方式实质上并非合法地再婚，而是一种典型的钱色交易：身为大学教授的他，遵循公平契约原则，付费获得性生活。从库切提供的描述(未有阳光暴晒痕迹却有"蜂蜜色"的肤色)来看，交易的另一方索拉娅显然是有色人种。卢梭曾经说过，"人是生而自由的，但却无往不在枷锁之中。自以为是其他一切的主人的人，反而比其他一切更是奴隶"(Rousseau 165)。卢里恰恰是这种自以为是的人，他自以为遵守着理性交换原则，成了索拉娅的主人，而后者交易时间内的表现支持了他的幻觉。然而，在交易时间外与后者偶遇、目光交织后，他的幻觉消失。索拉娅透露出的冷淡、卢里感受到的顾客地位，使卢里标榜满意的性生活变得索然无味，两人关系变得十分不自在，这时的他醒悟过来，明白自己的所谓“自由”实质上是金钱支撑之下“动物性欲望”（巴塔耶 47）的满足而已。他无法成为自己的主人，反倒切实地成为了自己欲望的奴隶。自以为崇尚“随性情而为”（2）、能够依据契约原则自由支配他人的卢里，在黑人新政权下已经失去了为所欲为的地位。

如果说与索拉娅以及护花公司提供的另一个“稚嫩”而“粗俗”的“索拉娅”（8）之间的关系是一种合法的契约买卖关系，与系秘书道恩的性关系仅是一种排遣无聊的随兴行为的话，那么，与梅拉妮·艾萨克斯的关系就无法用契约或理性来解释，只能采用巴塔耶“人性与兽性”博弈的“欲望身体观”（赵一凡 808）和尼采的“权力意志”（Nietzsche 333）来阐释。

梅拉妮与卢里之间是师生关系，这种关系同时表现为一种伦理关系，因为教师与学生构成一个特殊的道德共同体，各自承担一定的伦理责任，履行一定的伦理义务。然而，身为大学教授的卢里，却煞费苦心地引诱梅拉妮与其发生了性关系，这就违背了师生伦理关系原则和性爱关系准则，即相爱和自愿的原则。如果说第一次在卢里家里地板上的性爱是梅拉妮被教授诱惑而被动接受的行为的话，那么，第二次在梅拉妮的寓所里的性爱却直接背离了性伦理道德原则——灵肉融合的性爱原则、自由自律的私事原则、理解尊重基础上的无伤原则。显而易见，梅拉妮对其强迫性性行为十分反感，在这种情况下的性生活给她带来的只有精神、感情和心理上的伤害。梅拉妮虽没有决意反抗，但已经以明确的话语表现出自己的不愿意，这为小说后部露西的被强奸情节埋下了比对的伏笔。

为此，库切用了一整段对卢里的行为进行了评述：“这不是强奸，不完全是，但不管怎么说，违背了对方意愿，完全违背了对方的意志……在整个过程中[她]内心彻底地死了，就像一只脖子被狐狸的利牙咬住了的兔子。”（25）这时，如果用“性享受”与“性消费”是“人的权利”等等“性哲学”来解释卢里的行为，那就可能只强调了处于优势的大学教授地位的白人卢里的“权利”，而忽略了处于劣势弱者地位的有色人种女学生作为“人的权利”。卢里在这里表现的应该是尼采所说的“权力意志”，即“贪得无厌地要求显现权力，或者作为创造性的本能来运用、行使权力”（Nietzsche 333）。这种白人教授对学生权力的行使，显示的是人类性的自然属性，与社会的性伦理道德不相符合。

神经科学专家特拉伯教授曾经说过，“白人与生俱来的种族主义观念将自己归类于'文明人'以示区别于野蛮他者，通过法律保护白人的利益与特权来维护话语权"(Traber 23)。白人教授卢里在此个案中最不明智的是，他没有意识到，后种族隔离时代的新南非人已经觉醒，护佑白人利益与特权、维护白人霸权话语的那些不合理的法律已经废止，昔日的"野蛮他者"已经成为与白人平等的公民。库切仿佛不经意地描述了人们对此事的反应：校园女性反抗暴力组织自发地展开了对禽兽教授的声讨以及对受害者的声援活动，媒体对"性骚扰案"的报道显然没有姑息这位白人教授。在校方调查委员会的听证会上，他违背师德、运用教授的权力私自给未参加考试的梅拉妮70分的丑闻被揭出，随之，他不愿直视却无法掩盖的性丑闻被挑明，卢里下意识里保持的那份白人原有的矜持已经无法避免他声名狼藉的命运，正如卢里的前妻罗萨琳所预见的："没有人同情你，没有人可怜你，这年头，这时代，你就别指望了。人人的手指都会朝你戳着点着，干嘛不呢?"(44)虽然卢里认错道歉却坚持不悔过，没有意识到本能的性欲满足与为人道德以及"性伦理"已经严重相抵牾，但是，库切终究让读者清楚地看到，卢里的悲剧无可挽回，他无法逃脱自我放逐、自我他者化的命运。

虽然"批评界将注意力转向戴维·卢里的道德地位，有些评论对他孤独反抗社会和大学的责难表示同情"(Kissack 51)，但是，库切在小说中并没有表现出对当事者的同情，他对白人卢里的"耻辱"的深度揭示，明显带有批判性眼光。他对自以为是的白人桩桩件件令人不齿的行为所作的冷峻描述，使读者认识到，卢里的行为显然带有白人失去主导话语权后滞后反应的时代印迹。

(二) 历史重负与个体责任

如果说库切利用卢里在开普敦的经历对性伦理和人性道德进行了反思的话，那么，在小说《耻》的农场情节中，库切则利用卢里的女儿露西被抢劫轮奸事件，反思了后种族隔离时代从主导话语地位跌落到边缘他者地位的白人应该为历史的记忆付出什么样的代价、承担何种责任的问题。

卢里失去大学教职后来到女儿露西农场，在这里他亲眼目睹和亲身经历的事件，为库切的反思提供了充分的原始资料。如上文所述，白人同性恋者露西遭到了三个黑人青年的抢劫和轮奸。这个事件在后种族隔离时代的南非具有共性特征。300多年的白人种族压迫史、近半个世纪的野蛮种族隔离史、长期形成的黑人抵抗文化传统，使黑白种族之间矛盾尖锐而无法调解。库切在小说中描述的许多问题正是南非社会现状的真实写照：随着 1991 年 2 至 6 月南非议会宣布撤销《土著土地法》、《特定住区法》、《人口登记法》等 80 多项种族主义法律以来，保留地制度即黑人家园制度已经不复存在，但是，这颗种族主义历史毒瘤残留的余毒并未随着种族隔离制度的消失而消失，它仍然在今天的新南非肆虐不已。就土地改革而论，黑人新政府的土改政策造成了土地所有权变更，这项举措显然令黑人欢欣鼓舞，但是，由于平衡各方利益的复杂性，政府主导的改革进程无法使所有黑人满意，黑人因此抱怨政府改革缓慢，致使下层贫苦黑人无法迅速分到土地和财产。而且，黑人的诉求明显带有肤色革命胜利者清算白人历史旧账的姿势，因而南非发生过无数起黑人不满土地改革而抢劫杀害白人农场主的案例。

露西财产被抢劫、自己被轮奸这个情节以及之后她对父亲表述的困惑，实际上是库切针对新南非黑人政权领导下进行国家重建时如何对待沉重的历史负担问题提出的思考。他利用卢里的答话清楚地提出了自己的观点：“他们的行为有历史原因……一段充满错误的历史……这事看起来是私怨，可实际上并不是。那都是先辈传下来的。”(156)确实，南非黑人在近代史上经受了无尽的被殖民被压迫被剥削的磨难，欧洲白人对南非黑人犯下了罄竹难书的罪恶。种族隔离制的全面实行，是以最残酷的暴力为基础。镌刻在黑人种族记忆深处的痛苦无法在短时间内消除，黑人种族对白人的仇恨以及希冀报复的心理无法缓释，黑人新政权通过的“黑人经济振兴法案”虽损害了白人的既得利益、保护了黑人利益，但并未达到立竿见影的效果，除了激起有技术、高学历的白人移民他国的浪潮外，没有让黑人感受到切实的利益，因此，昔日掌控话语权如今沦落为边缘他者的白人，成了黑人泄愤的对象，他们占有的巨大财富成为黑人愤愤不平的原因之一，后者认为这原本属于南非人民，应该被无情地剥夺，归还南非黑人。客观地说，黑人新政府并没有出台相应的政策来处理白人的财产，倒是黑人自发地按照自己的意愿在进行着对白人的剥夺，于是，新南非针对白人的犯罪率居高不下，造成不分黑白的公民都缺乏人身安全感的后果。为了国家长治久安，南非黑人政权决定实施种族和解政策。1995 年，黑人大主教图图建立起“南非真相与和解委员会”，试图消弭黑人与白人之间的矛盾。然而，社会变革时期出现的磨难与阵痛无可避免，新旧社会观念在融合过程中发生剧烈碰撞在所难免。

库切安排露西对抢劫强奸事件的反应，实际上寄托了作者对南非种族之间和解的希望。"宽恕与和解话语在过去十年中作为与殖民主义遗产不断斗争的国家的种族之间谈判最有力的话语。"(McGonegal 1)面对黑人对白人的强烈仇恨,面对黑人在反种族隔离制度胜利后的种种报复白人的行动,是针锋相对地进行"正义"的讨伐、坚决的惩罚,还是隐忍宽恕,这对于南非能够实现民族复原、种族间的和解的伟大事业,能否成功地卸载历史留下的沉重负担,轻装上阵地建设人际关系和谐的新南非,对人类是否能够正常地过上民主自由的生活,至关重要。正如法国哲学家利科所说,"宽恕是记忆的一种康复药,是其服丧期的结束。记忆从负重状态下解脱,便获得开始大事业的自由。宽恕赋予记忆以未来"(Ricoeur 144)。在种族隔离制度消失之后,如何赦免罪恶的问题,如何赔偿白人犯下无法形容的恐怖事件造成的伤害问题,如何为白人所犯下的暴行寻求补偿办法并得到黑人的宽恕,是萦绕在小说《耻》中挥之不去的主题。尽管库切在《耻》中没有突显小说与历史真实性之间的关系,读来令人感到复杂模糊,困惑不解,但是,小说对可能发生的宽恕、重生和赔偿等问题所做出的思考应该是非常有益。

小说人物卢里对露西隐忍态度和不追究黑人责任的行为所表现出的不理解从一个侧面表明了大多数白人在新南非所遭遇的困惑:祖辈荷裔布尔殖民者对南非的殖民侵略、前辈白人对黑人的种族压迫与剥削等犯下的种种罪行,是否要由当代新南非白人承担?黑人在过去黑暗制度之下遭受过的痛苦和磨难是否应该让当下的白人再重新经历一番?库切在小说中并没有提供答案,但是,"慈善"与"宽恕"是库切在讨论南非种族关系时一直强调的两个关键词。他在接受德里克·阿特里吉教授采访时曾经说过,"使我免于做纯粹愚蠢的蠢事的办法,我希望,是一种慈善的方法,我猜,那是一种宽恕得以在这个世界上寓言化的方法"(Coetzee 1992:246)。

如果我们将卢里在小说前半部对梅拉妮的性行为与后半部的黑人对露西的性行为的后期处理做一比较的话,就可能发现一个有趣的现象:库切笔下的卢里在丑闻暴露后虽不悔过,但认罪伏法,接受惩罚,后来竟只身来到艾萨克斯家,乞求被害者家人的宽恕。虽然被害者并不在场,虽然在他的乞求中较多地涉及自己为此付出的耻辱代价,没有考虑到梅拉妮为此受到的鄙视和耻辱,艾萨克斯一家实际上最终还是以博大的胸怀宽恕了卢里;而白人女同性恋者露西受辱后迅速清除掉犯罪现场的痕迹,拒绝承认被性侵的事实,在巨大的痛苦中没有思索着如何去进行符合"公理"与"正义"的报复性行为,却一直在反思为什么黑人对白人如此仇恨的问题,反思在殖民地时代、种族隔离时代白人对黑人加害者曾经有过的伤害，并且在痛定思痛之后做出了令人惊诧的决定。德里达认为，“宽恕的权利最终只是受害者的，绝对受害者的”（qtd in McGonegal 135）。虽然库切并没有安排卢里与佩特鲁斯之间宽恕与和解的可能性，但是，露西的决定客观上起到了黑白和解的效果。在黑人掌控了南非政治话语权的当下，失去话语权的白人不能总是沉溺在过去优势地位时的辉煌无法自拔，不能紧紧抓住白人种族控权时的意识形态不放，应该接受白人已经被边缘化这个事实，接受自己已经成为他者的现实，以宽恕和解之心对待过去自以为劣等的黑人，以平等的姿态对待别人，只有这样，种族和解的实现才有可能。

（三）关爱动物与种族和解

后种族隔离时代黑白两个种族的关系问题，是库切关注的重大问题。作者利用主人公卢里从怀着白人优越感、大学教授的高傲、对卑贱者的蔑视与乡下人佩特鲁斯相处，到遭受抢劫后脱胎换骨的变化（为先前自己不齿者当下手，开始同情弱势动物等）说明，曾几何时，殖民者便失去了过去的蛮横与自大：说英语带着明显德国口音的白人老头爱丁杰得随身佩枪，住所防护设施周密，但依然无法确保性命无虞；卢里的女儿露西遭到黑人轮奸后忍辱沦为原帮工佩特鲁斯的情妇；欧洲殖民者的强势话语载体——西方文明语言竟然“像头陷在泥潭里垂死的恐龙，变得僵硬起来”（117），倒是索托语、科萨语等当地语言活力四射，恰如其分地表达着当时当地人民的真情实感。库切通过这一系列的倒置安排，使原先白人眼中的他者在自己的土地上恢复了应有的话语地位，而原先的白人话语权拥有者在当时当地的他者化衬托了后殖民、后种族隔离时期的乾坤颠覆。

在此语境之下，在黑白对立状况没有得到根本好转的时刻，库切强调人与人之间应该讲究宽恕，希望种族与种族之间应该和解，但是，他并没有采用直白说教的方式进行，尽管他也利用露西直言不讳地告诉读者，时代改变了，南非已不再是白人主导话语时代的南非。他要求宽恕和解的方式是“寓言化的方式”。这种方式表现在文本中，除了通过露西决定与佩特鲁斯结合这种寓意深刻的情节之外，主要通过大学教授卢里对动物的态度改变来显现。

库切安排卢里第一次来到“动物福利会”诊所时，显然没有让他对动物表示出任何兴趣。当贝芙·肖觉得他喜欢动物时,他的回答是否定的。然而,在小说中,库切安排了不少与动物相关的场景,如露西被轮奸时七条狗被黑人青年残忍地枪杀等,但最令人印象深刻的当属库切的两处描述:一处是卢里与两只待宰杀的黑面波斯羊的关系变化,一处是在死去的动物焚烧前卢里的见闻与决定。两处都以貌似随意的笔触,展示了人与动物的关系,前者是人对待将死的动物的态度,而后者是对死后动物的态度。无论对待哪一种状态的动物,人类都没有显示出人道的精神,没有把动物当作自然界生物的一种,而是下意识地认为动物是低级、低劣的,无需得到人类的尊重。所以,就出现了前者待宰前被拴住空旷的泥地上,没有水,没有草,还要经受阳光的暴晒;出现后者死后尸体自然僵硬时,"工人就在装尸体前先用铁锨背把尸体狠劲拍一遍,把僵直的四肢敲折了再送进去"(144-145)。应该说,如果按照刚到乡村的卢里的逻辑,对于这种司空见惯之事,人们下意识中不会产生任何反应的。然而,在经历种种事件后的卢里,开始同情动物、尊重生命尊严。虽说给羊松绑并将之撵到草地水池边仅举手之劳,亲手去处理焚烧动物尸体虽有点费事却也并非不可为,但是,库切如此安排应该别有用心。卢里的内心意识外化泄露了天机:"要为现实中的世界,或是为理想中的世界尽力,肯定还有许多其他更有成效的事情可做。"但是,"那就是为他自己。为他自己理想中的世界,这世界里的人们不用铁锨把尸体打平了处理"(146)。他对待动物态度的转变,实质上也表现了库切对大自然一切生命的看法。

库切刻意将传统意识中高等动物"人"与自然界的低级动物羊、狗并置,讨论他们之间的关系。正如他在《伊丽莎白·科斯特洛:八堂课》中利用女主人之口所说,"尊重所有人的世界观、母牛的世界观、松鼠的世界观,所有生物的世界观"(Coetzee 2003: 91-92)。大自然里,物种并无高低贵贱之分,都有和谐共存共生的权利。在后种族隔离时代新南非,人们确实需要重新思考人生问题、个人身份问题。过去的白人比黑人优越的意识,已属历史的记忆,不应永远萦绕于怀,而确应像露西一样,断然与其告别,开始新生;应该像卢里尊重动物生命与尊严一样,对待新南非的一切。库切的寓言化手法,以高超的隐喻,表达了作者心中人人平等自由的渴望,渴望白人与黑人不要被沉重的历史包袱所累,实现种族之间的和解。库切通过科斯特洛说出,"在历史上,对人类地位的信奉导致过这样的结局,即杀戮或奴役一个神圣的族类、一个由神创造的族类,因此导致我们自己遭到诅咒"(Coetzee 2003: 103)。这种悲剧不应重演,因为,正是人类将主观意志强加给人、将生物分成高低不同的做法,使希特勒的暴行得以实现,使犹太人受到集中营的虐待，“正是芝加哥的牲口围场使纳粹学会了处理人体的方法”。人类社会“理性地”把动物归为异类、把战俘归为异类，为所欲为的虚伪历史应该到了终结之时。

结 论

库切在小说《耻》中，通过后种族隔离时代黑人掌控话语权后新南非乾坤倒置、白人话语权缺失后的新历史语境下历经的种种遭遇，采用寓言化手法展示了新南非黑白之间的真实关系，对以犯下“道德之耻”的白人教授卢里和为祖辈殖民侵略、荼毒黑人的可耻历史被动偿还旧账的露西为代表的白人在往昔优势地位被颠覆成为落差很大的他者心态进行生动的描写，通过处于不同感受层面的白人代表卢里与露西的矛盾冲突，揭露了层层悖论下理性社会的荒谬与虚伪，拷问了历史记忆与个人责任问题，新南非的理性原则和道德原则问题。库切怀着对南非大地的热爱，对南非后种族隔离时代黑白种族应该和谐相处的信念，以隐喻的方式向通过人物的活动与话语，对南非社会黑人与白人提出了宽恕和解、共存共生的希望。他并不希望黑人在掌控了权力话语后对被边缘他者化的白人进行无情的打击报复，不希望以牙还牙、以血还血的血腥场面一再出现；也不希望被颠覆了话语权的白人念念不忘享尽优越条件的时光，不希望他们坚持多年来形成的固有意识形态，而是希望他们认清当下的语境、当下的南非。库切利用白人对动物观念转变这一寓言性很强的情节，传达了物种平等、自然需要和谐的思想。

参考文献：

Aristotle. *Politics*. Trans. Benjamin Jowett. Kitchener: Batoche Books, 1999.

Attridge, Derek. J. M. Coetzee's *Disgrace*. *Interventions* 4.3 (2002): 315 - 320.

Barnard, Rita. J. M. Coetzee's *Disgrace* and the South African Pastoral. *Contemporary Literature* XLIV. 2 (2003): 199 - 224.

Boehmer, Elleke. Not Saying Sorry, Not Speaking Pain: Gender Implications in *Disgrace*. *Interventions* 4.3 (2002): 342 - 51.

Boehmer, Elleke. Sorry, Sorrier, Sorriest: The Gendering of Contrition in J. M. Coetzee's

Disgrace. *J. M. Coetzee and the Idea of the Public Intellectual*. Ed. Jane Poyner. Athens, Ohio: Ohio UP, 2006. 135 – 147.

Buikema, Rosemarie. Literature and the Production of Ambiguous Memory. *European Journal of English Studies*. 10. 2 (2006): 187 – 197.

Coetzee, J. M. Interview. *Doubling the point: Essays and Interviews*. Ed. David Attwell. London Harvard UP, 1992. 243 – 250.

——. *Disgrace*. London: Vintage Books, 2009.

——. *Elizabeth Costello Eight Lessons*. Sydney: Knopf, 2003.

Cooper, Pamela. Metamorphosis and Sexuality: Reading the Strange Passions of *Disgrace*. *Research in African Literatures* 36. 4 (Winter 2005): 22 – 39.

Cornwell, Gareth. Disgraceland: History and the Humanities in Frontier Country. *English in Africa*, 30. 2 (Oct. 2003): 43 – 68.

Freud, Sigmund. *Beyond the Pleasure Principle*. Trans. James Strachey. New York, London: W. W. Norton and Company, 1961.

Kissack, Mike & Michel Titlestad. The Dynamics of Discontent: Containing Desire and Aggression in Coetzee's *Disgrace*. *African Identity*. 3. 1 (2005): 51 – 67.

Kossew, Sue. The Politics of Shame and Redemption in J. M. Coetzee's *Disgrace*. *Research in African Literatures* 34. 2 (Summer 2003): 155 – 162.

McDonald, Peter D. Disgrace Effects. *Interventions* 4. 3 (2002): 321 – 330.

McGonegal, Julie. *Imagining Justice: The Politics of Postcolonial Forgiveness and Reconciliation*. Ottawa: Library and Archives Canada, 2004.

Nietzsche, Friedrich. *The Will to Power*. Trans. Kaufmann, Walter and R. J. Hollingdale. Ed. Walter Kaufmann. New York: Random House, 1967.

Pienaar, Hans. Brilliant yet aloof, Coetzee at last wins Nobel prize for literature. *The Independent*. 3 October 2003. < http: //www. independent. co. uk/arts-entertainment/books/news/brilliant-yet-aloof-coetzee-at-last-wins-nobel-prize-for-literature-581951. html > (accessed 2011 – 10 – 29).

Ricoeur, Paul. *The Just*. Trans. David Pellauer. Chicago and London: University of Chicago Press, 2000.

Rousseau, Jean-Jacques. *The Discourse on the Sciences and Arts* and *The Social Contract*. Trans.

Susan Dunn. New Haven and London: Yale University Press, 2002.

Sanvan, Charles. Disgrace: a Path to Grace. *World Literature Today*. 78.1 (2004): 26-29.

Segall, Kimberly Wedeven. Pursuing Ghosts: The Traumatic Sublime in J. M. Coetzee's *Disgrace*. *Research in African Literatures* 36.4 (Winter 2005): 40-54.

Traber, Daniels S. *Whiteness, Otherness, and the Individualism Paradox from Huck to Punk*. New York: Palgrave MacMillan, 2007.

Tran, Danielle. "Swine! The Word Still Rings in the Air": David's Reaction and the Perpetuation of Racial Conflict in J. M. Coetzee's *Disgrace*. *Postamble* 7.1 (2011): 1-6.

Wood, James. Parables and Prizes. *The New Republic*. December 20, 1999:42-46.

巴塔耶. 色情史. 刘辉,译. 北京:商务印书馆,2003.

波伏娃. 第二性. 陶铁柱,译. 北京:中国书籍出版社,2004.

赵一凡. 西方文论关键词. 北京:外语教学与研究出版社,2006.

(原载《英美文学研究论丛》2012 年总 17 期,中国人民大学书报资料中心复印报刊资料《外国文学研究》2013 年第 4 期全文转载)

后基督时代的沉默他者

——评论《迈克尔·K 的生活与时代》

摘要：在小说《迈克尔·K 的生活与时代》中，库切采用沉默的他者形象，展示了南非被边缘化个体在后基督时代的生存状态以及抵抗方式，表现出作者在揭示人类社会的残忍暴力、相互隔绝、彼此仇恨、愚昧自欺，检视西方文明理性正义本质、批判其道德伦理的同时，为遭受压迫和蹂躏的边缘化他者弱势群体仗义言说，为南非人民在历史社会中所经受的创伤、南非沉重的历史、权力话语、规训与惩罚等话题进行深刻反思。

关键词：库切；《迈克尔·K 的生活与时代》；沉默；他者

中图分类号：I07　**文献标示码**：A　**文章编号**：2095－5723(2013)02－0050－08

一　导　言

J. M. 库切首部荣获英联邦布克奖和法国费米娜外国小说奖的小说《迈克尔·K 的生活与时代》(1983，下简称《迈克尔》)，采用寓言形式，成功地隐匿了时代背景，通篇只字未提人物的肤色，而是通过一个离群索居、沉默寡语的他者——天生兔唇、智力残缺、谜一般难解的小人物迈克尔·K 的"反英雄"情节，展示出一幅标准的后现代卡夫卡式图景，被评论界认为是一部"后基督时代神话"(Marijke 2005：94)。小说通过揭露现代文明社会中人的种种原始野蛮行为，展现被边缘化的他者在被异化的状态中所感受到的极度孤独与绝望情绪，以及他采取主动沉默方式进行抗拒权威意志，争取人性自由的反抗行动，表现出现代现实社会的荒诞和南非广漠大地上的世界末日感，给读者带来无尽的思索。

研究发现，在《迈克尔》中，库切将笔触伸入话语权缺失的下层社会，采用冷峻的语言、近乎白描的表现方式，通过历经劫难、自由理想信念不改、外表愚钝、内心细腻坚强的被边缘化他者形象，震撼人心地展示了在南非种族隔离政策逐渐成形、继而猖獗的年代普通人的生存状态。小说通过一系列诸如孤独、逃逸、异化、荒诞等卡夫卡式寓言主题呈现，展示了战争迫近时南非下层小人物迈克尔·K 这个典型的卑贱他者的经历以及他那近乎卑微的诉求——过上有人格尊严的生活。迈克尔·K 自认与战乱频仍、社会动荡无涉的"异类"思想、他以独特的沉默方式对威权话语势力所进行的抗争，他反复坚持以羸弱的生命主体回归自然的举措，无不表现出作者在揭示人类社会的残忍暴力、相互隔绝、彼此仇恨、愚昧自欺，检视西方文明理性正义本质、批判其道德伦理的同时，为遭受压迫和蹂躏的边缘化他者弱势群体仗义言说，为南非人民在历史社会中所经受的创伤、南非沉重的历史、权力话语、规训与惩罚等话题进行深刻反思，提出常人能否在历史社会中沉默隐身，他者在与环境的冲突中能否有自己的诉求等问题。

二 后基督时代的暴力动乱社会

"上帝死了。"(Nietzsche 2001：109)西方现代哲学开创者尼采的一句名言，对上帝进行了无情无畏的批判，指出了基督教衰落的历史必然性。随着现代科学与技术的崛起，连神学家们也不得不承认，基督教文化中的神已不再具有超越凡俗的力量，因为现代科学已经凌驾于基督教之上，社会与神的宏旨无关。世界已经进入了后基督时代，上帝已经无法成为人类社会道德标准与终极目的，人们的价值观、世界观不再受制于基督教理念。

20 世纪 80 年代的南非处于新旧交替时代，是一个受制于基督教理念的后基督时代，是一个种族隔离政策影响下战争频仍、暴力不断的恐怖时代。库切引用公元前 6 世纪希腊哲学家赫拉克利特的话，为《迈克尔》加上题记："战争是万物之父、万物之王。他将有些显示为神，其他显示为人。他将有些造就为奴隶，其他为自由者。"(Coetzee 1985：1)题记在某种程度上为小说的展开提供了前景，说明了战争在小说中的重要作用。战争，用军事理论家和军事历史学家克劳塞维茨的话说，"仅仅是大规模的决斗，……是一种暴力行为，意在迫使我们的敌手屈服于我们的意志"(Clausewitz 2007：13)。弗雷泽认为，现代国家很特别，"因为它们成功地垄断了对暴力的合法使用"(Frazer 2008：91)。

库切的小说《迈克尔》通篇都处于这种暴力行为之中，人们在使用暴力手段对现有秩序进行破坏或维护，意欲推翻、重建秩序。客观地说，这种暴力行为虽然从理论上说对人类文明的发展和进步起着催化和促进作用，但却时刻威胁着人类自身的生存。南非的历史是一部殖民者暴力入侵的历史，是各殖民者之间争夺霸权的历史，是威权统治者暴力压制人民的历史，也是人民争取权利而采取暴力抗争的历史。马克思说过，"当机会来临时，竞争国允许自己进行各种暴力行为"(Marx 1999：1489)。从1652年荷兰东印度公司占领开普半岛，到1657年荷兰首批移民（布尔人）侵占南非最古老居民科伊人土地，到18世纪70年代布尔人在古老南非大地上继续疯狂殖民扩张，无不通过惨烈暴力完成。究其原因，用马克思主义者辩证唯物的观点，即对抗性的经济利益冲突。南非人为了保卫自己的家园，奋起殊死反抗，同荷兰殖民者进行了持续百年之久的战争。18、19世纪之交英国两度占领开普殖民地，同样，南非人在半个多世纪内进行了6次反侵略战争；19世纪60和80年代，蕴量丰富的金刚石矿和金矿的发现使南非吸引了大批欧洲移民，同时也加剧了殖民者之间的暴力争夺。两次布尔战争、世界大战，乃至后来的索韦托惨案，无一不是为了一方利益而采用暴力手段试图迫使敌手屈服于自己的意志，结果是，无辜的人民被拖入持久深重的灾难之中，饱受战乱之苦，颠沛流离，前途绝望。

三　暴力动乱时代他者的沉默

库切在《迈克尔》中，没有像有些评论者提出的那样，选择被迫离开家园、任其在骚乱中倾废的中产者比尔曼夫妇为主人公，也没有考虑从战乱年代改造营、拘留营的被扭曲的监禁者角度选择主人公，去"追踪诺埃尔的心路历程"(翟业军、刘永昶 2006：70)，而是采用迈克尔·K这个异化弱者形象为主人公。虽然战争给这个社会的每一个人都造成了难以愈合的创伤，从无奈弃家的中产者角度去表现这种创伤可能对比度更为强烈；虽然监禁者其实与被监禁者一样，在监禁他者的过程中自己"其实成了战争的囚徒"(157)，一样无休无止地处于不自由之中，个体性格在监禁与反监禁的循环中很容易扭曲，从这个角度反映南非纷乱骚动时代的酷烈效果亦非一般，但是，库切毅然选择艰辛地逃离动乱的开普敦却陷入逃无所逃境地的迈克尔·K为主人公，以主人公辗转过程中不舍不弃微末希望、遁入无声无息的寂静，以呈现主体"失声"的沉默为象征，表现南非被边缘化他者的处境及其与命运的抗争。

有人将小说评论为"一幅不谙世事、反抗权力崇拜……令人心寒的图景"（Kratz 1984：462）。确实，库切呈现的迈克尔的生活与时代让人读来感到锥心般痛楚，他并没有花费大量篇幅来直接描写这个时代的乱象，然而，道路上不时驶过的军车，到处有士兵把守的关隘，空中尖啸而过的喷气式战斗机，大量存在的改造营和拘留营，医院里人满为患的伤病员，街道上常常发生的枪战械斗，都在不断地提醒读者，这里是充满喧嚣和骚动的地方，这里时时刻刻都可能发生流血事件，这里的生命没有任何安全保障。因此，逃亡、逃离危险成了南非生活中正常的主题，动乱是小说常态背景。

作者没有引用他者的声音来反抗威权，因为一般说来支配性与否定性总是与语言密切相连，而是采用冷峻笔调，表现了乱世之中边缘化他者在逃离社会过程中看似消极却极为有效的应对策略——沉默，即交际中言语形式的缺失。沉默固有的模糊性和它创造的话语空间，激荡着人们的各种想象力。黑德说，"K令人难以捉摸的另一面即是他的沉默，沉默既是被剥夺公民权的标志，也是抵抗的表现形式"（Head 1997：98）。K的沉默充满了不能言说的故事。库切在描述迈克尔·K这个人物的沉默时，采用了多层次的表现方法。在这里，作者倒没有标新立异，他基本上循规蹈矩地表现了K沉默性格的形成过程：童年由于身体缺损（兔唇与裂鼻）而受到同伴的歧视和侧目，长期压抑的结果使他通常情况下保持沉默，而他从事的工作（园丁-守夜人-园丁）客观上造成了交际机会短缺；在陶思河营地时，他积极为逃离做准备，更需要保持沉默。因此，"沉默并不是话语的终结，而是相对于话语而存在的另一种表达意义的方式"（Foucault 1978：27）。沉默决不意味着意义的缺无，在很多情况下恰恰暗示着意义的多元和深刻。

库切笔下K在不同场合下的沉默，不仅具有话语意义，传送言语信息，还能真实反映K的心理活动过程。心理语言学研究表明，"一切意义的根源在于沉默在谈话中出现的位置，以及由此而产生的受会话结构影响的预期"（Levinson 1983：329）。K的沉默有其鲜明的特征：在维萨基农场，实际上是在无人之境，他日出而作日入而息，超然于时代之外，无需语言来证明他的存在，或者说语言在这里已经失去交际功能，但这绝不代表思考的停止，不意味着K停止用语言去思想，虽然开普敦、战争以及来这个农场的过程，对于他来说正在淡忘。

维萨基的孙子出现，使语言交际成为可能，然而，K却十分机智地假装哑巴、装傻充愣。这里的"沉默"表达的是一种有意识的自我控制行为，蕴含着说话人不愿意表达的心态，掩盖的是隐秘的真相。而维萨基的孙子试图将他变成奴仆时，他一语不发地离开。这时的K保持"沉默"，显然是为了他所珍爱的自由，他借助沉默的力量来抵抗管制话语，宁可逃入群山，进入无人的自由之境，也不愿待在维萨基那座能避风挡雨的宅子里。

山顶洞里的食物匮乏使K在极度虚弱的情况下被迫回归人群，来到阿尔伯特王子城，他旋即被带到警察局，为了避免被权力话语掌控，最大限度地实现主体的话语救赎，作者确实安排了一些策略，"这些策略中最有效的就是沉默"(Marais 1996：73)。如前文所说，沉默绝不是思想的中止，而是意识的延伸。K被送往医院后，他的意识外化即是最好的说明："医院是一个为了身体而存在的地方，而在这里身体总是在维护自己的权利。"(71)

K在加卡尔斯德里夫营地的表现，同样证明了这个观点。尽管作者安排了他与不同人物的简短对话，同时又反复地对准他的深度心理作直接的描摹，但是，K骨子里是沉默不语的。他清楚地知道，要避免被主流话语捕获，就必须采取措施。他明白，自己不是囚犯，不应该受到限制自由的待遇。可是，那里规定"不许离开营地，禁止探望、禁止外出、禁止郊游野餐，早晚点名报到"(92)。然而，他虽然渴望自由生活，但是，当他在温暖的灰色沙地上躺下，眯缝着眼睛看着天空中太阳射出的七色彩虹时，却开始意识到自己"像一个不知道洞穴在哪里的蚂蚁"(83)。这为K的隐形生活做出了铺垫。

逃离加卡尔斯德里夫营地的迈克尔·K二次来到维萨基农场的经历，是小说重要的事件。这时的K自然又回到客观的沉默状态之中，他超越语言而存在，语言的缺场帮助他逃脱外在的压迫。为保护那来之不易的自由，他舍弃维萨基的住宅，在水坝边掘洞而居，开始种植南瓜和西瓜，捕获昆虫、蜥蜴、蚂蚁和蚂蚱以维持生命；他没有像笛福小说的鲁滨逊那样在大树上留下计算时间的刻痕，也没有去记录月亮的圆缺，仿佛整个成了世外生物。他意识到，自己脱离了人类社会，然而，他明白即便是这种状态的自由，也要比不自由强得多。他把自己比作"在香肠中打瞌睡的寄生虫"、"伏在石头下的蜥蜴"(116)。这种比喻把时代寒霜般的剑戟以及剑戟凭陵下生命的坚韧表现得淋漓尽致。他对谁是主人、谁是寄生虫的问题的思索进一步鞭挞了这个威权社会。

库切仿佛觉得客观再现迈克尔·K的边缘化他者生活还不足以最大限度地批判时

代的罪恶。于是,在进入第二章时,他从第一章第三人称全知全能叙事视角转入第一人称限制叙事视角,隐身于营地医官背后,近距离观察 K 的生活与沉默,以医官/隐含作者身份直接参入故事,直接言说评论。这里,他巧妙地为迈克尔的名字加上字母 S,营地管理者诺埃尔少校提到 K 时都说迈克尔斯,医官/隐含作者亦然。当主人公意识到他们在说自己时,曾有过话语纠正的表现,这应该可以被视作是试图恢复主体身份的努力,但事实证明这个被边缘化的他者的努力是徒劳的。营地的管理者是权威话语者,代表的是政府的利益。他们收留 K 并非出于慈善目的,而是希冀通过与 K 的对话来获取当地游击队的信息,以便政府军去镇压。在这种情况下,K 的主体身份客观被剥夺,这就成了无法避免的现实,对于这样的现实,K 此后虽不愿接受,但也只能以沉默来抗拒。

库切笔下 K 的沉默很难说是他因为看穿了营地用意后的刻意抵抗。作为比小说人物掌握更多信息的读者明白,事实上他确实与游击队没有任何关系,并不掌握有价值的游击队行动信息。他采取沉默的办法,在某种程度上是出于本能的抗拒。任凭少校说得天花乱坠,任凭助纣为虐的医官说得苦口婆心,K 一语不发。尽管长时间的沉默表面上使得这个被异化的他者在权威话语面前显得软弱无力,但是,正是因为他对正统话语的弃置,这种策略才起到保持他者他性的作用。每当他不想言说,他就倔强地闭上那张不能完全闭上的嘴,愤怒地注视着权力话语掌控者——少校和医官,有时竟像石头一样冷冰冰地回看着花言巧语的医官。正如赫尔曼指出的那样,沉默预示着“人物的相互敌视,也创造着冲突”(Herman 1995: 93),昭示着冷漠、拒绝和抵抗。“K 本能地知道,成为被施舍的对象就意味着放弃自己想要尊严和自主的主张,承认自己无助、完全依靠别人。”(Dragunoiu 2006: 70)最终发出的声响“我不在战争中”(138)虽然使权威话语者气急败坏,耐心尽失,但是,一个不容忽视的事实是,他这种抵制权威话语的沉默手段起到了意想不到的效果。库切隐身在医官背后评论到,“他不是生活在我们的世界里。他生活在一个完全属于他自己的世界里”(142)。

在《迈克尔的生活与时代》中,库切不仅十分在意人物的心理嬗变过程,而且非常重视意象的内涵演变过程,颇为巧妙地将两者结合成一个艺术整体。在刻画人物心理嬗变的过程中,作者始终保持了一种优裕而节制的叙述姿态,对“沉默”的调度和掌控游刃有余,恰到好处地表现出话语与沉默的强大功能。

库切对“沉默”策略的调度,除了上文讨论过的对言语的抗拒外,还体现在他设计的迈克尔·K 的身体的“沉默”,即在最后的集中营里,K 的身体对集中营里的食品的抗拒性物理反应。从拒绝话语到拒绝食物，标志着库切"沉默"艺术运用上的一种质的飞跃，也是库切调度"沉默"策略达到炉火纯青地步的标志。一般而言，保持沉默是主体的理性选择，即便说K在诺埃尔少校面前由于信息不对称而出现的沉默存在本能抗拒的成分的话，那种抗拒的理性成分也该大于本能。但是，库切仿佛觉得这样做还不能够完全表现这种抗拒的力量，他设计的身体的"沉默"这种反应，表现的并不是K有意的选择，而是身体本能的抗拒，与意识无涉，纯属自然的力量。这种与他对于自由的向往一样，并非理性的追求，而是一种天生本能的需要。然而，正是这种自然的本能，却有着让人战栗的威慑力量。至此，库切已经进入了一个高境界，他采用寓言体小说表现的卑微他者即刻得到了升华，K的追求不再是令人不解的怪诞想法，而是值得推崇的人类理想。为了进一步强化这一主题，作者还特地安排了囚禁他的人的意识流，让读者清晰地看到，这种本能具有强大的震撼力，甚至连囚禁他的人都后悔自己没有勇气跟着K一起逃走。自由，这一人类持续追求的崇高理想，在沉默中得到了张扬。

四 沉默他者引发的反思

在《迈克尔》中，库切在表现人物沉默抵抗权威话语的同时，采用叙事者全知全能叙述与人物意识流动相结合的手法，或直接叙述或隐身在被他者化了的沉默主人公之后，利用主人公的遭遇并根据其经历进行引申，对创伤、历史、权力、规训等问题进行了深刻的反思。

南非漫长的种族隔离史，在人们的心灵中遗留下似乎永不磨灭的创伤记忆，这种记忆既有个体的创伤，也有群体的创伤，既有身体的创伤，也有精神的创伤，既有直接的创伤，也有间接的创伤。疯狂肆虐、无限循环的暴力给南非大地上无辜的人民带来深重的灾难和巨大的创伤。库切钟情于用寓言的方式表现创伤性的现实故事，因为那"既是一种表现创伤性重负的方式，也是努力释放这种重负抑或是对这一事件精心掌控的方式"(Macarthur 2005：11)。

库切在这部小说中，设法隐匿时代背景，通篇不提人物肤色，却使用兔唇裂鼻的异形人物作为小说主人公，不能不说作者有其独特的用意。既然是寓言形式，那么，"兔唇"就不仅仅是任意身体缺陷这么简单。虽然南美洲有上帝之吻造就兔唇的传说，然而，当代大量神话研究表明，兔唇意蕴指向恰恰相反，如法国结构主义神话学家列维-斯特劳斯认为，兔唇与孪生关系密切，前者在母体中出现本体分裂，而后者在母体中实现彻底分裂。在有些部落习俗里，兔唇儿与孪生子一样被认为是怪胎、是野兽或人兽转生，或与恶灵和魔鬼有关，"在出生时被弄死"(Levi-Strauss 1980：42)否则将会成为妖孽。在由拉康式"凝视"的权力所绘制的肖像画中，"兔唇"成为"缺陷"的别名，成了一种被冷漠被他者化后的象征。

众所周知，库切经历过反霸权、反中心、重视边缘、倡导对话精神的后现代思潮的洗礼。他用心良苦地选择异形人作主人公，实际上是选择边缘人作为表现对象。在南非，白人虽仅占总人数的9.1%(2010年统计数据)，但代表了主流群体，被边缘化、他者化的却是占人口绝大多数的人种。因此，库切选择边缘化的K作为主人公，其用意不证自明。戈迪默曾直截了当地指出，"《迈克尔·K的生活与时代》是数百万南非黑人的生活与时代的写照，他们常常迁移、被遗弃，四处游荡，因《种族区域法》下的外出背书条款而隐身。迈克尔·K就是其中之一，代表了全部"(Gordimer 1996：xi)。虽然说在库切刻意抹去主人公肤色的情况下，给出K即黑人的代表或有色人的代表的定论稍有武断之嫌，但是，库切在作品中展示K的创伤，实际上是展示被边缘化的族裔的创伤，亦即展示后殖民时代背景下由于殖民者的越界而造成生存危机的弱势群体的创伤，这一点应该是没有异议的。

我们应该还记得，K出生时就被打上了边缘人的烙印，兔唇裂鼻如同黑人的肤色一样，受到人们的歧视。作为下层劳动者的母亲在别人的嬉笑和私语声中断绝了K与其他孩子的来往，"看着母亲在擦亮别人家的地板，他学会要一声不吭"(4)。表达自由的被管制和被剥夺，即意味着个体自主性和自由度的匮乏和丧失。创伤理论研究专家赫尔曼认为，"最重大的心理创伤体验是被剥夺权利、被剥夺与他人的联系"(Herman 1997：133)。K的基本话语权利以及与别人交往的权利从小就被剥夺，库切为他长大后先后安排的园丁与守夜人工作，进一步强化了这种权利剥夺。这就不得不使人联想起南非种族隔离制度，想起这个制度对白人与非白人(包括黑人、印度人、马来人及其他混血种族)进行分隔并在政治经济等各方面给予的区别性歧视待遇。K的母亲——安娜的遭遇则验证了上述观点。她在开普敦萨默塞特医院所遭受的屈辱与不公，她庆幸"逃出这个人间炼狱"(5)后，却不幸地与儿子共同分担的种种非人经历，以及最终死在归乡路上某个医院冷冰冰的病床上的情形，记录了一位下层劳动妇女充满创伤的一生，也是南非种族隔离制度下被边缘化的他者共同的创伤记录。

库切通过展示K与母亲在医院的经历，影射抨击了为区别白人和非白人的"隔离设施法"；以K携母归乡途中的种种经历，不动声色地指出了以人种作为居住地区限制的"集团地区法"的荒谬。南非人民在这种非人的制度下所受的创伤在《迈克尔》里都能找到影子。然而，库切并没有沉溺于揭开创伤的自怨自怜之中，他采用寓体书写手法揭示迈克尔·K的创伤，将K置于困境之中，在其卑微的生命遭受被追逼、被监禁的肉体精神双重折磨，处于潦倒落魄、甚至连生存都无以为继的尴尬境况下，却表现出他没有向命运低下高贵的头颅，没有失却隐忍的力量，也没有放弃自己理想之中要做的事，一个始终不懈地在精神炼狱中寻找生存罅隙的单薄而又坚韧的生命体便因此而跃然纸上。库切的这种做法为我们标示出了人之为人的精神底线，不仅揭示了人的存在与本质，而且彰显出他信奉的人道主义所独有的深刻。

库切在小说文本中反复再现历史创伤，回忆、反思南非动荡的历史，探索、思考、还原历史之真，透示出他对南非人那种深切的人文关怀。按照新历史主义的观点，历史是一个延伸的文本，而文本则是一段压缩的历史。在这政治隐喻性很强的文学文本中，库切对南非社会历史的反思深刻而透彻。他在接受耶路撒冷文学奖时曾经将南非社会总结为"主奴社会"，认为"奴隶因为不是自己的主人而不自由，主人因为没有奴隶一事无成也不自由"(Coetzee 1992：96)。在这样的社会里，大家都"不自由"是典型的特征。这自然而然地让读者将此与南非种族隔离政策造成的罪恶现实、南非人的历史境遇联系到一起。南非人，尤其是社会底层的普通人，在政治、经济、社会生活等诸多方面受到歧视，生存状态令人悲哀，他们支离破碎的生活痛苦不堪，缺乏身体和精神的自由，无法排遣内心的孤独，人格常常被扭曲。他们在抗议社会的不公时往往遭到政府派出的军队残酷镇压，那是一个充满血腥、残暴、冷酷的时代，形成了南非独特的历史文化语境。

生于斯、长于斯的库切，对南非的历史状况了如指掌，对种族隔离制度深恶痛绝。然而，他清楚地知道，对于历史事件的记录与评价需要权威话语。他在小说中旗帜鲜明地表示出这样的理念：历史事件的客观性和合法性是由叙事行为赋予的，而叙事行为受到意识形态和个人主观愿望的控制，因此，建立在特定的意识形态基础上的虚构就不可避免。与此同时，社会中的个体，尤其是处于边缘他者的弱势个体就无法指望逃脱虚构历史的束缚。

库切在小说中展示的迈克尔·K的遭遇表明，边缘化他者的历史并非文字再现的真实，而是由权威话语者杜撰而成的虚构。K是一个卑微的生命体，沉默无息地生活在这个乱象丛生的社会里，然而，他却偏偏被当作“暴动分子”关了起来，可悲的是，“他还不知道当下在打仗”(130)。“他的历史”被记录成“纵火犯”、“劳工营的逃犯”和游击队的食品提供者。读者明白，这样的历史绝不是事实的记录，仅仅说明一个处于弱势个体的历史不得不任由他人虚构、任凭他人摆布。这幅表面看来平淡无奇的图景实质上极具持续的震撼力，使读者对历史理念禁不住产生颠覆的冲动。

库切隐身在营地医官身后所作的评论，更强化了作者认同的历史束缚性的观点。库切笔下的营地医官据称是唯一理解沉默无声的迈克尔·K的人。他对K的认知比较客观，认为后者习惯于自己的简单生活，全然不在意远处什么地方“历史的车轮在继续隆隆转动”(159)。对于这样的人是否能逃脱这种虚构历史的束缚？库切采用了较大篇幅来肯定、赞美K摆脱历史羁绊的努力。同时，他坚持指出人在历史中的无奈：“你会默默无闻地死去，并且要被埋在这个赛马场的一个角落里……除了我，没有人会记得你，除非你屈服并最终张开你的嘴。”他最后的呼吁“迈克尔斯：屈服吧”(152)清楚地表明，人，尤其是失去话语权的边缘他者，在人为的历史面前是多么的渺小和无能为力。

库切对权力的反思在某种程度上强化了以上观点。提到权力，人们往往会想到福柯的权力话语理论：“权力不是制度，不是结构，也不是天赋的某种力量，而是在特定社会里所处的复杂而至关重要的位置名称。”(Foucault 1978：93)这种位置具有对人们思想行为的控制力和支配力，并且在不同的文化和历史时期会不断发生变化。福柯从压抑机制上分析权力，将权力视为一种压抑性的力量。当然，权力会压抑自然、压抑本能、压抑个人，也压抑阶级。小说中，这种压抑性权力随处可见，南非人未经许可不得离开原地方行政管理区，高速公路沿线禁止停留，如果被发现在别人的草原上哪怕是在睡觉都有可能被枪杀，宵禁、路障、警车、如匪徒般的士兵，无一不昭示着种族隔离时代的控制与支配，无一不表现出南非当局的恐怖性威权。库切在检视弥漫在南非空气中的这些威权时，主要还是采用寓言体书写方式，除了揭示上述标志性压抑机制外，还采用大量诸如压迫蛤蟆的大石头等隐喻。不过，最明显的威权展示当属营地。大量安置营、改造营、拘留营的存在，标志着这个社会的压抑机制、隔离机制的完备。

库切刻意描写了一个兼作安置与改造的营地——加卡尔斯德里夫营地，以图诠释营地的威权运行机制。那里，“营地的周围是一道三米高的围栏，上面覆盖着一层蒺藜铁丝网”(73)。那里，有凶神恶煞模样全副武装的卫兵把守。不过，库切显然并没有想让读者将此地误解成监狱，因为，作为营地成员，被关进这里的人们"为了获得食物，得像营地里的所有人一样干活"(77)。因为，这里的人们可以在营地内活动，虽然不能随意离开营地。

这里的情境实际上就是黑人隔离居住区的写照，因为它具备了大型劳役营的特点，因为它与南非种族学会倡导的核心理论观点惊人地相似："所有班图人都在保留地有其固定的家园……班图人一出保留区既没有土地，也没有政治权利。"(Jaenecke 1981：153)因为这种理论，保留地以外的黑人都变成了自己国家的异己；因为这种理论，南非当局试图把所有黑人都赶进"家园"，希冀将70%的南非居民挤到占整个领土的13.7%的土地上。在这里，受威权压抑是常态，他们的基本人权缺失，唯有的权利就是干体力活。库切对营地的描写暴露了南非当局的权力机制运作，或者说规训的运行机制，在反思权力的同时，仿佛不经意间反思了当局的规训机制及其后果。

南非当局的权力运作机制，除了在主人公K的营地生活中得到诠释外，还典型地表现在库切描述的罗伯特入营经历上：此人曾经在农场工作，由于羊毛市场不景气而丢掉了工作，居无定所，被迫流浪，却被警察抓住，"关到加卡尔斯德里夫的铁丝网里面"(80)，因为当局不能容忍居民流动，因为流动人群会脱离规训的控制。美国著名女社会活动家胡克斯曾一针见血地指出，权力就"等于对人或物的统治与控制"(Hooks 1984：83)。要维护统治者的利益，就必须对失控对象强行安置。人们进入营地后，就当然失去了主体身份，失去了自由，每天都被当作潜在对象处于权威性监视之下。营地的本质特征是劳役，强制性劳动使营地成员筋疲力尽、无力进行其他思考，而权威话语权者认为，这才是规训所应该达到的效果，才能体现权力的威严。只有当威权者满意，营地成员才可能平安无事地待在这种被隔绝的"家园"之中，否则就有可能会遭遇更糟糕的命运，甚至丧失生命本体："你要是不合作，你就会到一个比这里更差的地方去……如果你活不下来，命不好，他们就把你的号码从名单上划掉，那就是你的下场!"(138)这并不是简单的威胁，而是南非现实生活中无法否定的客观存在。

库切还安排牧师布道，从宗教角度进一步强化了当局的威权和规训的合法性。牧师要求虔诚的信众"决不对任何人怀有怨恨，下决心生活在一起，追随你[上帝]的名，服从你的诫令"(83)。牧师的布道散发出一种潜移默化的规训气息，要求信众隐忍一切无法容忍之事，对于压抑性威权要逆来顺受，对于自由的丧失要认定是上帝的安排。这样，南非当局就可以顺利地控制、驾驭着营地成员的思维行动，使营地所有活动都纳入这种特定权力话语的限制之中。然而，库切采用K令人震撼的身体本能的反抗，最终成功逃离营地，走向自由世界的情节，特别是营地管理者对K争取自由并最终挣脱束缚获得自由的羡慕之情，彻底颠覆了营地医官原先的规训以及营地威权压制的合理性。

库切对创伤、历史、权力、规训等方面所作的反思，从根本上反映了作者对南非种族隔离制度下南非现状的深刻认识。殖民与种族隔离政策给南非人民留下的是一部创伤累累的历史，统治者们滥用威权，滥用规训，使得被边缘化他者大众生活在水深火热之中，当局还在一味掩盖真相。库切在《进入黑暗封闭的空间：作家与南非现状》一文中写道："如果人民在挨饿，那么就让他们远远地到丛林里去挨饿，在那里他们瘦骨嶙峋的身体不会受到责备；如果他们没有工作，如果他们迁徙到城市里，那么就设置起路障，发布宵禁令，就制定法律来反对流浪、乞讨和擅自占用土地，就将那些违法者关起来，这样就听不到他们、看不到他们。"(Coetzee 1992：361)库切对荒诞的当代现实社会的揭露和批评，对南非广漠大地上的世界末日感的展示，为时代、为世人认识这块土地、了解这里的生存状态提供了不可多得的借鉴，他在第三章以寓言的形式告诉读者，身处边缘他者地位的人群，可以利用沉默作为反抗的手段，可以提出自己的诉求，因为自由是弥足珍贵的，需要人们坚守自己的理想信念，需要人们的韧性追求。

五 结 语

库切在《迈克尔》中，利用边缘他者K"与其他人之间缺乏有意义联系"的经历，以寓言体书写形式，以"阿米巴变形虫"、竹节虫、蝼蚁等形态为隐喻来表现后基督时代暴力社会下层大众的生活状态，以沉默的卑微小人物与命运抗争、坚守自己的自由信念的故事感动读者，对后殖民语境下种族隔离思维中南非现状进行了批判性揭示。库切笔下的沉默他者具有撼人心魄的力量，最后的结局中"博大静谧、蔚蓝而空旷幽远的天空下……蓦然见到的一抹鲜绿"(183)和K有水"就能活命"(184)的乐观见地，给人以无尽的自由希望，这种希望不是罪恶的南非种族隔离制度能够扼杀的，它给了在困境中挣扎的边缘他者以活下去的勇气和信心。与《非洲共产党人》上署名文章观点恰恰相反的是，那些对认识和改造南非社会有兴趣的人应该能从迈克尔·K的生活和时代中得到深刻的启示。

参考文献：

Attwell, David. *J. M. Coetzee: South Africa and the Politics of Writing*[M]. Berkeley: University of California Press, 1993.

Clausewitz, Carl von. *On War*[M]. New York: Oxford University Press, 2007.

Coetzee, J. M. *Doubling the Point*[M]. ed. David Attwell. Cambridge, Massachusetts: Harvard University Press, 1992.

Dragunoiu, Dana. J. M. Coetzee's Life & Times of Michel K and the Thin Theory of the Good [J]. *The Journal of Commonwealth Literature* 41 (2006): 69 - 92.

Foucault, Michel. *The History of Sexuality*[M]. Trans. Robert Hurley. New York: Pantheon Books, 1978.

Franssen, Paul. Fleeing from the Burning City: Michel K, Vagrancy and Empire[J]. *English Studies* 5 (2003): 453 - 463.

Frazer, Elizabeth & Hutchings, Kimberly. On Politics and Violence: Arendt Contra Fanon[J]. *Contemporary Political Theory* 7 (2008): 90 - 108.

Gordimer, Nadine. Preface[A]. *Critical Perspectives on J. M. Coetzee*[C]. ed. Graham Huggan and Stephen Waston. London: Macmillan Press Limited, 1996. i - xii.

Head, Dominic. *J. M. Coetzee*[M]. Cambridge: Cambridge University Press, 1997.

Herman, Judith. *Trauma and Recovery*[M]. New York: Basic Books, 1997.

Herman, Vimala. *Dramatic Discourse: Dialogue as Interaction in Plays* [M]. London: Routeledge, 1995.

Hooks, Bell. *Feminist Theory: From Margin to Center* [M]. Boston USA: South End Press, 1984.

Kaplan, E. Ann. *Trauma Culture: The Politics of Terror and Loss in Media and Literature* [M]. London: Rutgers University Press, 2005.

Kratz, Henry. Review of *Life and Times of Michel K*. [J] *World Literature Today* 3 (1984): 461 - 462.

Levinson, Stephen C. *Pragmatics*[M]. Cambridge: Cambridge University Press, 1983.

Locke, John. *Two Treatises of Government* [M]. ed. Peter Laslett. Cambridge: Cambridge University Press, 1960.

Macarthur, Kathleen Laura. *The Things We Carried: Trauma and Aesthetic in Contemporary*

American Fiction[D]. George Washington University, 2005.

Marais, Michel. The Hermeneutics of Empire: Coetzee's Post-colonial Metafiction [A]. *Critical Perspectives on J. M. Coetzee*[C]. ed. Graham Huggan and Stephen Waston. London: Macmillan, 1996: 66 - 81.

Marijke, Van Vuuren. Beyond Words: Silence In William Golding's Darkness Visible and J. M. Coetzee's *Life and Times of Michel K*[J]. *English Studies in Africa* 1(2005): 93 - 106.

Marx, Karl. *Capital*[M]. Trans. Samuel Moore & Edward Aveling. marxists. org, 1999.

Nietzsche, Friedrich. *The Gay Science* [M]. ed. Bernard Williams. Cambridge: Cambridge University Press, 2001.

李维斯陀. 神话与意义. 王维兰,译. 台北:时报文化出版企业公司,1980.

耶内克. 白人老爷. 赵振权,董光祖,译. 北京:世界知识出版社,1981.

翟业军,刘永昶. 无神时代的约伯——论库切的《迈克尔 · K 的生活和时代》[J]. 外国文学,2006, 2: 70 - 72.

（原载《外文研究》2013 年第 2 期）

《夏日》:后现代另类"他传"小说

摘要:诺贝尔文学奖获奖小说家 J. M. 库切在移居澳大利亚后发表的重要小说《夏日》中,又一次独辟蹊径,隐身于叙事之外,设计了假设自己死亡后别人为自己作传、由与自己相关联的人物从不同视点评价还原自己形象的另类"他传"。作者在模式的革新、传主的隐身和客体化叙述表现、受访者的主体意识与对传主的碎片化记忆,在注重展示传主主导性方面真实可信的同时,强化细节的生动可读,在召唤读者参与解读、完成意义实现的过程中,为世界传记文学提供了新的样式。

关键词:库切;《夏日》;后现代传记;他传

中图分类号:I106.4 **文献标示码**:A **文章编号**:1005-7242(2013)04-0098-04

锐意创新的多产作家库切,在其至今已长达38年的文学创作过程中,不间断地进行充满他性的书写试验,发表小说、传记、评论集等21部风格特异的作品,显示出永不枯竭的活力。库切的每一部作品面世都给读者带来惊喜,带来别样的感受。"[库切]拒斥线性情节、完美人物、清晰背景与封闭式结尾等现实主义手法"(Canepari - Labid 2005: 15),对文学文本从情节安排、人物塑造、环境设计到叙事方式都进行过大量创新,包括文类借鉴混杂、文本相互指涉等文本形式革新。虽然大家明白,"如今,他被认为已跻身于当代小说家前沿队伍之中"(Attwell 1992: 1)。但是,他的新作问世在不断为大家带来惊喜的同时,依然会一如既往地受到读者和评论家质疑,通常情况下,人们质疑库切的文学创作能否归属小说样式。在近作《夏日》中,库切利用自己日记片段讲述了一个作家的故事,引起广泛关注,出版当年就毫无悬念地进入布克奖决选名单,然而,人们却在持续追问着该作品的样式问题。小说封底上引用的《每日电讯》评论代表了这种质疑的声音:“对于这本书,读者最想问的是:它到底是一部虚构的小说,还是一部回忆录?”

一般认为,《夏日》与先前出版的《男孩》(1997)和《青春》(2002)共同构成库切的自传三部曲,这可能与作者在几部书名下都加上“外省生活场景”字样有关系,当然从内容上看这三部作品记录的是传主从童年到壮年的历时相关经历。不过,这部书是否符合“自传是个体生活的历史与故事,趋于主张客观真理”(Vambe 2009:81)的标准?如果符合,是什么意义上的符合?这个问题倒确实值得研究。虽然作者在小说中采用了与《男孩》和《青春》同样的手法,将传主称作“他”而非“我”,亦即采用第三人称单数代替第一人称单数叙事,但是《夏日》与前两部传记的写作模式还是存在着巨大的差异。在小说中,库切又一次独辟蹊径,隐身于叙事之外,设计了假设自己死亡后别人为自己作传、由与自己相关联的人物从不同视点评价还原自己形象的另类“他传”。这种手法仿佛在读者面前展示了这样一幅画面:库切安排了自己的笔记,安排了传记作家的采访,安排了被采访者的话语,而他自己站在文本之外,看着各色人等的表演,口中得意地念念有词,自传是“他传或另一个自我的叙说”(Coullie 2006:1)。

众所周知,传记与小说的最大区别在于真实性与虚构性。《英国文学词典》强调传记应该注重真实权威性,认为“传记是历史的分支”(Wynne-Davies 1997:63)。英国著名作家、批评家“戴斯蒙德·麦卡锡(Desmond MacCarthy)将传记作家定义为发过誓的艺术家”(Garraty 1964:19)。传记是否真实已经成为衡量作品优劣的重要标准之一,传记需要保证以事实为本展示真相,而不是任意编造故事。人们在研究传记文学时,也往往不由自主地将注意力集中于真实与虚构问题上。然而,在后现代语境下,有些传记作家开始先锋派实验,他们或者利用真实的传记材料建构小说的主人公,用虚构小说形式来探讨传记相关问题①,也有作者独出心裁地将自己编织进传记文本中,竟然将自己想象成一个犹如英国著名传记作家鲍斯韦尔一样的年轻人,与当代美国政要展开访谈对话,为后者撰写回忆录②。因而,有学者说,“在后现代理论思潮的影响下,当代西方传记无论是在观念上,还是在形式上都活跃在纪实与虚构、传统与发展的边缘上”(唐岫敏

① 如英国作家 Julian Barnes1984 年发表的《福楼拜的鹦鹉》(*Flaubert's Parrot*),A. S. Byatt1990 年发表的《占有》(*Possession*)和 2001 年发表的《传记作家的故事》(*A Biographer's Tale*)等。

② 见美国当代传记作家 Edmund Morris1999 年发表的《荷兰人:罗纳德·里根回忆录》(*Dutch: A Memoir of Ronald Reagan*)。

2009：4）。对于现代社会中过分实验的传记形式，学界并不欣然认同，美国文学理论家斯坦利·费希应该算是这方面较为突出的代表人物，他曾采用激烈的言辞对此类实验批评说，"传记作者……只会不可靠，只会错误百出，只会说谎，只会拿自己的故事顶替公开传主的故事"（Fish 1999：A23）。不过，库切的自传三部曲应该不在费希批评之列，这在《夏日》中作者利用人物对话表现出的创作态度可以发现端倪。美国文学批评家罗利森曾经以欣喜的口吻说，"库切的《夏日》全然是一个意外"。"传记作者的采访对象，代表了不同年龄、不同国籍、不同性别、不同职业，却引人注目地得出了相似的结论。"（Rollyson 2010：71－72）这种意外除了上述原因外，还表现在，它既不像20世纪传记作家利顿·斯特拉奇批评19世纪传记时说的"[传记]是传主乏味的纪念碑"（Wynne-Davies 1997：64），也不像费希批评的当代实验传记作家那样置传主的事实真相于不顾，而是如英国后现代叙事研究者马克·柯里所说的那样，"选择能表现我们特性的事件，并按叙事的形式原则将它们组织起来，以仿佛在跟他人说话的方式将我们自己外化，从而达到自我表现的目的"。同时，"从外部，从别人的故事，尤其是通过与别的人物融为一体的过程进行自我叙述"（Currie 1998：17）。

库切在传记小说《夏日》中，刻意采用不同叙事模式，从不同叙事视角来建构小说的整体结构。全书共分三部分，头尾两部分为笔记，中间为访谈，客观上形成一种以客体化的传主意识记录包裹他人陈述言论的"三明治"格局。在这部出人意料的后现代文学文本中，第一部分聚合了8段"约翰·库切1972年至1975年间的笔记"（Coetzee 2009：19，下文此书引文只标页码）①。这些笔记革新记录方式，将记录者客体化后以第三人称"他"来替代自述记录，用"外化自我"的形式来表现自我。这些记录既包括仿佛客观地记录的南非生活中的暴力事件、库切的房屋修缮工程、南非诗人布莱顿巴赫、日本导演黑泽明的早期电影、遗嘱条款语言的解读、白人基督教文明、邻居与城市发展等，也包括采用斜体呈现的库切自己撰写的主观性评论备忘。第二部分是由英国青年传记作家文特森采访5位被访者的访谈录，即"从外部，从别人的故事"来叙述。这里有曾经与库切发生婚外情的现加拿大精神治疗师朱莉娅·弗兰克尔，与库切关系密切的表姐玛戈特·琼克尔，指责库切试图勾引在其英语补习班学习的玛丽娅·瑞吉娜和自己的巴西人艾

① 括号内数字为小说《夏日》页码，出自"*Summertime* by J. M. Coetzee, published by Harvill Secker in London in 2009"，中文为自译。

德里安娜·纳西门托太太。还有两位库切在开普敦大学曾经的同事,一位是曾经参加同场面试竞聘同一职位、"20世纪70年代离开南非再也没有回去过的"南非裔英国公民马丁,另一位是曾经与他在70年代"合作开设过非洲文学课"(221)并保持过一段情人关系的索菲·戴努埃勒太太。这些采访的时间跨度为8个月(2007年底至2008年中),空间跨度为美非欧(加拿大、南非、巴西、英国、巴黎)三大洲。几位被访者在讲述她/他们与库切的故事的同时,从不同侧面中叙述他们对库切的印象,直接评价库切的各个方面。第三部分又回归"用外化自我"形式表现自我的做法,在这里呈现了5段标有"未标明日期的片段"字样的笔记,这些片段与第一部分的片段的记叙方式几近相同,同样的客体化叙述者,同样的评论性备忘。不同的是,几个片段几乎都在讲述库切与父亲的经历与故事——父子俩的孤独与冲突,库切对父亲的愧疚与理解,当然也有对故事构想的勾勒和写作方式的展示。

作者设计的这三个部分之间应该说存在着逻辑关联:第一部分是看上去互不相关的散乱笔记与库切的备忘性记录,一方面见证了作家库切作为独立个体的社会意识,另一方面以传主的意识形态和生活经历记录为叙述者提供了全方位采访、深入了解传主的契机。在第二部分,这些采访对象之间仿佛毫无关系,传记作家选择她/他们,表面上存在着随意性和偶然性,而且这些人物的叙述也好像充满不确定性和非中心性。但是,传记作家文森特对这些人的选择并非盲目随机,而是因为他/她们各自与传主存在扯不断的关系,而且,他/她们提供的片段甚至碎片式零星印象,拼贴起来就可能会形成一个完整的形象。第三部分似乎过多地着墨于传主的父亲,但是,隐含在深处的联系却不应该被忽略:作者在展示传主父亲孤独无助的同时,难道没有暗示传主自己的孤僻不合群?在表达传主对父亲不恭后感受到的悔恨、在面对父亲需要护理而不得不作出抉择时突兀地结束时,难道不是召唤着读者在阅读中对这未定点进行确定、对这刻意的留白进行填补?

事实上,传主约翰·库切在这部"他传"小说中一直处于一个十分独特的地位。作者刻意设计的传主死亡,从客观上使所有相关人物都处在回溯往事状态之中,无论从时间还是从空间上都与传主拉开了距离,使他们在回忆中更加理性地评价传主。不过,作者从来就不是循规蹈矩的人,他那一反常规的"三明治"式构架设计,文本中各部分内容呈现方式的标新立异,使受众惊愕的同时忍不住卷入其中,因为,无论是位于前后客体化的传主笔记还是置于中间的他人叙说和评论都呈现出零散、片段,甚至游离状态,需要读者去搜索、去拼贴相关叙述与评述。库切为读者提供了参与诠释的机会，这应该符合后现代文学的互动特征，符合文学接受理论家伊瑟尔的“交流”①观点。

传主的前8段记录以第三人称单数叙述，明显可以看出传主试图抽身而出、客观表现的愿望，然而，斜体部分评论性备忘仿佛有意无意地泄露了他的存在。正如前文所述，作者选择的这些记录集中在20世纪70年代，而这个时代用受访者茱莉亚的话来说是“南非种族隔离最残酷的时期”(21)，这与传主笔记中对当时非洲的定位——“非洲：一个饿殍遍野、嗜血如命的小丑骑在百姓头上作威作福的地方”(4)——遥相呼应，形成时空相互印证、互相勾连的文本。在这个时代里，任何人不可能无动于衷，不可能置身之外。笔记涉及父亲对南非暴力政治的轻蔑和不屑，以沉湎于板球比分来应对南非丑恶的政治，涉及传主从创造性工作退却到无需费脑的劳作之无奈，涉及人们对南非诗人布莱顿巴赫那种羡慕妒忌恨的态度以及对黑泽明电影《生之欲》近乎本能的反应，所有这一切无不清楚地表明，零散的片段内藏深意，碎片召唤着读者的参与，无怪乎美国后现代主义作家巴塞尔姆借小说中的一个人物之口说出了碎片是我信任的唯一形式的创作宣言。这里，传主的片段性笔记至少可以用作拼贴构建其完整形象的导引和受访者深入讨论的缘由，而斜体备忘则如超小说中的作者直接跳出言说一样发挥了警醒受众的作用。在访谈部分，读者常常看到，受访者在以自己为中心展开叙事，全然不在乎传主在其中的中心地位。在这里，谁是主角已然失去了重要性，重要的是让文本各个相关者注意到有关传主的片段信息，注意到拼贴建构信息的原则，注意到独特的库切式“他传”的构建方式。

访谈录中，作者已然隐身缺场，“从外部，从别人的故事进行自我叙述”。库切仿佛将话语权悉数交给了传记作家文森特和不同的受访者。这些人的叙述、对话或内心独白，共同构建了一个不修边幅、孤独而固执的形象。在茱莉亚眼里，库切“像是一只失去活力的鸟，身上有着衰败的气息”(21)，他“面对这个世界，充满警觉、自我防卫”(25)，“像是一种孤独症患者”(53)，“通常他那颗心裹在铠甲里”(83)。玛戈特认为，传主“害羞并不清高。喜欢独处”(100)。他“封闭着自己的心扉”(102)，“没有计划、没有野心，只有一些不着边际的渴望”(128)。在艾德里安娜看来，库切先生“衣着很差、头发剪得很糟，还

① 沃尔夫冈·伊瑟尔在评价现代文学时说，“文学作品是一种交流形式”(Iser ix)，认为文学文本的意义需要读者的参与交流才能实现。

留着胡子……就像一个僧侣似的，失去了男性气质……看上去一副心神不宁的模样”(160)；他是“孤僻的”(171)，“一个孤独而怪癖的年轻人，整天埋头读古老的哲学书”(191)，“此人灵魂脱离了肉体”(198)。索菲对他的印象是“比较严肃、比较内向”(224)。“他天生是一个非常谨慎的人，很像一只乌龟。”(238)“他完全不是搞政治的材料。”(228)五位受访者中唯一的男性马丁对库切的评价是“不合时宜的人，骨子里是一个谨慎的人”(215)。库切的政治倾向、生活态度、宗教信仰等等皆散落在这些受访者的叙述之中，需要读者去从仿佛海量的信息中去攫取，然后拼贴，因为，这些受访者从自己的视角出发，有时采用独白形式呈现往昔记忆、当时的意识流动，有时又在与采访者互动对话中拓展思绪。这里的评论、平等对话既有超小说的特点，又有复调小说的众声喧哗特征，更有与传记、自传大相径庭的写法。确实，在仿佛主次颠倒的情节和记录中，库切突出地表现了自己认定的“他传”特征。

在这种“他传”小说中，虽然作者隐身离场，但是，毕竟这里传记作者和采访者的话语都是作者精心设计的，他掌握着对话双方的话语脉络，更显示出他自己独特的“他传”立场。库切对传主的评价是有节制的，体现了他一贯低调为人的风格。在受访者的队伍里，他最后安排了批评家索菲，而索菲对传主的评价应该是作者的自画像：

> “我知道他有许多仰慕者，他的诺贝尔奖不是凭空得来的。可是，……我并没有从他那儿得到那蓦然照亮世界的灵光的启迪。……我觉得约翰很聪明，我觉得他知识面很广，我在许多方面都很佩服他。作为一个作家，他知道自己在做什么，他有某种风格，而风格就是与众不同的开端。……他只是一个人，是他那个时代的人，有才干，甚至天分很高，但是，坦白说，不是一个巨匠。”(242)

库切的创作态度是严谨的，用索菲的话说，他的作品“过于沉稳、过于规整”(242)。他不允许传记作者胡编乱造，安排玛戈特直截了当地对传记作者说，“现在我得提抗议了。你真的太过分了。我根本没有说过这么离谱的话。你是把自己的话塞进了我的嘴里”(119)。这种抗议虽然并不经常出现，但清楚地表明了作者的“他传”立场，库切可以容忍传记作品中以不同视角看待问题，可以容忍述说的形象不够完整，也可以容忍无意出现的记忆错误，但无法容忍有意或者恶意编造，除了抗议之外，他还利用受访者公开地制止此类行为,说,"你不能这么写。你不能这么来。你这是在编造故事。"(137)以此来明确表现自己坚决而认真的态度。如果说受访者的这些声音还不够有分量的话,那么,库切安排的文森特的即时回应应该强化了这种观点:"对不起我渲染得太过分了。我会修改的。我会把调子处理得缓和一些。"(119)他明确表示,"我会删掉的"(137)。不过,库切明白,他在这里推出的是一位作家的传记,而不是历史大事记载,在无碍大局的细微之处采用一些虚构的手法应该也无伤大雅。比如,他让茱莉亚在生动地回顾了三四十年前的琐细对话后,理直气壮地对传记作家文森特说,"坦白地说,这里涉及的对话部分,我一般都是编的。我觉得应该允许这样,因为我们是在谈论一个作家"(32)。他甚至让后者坦率地说,"我加一两个细节,以便让场景更生动一些"(105)。因为,这是文学文本自身的需要,在他看来,"他传"小说绝非"传主枯燥乏味的纪念碑",为了作品的可读性,可以适量增加细节的生动性;而且特别需要注意的是,叙述者应该采用适当的叙事视角与叙事语调。这就是为什么他安排文森特对玛戈特说,"由于你的叙述太长,我在各处作了一些改编,让人物用自己的口吻说话"(87)。《夏日》的语调是丰富生动的,为库切的"他传"小说理念增色不少,限于篇幅,恕不展开。

库切在非同凡响的《夏日》中利用人物谈及文学创作时指出,这是"面对时间的一种拒绝姿态,是面向永恒的努力"(61)。他以自己独特的方式在面向永恒进行着努力,因为"我要不写作就会感到很压抑"(60)。作者不断地创新,以独特的风格表现了自己心目中的"他传"小说。这种独特,表现在模式的革新、传主的隐身和客体化叙述表现、受访者的主体意识与对传主的碎片化记忆,在注重展示传主主导性方面真实可信的同时,强化细节的生动可读,在召唤读者参入解读、完成意义实现的过程中,为世界传记文学提供了新的样式。

参考文献:

[1] Attwell, D. Editor's Introduction[C]. *Doubling the Point: Essays and Interviews*. Cambridge, Massachusetts; London, England: Harvard University Press, 1992.

[2] Canepari-Labid, M. *Old Myths-Modern Empires: Power, Language and Identity*[M]. Bern: Peter Lang, 2005.

[3] Coetzee, J. M. *Summertime* [M]. London: Harvill Secker, 2009.

[4] Coullie, J. L., S. Meyer, T. H. Ngwenya & T. Olver. *Selves in Question: Interviews on Southern*

African Autobiography: Writing Past Colonialism [M]. Honolulu: University of Hawaii Press, 2006.

[5] Currie, M. *Postmodern Narrative Theory*[M]. London: Macmillan Press Limited, 1998.

[6] Fish, S. Just published: Minutiae without meaning[J]. *The New York Times* 7 September 1999.

[7] Garraty, J. A. *The Nature of Biography*[M]. New York: Vintage Books, 1964.

[8] Rollyson, C. A biographer's virtues[J]. *The New Criterion* 5 (2010): 71 - 72.

[9] Vambe, M. T. Fictions of Autobiographical Representations[J]. *Journal of Literary Studies* 25.1 (2009): 80 - 97.

[10] Wynne - Davies, M. *Dictionary of English Literature*[M]. London: Bloomsbury Publishing plc, 1997.

[11] 唐岫敏. 斯特拉奇与"新传记"——历史与文化的透视[M]. 太原：山西人民出版社,2009.

[12] 伊瑟尔,沃尔夫冈. 虚构与想象——文学人类学疆界[M]. 陈定家,等,译. 长春：吉林人民出版社,2003.

（原载《外语研究》2013 年第 3 期）

论 J. M. 库切的小说创作

摘要：2003 年诺贝尔文学奖得主 J. M. 库切自首部小说《幽暗之地》问世到最新小说《凶年纪事》发表为止，一直在不停地进行着创新实验。这些跨越 30 余载的小说充满着他性的辉光，不断地给读者带来惊喜，为深化小说样式内涵、拓展小说外延起到积极的作用，为当代小说创新提供了极其可贵的启示。

关键词：J. M. 库切；他性；小说创作

中图分类号：I106.4　**文献标示码**：A　**文章编号**：1671－2129(2013)02－0069－05

J. M. 库切的文学创作往往以出人意料的创新性而著称于世，他以其特立独行的他者风格，写出大量“篇幅有限而范围无限”的作品，被称为是能够“想象出无法想象的东西”的“后现代寓言家”①。早在《幽暗之地》1974 年发表之时，南非著名评论家乔纳森·克鲁就在南非文学杂志《对比》上刊文热情地称其为南非第一次出现的现代小说。评论家黑德则走得更远，他在《剑桥库切入门》中直接宣称，“后现代主义据说是随着 1974 年 J. M. 库切第一部小说《幽暗之地》发表而来到非洲的”②。这种评论是否精准可能有待商榷，但是，库切的小说处女作带给南非文学界的影响决不能低估。

既然评论家将库切的小说发表与南非文学创作的后现代主义联系在一起，那么，我

① Wästberg，Per. Award Ceremony Speech [EB/OL]. 6 June 2013 <http：//www.nobelprize.org/nobel_prizes/literature/laureates/2003/presentation-speech.html>.

② Head，Dominic. *The Cambridge Introduction to J. M. Coetzee* [M]. Cambridge：Cambridge University Press，2009. ix.

们有理由相信，这部小说应该给南非文学带来了推动性力量，这种力量必定与南非文学传统不相一致但却与世界文学发展趋势合辙。库切研究专家斯蒂芬·沃森的评论不仅重新界定了克鲁的说法，认为克鲁说的"现代小说"实际上应该是"现代主义小说或后现代主义小说"，而且旗帜鲜明地支持了黑德的观点，认为"从来没有一部南非小说如此明显、甚至有意识地摆脱现实主义传统，如此坦诚地宣布自己的非真实性、虚构性"[①]。众所周知，南非50年代黑人文学通常不会显露政治意识形态，作家善意地期待着各民族之间的对抗会促成一个多民族和平相处、共生共存的和谐局面；60年代南非文学倾向性较为明显，自从臭名昭著的沙佩维尔惨案[②]发生后，文学作品大力表现的是黑人反抗种族歧视，探讨的是作家们的共同感受——他们不再试图维持那种由善意的白人和有耐性的黑人共同努力来改善政治生态的虚妄幻想。其实，南非文学在相当长时间里就是在采用现实主义手法表现幻想与幻灭，主题较为局限，形式较为传统。

《幽暗之地》的问世，不仅为南非文学界带来全新的主题，而且带来别样的文学样式。这部小说首先突破了文学范式、叙事模式的制约，采用将相隔两个世纪仿佛毫不相干的故事并置，以隐喻的方式展示"厌恶人类的两种形式，其一为知性与夸大狂式的厌恶，另一为充满原始活力的厌恶，两者之间互为映照"[③]。库切的小说因而跳出了南非传统文学创作的禁锢，突破了狭隘的南非黑白之间争斗的主题，突破了小说创作的头身尾线性发展模式，作家审视的目光不再仅仅注视着南非本土黑白的争斗，而是投向世界，关注人性疏离异化等人类共同的话题。库切将以元小说特征明显的文本与他性充分的虚拟译本并置，因而便穿梭在两个世纪之间、穿梭在美国人与布尔人[④]之间，这种具有典型后现代文学特征的小说出现在20世纪70年代的南非，无疑对南非文学造成震撼性影响。库切能写出当时如此先锋派的小说，与他本人此前的经历与所受的影响不无关系。

① Waston, Stephen. Colonialism and Novels of J. M. Coetzee [C]// Huggan, Graham, Stephen Watson. *Critical Perspectives on J. M. Coetzee*. London: Macmillan Press Ltd., 1996. 15.

② 南非白人种族主义政权大规模屠杀非洲人的惨案。1960年3月21日，南非德兰士瓦省沙佩维尔镇的非洲人举行大规模的示威游行，反对南非白人当局推行种族歧视的"通行证法"。南非当局出动大批军警镇压示威群众，致使72名非洲人被枪杀，240多名被打伤，造成了震惊世界的"沙佩维尔惨案"。

③ Engdahl, Horace Oscar Axel. The Nobel Prize in Literature — Press Release[J]. (2003-10-2)[2013-6-6]. http://www.nobelprize.org/nobel_prizes/literature/laureates/2003/press.html.

④ 南非的荷兰、法国和德国白人移民后裔形成的混合民族。来源于荷兰语Boer(农民)一词。今布尔人的后裔多指阿非利堪人(Afrikaner)。

在英国工作期间他于1962—1963年对著名作家福特的研究①,1965年赴美国德克萨斯大学采用计算机语体分析方法对荒诞派戏剧创始人之一和集大成者塞缪尔·贝克特的研究②,博士毕业后在美国纽约州立大学的文学教学经历,作为南非人在美国反越战抗议以及随后的遭遇、长时间内浸淫在英美文化中的感受,使库切对当代意识形态、文学创作理论与实践产生了独特的认识。尤其是他对贝克特的潜心研究给他留下的沁入骨髓的影响,使他在尝试文学创作伊始就站在了时代的前列。

从库切的回忆来看,他研究福特是因为美国著名现代派诗人、意象派代表人物埃兹拉·庞德认为福特是"当代最优秀的散文文体家"。他经过研究后发现,"福特给人的印象是,他从英国统治阶级内部写作,但事实上,他是作为一个局外人、作为一个对此有点渴望的局外人在写作"③。这种局外人书写的视角,确实也影响到了他的创作。这种影响并没有让库切在创作中模仿福特的风格,而是启发他注意到如何更有效地利用局外人立场,使他站在他者的立场上书写,而这种站在他者立场上进行他性书写的风格在其以后的文学创作中一直占有重要的地位。

其实,影响库切最大的应该是贝克特。他在博士论文之外还曾写过一系列文章专门谈论贝克特,这些评论性文章清楚地表明了他对贝克特的认知和欣赏。阿特维尔采访时曾对库切说"你对贝克特的评论似乎不仅回应了设计重复的活动,而且回应了你的虚构"④。库切明确地告诉阿特维尔,"贝克特对于我自己的写作意义重大——那一定是毫无疑问的……我对贝克特的评论不仅是学术训练……而且是企图接近一种秘密——我想要拥为己有的贝克特的秘密"⑤。其实,库切通过严格的学术训练获得了贝克特的精髓,而且,在汲取运用这些精髓时得到了无比的快乐。"贝克特的散文……给了我感官的快乐,这么多年来这种快乐一直没有暗淡过。我对贝克特所作的批评来源于这种

---

① 1963年,库切以一篇研究福特·马多克斯·福特的论文获得开普敦大学文学硕士学位。其英国经历后来出现在自传三部曲的第二部《青春》(2002)中。

② 该研究论文于1969年帮助库切获得德克萨斯大学语言学博士学位。

③ Coetzee, J. M. *Doubling the Point* [M]. Cambridge, Massachusetts: Harvard University Press, 1992. 20.

④ Coetzee, J. M. *Doubling the Point* [M]. Cambridge, Massachusetts: Harvard University Press, 1992. 22.

⑤ Coetzee, J. M. *Doubling the Point* [M]. Cambridge, Massachusetts: Harvard University Press, 1992. 25.

感官反应。”[①]这种快乐潜移默化地影响了他的小说创作，而后他创作大量的寓言体小说虽然说与南非政治生态不无关系，但是，最重要的还是与他的贝克特研究相关。

上述讨论可以看出，库切的《幽暗之地》创作别出机杼有据可依，而初试身手就在南非文坛引起巨大反响，激发了库切的创作热情，也促使库切走上了一条不断挑战自我、挑战文学模式和叙事方式之路，而且每一次新的尝试都为阅读大众和创作者、评论者群体带来惊喜，他的特殊身份[②]使其一直站在局外人的立场冷眼看世界，而体现其不断追求的文学创作则永远给人以别样的感受。结果，“他尽管每一部小说都聚焦于南非，但是，他的后现代、超小说关注无疑使他比大多数作家更加国际化，使他获得世界范围内认可”[③]。

库切破冰式小说《幽暗之地》虽然触动了南非文学界，但第一次真正使库切获得国际声誉的小说还是诺贝尔文学奖颁奖词中提到的“有康拉德遗风的政治惊悚小说”[④]《等待野蛮人》(1980)。该小说在出版当年就获得英国最古老的文学奖“詹姆斯·泰特·布莱克纪念奖”，次年又获得英国费伯小说纪念奖。这部在库切获得诺贝尔文学奖后被企鹅丛书收入“20 世纪伟大图书”的小说深得贝克特等人真传，“《等待野蛮人》在很多地方与卡夫卡(《在流放地》)、霍桑和无处不在的贝克特文本产生互文”[⑤]。这与库切所受影响相关，也与他追求独特的他者写作风格有关。正如库切研究专家多维所说，“库切小说利用拉康被割裂的主体的观念(在文本与叙事之间割裂)，设法达到逃离与主流话语共谋的目的”[⑥]。小说采用后现代政治寓言形式，“通过将野蛮人建构成精

---

① Coetzee, J. M. *Doubling the Point* [M]. Cambridge, Massachusetts: Harvard University Press, 1992. 20.

② 库切是南非出生的荷兰人后代，自小在南非黑白对抗的环境中接受英语教育，开普敦大学毕业后去英国做计算机程序员的工作，后去美国德克萨斯大学攻读博士学位，后留美担任大学文学教师，因抗议越战而导致绿卡申请被拒，回到开普敦大学教授文学。成长经历造就了他一直处于边缘、局外的感觉。

③ Canepari - Labib, Michela. *Old Myth — Modern Empires Power: Language and Identity in J. M. Coetzee's Work* [M]. Oxford, Bern, Berlin: Peter Lang, 2005. 14.

④ Engdahl, Horace Oscar Axel. The Nobel Prize in Literature — Press Release[J]. (2003 - 10 - 2) [2013 - 6 - 6]. http://www.nobelprize.org/nobel_prizes/literature/laureates/2003/press.html.

⑤ Newman, Judie. Intertexuality, Power and Danger: *Waiting for the Barbarians* as a Dirty Diary [C]// Sue Kossew. *Critical Essays on J. M. Coetzee.* New York: G. K. Hall & Co., 1998. 127.

⑥ Dovey, Teresa. J. M. Coetzee: Writing in the Middle Voice [C]. Sue Kossew. *Critical Essays on J. M. Coetzee.* New York: G. K. Hall & Co., 1998. 19.

致而荒唐的想象而破解了'文明/野蛮'二元论"①。从传统意义上看,文明人建立在假想野蛮人存在的基础之上,而文明的标准通常是由主流权威话语者制定,欧洲白人与非洲有色人种因而被轻而易举地建构成"文明/野蛮"二元论的两极。小说中,库切站在南非被欺压、被蹂躏者的立场,通过暴露欧洲白人文明者的野蛮行径形式,表现霸权时代的种族他者、性别他者和身份他者的遭遇,揭秘殖民霸权时代帝国文明的真相。这部形式特别、寓意深刻的他性小说为南非文学、世界文学提供了切实可行的小说样式。

三年后发表的小说《迈克尔·K的生活与时代》(1983)堪称库切文学成就的第一个高潮,该小说甫一出版便不同凡响,被认为是"肯定生命的小说",进入决选名单后击败呼声最高的萨尔曼·拉什迪的《耻辱》,一举获得当年英国文学最高奖——布克奖。该小说明显地受奥地利作家卡夫卡影响,将寓言体小说发展到一个新的高度。黑德的评论代表了学界的观点:"很清楚,库切处理边缘化和异化的手法与卡夫卡相似。"②库切在小说中对局外人或者说边缘化他者的处理到达了几乎出神入化的地步,为南非后现代文学注入了新的范本,同时也为小说的经典化奠定了稳固的基础。库切本人并不否认卡夫卡作品对小说《迈克尔·K的生活与时代》创作的影响。在一次访谈中,他曾经明确地说,"你问到卡夫卡对我小说的影响,我承认这种影响。"不过,"字母K并非只有一种解释。"③库切的说法真实可信,确实,他的小说受到过卡夫卡的影响,受到过贝克特的影响,但是,正如前文所述,这种影响是库切在深入研究过这些作家后沁入骨髓并化为自己意识的影响,没有任何模仿别人的痕迹。他从局外人视野解读南非种族隔离制度下社会的动荡、人民的苦难,为被边缘化他者化的普通人仗义执言,为话语权缺失的人们呐喊。小说蕴含丰富,寓意深刻,任何一种单向度的解释都将流于片面,给南非文学界带来的启示重大,意义深远。

库切接下来推出的小说《福》(1986)显示出鲜明的后现代主义特征。作者采用去

① Ashcroft, Bill. Irony, Allegory and Empire: *Waiting for the Barbarians* and *In the Heart of the Country* [C]// Sue Kossew. *Critical Essays on J. M. Coetzee*. New York: G. K. Hall & Co., 1998. 107.

② Head, Dominic. *The Cambridge Introduction to J. M. Coetzee* [M]. Cambridge: Cambridge University Press, 2009. 56.

③ Coetzee, J. M. *Doubling the Point* [M]. Cambridge, Massachusetts: Harvard University Press, 1992. 199.

经典的方式将有英国启蒙时期现实主义小说家、被誉为“英国和欧洲小说之父”的作家笛福(Defoe)姓氏前缀“de”[①]去除(有趣的是,“de”本身除经常与贵族姓氏相连外就有“去除”的意思),大有去经典、去贵族化、去规范化、去传统性的意思,使作家“笛福”还原成作家“福”。当然,《福》与笛福的《鲁滨逊漂流记》之间明显的互文关系无法否认。虽然它紧随在布克奖获奖小说之后出版,不免使读者对其存在更多的期待,因而使一些人感到失望,但是,在这部“去”字当头的小说中,库切显现出非同寻常的他性特征,用哈根与沃森的话说,“他[库切]的小说好像有意这样建构,以图逃避任何一种阐释框架”[②]。他选取白人女性苏珊作为主要叙述人物,引入女性声音以填补笛福小说中缺席的声音,试图以此与男性声音相抗衡,尽管“性别与[苏珊]缺乏叙事权威相关”[③]。除了在文本中重构女性话语、挑战白人男性作家权威以外,作者还特别注意表现沉默黑人男性的觉醒,揭秘历史写作中的权力结构,试图解构父权与殖民霸权,为女性群体和殖民地弱势群体寻求话语权。在文本中,作者采用诸如拼贴、互文、超小说、开放式结局等后现代主义创作手法,展示历史的多面性、复杂性并提供解构历史的新路径。小说为读者提供多重阐释空间的同时,为南非文学提供了文学新品。

1994 年因为种族隔离制度被废除而在南非历史上十分重要,而这一年发表的《彼得堡的大师》也“标志着库切文学生涯的转折点”。库切的这种转折体现在他在作品中表现的与前一部小说《铁器时代》一样的“政治相关性与迫切性”[④],正如毕晓普所说,“在这部作品的进程中,库切对政治身份的关注变得越来越明显”[⑤]。同时,这种转折还表现在他的创作手法的运用上。他借用自美国回到南非开普敦大学教授文学时的俄罗斯文学研究成果,尤其是陀思妥耶夫斯基专题研究成果,在小说中创造了一个具有

---

① 笛福原姓福,1703 年后自己在姓前面加上听起来如同贵族的“de”的前缀,形成笛福(Defoe)这一笔名。

② Huggan, Graham, Stephan Watson. Introduction [C]// Huggan, Graham, Stephen Waston. *Critical Perspectives on J.M. Coetzee*. London: Macmillan Press Limited, 1996. 1.

③ Hutcheon, Linda. The Politics of Impossible Worlds [C]// Mihailescu, Calin - Andrei, Walid Hamarneh. *Fiction Updated: Theories of Fictionality, Narratology, and Politics*. Toronto: U of Toronto P, 1996. 218.

④ Head, Dominic. *The Cambridge Introduction to J. M. Coetzee* [M]. Cambridge: Cambridge University Press, 2009. 72.

⑤ Bishop, Scott G. “J. M. Coetzee's Foe: A Culmination and a Solution to a Problem of White Identity.” [J] *World Literature Today* 64(1990): 56.

自主意识的陀思妥耶夫斯基形象。库切将这位文学大师设计成因继子巴维尔(Pavel)亡故来到彼得堡,而在调查中,与巴维尔相关的一些人物包括无政府主义者涅恰耶夫(Nechaev)、帝国警察马克西莫夫(Maximov)都自然进入陀思妥耶夫斯基的精神生活,使作者无法不与政治相牵连。此外,库切在叙事形式上进行大胆革新,他采用现在时共时叙事向传统叙事规约提出挑战,使包括陀思妥耶夫斯基在内的人物具有独立的声音、开放的他人意识,不断发出有价值的议论,与作者形成多重平等的对话关系。巴赫金在谈到陀思妥耶夫斯基长篇小说基本特点时说,"有着众多的各自独立而不相融合的声音和意识,由具有充分价值的不同声音组成的真正复调"①。而《彼得堡的大师》不仅具有所有这些特征,并且将陀思妥耶夫斯基拉入对话关系之中,故被认为是复调的复调,库切的创作因此而表现出独特的他性特征。

帮助库切第二次获得英联邦布克奖的小说《耻》(1999)代表着作者创作的第二个高潮。与作者早期作品相比,该小说现实意识更强。作者站在他者的立场,冷眼审视南非社会转型时期——后种族隔离时代的严峻社会现状。长期以来的殖民主义、种族隔离时代产生的历史伤痛记忆在人们心灵中已经留下难以泯灭的创伤,这些创伤并不会随着白人统治结束而被人遗忘。当原先的主体与他者之间关系被人为地颠倒后,如何认识历史变迁后新时代中的黑白关系,失去殖民政策护佑的白人殖民者后裔如何与这片黑人聚集之地上的原始居民和平共处,饱受种族隔离历史创伤之痛的南非人民怎样才能走出心灵创伤的阴影,是小说关注的重点。作者以"耻"为引,展示耻的内涵,这里既揭示了个体层面之耻,更暗示着群体层面之耻。他不仅探讨帝国主义殖民造成的历史旧账与殖民者后裔个体应当承担的责任问题,而且在设法探究如何解决问题的途径。不过,在探讨人类和解之途时,小说《耻》沿袭了《铁器时代》和《彼得堡的大师》中的宽恕主题,而宽恕通常与忏悔联系在一起,然而,"忏悔当时成为管控社会禁锢个人意识的一种工具,其真实目的因而被消解。"作者明白工具性忏悔无法得到宽恕,永远达不到和解的目的,故而,"库切一直在试验着忏悔模式,而在这里他采用不同的方式接近这个问题"②。他从被颠覆的他者视角出发,表现自己对黑人文化取代白人文化并

① [前苏联]巴赫金. 陀思妥耶夫斯基的诗学问题[M]. 白春仁,顾亚玲,译. 北京:生活·读书·新知三联书店,1988. 29.

② Head, Dominic. *The Cambridge Introduction to J. M. Coetzee* [M]. Cambridge: Cambridge University Press, 2009. 77.

没有带来观念进步和社会和谐而感到的困惑，在展示后种族隔离时代南非的矛盾冲突之时，注重呈现殖民者后裔在白人统治结束后沦为地位被颠覆的他者的境遇，通过人物露西和受害女生之父的言论与行为，反思殖民者的作为，寄托和谐之愿望。

移居澳大利亚阿德莱德后发表的第一部作品《伊丽莎白·科斯特洛》(2003)他性特征更加鲜明，这部可谓是讲座式小说或小说式讲座是库切为文学长廊提供的新画卷。在此式样新颖的画卷上，他者作用得到更加充分的发挥，在他性十足的女作家与不同角色的不断抗争中，在对其进行质疑挑战的过程中，库切不仅讨论了非洲文学创作、非洲人文学科问题，而且讨论了人类、自然界诸多热点问题，在这部篇幅不大的作品里，库切讨论哲学、伦理学、心理学、人类学、诗学、动物生命等充满思辨色彩的众多话题，涉猎之广，令人诧异，他似乎想利用作品人物告诉读者，哲学语言或许并非女作家科斯特洛的强项，她在讲座中不能自如地运用哲学语言说服听众纯属正常，但是，学术讨论并非仅有哲学语言，采用诗学语言、虚构故事形式讨论哲理性问题同样能够帮助思考、探索真理，并且可以取得意想不到的效果。这部引起学者和批评家争论其文类归属的作品，以其特有的他性色彩，为文学创作和批评拓展了小说范畴，增加了新的样式。

如果说《伊丽莎白·科斯特洛》在小说样式上进行了富有争议的创新的话，《凶年纪事》(2007)在叙事模式上的革新则应该是标新立异之举。因为，前者采用了将讲座与故事相融合的方式来构建新的小说样式，这种建构虽然他性明显，但依然具有小说的基本要素，即作者创造了一以贯之的人物，讲述了她在不同时间不同地点讲座的经历，这里有人物塑造，有情节发展，有矛盾冲突，有高潮有结局，有对话关系有心理活动等等，当然还有传统小说所不具备的成分，即作者通过不同的"课"来明确传达讲座之内核；而后者虽然也不乏传统小说的基本成分，但作者表现这些成分时采用的手法出乎读者意外，他为读者刻意设置了阅读障碍。库切在作品中采用的是以技术手段来造成视觉冲击的手法，以鲜明的他性视图——在书页里加平行线，在叙事中形成客观上的共时特征，即上中下三栏同时发生、共时发展的方式，边发表言论、记录思想边推进故事，在众声喧哗中完成创作意图。作者因此为读者与评论界留下了"不穷尽小说样式誓不停止文学创新实验"的印象。

库切自投身文学创作以来，共发表小说 12 部以及其他大量作品①。这些作品不仅奠定了他在南非文学中的地位(三次获得南非最高文学奖"CNA 奖")，更重要的是获得了世界文学的认同，先后获得英联邦最高文学奖"布克奖"(1989，1999)、法国费米娜奖、以色列耶路撒冷奖、《爱尔兰时报》国际小说奖等国际重要奖项，并于 2003 年荣膺诺贝尔文学奖。诺贝尔文学奖颁奖委员会在评价库切时以高度凝练的语言评说他是"一位审慎的怀疑者"，认为他"以无数姿态表现了局外人令人诧异的牵连"，"无情地批判了西方文明中残酷的理性主义和肤浅的道德观"②。

确实，"库切常被人贴上'与众不同'作家的标签，他的小说常常会引起评论家们的直接反对意见"③。他自己在大众面前最常见的形象是"难以捉摸"、"难于描述"。他常常把自己置于大众视野之外，以旁观者/局外人的身份来审视南非殖民主义、后殖民主义、后种族隔离制度，审视当下这个荒诞不经的世界，揭示在非正义制度下的种种暴力行为，揭示被边缘化他者所遭受的压迫与痛苦，揭示人类生存的困惑、焦虑、孤独以及现代社会中人们丧失自主意识后的悲哀。在表现自己的哲思时，库切不断试验新的文学样式、叙事方式，故而其作品充满了他性，为读者、批评者增添了解读空间。文学评论界运用各种不同文学、哲学理论对库切作品进行了大量的解读，然而，无论哪一种文学、批评理论都无法涵盖其全部作品，因为他用不间断的文学实验创新永远走在超越自己的道路上。他的文学成就因此在南非文学史上占有重要的地位。

[原载《南京航空航天大学学报(社会科学版)》2013 年第 2 期]

---

① 发表《男孩》(1997)、《青春》(2002)和《夏日》(2009)等传记 3 部，2011 年以《外省生活场景》为名将 3 部传记结集出版；发表非小说类作品 5 部，其中包括《白色书写：论南非的文人文化》(*White Writing*: *On the Culture of Letters in South Africa*，1988)、《双重视角：散文和访谈集》(*Doubling the Point*: *Essays and Interviews*，1992)、《冒犯：论书刊审查制度》(*Giving Offense*: *Essays on Censorship*，1996)、《异乡人的国度：文学评论集》(*Stranger Shores*: *Literary Essays*，*1986－1999*，2002)、《内心活动：文学评论集》(*Inner Workings*: *Literary Essays*，*2000－2005*，2007)，计划发表作品《此地此时》(*Here and Now*，2013)；出版翻译作品 3 部，为丹尼尔·笛福、索尔·贝娄、塞缪尔·贝克特等人的 6 部经典著作再版撰序。

② Engdahl, Horace Oscar Axel. The Nobel Prize in Literature — Press Release[J]. (2003－10－2)[2013－6－6]. http://www.nobelprize.org/nobel_prizes/literature/laureates/2003/press.html.

③ Canepari－Labib, Michela. *Old Myth — Modern Empires Power*: *Language and Identity in J. M. Coetzee's Work* [M]. Oxford, Bern, Berlin: Peter Lang, 2005. 15.

2. 2003年诺贝尔文学奖新闻发布会上的讲话

2003年诺贝尔文学奖授予"以无数姿态表现了局外人令人诧异的牵连"的南非作家约翰·麦克斯维尔·库切。

约·麦·库切的小说以精致巧妙的构思、意味深长的对话、卓越超群的分析为特色。然而,他同时又是一位审慎的怀疑者,无情地批判了西方文明中残酷的理性主义和肤浅的道德观。他那理智的正直使慰藉的所有基础逐渐丧失,不可能采用悔恨、忏悔等去达到华而不实的戏剧效果。即便当他自己坚定的信念浮出水面时,比如在他捍卫动物权利时,他也预设了这些权利存在基础这样的前提,而不是为它们争辩。

库切的兴趣主要指向区分真理与谬误的情境,十分清楚的是,可以被视作没有任何意图。诚如勒内·马格利特名画中的那个面对镜子打量自己脖子的人,在关键时刻,库切的人物站在自己身后一动不动,无法投入自己的行动之中。然而,被动并不仅仅是吞噬人格的黑色雾霾……在探究弱点和失败中,库切抓住了人类神圣的火花。

他最早的小说《幽暗之地》就是表现移情能力的第一个例证,这种能力使库切一次又一次地深入异己者与憎恶者内心深处。一个在越战期间为美国政府工作的人梦想着发明一种无敌的心理战装置,与此同时,他的私密生活被弄得四分五裂。他经过深思熟虑后的观点与开发非洲土著人土地的远征报告并列在一起,而后者声称是由18世纪一位布尔人开拓者写下的。厌恶人类的两种形式,其一为知性与夸大狂式的厌恶,另一为充满原始活力的厌恶,两者之间互为映照。

他的下一部小说《内陆深处》中一个要素是心理刻画。一个与父亲同住而饱受忧虑折磨的老处女,十分厌恶地发现了前者与一个年轻的有色女人之间的恋情。她幻想着将他们俩都谋杀了,但是,一切似乎表明,她更准确地说决定将自己禁闭在与奴仆有悖常情的契约之中。实际上的连续事件无法断定,因为读者唯一的信息源是她的笔记,而她的笔记中谎言和真话、粗野话语与文雅谈吐在字里行间任意交替出现。华而不实的爱德华时代文学风格的女性独白与周围的非洲景色十分奇怪地交织在一起。

《等待野蛮人》是有康拉德遗风的政治惊悚小说。其中,理想主义者的天真开启了通向恐怖的大门。嬉戏一般的超小说《福》讲述了一个有关文学与生活互相矛盾又不可分离的故事。讲述者是一位妇女,渴望成为主要叙事部分,而事实上她只提供了微不足道的叙事。

有了根植于笛福、卡夫卡和贝克特的小说《迈克尔·K的生活与时代》,库切是孤独作家的印象就变得更加清晰。小说涉及一个无足轻重的市民的逃亡经历,他逃离日益动荡的局势和不断迫近的战争,结果变得对一切需求漠不关心,沉默寡语,否定了权力的内在联系。

《彼得堡的大师》阐释了陀思妥耶夫斯基的生活和小说世界。为在心中远离世界而逝,库切想象中的人物所面临的诱惑证明是恐怖主义昧良心的自由法则。在这里,作者与邪恶问题的斗争带上了妖魔论的色彩,这种因素在他最近出版的作品《伊丽莎白·科斯特洛》再次出现。

在《耻》中,库切让我们参与到在南非白人优越观念消失后的新环境中一位声名狼藉的大学教师为捍卫自己和女儿的声誉所进行的抗争之中。小说涉及他作品中的一个中心问题:是否可能逃避历史?

他的自传体小说《少年时代》主要围绕父亲的屈辱以及这种屈辱对儿子造成的心理分裂进行,不过,该书也传达了守旧的南非乡村生活不可思议的印象,那里布尔人与英国人之间、白人和黑人之间永远有着矛盾冲突。在其续篇《青春》中,作者详细剖析了自己,把自己解读为一个残忍的青年,为能够与他实现认同的任何人提供慰藉。

库切作品中形式丰富多样。从来没有两本书采用相同的创作方法。广泛阅读显示了一个反复出现的模式,他认为螺旋下降的历程对于他的人物的救赎很有必要。他的作品主人公常常被沉沦的冲动所征服,不过,他们往往自相矛盾地在被剥夺了一切外在尊严时获得力量。

瑞典皇家学院

3. 2003 年诺贝尔文学奖颁奖词

斯德哥尔摩音乐厅2003年诺贝尔文学奖授奖仪式上的讲话

佩尔·沃兹伯格

尊敬的国王和王后陛下、殿下，尊敬的诺贝尔奖得主们，女士们、先生们：

写作就是要唤醒内心各种相反的声音，敢于与它们进行对话。内心自我的这种危险的吸引力就是约翰·库切的主题：人民的意识和身体，非洲的内在状态。“想象无法想象的东西”是作家的责任。作为一位后现代寓言作家，库切明白，不设法模仿现实的小说，使我们确信现实客观存在。

库切看透了历史令人厌恶的矫揉造作和虚假炫耀，为被噤声者和受人蔑视者发声。他谨慎而坚定不移地捍卫着诗歌、文学和想象的伦理价值。如果这些缺失，我们将会什么也看不清，成为灵魂的盲者。

约翰·库切的人物在权力范围之外寻找庇护。《迈克尔·K的生活与时代》呈现了一个生活在人类共存基础之外的个体的梦想。迈克尔·K是一位纯真的个体，通常在无尽的迁徙中看世界。尽管暴露在种族主义专制的暴力之下，他通过被动应对获得了一种自由，挫败了种族隔离制度当局和游击队的势力，只是因为他什么都不需要：既不需要战争也不需要革命，既不需要权力也不需要金钱。

《等待野蛮人》是一个扰乱心境的爱情故事，讲述了占有他人的渴望，希冀将那个人彻底了解，仿佛那是一个需要解开的谜。认识到极权主义威胁、感觉到拥有他人的渴望的任何人，都会从库切的黑色寓言中学到东西。他采用极度详尽、言辞规范的绝望情绪，处理了长期以来的一个重大问题：理解暴行、折磨和非正义的驱动力。

谁在写作？谁在通过执笔掌握权力？黑人的经验能否由白人描写？在《福》中，星期五是非洲人，已经被笛福剥夺了人的基本特性。如果让星期五具备说话能力，他就可能会受到控制，因而失去仅存的正义感。《等待野蛮人》中的女孩用一种难以理解的语言在言说，同时又因折磨而被弄瞎了眼睛；迈克尔·K 长着兔唇，星期五的舌头被割掉了。他的故事由苏珊·巴顿叙述，即通过"白色书写"（库切的一本书的标题）来进行。

无论我们多么努力地去掌握迈克尔和星期五，他们都已经被库切塑造完成，不受阐释的玷污。他们保持沉默。但是，在字里行间，在没有言说的话语之中，存在着一种当代文学中不常见的情感升华。

荒岛上幸存者的神话是唯一现存故事，库切曾经说过。他的几本书都涉及相同的孤独话题。有没有可能置身于历史之外？来自专制统治当局的自由是否存在？"我不喜欢共谋。上帝啊，别管我，"第一部小说《幽暗之地》中的雅各布·库切说，他喜欢被遗弃的感觉。但是，他一直是历史的工具，迫使土著人认真对待他的原因是他得胜的暴力。不过，他确实自问，黑人是否居住在一个自己意识不到的奇妙世界里："可能，我已经扼杀了一些价值无法估量的东西。"

库切的作品就像越过不友好的南非风景上的一道高压电缆。《铁器时代》中的固伦太太目睹了骇人听闻的暴行，但是无法采用别人的话语来谴责这些暴行。库切自己也绝不会写请愿书或参加政治集会。

在反乌托邦小说《耻》中，戴维·卢里受到自己的羞耻和历史的耻辱双重影响，直到被剥夺了所有尊严后才真正获得创造力和自由。在这部作品中，库切总结了自己的主题：种族和性别，拥有权与暴力，以及每个人在解放与和解的语言没有任何意义的边界地区与道德和政治之间的牵连。

库切的每一部新书都令人震惊地与其他作品不一样。他侵入读者荒芜的空间。在其自传中，他无情地反思了先前的自己。在他的散文小说《伊丽莎白·科斯特洛》中，他带着前所未有的幽默和讽刺，将当代叙事与神话、哲学与流言结合在一起。

亲爱的约翰·库切，

你的作品篇幅有限、范围无限。我用瑞典语对在场各位说的可以用以下话语总结：“别听我说，马上回家去读，有些形象会与你永远在一起。”

在你自己的生活中，你最近已经沿着那条连接开普敦和阿德莱德的纬度运动。你可能已经离开了南非，南非却永远不会离开你。对于瑞典皇家科学院来说，民族根源没有多大关系，我们并不认同欧洲人常常称之为文学边缘的说法。

你是自己的真相与和解委员会，你以表达对我们最深切的关注为基本出发点。你深入探究人类残忍而孤独的环境土壤。你赋予处于各个权势等级之外的那些人以声音。你带着知识分子的真诚和复杂的情感，采用精密得无情的散文形式，揭橥了我们文明的面具，揭示了罪恶的表征。

此时此刻，我请求您从皇帝陛下手中接受本年度诺贝尔文学奖，同时想要表达瑞典皇家学院最热烈的祝贺。

4. 他与他的人——库切诺贝尔文学奖获奖演说辞

还是回过来说说我的新同伴吧。与他在一起我很欣慰。为了让他能干有用,成为我的帮手,我事事都亲力亲为地教他。不过,最紧要的还是教他说话,让他听明白我说话。他是个最有悟性的学生。

丹尼尔·笛福《鲁滨逊漂流记》

波士顿坐落在林肯郡海边,是一座漂亮的城,他的人写道。那儿耸立着全英格兰最高的教堂尖顶,海上引航员用它来导航。波士顿周围是沼泽地。麻鳽随处可见,这寓意不祥的鸟儿发出钝重的呻吟与哀鸣,两英里开外听到都不觉战栗,疑是听到放枪的声音。

沼泽地还是其他很多鸟类的家园,他的人写道,普通野鸭、绿头野鸭、短颈野鸭和赤颈野鸭都可以在这里觅到踪迹。为了逮住这些野鸭,沼泽地的人(泽人)驯养出了一种鸭子,他们称之为诱饵鸭,或是囮子。

沼泽即大片的湿地。欧洲乃至全世界都不乏大片大片的湿地,但却没有一处被称为沼泽。"沼泽"是英格兰的叫法,不会外传。

林肯郡的这些囮子是在诱饵塘里养大的,他的人写道,它们经人喂养而得以驯服。等捕获季节一到,这些诱饵鸭便会被送往国外,送到荷兰和德国。在荷兰和德国,它们遇到自己的同类,亲眼目睹当地鸭子的生活是何等悲惨不幸,它们的河流被冻得如何严实,它们的陆地如何被大雪覆盖。这些诱饵鸭挖空心思,靠着某种让当地鸭听得懂的语言,叫它们明白自己故乡英格兰的情形截然不同:英格兰的鸭子有许多海岸,海岸食物丰盛且营养丰富,那里潮水自由自在地涌上河湾;那儿有湖泊,有泉水,有无遮无掩的池塘,也有绿树掩映的河塘;那里田地间满是拾穗人遗落下的谷物;那里没有冰霜没有飞雪,即便有,也就一丁点。

这些诱饵鸭或是囮子通过完全采用鸭语描绘出这般景象，他写道，集结起大群大群的水禽，说穿了就是诱拐了它们。诱饵鸭带领它们从荷兰和德国漂洋过海，抵达林肯郡的沼泽地，在诱饵鸭塘安顿下来。诱饵鸭嘎嘎声不断，用自己的语言喋喋不休地告诉同伴们，说这就是它们一直念叨的池塘，大家在这里可以过上悠然自得的日子。

正当它们忙于安定的时候，驯鸭人——诱饵鸭的主人们蹑手蹑脚地潜入沼泽地里他们用芦苇搭的隐秘藏身之处，悄悄地将一把把谷物投入水中。诱饵鸭或囮子引领它们的外国客人紧紧跟上。就这样，两三天后，它们引着来客进入越来越窄的水道，一路上不断地招呼它们看我们在英格兰生活得多么惬意，将它们引向一个罗网密布的地方。

这时候，诱饵鸭的主人放出诱饵犬。这些犬训练有素，能在水禽后游泳，一路游一路狂吠不已。鸭群被这可怖的牲畜惊得走投无路，扑棱着翅膀飞起来，无奈被头顶上架着的拱网撞落水中。在网下面，群鸭要想活路就得游。可是，网越来越小，像钱袋一样，尽头站着的是下饵人，他们将失去自由的鸭子一只接一只地拽出来。诱饵鸭得到了爱抚和悉心照料，而那些作客的鸭子，却当场受到棒击，褪毛后成百上千地被卖掉。

林肯郡的这一切新闻都是他的人简洁而敏捷地完成的，每天动笔之前，他总会拿他的小折刀将羽毛笔削得尖尖的。

在哈利法克斯曾经竖立过一台行刑架，詹姆士一世执政时期才被移走，他的人写道。犯人的头被固定在断头台的十字基座或杯状装置上，接着，行刑人敲开卡着沉重铡刀片的销栓，铡刀从教堂门那么高的横梁上轰然落下，砍头过程就像屠夫剁肉一样干净利索。

然而，哈利法克斯有个习俗，要是犯人能在销栓启开到铡刀落下的当口一跃而起，奔下山岗，游过河去，并且没有被行刑人再次逮住的话，就可以重获自由之身。不过，行刑架竖立在哈利法克斯这么多年，这样的事儿还从未发生过。

他（现在是他，不是他的人）在布里斯托尔端坐在河畔房间里读这篇文字。他日渐老去，现如今差不多可以说老态龙钟。在用棕榈叶或蒲葵叶做阳伞为自己遮阴之前，他脸上的皮肤几乎已经被热带阳光晒黑。虽然脸皮现在显得有点苍白，可还是像羊皮纸那样坚韧。鼻子上有一块愈合不了的晒伤。

那把遮阳伞如今还立在房间角落，一直陪伴着他，而和他一同回来的鹦鹉却已不在人世。“可怜的鲁滨！”那只鹦鹉会从它栖息之地——他的肩上大声喊道。“可怜的鲁滨·克鲁索！谁来拯救可怜的鲁滨！""可怜的鲁滨"声日以继夜地响着，他的妻子没法忍受鹦鹉哀切的鸣叫。"我真该拧断它的脖子，"她说道，可她没胆子那么干。

当他带着鹦鹉、阳伞和装满财宝的大箱从岛上回到英格兰后，他和老妻在亨廷顿新置办的房子里过了一段平静安宁的日子。那时的他已经是有钱人了，等到那本漂流奇遇记出版后，他变得更加富有。可是，荒岛生活的那些岁月以及后来与仆人"星期五"旅行的那些年头，使他觉得陆上绅士生活无比枯燥（可怜的"星期五"，他悲戚地嘟囔着，呱呱——呱呱，因为鹦鹉从来都不会叫"星期五"的名字，只叫他的名字）。而且，倘若实话实说，婚姻生活也让人失望透顶。他不知不觉愈加频繁地去马厩伺弄马匹，幸好那些马儿不会唠叨，看到他来最多轻轻地哼几声，表示认得他是谁，然后就归于平静。

在"星期五"到来之前，他一直孤身在荒岛上过着沉默无语的日子。回来后，他仿佛觉得这个世界太过喧闹。躺上妻子在侧的床，他觉得窸窣声、唠叨声不绝于耳，就像是一阵卵石雨倾倒在自己脑袋上，而这时他最渴望的只是睡觉。

所以，当老妻魂归天国之时，他为之哀悼，却不遗憾。他安葬了妻子，过了好久后，在布里斯托尔码头区的"欢乐水手"客栈租下一间屋子，将亨廷顿的住宅交给儿子打理。他临走时只带了那把让他成名的荒岛阳伞，那只固定在栖枝上的死鹦鹉和一些生活必需品。从此以后，他在这里过上了孤身一人的生活，白天在码头上散散步，抽抽烟斗，向西凝望无际的大海——他的目光还算锐利。至于饮食，他让人一日三餐送到自己的房间，因为习惯了岛上的独居生活，他不觉得社交有什么乐趣。

他不看书，对书已失去兴致。不过，记录自己的冒险经历让他养成了写作的习惯，这是足以令人愉悦的一种消遣。晚上，在烛光的映照下，他会铺开纸，削尖羽毛笔，写上一两页"他的人"。此人送来了林肯郡诱饵鸭传说、送来哈利法克斯大行刑架报告，说犯人若能在可怕的铡刀落下前一跃而起冲下山岗便可以重获自由，他还带来诸多此类消息。每到一处，他的这位大忙人都会寄来些见闻，那是他的首要工作。

漫步在港口岸壁上，回想起哈利法克斯的行刑架，他，鲁滨，那只鹦鹉习惯叫他"可怜的鲁滨"，扔出一枚石子，听它落水的声响。一秒钟，甚至不消一秒钟时间，石头就落入了水中。上帝的恩慈倏忽而至，可恩慈的降临能快得过那把钢刃，那把涂过动物油脂远比石子要重的回火钢刃么？我们如何才能逃脱？究竟是怎样的一类人才会成日在帝国里四处奔波忙忙碌碌，辗转于一个又一个的死亡场景（棒击、砍头），而后寄来一份又一份的报道？

一个生意人吧，他暗自思量。不妨让他当个谷物批发商或者皮革商人吧，要不就在某个出产黏土的地方，比方说沃平，做个瓦片制造商或是承办商，他得是个为生意到处奔走的人。让他生意兴隆，给他一个爱他的妻子，不会过于唠叨，为他生养孩子，主要是女儿。给他一份合乎情理的幸福，然后让那份幸福戛然而止。泰晤士河冬天突然涨水，烧制好瓦片的窑被水冲走，遭此劫难的或是谷仓，或是皮革厂。他毁了，他的这个人。债主们像苍蝇像乌鸦一样对他紧追不放。他不得不抛下妻儿，逃离家门，隐姓埋名地在条件最恶劣的穷街陋巷里躲躲藏藏。一切的一切——大水，破产，逃亡，身无分文，衣衫褴褛，孤苦无依——重演了失事船骸和荒岛上的景象。可怜的鲁滨，就这样与世隔绝了 26 年，差点儿就精神错乱（事实上，从某种程度上看，谁能说他没疯呢）。

或者让这个人成为一个马具商，在白教堂区拥有一个家、一间铺子、一座仓库，让他下巴上长一颗痣，给他一个爱他的妻子，不会过于唠叨，为他生养孩子，主要是女儿。让他享有巨大幸福，直到瘟疫降临这个城市。那是 1665 年，伦敦大火还不曾发生。瘟疫降临伦敦：每个教区的死亡人数都在与日攀升，富人和穷人都难逃厄运，瘟疫可不管什么阶层，马具商的所有世俗财富都不会保住他的性命。他将妻女送往乡下，打算筹划自己的逃亡，不过随后打消了这个念头。“汝勿惧畏暗夜之惊骇，”危难关头，他翻开《圣经》，诵读经文：“勿惧畏白日之飞箭；汝勿惧畏行于暗夜之瘟疫，勿惧畏午间毁人之毒病。纵有千人扑于汝侧，万人伏于汝旁，灾亦不得临近汝身。”这安度厄难的兆示使他振作，他留在疫症肆虐的伦敦，着手撰写报道。我在街上偶遇一群人，他写道，其中一个女人手指向天空。“看啦，”她大声呼喊：“白衣素身的天使挥舞着冒着火焰的剑！”“真是这样，”那群人跟着点头附和：“一位舞剑的天使！”可是他，这个马具商，根本没看见什么天使，也没看见什么宝剑。他所看见的只是一片形状怪异的云彩，因阳光照射之故，一边比另一边鲜亮些而已。

“这是一个象征！”街上那女人喊道，可他看不出代表他生命的任何象征。因此，他将此事写进了报道。

又一天，他的人——这个曾经的马具商、如今的无业者——走在沃平的河畔，看到一个女人怎样在自家门口朝一个驾着平底小渔船的男人喊：“罗伯特！罗伯特！”那人怎样将船泊岸，从船里拎出一个麻袋，靠在岸边的一个石头上，然后又把船划走。那女人怎样走到河边，将麻袋拖回家去，脸上写满悲伤哀戚。

他与那个叫罗伯特的男人搭腔。罗伯特告诉他，那女人是自己的妻子，麻袋里装的是老婆孩子一个星期的供给，肉食、粗磨粉和黄油。但他不敢靠得太近，因为家里所有人，无论老婆还是孩子都已经染上了瘟疫，这让他的心都碎了。这一切——靠着隔河呼叫来保持联系的罗伯特夫妇，留在河边的那个麻袋——自然代表了事件本身，但也象征着他的一个人物形象，鲁滨逊的形象，他在荒岛上的形影自吊。在岛上最为黑暗绝望的时日，隔着海浪呼唤他在英格兰的亲人来救他，其余时间则游到失事船只的残骸上搜寻日用品。

有关悲惨岁月的报道还在继续。因不堪忍受腹股沟和腋窝肿胀的疼痛——瘟疫的征兆，一个男人赤裸着身子，号叫着奔到大街上，冲进白教堂区的哈罗巷。在那里，他的人(那个马具商)亲眼目睹那男人时而跳跃，时而腾跃，并且做出许多怪异的姿势，他的妻儿跟在后面一路狂追，叫喊着让他回去。这种跳跃和腾跃有其自身的象征寓意。那艘船不幸失事后，他在岸边四处搜寻船上同伴的踪迹，可除了找到两只不成对的鞋子外，其他一无所获。自那以后他明白，自己孤身一人被冲到了一个渺无人烟的荒岛上，很可能会丧生，没有获救的希望。

(令他茫然不解的是，他所读到的这个饱受折磨的可怜人，除了忧伤悲怆外，还会在背地里吟唱什么？越过茫茫大海，越过经年岁月，他不为人知的内心之火在呼唤着什么?)

一年前，他(鲁滨逊)付两畿尼给水手买了一只鹦鹉，那个水手说鹦鹉是他从巴西带回来的。鹦鹉不如自己心爱的那只出类拔萃，不过也算令人满意，翠绿的羽毛，猩红的羽冠，还是个口舌灵巧的主，倘是水手的话可信的话。那只鸟会坐立在他客栈房间的栖枝上，腿上拴了一条细细的链子，以防它设法飞走。那鸟只会叫"可怜的波尔！可怜的波尔!"叫了一遍又一遍，直到迫不得已给它套上罩子才会消停。不过，其他词怎么教也不会，譬如"可怜的鲁滨!"也许是它太老了，学不进去。

可怜的波尔，透过狭窄的窗凝望着一根根桅杆的顶端，目光越过桅杆顶，停落在汹涌澎湃的大西洋上，停落在大西洋灰蒙蒙的波涛上。"这是什么岛?"可怜的波尔问，"我被抛弃到这里，这般寒冷，如此乏味？在我最迫切需要你的时候，你在哪里啊，我的救主?"

有天夜深了，一个男人喝得醉醺醺的（他的人的另一份报道），倒在跛子门[1]的门口睡着了。运尸车一路开过来（我们还在瘟疫那年），邻居们以为这个人死了，将他抬上运尸车，混在尸体堆里。过了一会儿，运尸车开到了芒特米尔的埋尸坑。运尸车车夫脸上裹得严严实实以抵挡恶臭，他一把抓住那男人，将他丢进坑里。那人摔醒了，茫然地挣扎起来。“我在哪？”他说。“差点儿把你和死人一同埋了。”车夫说。“可是我就这样死了么？”那人说。这无疑是荒岛上的他的又一形象。

一些伦敦人继续做着生意，感觉身体健康，想着瘟疫将会过去。殊不知，瘟疫早已于不知不觉中潜进他们的血液：一旦心脏遭到感染，便会猝然死去，好像突然被闪电击中一般，他的人这样描述。这是生命本身的形象，整个人生的形象。未雨绸缪。我们要为死亡早作准备，否则面临死亡我们会不堪一击，正如上苍让他——鲁滨逊在荒岛上突然有一天看到沙滩上有一个人的脚印时顿悟到的一样。这是一个印迹，因而是一个标志：一只脚的标志，一个人的标志。不过，这标志还蕴藏着更多的意义。“你并非只身孤影，”标志显示；而且，“无论你航行多远，无论你身藏何处，都会被人搜寻出来。”

在瘟疫蔓延的日子里，他的人写道，另一些人出于恐惧，抛弃了一切。他们遗弃了自己的家、妻子儿女，竭尽所能远离伦敦。等到瘟疫过去，他们的逃跑行径遭到谴责，处处被人骂作懦夫。可是，他的人写道，我们忘记了面对瘟疫时需要唤起的是怎样的勇气。这不仅仅是战士的勇气，那种抓起武器向敌人发起攻击的斗志，而是向骑着灰白骏马的死神自身发起进攻的勇气。

他的荒岛鹦鹉（两只鹦鹉中他更喜欢的那只）即便在最佳状态也不会叫出主人没有教过的词。他的这个人，不过是鹦鹉学舌之辈而且不怎么受待见，何以写出和主人一样好乃至更胜主人一筹的文章？毫无疑问，是因为他的人握着那支生花妙笔。“就像骑着灰白骏马的死神自身。”他自己从账房学来的那点本事，不过是记账算账，而非遣词造句。“骑着灰白骏马的死神自身”：这样的词句他根本想不到。唯有他拜服于他的人时，这样的妙语才会出现。

---

①　跛子门：伦敦八座城门之一。鲁德门（Ludgate）、新门（Newgate）、参事门（Aldersgate）、跛子门（Cripplegate）、高沼门（Moorgate）、主教门（Bishopsgate）和无税门（Aldgate））这七座城门于十八世纪六十年代被拆除。

还有诱饵鸭或是囮子。鲁滨逊了解这些诱饵鸭的故事么？完全不了解，直到他的人开始送出相关报道他才知晓。

林肯郡的沼泽诱饵鸭、哈利法克斯的大行刑架，这些报道取材于他的这个人游览不列颠岛的经历，也是他乘着自制小船环游荒岛的写照。环岛之行探明岛的那一边陡峭、昏暗且荒凉，他之后总是避开那地方。不过，将来若有殖民者抵达那个岛屿，他们没准会开发荒岛，在那里定居下来。那将是另一种形象，关乎灵魂的阴暗面和光明面。

第一伙剽窃者和模仿者盯上了他的荒岛经历，将他们杜撰出来的海难逃生故事强加给公众。对他而言，那伙人无异于一帮扑向他的肉体、取他性命的食人生番，他这样说丝毫没有顾忌。“那些食人生番企图将我打倒在地，烘烤我、吞食我。当我自卫抗拒他们荼毒时，”他写道：“我想我自卫抗拒这件事本身的侵害。我一点都没想到，那些食人生番不过是更残忍更贪婪的家伙，他们噬啮的正是真理的实质。”

可如今，再往深处想想，他心底竟暗生出一丝对模仿者的惺惺相惜之情。在他看来，世上仅有为数不多的故事，如果不让年轻人掠夺老人的话，他们必定会默默无闻了。

因此，在他那部荒岛历险记里，他描述了一天夜里自己如何在惊恐中醒来，确信魔鬼化身为一条大狗跳上床扑在他身上。他一跃而起，抓起一把短弯刀左挥右砍进行自卫，而睡在床边的那只可怜鹦鹉惊得尖叫起来。很多天后他才弄明白，压在他身上的既不是什么大狗也不是什么魔鬼，而是某种短暂性麻痹使腿无法动弹，以至于幻想出有什么东西压在身上了。从这事中似乎得到一种教训：包括麻痹在内的一切痛苦都来自魔鬼，而且是魔鬼本身；疾病的造访可以看成是魔鬼的降临，或是幻化成狗形的魔鬼的降临，反之亦然，在马具商对瘟疫的记载中，造访代表了疾病。因此，写魔鬼故事的人也好，写瘟疫故事的人也罢，都不该立即被指责为造假剽窃之流。

多年前，他决定铺开纸张记述荒岛经历时发现，文辞匮乏、书写不畅，手指僵硬不听使唤。不过，他一天天地逐渐掌握了写作的要领，写到与鲁滨逊在冰封的北方冒险时，已是文思泉涌，笔酣墨饱。

天哪，原先写作的那种轻松自如竟弃他而去。他坐在窗前的小写字台边，眺望布里斯托尔港湾，手又僵硬起来，笔头生出一如从前的陌生之感。

他（另一个人，他的那个人）觉得写作这活轻松么？他写的那些诱饵鸭、断头台还有瘟疫肆虐伦敦的故事如行云流水般酣畅。不过，自己的故事也曾流畅过。或是自己错看了他。那个衣冠楚楚、步履轻快、下颏有痣的小个子男人，也许此时此刻正孤零零地坐在辽阔王国某处一个租屋里蘸着笔，蘸了又蘸，满心疑虑，踌躇不定，思忖再三。

他和这个男人，该怎么形容他们的关系呢？主人和奴隶？兄弟，孪生兄弟？战友？抑或是敌人，仇敌？他该给这个无名同伴取个什么名字呢？这个日落后与他相伴，有时陪他一同度过漫漫长夜的男人，只在白天消失不见。当他——鲁滨漫步于码头观察新来船只之时，他的人正驰骋于王国各地进行着他的观察？

这个人在旅行途中会来布里斯托尔么？他渴望见到这个家伙的真身，握握他的手，与他一同在码头周围散散步，倾听他述说孤岛神秘北方之行或他笔下的各种奇遇。可是，他担心他们不会相遇，今生今世都不会。如果非要找个喻体来描绘他俩——他和他的人之间的关系，他会这样写：他们就像两艘反向行驶的船，一艘向西，一艘往东。或者更准确地说，他们是养护索具的甲板水手，一个在西驶的船上，一个在东行的船上。他们的船擦身而过，近得足够打个招呼。可是，海上波涛汹涌，暴风骤雨席卷而来。浪花飞溅上眼睛，绳索勒伤了双手，他们彼此错过，忙得甚至都没有挥一挥手。

（李栋飏译　石云龙审校）

5. 库切作品列表

Fiction

Dusklands (1974)《幽暗之地》

In the Heart of the Country (1977)《内陆深处》

Waiting for the Barbarians (1980)《等待野蛮人》

Life & Times of Michel K (1983)《迈克尔·K的生活与时代》

Foe (1986)《福》

Age of Iron (1990)《铁器时代》

The Master of Petersburg (1994)《彼得堡的大师》

The Lives of Animals (1999)《动物的生命》

Disgrace (1999)《耻》

Elizabeth Costello: Eight Lessons (2003)《伊丽莎白·科斯特洛：八堂课》

Slow Man (2005)《慢人》

Diary of a Bad Year (2007)《凶年纪事》

Fictionalised autobiography

Boyhood: Scenes from Provincial Life (1997)《少年时代：外省生活场景》(又译《男孩》)

Youth: Scenes from Provincial Life II (2002)《青春：外省生活场景Ⅱ》

Summertime (2009)《夏日》

Non-fiction

White Writing: On the Culture of Letters in South Africa (1988)《白色书写：论

南非的文人文化》

Doubling the Point: *Essays and Interviews* (1992)《双重视角：散文和访谈集》

Giving Offense: *Essays on Censorship* (1996)《冒犯：论书刊审查制度》

Stranger Shores: *Literary Essays*, *1986 - 1999* (2002)《异乡人的国度：文学评论集》

Inner Workings: *Literary Essays*, *2000 - 2005* (2007)《内心活动：文学评论集》

Translations and introductions

A Posthumous Confession by Marcellus Emants (Boston: Twayne, 1976 & London: Quartet, 1986) Translated by J. M. Coetzee.

The Expedition to the Baobab Tree by Wilma Stockenström (Johannesburg: Jonathan Ball, 1983 & London: Faber, 1984) Translated by J. M. Coetzee.

Landscape with Rowers: *Poetry from the Netherlands* Translated and Introduced by J. M. Coetzee (2004)

Introduction to *Robinson Crusoe* by Daniel Defoe (Oxford World's Classics)

Introduction to *Brighton Rock* by Graham Greene (Penguin Classics)

Introduction to *Dangling Man* by Saul Bellow (Penguin Classics)

6. 库切大事年表

1940 年　库切于 2 月 9 日出生在南非开普省开普敦市，父系祖先可追溯到 17 世纪荷兰移民，母系祖先可追溯到波兰移民。父亲扎查里阿斯·维梅厄（Zacharias Wehmeyer）是市政府律师，母亲维拉·维梅厄（Vera Wehmeyer）是教师。

1948 年　库切的父亲因对国家种族隔离政策持有异议而失去政府律师工作，全家迁移至沃赛斯特（Worcester）。

1951 年　库切全家搬回开普敦，在那里，父亲扎查里阿斯开设起一间小的律师事务所，后因经营不善而倒闭。

1956 年　库切被大学录取。

1957 年　库切进入开普敦大学学习英语与数学。

1960 年　库切获得开普敦大学英语本科荣誉学位。

1961 年　库切获得开普敦大学数学本科荣誉学位。

1962 年　库切离开南非，前往英国伦敦，受聘于 IBM 公司伦敦总部，任职计算机程序员至 1965 年。

1963 年　库切以一篇题为"论福特·马多克斯·福特作品尤其是小说"的论文（"The Works of Ford Madox Ford with Particular Reference to the Novels"）获得开普敦大学文学硕士学位。

同年，库切与菲莉帕·嘉伯（Philippa Jubber）结婚。

1965 年　库切获富布赖特项目（Fullbright Programme）奖学金，赴美国德克萨斯大学奥斯汀分校攻读博士学位。

1966 年　儿子尼古拉斯·库切（Nicolas Coetzee）出生。

1968 年　库切受聘于纽约州立大学布法罗分校，讲授英语文学。

女儿吉塞拉·库切（Gisela Coetzee）出生。

1969 年　库切的博士论文“萨缪尔·贝克特作品计算机文体分析”(Computer Stylistic Analysis of Samuel Beckett)通过答辩,获得德克萨斯大学语言学博士学位。

开始创作其第一部小说《幽暗之地》(*Duskland*s)。

1971 年　库切申请美国永久居住权(绿卡),因曾参与反对越南战争抗议活动而遭拒。

1974 年　南非共和国政府颁布《阿非利堪斯语媒体法》(Afrikaans Medium Decree),规定在黑人家园以外的地区,阿非利堪斯语在学校授课中要达到 50%的使用比例。

库切第一部长篇小说《幽暗之地》(*Dusklands*) 出版,获南非文学大奖默夫洛-波洛墨奖(Mofolo-Plomer Prize)。

1977 年　库切小说《内陆深处》(*In the Heart of the Country*) 出版,摘取南非文学最高荣誉——中央通讯社文学奖(The Central News Agency Literary Award)。

1980 年　库切小说《等待野蛮人》(*Waiting for the Barbarians*)出版,获中央通讯社文学奖、杰弗里·费伯纪念奖 (Geoffrey Faber Memorial Prize)及英国最古老的文学奖——詹姆斯·泰特·布莱克纪念奖(The James Tait Black Memorial Prize)。

库切与妻子菲莉帕·嘉伯离婚。

1983 年　小说《迈克尔·K 的生活与时代》(*Life & Times of Michel K*)出版,荣膺当年英语文学界最高荣誉英国布克奖(The Man Booker Prize)。

1984 年　库切升任开普敦大学英语文学教授。

小说《迈克尔·K 的生活与时代》获中央通讯社文学奖。

1985 年　电影《尘土》(*Dust*)上映,该电影改编自库切小说《内陆深处》。

小说《迈克尔·K 的生活与时代》获法国费米娜外国小说奖(Prix Femina Étranger)。

1986 年　库切小说《福》(*Foe*)出版。

1987 年　因为对“社会个体自由”贡献突出,库切被授予以色列耶路撒冷奖 (The Jerusalem Prize),成为第一位获得该奖项的南非人。

1988 年　库切文学评论集《白色书写:论南非的文人文化》(*White Writing: On the Culture of Letters in South Africa*)出版。

1989 年　德克拉克担任南非总统,释放反对种族隔离政策而入狱的曼德拉。

儿子尼古拉斯·库切遭遇意外事故,不幸丧生,年仅23岁。

1990年 南非总统德克拉克解除戒严。

库切小说《铁器时代》(*Age of Iron*)出版,获英国《星期日快报》年度好书奖(the Sunday Express Book of the Year Award)。

1991年 南非共和国废止人口登记法、原住民土地法与集团地区法,在法律上取消了种族隔离政策。

1992年 库切文学评论集《双重视角:散文和访谈集》(*Doubling the Point: Essays and Interviews*)出版。

1993年德克拉克与曼德拉同获颁诺贝尔和平奖。

1994年 小说《彼得堡的大师》(*The Master of Petersburg*)出版。

1995年 小说《彼得堡的大师》获爱尔兰时报国际小说奖(Irish Times International Fiction Prize)

1996年 库切文学评论集《冒犯:论书刊审查制度》(*Giving Offense: Essays on Censorship*)出版。

1997年 库切第一部自传体小说《少年时代:外省生活场景》(*Boyhood: Scenes from Provincial Life*)出版。

1999年 库切出版小说《耻》(*Disgrace*),二度荣获布克奖。该书同年还获美国全国书评家协会小说奖(National Book Critics Circle Award)提名,被评为《纽约时报书评》(*The New York Review of Books*)年度最佳图书。

库切小说《动物的生命》(*The lives of Animals*)出版。

2000年 小说《耻》获英联邦作家奖(Commonwealth Writers' Prize)。

2002年 库切退休后离开开普敦,移居澳大利亚阿德莱德市,任阿德莱德大学英语系名誉研究员,同时在芝加哥大学"社会思想委员会"任客座教授。

库切自传体小说《青春:外省生活场景Ⅱ》(*Youth: Scenes from Provincial Life II*)出版。

库切文学评论集《异乡人的国度:文学评论集》(*Stranger Shores: Literary Essays, 1986 -1999*)出版。

改编自库切同名小说的电影《动物的生命》(*The lives of Animals*)上映。

2003年 库切小说《伊丽莎白·科斯特洛:八堂课》(*Elizabeth Costello: Eight*

Lessons) 出版，入围年度布克奖初选名单。

瑞典皇家科学院授予库切 2003 年度诺贝尔文学奖(Nobel Prize in Literature)。

2005 年　库切小说《慢人》(*Slow Man*) 出版，入围年度布克奖初选名单。

为表彰库切在文学领域对南非做出的突出贡献，南非政府授予库切南非最高荣誉马篷古布韦勋章(Order of Mapungubwe)。

2006 年　库切向澳大利亚移民部门提出申请，加入澳大利亚国籍。

2007 年　库切文学评论集《内心活动：文学评论集》(*Inner Workings: Literary Essays, 2000 -2005*)出版。

库切小说《凶年纪事》(*Diary of a Bad Year*)出版。

2008 年　改编自库切的同名小说的电影《耻》上映。

2009 年　库切自传体小说《夏日》(*Summertime*)出版，入围年度布克奖决选名单。

2011 年　库切自传体小说三部曲合集《外省生活场景》(*Scenes from Provincial Life*)出版。

2013 年　库切文学评论集《此地此时：2008—2011 年间信件》(*Here and Now: Letters, 2008 -2011*)。

库切小说《耶稣的童年》(*The Childhood of Jesus*)出版。

7. 国内外主要库切研究成果列表

学术著作：

Attridge, Derek. *J. M. Coetzee & the Ethics of Reading: Literature in the Event*. Chicago: University of Chicago Press, 2004.

Attwell, David. *J. M. Coetzee: South Africa and the Politics of Writing*. Berkeley, CA: University of California Press, 1993.

Barnard, Rita. *Apartheid and Beyond: South African Writers and the Politics of Place*. Oxford: Oxford University Press, 2006.

Bell, Michel. *Open Secrets: Literature, Education, and Authority from J-J. Rousseau to J. M. Coetzee*. Oxford: Oxford University Press, 2007.

Benson, Stephen. *Literary Music: Writing Music in Contemporary Fiction*. Aldershot, England; Burlington, Vt.: Ashgate, 2006.

Bewes, Timothy. *The Event of Postcolonial Shame*. Princeton, N. J.: Princeton University Press, 2011.

Black, Shameem. *Fiction Across Borders: Imagining the Lives of Others in Late-twentieth-century Novels*. New York: Columbia University Press, 2010.

Boehmer, Elleke. *Colonial and Postcolonial Literature: Migrant Metaphors*. Oxford; New York: Oxford University Press, 1995.

Boehmer, Elleke, Robert Eaglestone and Katy Iddiols (eds). *J. M. Coetzee in Context and Theory*. New York: Continuum International Publishing Group, 2009.

Bradshaw, Graham and Michel Neill (eds). *J. M. Coetzee's Austerities*. Farnham, UK and Burlington, VT: Ashgate Publishing Limited, 2010.

Canepari-Labib, Michela. *Old Myths-Modern Empires: Power, Language and

Identity in J. M. Coetzee's Work. Oxford; New York, NY: Peter Lang, 2005.

Cavalieri, Paola. *The Death of the Animal: a Dialogue*. New York: Columbia University Press, 2009.

Chambers, Iain and Lidia Curti. *The Post-colonial Question: Common Skies, Divided Horizons*. London; New York: Routledge, 1996.

Clarkson, Carrol. *J. M. Coetzee: Countervoices*. Basingstoke; New York, NY: Palgrave Macmillan, 2009.

Davis, Todd F and Kenneth Womack. *Mapping the Ethical Turn: A Reader in Ethics, Culture, and Literary Theory*. Charlottesville, Virginia: University Press of Virginia, 2001.

De Lange, Attie. *Literary Landscapes: From Modernism to Postcolonialism*. London: Palgrave Macmillan, 2008.

Dooley, Gillian. *J. M. Coetzee and the Power of Narrative*. New York: Cambria Press, 2010.

Eagleton, Mary. *Figuring the Woman Author in Contemporary Fiction*. New York; Basingstoke: Palgrave Macmillan, 2005.

Gallagher, Susan V. *A Story of South Africa: J. M. Coetzee's Fiction in Context*. Cambridge, MA: Harvard University Press, 1991.

Hall, Alice. *Disability and Modern Fiction: Faulkner, Morrison, Coetzee and the Nobel Prize for Literature*. London: Palgrave Macmillan, 2011.

Hamilton, Grant. *On Representation: Deleuze and Coetzee on the Colonized Subject*. Amsterdam and Atlanta: Rodopi Press, 2011.

Hayes, Patrick. *J. M. Coetzee and the Novel: Writing and Politics after Beckett*. Oxford: Oxford University Press, 2010.

Head, Dominic. *J. M. Coetzee*. Cambridge: Cambridge University Press, 1997.

——. *The Cambridge Introduction to J. M. Coetzee*. Cambridge: Cambridge University Press, 2009.

Huggan, Graham, and Stephan Watson (eds). *Critical Perspectives on J. M. Coetzee*. London: MacMillan Press Ltd., 1996.

Ingram, Penelope. *The Signifying Body: Toward an Ethics of Sexual and Racial Difference*. Albany, New York: State University of New York Press, 2008.

Irele, Abiola. *The Cambridge Companion to the African Novel*. Cambridge: Cambridge University Press, 2009.

James, David. *Modernist Futures: Innovation and Inheritance in the Contemporary Novel*. Cambridge: Cambridge University Press, 2012.

Kossew, Sue. *Pen and Power: A Postcolonial Reading of J. M. Coetzee and André Brink*. Amsterdam: Atlanta, GA. 1996.

—— (ed). *Critical Essays on Coetzee*. New York: G. K. Hall & Co., 1998.

Leist, Anton and Peter Singer. *J. M. Coetzee and Ethics: Philosophical Perspectives on Literature*. New York: Columbia University Press, 2010.

López, María J. *Acts of Visitation: The Narrative of J. M. Coetzee*. Amsterdam: Rodopi, 2011.

Marais, Mike. *Secretary of the Invisible: The Idea of Hospitality in the Fiction of J. M. Coetzee*. Amsterdam: Rodopi, 2009.

Masłoń, Sławomir. *Père-Versions of the Truth: The Novels of J. M. Coetzee*. Katowice: University of Silesia, 2007.

Mathuray, Mark. *On the Sacred in African Literature: Old Gods and New Worlds*. London: Palgrave Macmillan, 2009.

Mulhall, Stephen. *The Wounded Animal: J. M. Coetzee and the Difficulty of Reality in Literature and Philosophy*. Princeton, NJ: Princeton University Press, 2008.

Nashef, Hania A. M. *The Politics of Humiliation in the Novels of J. M. Coetzee*. New York, NY: Routledge, 2009.

Parker, David. *The Self in Moral Space: Life Narrative and the Good*. Ithaca, New York: Cornell University Press, 2007.

Penner, Dick. *Countries of the Mind: The Fiction of J. M. Coetzee*. New York, NY: Greenwood Press, 1989.

Poyne, Jane. (ed). *J. M. Coetzee and the Idea of the Public Intellectual*. Athens:

Ohio University Press, 2006.

——. *J. M. Coetzee and the Paradox of Postcolonial Authorship*. Farnham; Burlington, VT: Ashgate, 2009.

Quayson, Ato. *Aesthetic Nervousness: Disability and the Crisis of Representation*. New York: Columbia University Press, 2007.

Samolsky, Russell. *Apocalyptic Futures: Marked Bodies and the Violence of the Text in Kafka, Conrad, and Coetzee*. New York: Fordham University Press, 2011.

Stanton, Katherine. *Cosmopolitan Fictions: Ethics, Politics, and Global Change in the Works of Kazuo Ishiguro, Michel Ondaatje, Jamaica Kincaid, and J. M. Coetzee*. London: Routledge, 2005.

Su, John J. *Imagination and the Contemporary Novel*. Cambridge: Cambridge University Press, 2011.

Upstone, Sara. *Spatial Politics in the Postcolonial Novel*. Farnham, England; Burlington, VT: Ashgate, 2009.

Van der Vlies, Andrew. *J.M. Coetzee's 'Disgrace'*. New York: Continuum, 2010.

Worthington, Kim L. *Self as Narrative: Subjectivity and Community in Contemporary Fiction*. Oxford: Clarendon Press, 1996.

Wright, Laura. *Writing "Out of All the Camps": J. M. Coetzee's Narratives of Displacement*. New York & London: Routledge, 2006.

蔡圣勤. 库切研究与后殖民文学. 武汉：武汉大学出版社,2011.

段枫. 历史话语的挑战者——库切四部开放性和对话性的小说研究. 上海：复旦大学出版社,2011.

高文惠. 后殖民文化语境中的库切. 北京：中国社会科学出版社，2008.

王敬慧. 永远的流散者. 北京：北京大学出版社，2010.

博士论文：

Al-Sharqi, L. *The Rhetoric of Literary Rewriting: A Study in Postmodern Fiction by J.M. Coetzee, Michel Cunningham, Peter Huber and Bharati Mukherjee*. The University of Nottingham (United Kingdom), 2005.

Anantharayan, Parvathy. *Silence, Alterity and Synoptic Understanding*. University of Louisiana at Lafayette (United States of America), 2006.

Anker, Elizabeth S. *World Literature, Narrative Ethics, and the Discourse of Human Rights*. University of Virginia (United States of America), 2007.

Azzam, Julie Hakim. *The Alien Within: Postcolonial Gothic and the Politics of Home*. University of Pittsburgh (United States of America), 2007.

Barilla, James Jerome. The Nature of Homelands: Narratives of Restoration and Return. University of California, Davis (United States of America), 2004.

Birdi, Alvin. *Animals, Time and Space: the 'Political' Within the Works of Samuel Beckett and J.M. Coetzee.* University of Sussex (United Kingdom), 2006.

Black, Shameem. *Cosmopoetics: Global Imagination in Contemporary Writing*. Stanford University (United States of America), 2004.

Brouillette, Sarah. *Postcolonial Authorship in the Global Literary Marketplace*. University of Toronto (Canada), 2005.

Cabarcos, Maria Jesus. *Some Post-colonial Versions of the Pastoral*. University of Kansas (United States of America), 1999.

Carruth, Allison. *Global Appetites: Literary Form and Food Politics from World War I to the World Trade Organization.* Stanford University (United States of America), 2008.

Casey, John Shepard. *Self and Politics in the Novels of J. M. Coetzee.* University of Illinois at Urbana-Champaign (United States of America), 1994.

Clark, Emily. *Voiceless Bodies: Feminism, Disability, Posthumanism.* The University of Wisconsin - Madison (United States of America), 2013.

Comorau, Nancy. *Postcolonial Refashionings: Reading Forms, Reading Novels.* University of Maryland, College Park (United States of America), 2009.

De Boever, Arne. *Literary Sovereignties: The Contemporary Novel and the State of Exception*. Columbia University (United States of America), 2009.

Deyo, Brian Daniel. *We Have Never Been Human: J. M. Coetzee, the Enlightenment, and the Lives of Animals*. Vanderbilt University (United States of

America), 2008.

Durrant, Samuel Robin. "*Some Kind of Tomorrow*": *Postcolonial Narrative and the Work of Mourning*. Queen's University at Kingston (Canada), 2000.

Egerer, Claudia. *Fictions of (in) Betweenness*. Goteborgs Universitet (Sweden),1996.

Farrands, Peter James. *The Myth of the White Tribe*. University of Southampton (United Kingdom), 1994.

Flanagan, Joseph. *The Psychic Life of the Nation: Literature, Culture, and the Critique of Ideology*. University of Delaware (United States of America), 1999.

Gang, Joshua. *Behaviorism and Literary Modernity*, 1913－2009. Rutgers The State University of New Jersey-New Brunswick (United States of America), 2012.

Garrett, O. J. *Fictions of Ethics and Identity: Ideological Negotiations andRe-presentations in the Works of Joseph Conrad and J. M. Coetzee.* University of Exeter (United Kingdom), 2008.

Grayson, Erik. "*The Ones Who Cry*": *Aging and the Anxiety of Finitude in J. M. Coetzee's Novels of Senescence*. State University of New York at Binghamton (United States of America), 2010.

Hayes, P. *J. M. Coetzee and the Novel: Reading the Later Fiction*. University of Oxford (United Kingdom), 2007.

Helgesson, Stefan. *Sports of Culture: Writing the Resistant Subject in South Africa (Readings of Ndebele, Gordimer, Coetzee)*. Uppsala Universitet (Sweden), 1999.

Hogarth, Claire Milne. *Epistolary Constructions of Identity in Derrida's "Envois" and Coetzee's "Age of Iron"*. McGill University (Canada), 2002.

Iwuanyanwu, Obiwu. *In the Name of the Father Lacanian Reading of Four White South African Writers*. Syracuse University (United States of America), 2011.

Johnson, Jamie. *The Philosophy of the Animal in 20th Century Literature*. Florida Atlantic University (United States of America), 2009.

Johnson, Katyna. *Reframing Narratives and Reevaluating Bodies: Incorporating*

Disability into Narratives. The University of New Mexico (United States of America), 2009.

Kapstein, Helen Sarah. *The Castaway State: On Islands and Nation-building*. Columbia University (United States of America), 2002.

Kelly, Maria Michelle. '*So I Sing for My Keep*': *J. M. Coetzee and Confessional Narrative*. University of York (United Kingdom), 2008.

Kenny, Tobias. '*Coming Home to Roost*': *Some Reflections on Moments of Literary Response to the Paradoxes of Empire*. McGill University (Canada), 1998.

Koetters, Joseph T. *Authors Going Alien: Textual Production in the Novels of J. M. Coetzee*. University of California, Santa Barbara (United States of America), 1998.

Kossew, Susan Rachelle. *Pen and Power: A Post-colonial Reading of the Novels of J. M. Coetzee and Andre Brink*. University of New South Wales (Australia), 1993.

Lachman, Kathryn M. *The Music of Voice: Transnational Encounters between Music, Theory and Fiction*. Princeton University (United States of America), 2008.

Liatsos, Yianna. *Historical Catharsis and the Ethics of Remembering in the Post-apartheid Novel*. The State University of New Jersey - New Brunswick (United States of America), 2005.

Limbu, Bishupal. *Fiction, Theory, and Social Justice: Dispropriative Readings*. Northwestern University (United States of America), 2010.

Lin, Lidan. *The Rhetoric of Posthumanism in Four Twentieth-century International Novels*. University of North Texas (United States of America), 1998.

Love, Christopher D. *Creating Tragic Spectators: Rebellion and Ambiguity in World Tragedy*. University of Michigan (United States of America), 2009.

Macleod, Lewis Francis. "*The Way a Man does Do Things*": *Epic Masculinity, Grand Narrative and Ideological Discourse in Selected Twentieth-century Novels*. Memorial University of Newfoundland (Canada), 2002.

Macri, Linda C. *Revising the Story: A rhetorical Perspective on Revisionary Fiction by Women Writers*. University of Maryland College Park (United States of America), 2000.

Marques, Irene. *Four Writers Being Political on Their Own Terms: Feminist, Class and Cultural Identity Discourses across Continents (Mia Couto, Jose Saramago, Clarice Lispector, J. M. Coetzee)*. University of Toronto (Canada), 2005.

McGonegal, Julie. *Imagining Justice: The Politics of Postcolonial Forgiveness and Reconciliation*. McMaster University (Canada), 2004.

McLeod, Corinna M. *The Problematic Postcolonial Narrative: Intertextuality and Empire in African and Afro-Caribbean Fiction and Film*. University of South Carolina (United States of America), 2003.

Medin, Daniel L. *Three Sons. Franz Kafka and the Fiction of J. M. Coetzee, Philip Roth, and W. G. Sebald*. Washington University (United States of America), 2005.

Menon, Nirmala. *Remapping the Postcolonial Canon*. The George Washington University (United States of America), 2008.

Mishra Tarc, Aparna. *Literacy of the Other: Making Relations to Language*. York University (Canada), 2007.

Mohammad, Malek Hardan. *The Discourse of Human Dgnity and Techniques of Disempowerment: Giorgio Agamben, J. M. Coetzee, and Kazuo Ishiguro*. Texas A&M University (United States of America), 2010.

Neimneh, Shadi. *J. M. Coetzee's 'Postmodern' Corpus: Bodies/Texts, History, and Politics in the Apartheid Novels*, 1974 - 1990. The University of Oklahoma (United States of America), 2011.

Niemi, Minna Johanna. *Representations of History in African Diasporic Literatures and the Politics of Postmodernism*. State University of New York at Buffalo (United States of America), 2011.

Pearsall, Susan Middleton. *Aestheticized Politics in the Work of Nadine Gordimer and J. M. Coetzee*. The University of North Carolina at Chapel Hill (United States of America), 1999.

Popescu, Monica. *South Africa in Transition: Theorizing Post-colonial, Post-apartheid and Post-communist Cultural Formations*. University of Pennsylvania (United States of America), 2005.

Poyner, Jane. *The Fictions of J. M. Coetzee: Master of His Craft?* University of Warwick (United Kingdom), 2003.

Probyn, Fiona Susan. *Unsettling Postcolonial Representations of the White Woman*. University of New South Wales (Australia), 1999.

Rayneard, Max James Anthony. *Performing Literariness: Literature in the Event in South Africa and the United States*. University of Oregon (United States of America), 2011.

Readey, Jonathan Eric. *Written and Built Memorials: Postcolonial Literature and "Secondary" Commemoration in a Contemporary Age of Mass Tragedy*. University of Virginia (United States of America), 2012.

Roeschlein, Michel J. *Tarrying with the Transcendent: Forms of Religious Experience in Twentieth-century Literature*. The University of Wisconsin - Madison (United States of America), 2006.

Rother, Adeline Patten. *The Teeming and the Rare: Displacements of Sacrifice and the Turn to Insect Life*. Cornell University (United States of America), 2012.

Runia, Robin. *Hearkening to Whores: Reviving Eighteenth-century Models of Sensible Writing*. The University of New Mexico (United States of America), 2009.

Samantrai, Ranu. *The Erotic of Imperialism: V. S. Naipaul, J. M. Coetzee, Lewis Nkosi*. University of Michigan (United States of America), 1990.

Samolsky, Russell Evan. *Apocalyptic Futures: Inscribed Bodies and the Violence of the Text in Twentieth-century Culture*. University of Colorado at Boulder (United States of America), 2003.

Schatteman, Renee Therese. *Caryl Phillips, J. M. Coetzee, and Michel Ondaatje: Writing at the Intersection of the Postmodern and the Postcolonial*. University of Massachusetts Amherst (United States of America), 2000.

Schatz, Anna Marie. *Seeing Justice through Kafka: Knowing, Judgment and Faith*. State University of New York at Buffalo (United States of America), 1999.

Schiff, Jacob Laurence. *The Cultivation of Responsiveness*. The University of Chicago (United States of America), 2010.

Semler, Johanna Theresa. *Bare Life and Metamorphic Being: Nazi Propaganda, Agamben, Coetzee and Kafka*. The University of Chicago (United States of America), 2012.

Sood, Sujay. *Dharmic-ethics: The Ethical Sociality of the Self in Postmodernism and Post-colonialism*. Emory University (United States of America), 1997.

Stanton, Katherine Ann. *Worldwise: Global Change and Ethical Demands in the Cosmopolitan Fictions of Kazuo Ishiguro, Jamaica Kincaid, J. M. Coetzee, and Michel Ondaatje*. The State University of New Jersey - New Brunswick (United States of America), 2003.

Stokes, Katherine May. *Sexual Violence and the Authority to Speak: The Representation of Rape in Three Contemporary Novels*. McGill University (Canada), 2009.

Treiber, Jeanette. *The Construction of Identity and Representation of Gender in Four African Novels*. University of California, Davis (United States of America), 1992.

Turk, Tisha. *In the Canon's Mouth: Rhetoric and Narration in Historiographic Metafiction*. The University of Wisconsin - Madison (United States of America), 2005.

Van Wert, Kathryn. *Wars of Inflection: Imperial Violence and the Modern Voice*. University of Rochester (United States of America), 2012.

Vegari, Amy Neda. *Violence, Immediately: Representation and Materiality in Coetzee, Ellis, Cooper, Beckett, Godard, and Noe*. Brown University (United States of America), 2008.

Wade, J. P. *A Comparison of the Novels of Peter Abrahams and J. M. Coetzee*. University of Essex (United Kingdom), 1987.

Wenzel, Jennifer Ann. *Promised Lands: J. M. Coetzee, Mahasweta Devi, and the Contested Geographies of South Africa and India*. The University of Texas at Austin (United States of America), 1998.

Wheeler, Rebecca L. *Rewriting the Colonized Past through Textual Strategies of Exclusion*. Ball State University (United States of America), 2002.

Wright, Laura. *Writing "Out of All the Camps": J. M. Coetzee's Narratives of Displacement*. University of Massachusetts Amherst (United States of America), 2004.

Wright, Timothy. *Disconsolate Subjects: Figures of Radical Alterity in the Twentieth Century Novel, From Modernism to Postcolonialism*. Duke University (United States of America), 2012.

Yanaginio, Yukari. *Psychoanalysis and Literature: Perversion, Racism and Language of Difference*. The State University of New Jersey — New Brunswick (United States of America), 2008.

Yeoh, Gilbert Guan-Hin. *The Persistence of Ethics: Ethical Rreadings of Samuel Beckett, Primo Levi and J. M. Coetzee*. Harvard University (United States of America), 1998.

Yoo, JaeEun. *Ghost Novels: Haunting as Form in the Works of Toni Morrison, Don DeLillo, Michel Ondaatje, and J. M. Coetzee*. The State University of New Jersey-New Brunswick (United States of America), 2009.

Zainer, Leanne Christine. *Enduring Violence: Representation and Response in Contemporary Fiction*. The University of Wisconsin - Madison (United States of America), 1998.

Zanjani Henriksen, Lene. *Voice and Silence in Contemporary Fiction: Kazuo Ishiguro, J. M. Coetzee and Jeanette Winterson*. University of Sussex (United Kingdom), 2005.

蔡圣勤.孤岛意识：帝国流散群知识分子的书写状况.武汉:华中师范大学,2008.

段枫.历史话语的挑战者——库切四部开放性和对话性的小说研究.北京:北京大学,2010.

高文惠. 后殖民文化语境中的库切. 天津：天津师范大学，2007.

兰守亭. 人的困境与拯救——库切小说研究. 上海：华东师范大学，2010.

苗永敏. 拒绝妥协. 苏州：苏州大学，2010.

石云龙. 库切小说“他者”多维度研究. 上海：上海外国语大学，2012.

王敬慧. 永远的异乡客. 北京：北京语言大学，2006.

王旭峰. 解放政治与后殖民文学. 天津：南开大学，2009.

武娜. 库切小说中的他性表征与伦理重构. 郑州：河南大学，2010.

周桂君. 现代性语境下跨文化作家的创伤书写. 长春：东北师范大学，2010.

期刊论文：

Abbott, H. Porter. Time, Narrative, Life, Death, & Text-Type Distinctions: The Example of Coetzee's *Diary of a Bad Year*. *Narrative* 19. 2 (2011): 187 - 200.

Adelman, Gary. Stalking Stavrogin: J. M. Coetzee's *The Master of Petersburg* and the Writing of *The Possessed*. *Journal of Modern Literature* 23. 2(1999): 351 - 357.

Alsop, Elizabeth. Refusal to Tell: Withholding Heroines in Hawthorne, Wharton, and Coetzee. *College Literature* 39. 3 (2012): 84 - 105.

Andriolo, Karin. The Twice-Killed: Imagining Protest Suicide. *American Anthropologist* 108. 1 (2006): 100 - 113.

Anker, Elizabeth Susan. Human Rights, Social Justice, and J. M. Coetzee's *Disgrace*. *Modern Fiction Studies* 54. 2 (2008): 233 - 267.

——. Elizabeth Costello, Embodiment, and the Limits of Rights. *New Literary History* 42. 1 (2011): 169 - 192.

Ankersmit, F. R. The Ethics of History: From the Double Binds of (Moral) Meaning to Experience. *History and Theory* 43. 4 (2004): 84 - 102.

Attridge, Derek. Age of Bronze, State of Grace: Music and Dogs in Coetzee's *Disgrace*. *Novel: A Forum on Fiction* 34. 1 (2000): 98 - 121.

——. Ethical Modernism: Servants as Others in J. M. Coetzee's Early Fiction. *Poetics Today* 25. 4 (2004): 653 - 671.

Attwell, David. The Labyrinth of My History: J. M. Coetzee's *Dusklands*. *Novel: A*

Forum on Fiction 25.1 (1991): 7 - 32.

——. Coetzee's Estrangements. *Novel: A Forum on Fiction* 41.2 - 3 (2008): 229 - 243.

——. J. M. Coetzee and the Idea of Africa. *Journal of Literary Studies* 25.4 (2009): 67 - 83.

——. Mastering Authority: J. M. Coetzee's *Diary of a Bad Year*. *Social Dynamics* 36.1 (2010): 214 - 221.

——. Coetzee's Postcolonial Diaspora. *Twentieth Century Literature* 57.1 (2011): 9 - 19.

Barnard, Rita. Dream Topography: J. M. Coetzee's *Disgrace* and the South African Pastoral. *South Atlantic Quarterly* 93.1 (1994): 33 - 58.

——. Coetzee in/and Afrikaans. *Journal of Literary Studies* 25.4 (2009): 84 - 105.

——. J. M. Coetzee. *Research in African Literatures* 31.2 (2000): 214 - 216.

Barris, Ken. Miscegenation, Desire and Rape: the Shifting Ground of *Disgrace*. *Journal of Literary Studies* 26.3 (2010): 50 - 64.

Beard, Margot. Lessons from the Dead Masters: Wordsworth and Byron in J. M. Coetzee's *Disgrace*. *English in Africa* 34.1 (2007): 59 - 77.

Bethlehem, Louise. Aneconomy in an Economy of Melancholy: Embodiment and Gendered Identity in J. M. Coetzee's *Disgrace*. *African Identities* 1.2 (2003): 167 - 185.

——. Materiality and the Madness of Reading: J. M. Coetzee's *Elizabeth Costello* as Post-Apartheid Text. *Journal of Literary Studies* 21.3 - 4 (2005): 235 - 253.

Boehmer, Elleke. Coetzee's Queer Body. *Journal of Literary Studies* 21.3 - 4 (2005): 222 - 234.

Boletsi, Maria. Barbaric Encounters: Rethinking Barbarism in C. P. Cavafy's and J. M. Coetzee's *Waiting for the Barbarians*. *Comparative Literature Studies* 44.1/2 (2007): 67 - 96.

Brittan, Alice. Death and J. M. Coetzee's *Disgrace*. *Contemporary Literature* 51.3 (2010): 477 - 502

Bruns, Gerald L. Becoming-Animal (Some Simple Ways). *New Literary History* 38. 4 (2008): 703 - 720.

Buikema, Rosemarie. Crossing the Borders of Identity Politics: *Disgrace* by J. M. Coetzee and *Agaat* by Marlene van Niekerk. *European Journal of Women's Studies* 16. 4 (2009): 309 - 323.

Caracciolo, Marco. J. M. Coetzee's *Foe* and the Embodiment of Meaning. *Journal of Modern Literature* 36. 1 (2012): 90 - 103.

Carstensen, Thorsten. Shattering the Word-Mirror in *Elizabeth Costello*: J. M. Coetzee's Deconstructive Experiment. *The Journal of Commonwealth Literature* 42. 1 (2007): 79 - 96.

Castillo, Debra A. Coetzee's *Dusklands*: The Mythic Punctum. *PMLA* 105. 5 (1990): 1108 - 1122.

Caton, Steven C. Coetzee, Agamben, and the Passion of Abu Ghraib. *American Anthropologist* 108. 1 (2006): 114 - 123.

Chapman, Michel. The Politics of Identity: South Africa, Story-telling, and Literary History. *Journal of Literary Studies* 18. 3 - 4 (2002): 224 - 239.

——. Coetzee, Gordimer and the Nobel Prize. *Scrutiny2* 14. 1 (2009): 57 - 65.

——. The Case of Coetzee: South African Literary Criticism, 1990 to Today. *Journal of Literary Studies* 26. 2 (2010): 103 - 117.

——. Postcolonial Problematics: A South African Case Study. *Research in African Literatures* 42. 4 (2011): 60 - 71.

Chesney, Duncan McColl. Toward an Ethics of Silence: *Michel K*. *Criticism* 49. 3 (2007): 307 - 325.

Ciobanu, Calina, Coetzee's Posthumanist Ethics. *Modern Fiction Studies* 58. 4 (2012): 668 - 698.

Clarkson, Carrol. J. M. Coetzee and the Ethics of Reading: Literature in the Event. *Comparative Studies of South Asia, Africa and the Middle East* 27. 2 (2007): 492 - 494

——. J. M. Coetzee and the Limits of Language. *Journal of Literary Studies* 25. 4

(2009): 106 - 124.

Clowes, Edith. The Robinson Myth Reread in Postcolonial and Postcommunist Modes. *Critique: Studies in Contemporary Fiction* 36. 2 (1995): 145 - 159.

Coleman, Deirdre. The "Dog-Man": Race, Sex, Species, and Lineage in Coetzee's *Disgrace*. *Twentieth Century Literature* 55. 4 (2009): 597 - 617.

Collins, Walter. Open Secrets: Literature, Education, and Authority from J-J. Rousseau to J. M. Coetzee. *Studies in the Novel* 41. 2 (2009): 255 - 257.

Cooper, Pamela. Metamorphosis and Sexuality: Reading the Strange Passions of *Disgrace*. *Research in African Literatures* 36. 4 (2005): 22 - 39.

Cornwell, Gareth. Realism, Rape, and J. M. Coetzee's *Disgrace*. *Critique* 43. 4 (2002): 307 - 322.

——. J. M. Coetzee, Elizabeth Costello, and the Inevitability of "Realism". *Critique: Studies in Contemporary Fiction* 52. 3 (2011): 348 - 361.

Crocker, Thomas P. Still Waiting for the Barbarians: What is New About Post-September 11 Exceptionalism? *Law and Literature* 19. 2 (2007): 303 - 326.

Danta, Chris. "Like a dog ... like a lamb": Becoming Sacrificial Animal in Kafka and Coetzee. *New Literary History* 38. 4 (2008): 721 - 737.

De Jong, Marianne and John Hilton. Is the Writer Ethical?: The Early Novels of J. M. Coetzee up to *Age of Iron*. *Journal of Literary Studies* 20. 1 - 2 (2004): 71 - 93.

——. Maria Mouton in the Heart of the Country? *Journal of Literary Studies* 27. 2 (2011): 91 - 144.

De Villiers, Rick. Narrative (De)construction: Mr Coetzee, in the Basement, with the Quill: A Discussion of Authorial Complicity in J. M. Coetzee's *Foe*. *Journal of Literary Studies* 26. 2 (2010): 118 - 126.

DeKoven, Marianne. Going to the Dogs in *Disgrace*. *ELH* 76. 4 (2009): 847 - 875.

DelConte, Matt. A Further Study of Present Tense Narration: The Absentee Narratee and Four-Wall Present Tense in Coetzee's *Waiting for the Barbarians* and *Disgrace*. *Journal of Narrative Theory* 37. 3 (2008): 427 - 446.

Devarenne, Nicole. Nationalism and the Farm Novel in South Africa, 1883 - 2004. *Journal of Southern African Studies* 35. 3 (2009): 627 - 642.

D'Hoker, Elke. Confession and Atonement in Contemporary Fiction: J. M. Coetzee, John Banville, and Ian McEwan. *Critique: Studies in Contemporary Fiction* 48. 1 (2006): 31 - 43.

Diala, Isidore. Nadine Gordimer, J. M. Coetzee, and Andre Brink: Guilt, Expiation, and the Reconciliation Process in Post-Apartheid South Africa. *Journal of Modern Literature* 25. 2 (2003): 50 - 68.

Dooley, Gillian Mary. Alien and Adrift: The Diasporic Consciousness in V. S. Naipaul's *Half a Life* and J. M. Coetzee's *Youth*. *New Literatures Review* 40 (2003): 73 - 82.

Dragunoiu, Dana. Existential Doubt and Political Responsibility in J. M. Coetzee's *Foe*. *Critique* 42. 3 (2001): 309 - 326.

——. J. M. Coetzee's *Life & Times of Michel K* and the Thin Theory of the Good. *The Journal of Commonwealth Literature* 41. 1 (2006): 69 - 92.

Durrant, Samuel. Bearing Witness to Apartheid: J. M. Coetzee's Inconsolable Works of Mourning. *Contemporary Literature* 40. 3 (1999): 430 - 463.

Eagleton, Mary. Ethical reading: The Problem of Alice Walker's *Advancing Luna-and Ida B. Wells* and J. M. Coetzee's *Disgrace*. *Feminist Theory* 2. 2 (2001): 189 - 203.

Easton, Kai. Coetzee's *Disgrace*: Byron in Italy and the Eastern Cape c. 1820. *The Journal of Commonwealth Literature* 42. 3 (2007): 113 - 130.

Eckstein, Barbara J. The Body, the Word, and the State: J. M. Coetzee's *Waiting for the Barbarians*. *Novel: A Forum on Fiction* 22. 2 (1989): 175 - 198.

——. Postcolonial Narrative and the Work of Mourning: J. M. Coetzee, Wilson Harris, and Toni Morrison. *Modern Fiction Studies* 51. 3 (2005): 714 - 717.

England, Frank. Foes: Plato, Derrida, and Coetzee: Rereading J. M. Coetzee's *Foe*. *Journal of Literary Studies* 24. 4 (2008): 44 - 62.

Engle, Lars. Being Literary in the Wrong Way, Time, and Place: J. M. Coetzee's

Youth. *English Studies in Africa* 49. 2 (2006): 29 - 50.

Eze, Chielozona. Ambits of Moral Judgement: Of Pain, Empathy and Redemption in J. M. Coetzee's *Age of Iron*. *Journal of Literary Studies* 27. 4 (2011): 17 - 35.

Faber, Alyda. The Post-Secular Poetics and Ethics of Exposure in J. M. Coetzee's *Disgrace*. *Literature and Theology* 23. 3 (2009): 303 - 316.

Fan, Kit. Imagined Places: Robinson Crusoe and Elizabeth Bishop. *Biography* 28. 1 (2005): 43 - 53.

Fassin, Didier, Frédéric Le Marci, and Todd Lethata. Life & Times of Magda A: Telling a Story of Violence in South Africa. *Current Anthropology* 4. 2 (2008): 225 - 246.

Flint, Holly. White Talk, White Writing: New Contexts for Examining Genre and Identity in J. M. Coetzee's *Foe*. *Literature Interpretation Theory* 22. 4 (2011): 336 - 353.

Fokkema, Douwe. Literary Representations of Risk: Terror, Crime and Punishment. *European Review* 11. 1 (2003): 99 - 107.

Franssen, Paul J. C. M. Pollux in Coetzee's *Disgrace*. *Notes and Queries* 57. 2 (2010): 240 - 243.

Fuentes, Agustin. The Humanity of Animals and the Animality of Humans: A View from Biological Anthropology Inspired by J. M. Coetzee's *Elizabeth Costello*. *American Anthropologist* 108. 1 (2006): 124 - 132.

Gal, Noam. A Note on the Use of Animals for Remapping Victimhood in J. M. Coetzee's *Disgrace*. *African Identities* 6. 3 (2008): 241 - 252.

Geertsema, Johan. White Natives? Dan Roodt, Afrikaner Identity and the Politics of the Sublime. *The Journal of Commonwealth Literature* 41. 3 (2006): 103 - 120.

——. Coetzee's *Diary of a Bad Year*, Politics, and the Problem of Position. *Twentieth Century Literature* 57. 1 (2011): 70 - 85.

Glenn, Ian. Gone for Good - Coetzee's *Disgrace*. *English in Africa* 36. 2 (2009): 79 - 98.

Gough, Annette and Noel Gough. Environmental Education Research in Southern

Africa: Dilemmas of Interpretation. *Environmental Education Research* 10. 3 (2004): 409 - 424.

Gräbe, Ina. Writing as Exploration and Revelation: Experiencing the Environment, Whether Local or Global, as Envisioned by Different Role-players in J. M. Coetzee's Latest Novels. *Journal of Literary Studies* 17. 3 - 4 (2001): 120 - 144.

Graham, Lucy Valerie. Reading the Unspeakable: Rape in J. M. Coetzee's *Disgrace*. *Journal of Southern African Studies* 29. 2 (2003): 433 - 444.

Grayson, Erik. The Wounded Animal: J. M. Coetzee and the Difficulty of Reality in Literature and Philosophy. *Modern Fiction Studies* 56. 2 (2010): 439 - 441.

Green, Michel. Social History, Literary History, and Historical Fiction in South Africa. *Journal of African Cultural Studies* 12. 2 (1999): 121 - 136.

Hallemeier, Katherine. Secular Study and Suffering: J. M. Coetzee's *The Humanities in Africa*. *Scrutiny2* 16. 1 (2011): 42 - 52.

Hamilton, Grant. J. M. Coetzee's *Dusklands*: The Meaning of Suffering. *Journal of Literary Studies* 21. 3 - 4 (2005): 296 - 314.

Handler, Richard. Afterword to "Cruelty, Suffering, Imagination: The Lessons of J. M. Coetzee": Anthropologists as Public Intellectuals, Again. *American Anthropologist* 108. 1 (2006): 133 - 134.

Harrison, James. Point of View and Tense in the Novels of J. M. Coetzee. *The Journal of Commonwealth Literature* 30. 1 (1995): 79 - 85.

Hayes, Patrick. The Review of "English Studies" Prize Essay: 'An Author I Have Not Read': Coetzee's *Foe*, Dostoevsky's *Crime and Punishment*, and *the Problem of the Novel*. *The Review of English Studies* 57. 2 /3 (2006): 273 - 290.

Head, Dominic. Pen and Power: A Post-Colonial Reading of J. M. Coetzee and Andre Brink, and A Morbid Fascination: White Prose and Politics in Apartheid South Africa. *Research in African Literatures* 31. 1 (2000): 223 - 227.

Hedin, Benjamin. J. M. Coetzee's "Confession". *Salmagundi* 162 /163 (2009): 209 - 217.

Herron, Tom. The Dog Man: Becoming Animal in Coetzee's *Disgrace*. *Twentieth*

Century Literature 51.4 (2005): 467 – 490.

Heyns, Michiel. The Whole Country's Truth: Confession and Narrative in Recent White South African Writing. *Modern Fiction Studies* 46.1 (2000): 42 – 66.

Hirsh, Elizabeth. Educating the Heart: Realism, Reason, and the Novel. *Contemporary Literature* 50.4 (2009): 817 – 821.

Hook, Derek. Postcolonial Psychoanalysis. *Theory and Psychology* 18.2 (2008): 269 – 283.

Irlam, Shaun. Double Entendre: Listening for Angels. *Journal of Literary Studies* 25.4 (2009): 125 – 139.

Janes, Regina. "Writing without Authority": J. M. Coetzee and His Fictions. *Salmagundi* 114/115 (1997): 103 – 121.

Kerr, Douglas. Three Ways of Going Wrong: Kipling, Conrad, Coetzee. *The Modern Language Review* 95.1 (2000): 18 – 27.

Kissack, Mike and Michel Titlestad. The Dynamics of Discontent: Containing Desire and Aggression in Coetzee's *Disgrace*. *African Identities* 3.1 (2005): 51 – 67.

Klopper, Dirk. "We Are Not Made for Revelation": Letters to Francis Bacon in the Postscript to J. M. Coetzee's *Elizabeth Costello*. *English in Africa* 35.2 (2008): 119 – 132.

Kossew, Sue. The Politics of Shame and Redemption in J. M. Coetzee's *Disgrace*. *Research in African Literatures* 34.2 (2003): 155 – 162.

Krzychylkiewicz, Agata. The Reception of J. M. Coetzee in Russia. *Journal of Literary Studies* 21.3 – 4 (2005): 338 – 367.

Labuscagne, Cobi. Representing the South African Landscape: Coetzee, Kentridge, and the Ecocritical Enterprise. *Journal of Literary Studies* 23.4 (2007): 432 – 443.

Lenta, Margaret. Autrebiography: J. M. Coetzee's *Boyhood* and *Youth*. *English in Africa* 30.1 (2003): 157 – 169.

——. Coetzee and Costello: Two Artists Abroad. *English in Africa* 31.1 (2004): 105 – 120.

——. Group, Nation, State: J. M. Coetzee and Problems of Nationality in Postcolonial Countries. *Journal of Literary Studies* 27. 4 (2011): 1 - 16.

Lenta, Patrick. Discipline in Disgrace. *Mosaic: a Journal for the Interdisciplinary Study of Literatur*e 43. 3 (2010): 1 - 16.

Leusmann, Harald. J. M. Coetzee's Cultural Critique. *World Literature Today* 78. 3/4 (2004): 60 - 63.

Ley, James. A Dog with a Broken Back: Animals as Rhetoric and Reality in the Fiction of J. M. Coetzee. *Australian Literary Studies* 25. 2 (2010): 60 - 71.

Longmuir, Anne. Coetzee's *Disgrace. The Explicator* 65. 2 (2007): 119 - 121.

López, María. *Foe*: A Ghost Story. *The Journal of Commonwealth Literature* 45. 2 (2010): 295 - 310.

Lowry, Elizabeth. The Hermeneutic Reflex: Reading J. M. Coetzee's *Inner Workings* and Critical Constructions of Coetzee as "Public Intellectual". *Scrutiny*2 13. 1 (2008): 60 - 67.

Macaskill, Brian. The Ballistic Bard: Postcolonial Fictions, and: Colonization, Violence, and Narration in White South African Writing: André Brink, Breyten Breytenbach, and J. M. Coetzee. *Modern Fiction Studies* 43. 2 (1997): 530 - 534.

——. Authority, the Newspaper, and Other Media, including J. M. Coetzee's *Summertime. Narrative* 21. 1 (2013): 19 - 45.

MacLeod, Lewis. "Do We of Necessity Become Puppets in a Story?" or Narrating the World: On Speech, Silence, and Discourse in J. M. Coetzee's *Foe. Modern Fiction Studies* 52. 1 (2006): 1 - 18.

Marais, Michel. Coming into Being: J. M. Coetzee's *Slow Man* and the Aesthetic of Hospitality. *Contemporary Literature* 50. 2 (2009): 273 - 298.

Marais, Mike. "Omnnipotent Fantasies" of a Solitary Self: J. M. Coetzee's *The Narrative of Jacobus Coetzee. The Journal of Commonwealth Literature* 28. 2 (1993): 48 - 65.

——. Places of Pigs: The Tension between Implication and Transcendence in J. M.

Coetzee's: *Age of Iron* and *The Master of Petersburg*. *The Journal of Commonwealth Literature* 31.1 (1996): 83 - 95.

——. Introduction: The Novel and the Question of Responsibility for the Other. *Journal of Literary Studies* 13.1 - 2 (1997): 1 - 20.

——. The Novel as Ethical Command: J. M. Coetzee's *Foe*. *Journal of Literary Studies* 16.2 (2000): 62 - 85.

——. "Little Enough, Less than Little: Nothing": Ethics, Engagement, and Change in the Fiction of J. M. Coetzee. *Modern Fiction Studies* 46.1 (2000): 159 - 182.

——. Literature and the Labour of Negation: J. M. Coetzee's *Life & Times of Michel K*. *The Journal of Commonwealth Literature* 36.1 (2001): 107 - 125.

——. Reading against Race: J. M. Coetzee's *Disgrace*, Justin Cartwright's *White Lightning* and Ivan Vladislavic's *The Restless Supermarket*. *Journal of Literary Studies* 19.3 (2003): 271 - 289.

——. J. M. Coetzee's *Disgrace* and the Task of the Imagination. *Journal of Modern Literature* 29.2 (2006): 75 - 93.

——. J. M. Coetzee and the Ethics of Reading. *Modern Fiction Studies* 53.4 (2008): 910 - 912.

——. Violence, Postcolonial Fiction, and the Limits of Sympathy. *Studies in the Novel* 43.1 (2011): 94 - 114.

Mardorossian, Carine M. Rape and the Violence of Representation in J. M. Coetzee's *Disgrace*. *Research in African Literatures* 42.4 (2011): 72 - 83.

Mascia-Lees, Frances E. and Patricia Sharpe. Introduction to "Cruelty, Suffering, Imagination: The Lessons of J. M. Coetzee". *American Anthropologist* 108.1 (2006): 84 - 87.

Mason, Travis V. Dog Gambit: Shifting the Species Boundary in J. M. Coetzee's Recent Fiction. *Mosaic: a Journal for the Interdisciplinary Study of Literature* 39.4 (2006): 129 - 144.

Maus, Derek. Kneeling Before the Fathers' Wand: Violence, Eroticism and Paternalism in Thomas Pynchon's *V.* and J. M. Coetzee's *Dusklands*. *Journal of*

Literary Studies 15. 1 - 2 (1999): 195 - 217.

May, Brian. J. M. Coetzee and the Question of the Body. *Modern Fiction Studies* 47. 2 (2001): 391 - 420.

——. Extravagant Postcolonialism: Ethics and Individualism in Anglophonic, Anglocentric Postcolonial Fiction; or, "What Was (This) Postcolonialism?" *ELH* 75. 4 (2008): 899 - 937.

McDonald, Peter D. The Writer, the Critic, and the Censor: J. M. Coetzee and the Question of Literature. *Book History* 7. 1 (2004): 285 - 302.

——. The Ethics of Reading and the Question of the Novel: The Challenge of J. M. Coetzee's *Diary of a Bad Year*. *Novel: A Forum on Fiction* 43. 3 (2010): 483 - 499.

McKay, Robert. Metafiction, Vegetarianism, and the Literary Performance of Animal Ethics in J. M. Coetzee's *The Lives of Animals*. *Safundi* 11. 1 - 2 (2010): 67 - 85.

Mehrabadi, Mina and Hossein Pirnajmuddin. (Hi) story in Search of Author(ity): Feminine Narration in J. M. Coetzee's *Foe*. *Studies in Literature and Language* 5. 1 (2012): 27 - 32.

Meljac, Eric Paul. The Poetics of Dwelling: A Consideration of Heidegger, Kafka, and Michel K. *Journal of Modern Literature* 32. 1 (2009): 69 - 76.

——. Seductive Lines: The Use of Horizontal Bars by Josipovici and Coetzee, and the Art of Seduction. *Journal of Modern Literature* 33. 1 (2009): 92 - 101.

——. Love and Disgrace: Reading Coetzee in the Light (and Love) of Barthes. *Journal of Modern Literature* 34. 3 (2011): 149 - 161.

Meskell, Lynn and Lindsay Weiss. Coetzee on South Africa's Past: Remembering in the Time of Forgetting. *American Anthropologist* 108. 1 (2006): 88 - 99.

Michel Marais. From the Standpoint of Redemption: Aesthetic Autonomy and Social Engagement in J. M. Coetzee's Fiction of the Late Apartheid Period. *Journal of Narrative Theory* 38. 2 (2008): 229 - 248.

Monson, Tamlyn. An Infinite Question: The Paradox of Representation in *Life &*

Times of Michel K. *Journal of Commonwealth Literature* 38. 3 (2003): 87 – 106.

Morphet, Tony. Stranger Fictions: Trajectories in the Liberal Novel. *World Literature Today* 70. 1 (1996): 53 – 58.

——. Reading Coetzee in South Africa. *World Literature Today* 78. 1 (2004): 14 – 16.

Moses, Michel Valdez. "King of the Amphibians": *Elizabeth Costello* and Coetzee's Metamorphoric Fictions. *Journal of Literary Studies* 25. 4 (2009): 25 – 38.

Mukherjee, Ankhi. The Death of the Novel and Two Postcolonial Writers. *Modern Language Quarterly* 69. 4 (2008): 533 – 556.

Murphet, Julian. Coetzee's Lateness and the Detours of Globalization. *Twentieth Century Literature* 57. 1 (2011): 1 – 8.

——. Coetzee and Late Style: Exile within the Form. *Twentieth Century Literature* 57. 1 (2011): 86 – 104.

Murray, Jessica. A Post-colonial and Feminist Reading of Selected Testimonies to Trauma in Post-liberation South Africa and Zimbabwe. *Journal of African Cultural Studies* 21. 1 (2009): 1 – 21.

Nagy, Rosemary. The Ambiguities of Reconciliation and Responsibility in South Africa. *Political Studies* 52. 4 (2004): 709 – 727.

Nashef, Hania A. M. Becomings in J. M. Coetzee's *Waiting for the Barbarians* and José Saramago's *Blindness*. *Comparative Literature Studies* 47. 1 (2010): 21 – 41.

Nethersole, Reingard. Reading in the In-between: Prescripting the "postscript" to *Elizabeth Costello*. *Journal of Literary Studies* 21. 3 – 4 (2005): 254 – 276.

Nkosi, Lewis. Luster's Lost Quarter: Reading South African Identities (William Faulkner and J. M. Coetzee). *Journal of Postcolonial Writing* 41. 2 (2005): 166 – 178.

Nurka, Camille. Feminine Shame/Masculine Disgrace: a Literary Excursion through Gender and Embodied Emotion. *Cultural Studies Review* 18. 3 (2012): 310

-333.

Nuttall, Sarah. Reading J. M. Coetzee Politically. *Journal of Southern African Studies* 19.4 (1993): 731-735.

Oerlemans, Onno. A Defense of Anthropomorphism: Comparing Coetzee and Gowdy. *Mosaic: a Journal for the Interdisciplinary Study of Literature* 40.1 (2007): 181-196.

Ogden, Benjamin H. The Coming into Being of Literature: How J. M. Coetzee's *Diary of a Bad Year* Thinks through the Novel. *Novel: A Forum on Fiction* 43.3 (2010): 466-482.

O'Sullivan, Michel. Giving up Control: Narrative Authority and Animal Experience in Coetzee and Kafka. *Mosaic: a Journal for the Interdisciplinary Study of Literature* 44.2 (2011): 119-135.

Patton, Paul. Becoming-Animal and Pure Life in Coetzee's *Disgrace*. *Ariel* 35.1/2 (2004): 101-119.

Pellow, C. Kenneth. Intertextuality and Other Analogues in J. M. Coetzee's *Slow Man*. *Contemporary Literature* 50.3 (2009): 528-552.

Penfold, Tom. Public and Private Space in Contemporary South Africa: Perspectives from Post-Apartheid Literature. *Journal of Southern African Studies* 38.4 (2012): 993-1006.

Pimentel, Juan. Robinson Crusoe: the Fate of the British Ulysses. *Endeavour* 34.1 (2010): 16-20.

Poyner, Jane. Writing under Pressure: A Post-Apartheid Canon? *Journal of Postcolonial Writing* 44.2 (2008): 103-114.

Pughe, Thomas. The Politics of Form in J. M. Coetzee's *The Lives of Animals*. *Interdisciplinary Studies in Literature and Environment* 18.2 (2011): 377-395.

Rainey, Lawrence, David Attwell and Benjamin Madden. An Interview with J. M. Coetzee. *Modernism/modernity* 18.4 (2011): 847-853.

Randall, Don. The Community of Sentient Beings: J. M. Coetzee's Ecology in *Disgrace* and *Elizabeth Costello*. *ESC* 33.1-2 (2007): 209-225.

Rose, Arthur. Questions of Hospitality in Coetzee's *Diary of a Bad Year*. *Twentieth Century Literature* 57.1 (2011): 54-69.

Roy, Sohinee. Speaking with a Forked Tongue: Disgrace and the Irony of Reconciliation in Postapartheid South Africa. *Modern Fiction Studies* 58.4 (2012): 699-722.

Ryan, Pam. A Woman Thinking in Dark Times?: The Absent Presence of Hannah Arendt in J. M. Coetzee's *Elizabeth Costello* and *the Problem of Evil*. *Journal of Literary Studies* 21.3-4 (2005): 277-295.

Sanders, Mark. Undesirable Publications: J. M. Coetzee on Censorship and Apartheid. *Law and Literature* 18.1 (2006): 101-114.

——. J. M. Coetzee and the Ethics of Reading: Literature in the Event. *Modern Fiction Studies* 53.3 (2007): 641-645.

——. The Writing Business: "He and His Man", Coetzee and Defoe. *Journal of Literary Studies* 25.4 (2009): 39-50.

Sarvan, Charles. Disgrace: A Path to Grace? *World Literature Today* 78.1 (2004): 26-29.

Saunders, Rebecca. The Agony and the Allegory: The Concept of the Foreign, the Language of Apartheid, and the Fiction of J. M. Coetzee. *Cultural Critique* 47 (2001): 215-264.

——. Disgrace in the Time of a Truth Commission. *Parallax* 11.3 (2005): 99-106.

Scott, Joanna and J. M. Coetzee. Voice and Trajectory: An Interview with J. M. Coetzee. *Salmagundi* 114/115 (1997): 82-102.

Segall, Kimberly Wedeven. Pursuing Ghosts: The Traumatic Sublime in J. M. Coetzee's *Disgrace*. *Research in African Literatures* 36.4 (2005): 40-54.

Sheehan, Paul. The Disasters of "Youth": Coetzee and Geomodernism. *Twentieth Century Literature* 57.1 (2011): 20-33.

Silverstein, Stephen. The Discourse of Jewish Difference in J. M. Coetzee's *Disgrace*. *Jewish Social Studies* 17.2 (2011): 80-100.

Smuts, Eckard. Reading through the Gates: Structure, Desire and Subjectivity in J.

M. Coetzee's *Elizabeth Costello*. *English in Africa* 36. 2 (2009): 63 - 77.

Spencer, Robert. J. M. Coetzee and Colonial Violence. *Interventions* 10. 2 (2008): 173 - 187.

Splendore, Paola. "No More Mothers and Fathers": The Family Sub-Text in J. M. Coetzee's Novels. *Journal of Commonwealth Literature* 38. 3 (2003): 148 - 161.

Standish, Paul. Food for Thought: Resourcing Moral Education. *Ethics and Education* 4. 1 (2009): 31 - 42.

Stott, Graham St. John. Rape and Silence in J. M. Coetzee's *Disgrace*. *Philosophical Papers* 38. 3 (2009): 347 - 362.

Sulk, Kay. "Visiting Himself on Me"- the Angel, the Witness and the Modern Subject of Enunciation in J. M. Coetzee's *Age of Iron*. *Journal of Literary Studies* 18. 3 - 4 (2002): 313 - 326.

Swales, Martin. Sex, Shame and Guilt: Reflections on Bernhard Schlink's *Der Vorleser* (The Reader) and J. M. Coetzee's *Disgrace*. *Journal of European Studies* 33 (2003): 7 - 22.

Tarc, Aparna Mishra. Disturbing Reading: J. M. Coetzee's *The Problem of Evil*. *Changing English* 18. 1 (2011): 57 - 66.

Travis, Molly Abel. Beyond Empathy: Narrative Distancing and Ethics in Toni Morrison's *Beloved* and J. M. Coetzee's *Disgrace*. *Journal of Narrative Theory* 40. 2 (2010): 231 - 250.

Tremaine, Louis. The Embodied Soul: Animal Being in the Work of J. M. Coetzee. *Contemporary Literature* 44. 4 (2003): 587 - 612.

Turk, Tisha. Intertextuality and the Collaborative Construction of Narrative: J. M. Coetzee's *Foe*. *Narrative* 19. 3 (2011): 295 - 310.

Uhlmann, Anthony. J. M. Coetzee and the Uses of Anachronism in *Summertime*. *Textual Practice* 26. 4 (2012): 747 - 761.

Urquhart, Troy. Truth, Reconciliation, and the Restoration of the State: Coetzee's *Waiting for the Barbarians*. *Twentieth Century Literature* 52. 1 (2006): 1 - 21.

Van der Vlies, Andrew. Reading Banned Books: Apartheid Censors and Anti-

Apartheid Aesthetics. *Wasafiri* 22. 3 (2007): 55 - 61.

Vital, Anthony. Toward an African Ecocriticism: Postcolonialism, Ecology and *Life & Times of Michel K*. *Research in African Literatures* 39. 1 (2008): 87 - 121.

Vold, Tonje. How to "Rise above Mere Nationality": Coetzee's Novels *Youth* and *Slow Man* in the World Republic of Letters. *Twentieth Century Literature* 57. 1 (2011): 34 - 53.

Walton, Heather. Staging John Coetzee/Elizabeth Costello. *Literature and Theology* 22. 3 (2008): 280 - 294.

Wenzel, Jennifer. The Pastoral Promise and the Political Imperative: The Plaasroman Tradition in an Era of Land Reform. *Modern Fiction Studies* 46. 1 (2000): 90 - 113.

Wicomb, Zoe. Slow Man and the Real: a Lesson in Reading and Writing. *Journal of Literary Studies* 25. 4 (2009): 7 - 24.

Wittenberg, Hermann. The Taint of the Censor: J. M. Coetzee and the Making of *In the Heart of the Country*. *English in Africa* 35. 2 (2008): 133 - 150.

Wood, Michel. Centennial Odysseys: Longest Way Round. *Critical Quarterly* 47. 1 - 2 (2005): 165 - 172.

——. The Last Night of All. *PMLA* 122. 5 (2007): 1394 - 1402.

Woodward, Wendy. Dog Stars and Dog Souls: *The Lives of Dogs in Triomf* by Marlene van Niekerk and *Disgrace* by J. M. Coetzee. *Journal of Literary Studies* 17. 3 - 4 (2001): 90 - 119.

——. The Killing (Off) of Animals in Some Southern African Fiction, or "Why Does Every Animal Story Have to be Sad?" *Journal of Literary Studies* 23. 3 (2007): 293 - 313.

Wright, Derek. A Story of South Africa: J. M. Coetzee's Fiction in Context. *Modern Fiction Studies* 38. 2 (1992): 530 - 531.

Wright, Laura. "Does He Have it in Him to be the Woman?": The Performance of Displacement in J. M. Coetzee's *Disgrace*. *Ariel* 37. 4 (2006): 83 - 102.

——. Displacing the Voice: South African Feminism and J. M. Coetzee's Female

Narrators. *African Studies* 67.1 (2008): 11 - 32.

Wright, S. Tense Meanings as Styles in Fictional Narrative: Present Tense Use in J. M. Coetzee's *In the Heart of the Country*. *Poetics* 16.1 (1987): 53 - 73.

Yeoh, Gilbert. Love and Indifference in J. M. Coetzee's *Age of Iron*. *Journal of Commonwealth Literature* 38.3 (2003): 107 - 134.

——. J. M. Coetzee and Samuel Beckett: Ethics, Truth-Telling, and Self-Deception. *Critique: Studies in Contemporary Fiction* 44.4 (2003): 331 - 348.

Yuan, Y. The Subject of Reading and the Colonial Unconscious: Countertransference in J. M. Coetzee's *Waiting for the Barbarians*. *American Journal of Psychoanalysis* 60.1 (2000): 71 - 84.

Zembylas, Michalinos. Bearing Witness to the Ethics and Politics of Suffering: J. M. Coetzee's Disgrace, Inconsolable Mourning, and the Task of Educators. *Studies in Philosophy and Education* 28.3 (2009): 223 - 237.

Zimbler, Jarad. Under Local Eyes: The South African Publishing Context of J. M. Coetzee's *Foe*. *English Studies in Africa* 47.1 (2004): 47 - 59.

蔡圣勤. 两个隐喻：关于拜伦的歌剧和狗的出场——库切小说《耻》之再细读. 湖北社会科学,2009,1: 141 - 144.

——. 神话的解构与自我解剖——再论库切对后殖民理论的贡献. 外国文学研究,2011,5: 29 - 35.

段枫. 历史的竞争者：库切对传统现实主义的继承与超越. 当代外国文学,2006,3: 28 - 36.

——. 库切研究的走向及展望. 外国文学评论,2007,4: 139 - 145.

——. 聚焦和反聚焦：《耻》中的视角、对话和叙述距离. 外国文学评论,2008,3: 85 - 94.

——. 审讯室外的小说家. 外国文学评论,2009,2: 92 - 104.

高文惠. 边缘处境中的自由言说：J. M. 库切与压迫性权威的对抗. 外国文学研究,2007,2: 150 - 157.

——. "雅各布・库切的叙述"：审视帝国叙述和神话制造. 名作欣赏,2007,5: 96 - 100.

——. J. M. 库切与历史权威的对抗. 山东社会科学，2008，7：61－64.

——. 库切的自传观和自传写作. 外国文学评论，2009，2：116－126.

何卫华.《耻》：历史叙事中的时空冲突. 外国文学研究，2009，5：46－52.

黄晖. 叙事主体的衰落与置换——库切小说《福》的后现代、后殖民解读. 四川外语学院学报，2006，4：57－60.

——.《福》：重构帝国文学经典. 外国文学研究，2010，3：155－160.

姜小卫. 库切小说《耻》中的忏悔、宽恕与和解. 外国文学评论，2007，3：31－37.

兰守亭. 论《福》中星期五失语的象征性. 名作欣赏，2009，7：80－82.

李嘉娜. 走进“他和他的人”——评库切的小说创作. 文艺理论与批评，2005，6：90－95.

李茂增. 宽恕与和解的寓言. 外国文学，2006，1：58－62.

李倩. 记下历史转身的瞬间——解读南非当代小说家库切的小说《耻》. 扬州大学学报：人文社会科学版，2004，6：39－43.

——. 库切小说《等待野蛮人》核心价值理念解析. 名作欣赏，2006，10：62－65.

刘惠玲. 库切的后殖民书写. 外语与外语教学，2009，5：38－41.

刘静观. 论库切自传体小说中情感世界. 河南师范大学学报：哲学社会科学版，2012，2：234－236.

麦克唐纳，彼得. 阅读的伦理和小说家的角色：库切《凶年纪事》的挑战. 英文. 外国文学研究，2011，5：15－19.

毛颢. 探微文明社会的生命本能——库切作品《耻》真义管窥. 武汉大学学报：人文科学版，2007，6：852－856.

秦海花. 拓展小说极限，寻求新的主题——从《慢人》看库切的后现代主义小说观. 当代外国文学，2009，2：110－117.

——. 小说家的演讲——库切《伊丽莎白·科斯特洛：八堂课》评析. 外国文学，2011，3：3－10.

——. 论库切小说中的批评及其小说批评观. 当代外国文学，2012，1：23－32.

任海燕. 探索殖民语境中再现与权力的关系——库切小说《福》对鲁滨逊神话的改写. 外国文学，2009，3：81－88.

邵凌. 库切的政治观与文学创作. 外国文学，2010，6：78－84.

——. 库切与创伤书写. 当代外国文学,2011,1：36－44.
——. 从库切对现实主义态度的转变看库切创作的新方向. 外国文学,2011,6：61－66.
石平萍. 关注局外人的诺贝尔文学奖得主库切. 外国文学,2004,1：3－6.
——. 关于非洲后殖民文学的对话：评《小说在非洲》. 外国文学,2004,1：14－17.
石云龙. 他者·他性——库切研究. 外语研究,2011,2：95－100.
——. 约·麦·库切：为他者化的他者代言. 英美文学研究论丛,2011,15：67－80.
——.《凶年纪事》独特的后现代复调小说. 外语研究,2012,4：93－96.
——. 后种族隔离时代的颠覆他者——对库切《耻》的研究. 英美文学研究论丛,2012,17：40－56. 人大复印资料《外国文学研究》,2013,4：60－67.
——. 后基督时代的沉默他者——评论《迈克尔·K 的生活与时代》. 外文研究,2013,2：50－57.
——.《夏日》：后现代另类"他传"小说. 外语研究,2013,4：98－101.
田晓南. 从属下角度解读 J. M. 库切的小说《耻》. 四川外语学院学报,2006,6：38－42.
汪霖. 论库切的《耻》和人性的《耻》. 当代外国文学,2006,4：166－170.
汪正平. 库切小说《福》的叙事策略分析. 求索,2010,10：227－229.
王成宇. 流散者的爱——试析库切的新作《慢人》. 河南社会科学,2008,1：162－164.
——. 试析《福》的语言策略. 外国文学研究,2008,5：160－167.
王敬慧. 两种帝国理念的对照：论库切寓言体小说《等待野蛮人》. 外国文学研究,2006,6：153－158.
王黎生. 库切的聚焦：一曲坚忍、苦难与畅想的悲歌. 河南社会科学,2010,6：171－173.
王丽丽. 弱者哲学与反抗的叙事——论库切长篇小说《耻》中的连环叙事. 江汉论坛,2005,4：131－134.
王娜："库切研究与后殖民文学"国际学术研讨会综述. 外国文学研究,2011,2：171－173.
王旭峰. 库切与自由主义. 外国文学评论,2009,2：105－115.
——.《伊丽莎白·科斯特洛：八堂课》——与后殖民沟通. 南开学报：哲学社会科学版,2013,1：104－109.
卫岭. 论库切小说《耻》的后殖民主义话语特征. 四川外语学院学报,2006,2：29－33.

乍从巨. 三重主题及其完成:关于库切之《耻》. 当代外国文学,2006,1:64－72.

武娜. 伦理困厄下的精神突围. 由库切作品中的动物情结所引发的哲学思索. 名作欣赏,2010,1:94－96.

——. 约翰·马克斯维尔·库切后现代创作策略刍议. 江西社会科学,2012,1:119－121.

许志强. 老年C先生与"小故事"写作:读库切新作《凶年纪事》. 中国图书评论,2006,1:58－62.

颜晓川. 沉默的颠覆:《迈克尔·K的生活和时代》的后殖民解读. 东北大学学报:社会科学版,2001,2:183－188.

杨铭瑀. 论库切的动物权利焦虑. 暨南学报:哲学社会科学版,2008,2:84－87.

杨雪梅. 试析《等待野蛮人》中的文明冲突. 名作欣赏,2006,3:91－94.

尹锐. 沉默与逃避——论《迈克尔·K的生活和时代》中的风景. 东北大学学报:社会科学版, 2001,2:372－376.

袁盛财. 论《福》的叙事策略. 当代外国文学,2011,2:23－29.

翟业军. 无神时代的约伯——论库切的《迈克尔·K的生活和时代》. 外国文学,2006,2:70－72.

张冲. 越界的代价:解读库切的布克奖小说《耻》. 外国文学,2001,5:86－89.

张德明. 从《福》看后殖民文学的表述困境. 当代外国文学,2010,4:66－74.

张勇. 寻觅迷失中的自我——读J. M. 库切的《耻》. 名作欣赏,2005,1:17－22.

——. 殖民文学经典与经典改写——析库切小说《福》对《鲁滨逊》的后殖民改写. 国外文学,2011,1:152－158.

郑禄英. 西方父权帝国话语的颠覆者——《福》对《鲁滨逊漂流记》的解构. 江西社会科学,2012,9:90－93.

周长才. 风月所以惊世界——对库切小说的一种解释. 外国文学,2004,1:18－22.

周怡. 诺贝尔奖关注的文学母题——流亡与回乡. 文史哲,2005,1:117－122.

朱安博. 文化的批判与历史的重构——《耻》的流散文学解读. 外语研究,2007,5:89－92.

庄华萍.《凶年纪事》的叙事形式与作者时空体. 当代外国文学,2011,1:27－35.

邹涛. 从库切的《福》看传记性叙述的双层困境及对策. 外国语文,2012,5:14－18.

后　记

写下“后记”两字，我隐隐觉得，这个耗时费心数年的研究项目似乎应该告一段落了，竟不由得产生一丝异样的感觉，既有几分兴奋，亦有几分感慨。

该项目缘起2009年山东威海当代外国文学学术会议。该会议主题定为“20世纪以来获得诺贝尔文学奖作家作品研究”，要求“探讨其特有的文学观念、艺术品格和创作规律”。此前，我进行过康拉德研究、奥康纳研究，也尝试过爱尔兰文学研究，唯独没有研究过诺奖得主。参加该全国性学术专题研究会议，理应有这方面研究成果。鉴于本人求学经历中始终没有离开过英语语言文学专业这样的背景，我为自己将要开展的诺奖相关研究设定两条标准，一是选取当代作家作为研究对象，二是选取英语作家的作品作为研究文本。

经过查证相关资料，我发现，2000年至2009年10位诺贝尔文学奖获得者中，竟然有5位是离开本土定居别国的所谓“离散”作家，亦即移民作家。这个群体立即引起我强烈的兴趣，因为根据黑格尔“凡是合乎理性的东西都是现实的，凡是现实的东西都合乎理性”的说法，该群体存在必定有其合乎理性的一面。最终，我选定2006年入籍澳大利亚的南非英语作家约翰·麦克斯维尔·库切。选择库切，是因为这个作家实在与众不同：他是南非荷兰人后裔，接受的是英语文化教育，在出生地竟然有“他者”的感觉；成年后曾赴英国寻根，混迹白人群中却被发现是英国文化的“他者”，无法得到肤色相同的人群的认同；赴崇尚自由平等的美国攻读博士学位，却因参与反对越战的游行而遭到不公平的待遇，在申请美国绿卡时遭到拒绝，成了无法融入色拉文化的“他者”；上世纪70年代被迫回到南非后，罪恶的种族隔离制度依旧猖獗，在英美不同寻常的经历使他原本就存在的“他者”意识变得越发强烈；他来到澳大利亚的阿德莱德，这是一座宁静美丽、略带乡村气息但又不失现代与艺术气氛的城市，在这里他找到了自己的归属；但依然关注着“他者”的生存状况。

多年来，库切不断地追求自由平等，却处处感觉不到自由平等；他渴望个性自由，但常觉得被他者化。作为大学教授，他性情孤僻、不苟言笑；作为美国芝加哥大学“社会思想委员会”成员，他向来不接受记者采访。他进行了大量的文学创作，每部作品都在挑战自我，尝试不同的书写形式。所有这一切，造就了他作为西方“他者”的作家特质。库切作品呈现出鲜明的他性特征，表现出作家不应声附和文学主流传统、独立创新的他者精神。我抓住库切的这些特征，从研究他者视角出发，完成了一篇题为“他者·他性——库切研究”的论文，在威海会议上得到同行专家学者的好评。论文的发表，激发起我继续深入研究库切的热情。

这种想法得到我的导师、上海外国语大学英语学科学术委员会主任李维屏教授的大力支持。他认为从文学批评他者理论视角研究库切，可以深入发掘库切作品中的真实内涵，为自己的创新研究提供施展手脚的舞台，不仅对于在中国外国文学研究界建构自己的库切研究者学术面貌大有裨益，而且可以促进我国的库切研究及后殖民文学批评的发展，并可能在学界产生积极的影响。在他的鼓励下，我将库切研究作为自己阶段性主要项目，进行了锲而不舍的研究，并于次年(2010)参加了武汉“库切研究与后殖民文学”国际学术研讨会。感谢会议组织者蔡圣勤教授，他请我与郑云先生共同主持库切研究组讨论活动，这是我组织过的最为辛苦也最为兴奋的一场学术讨论，会上发言人数达到 21 人，参与讨论者不仅有牛津大学艾勒克·博埃默、彼得·麦克唐纳、约克大学德里克·阿特里奇、戴维·阿特维尔、澳大利亚莫纳什大学苏珊·科休、中国社会科学院陆建德、复旦大学汪洪章等知名教授、学者，而且有一批来自世界各地的库切研究者、博士等。学术讨论是富有成效的，我在会议论文“约·麦·库切：为他者化的他者代言”中提出的“他者”观点得到了专家与学者们的认同，并得到库切研究专家阿特里奇教授、阿特维尔教授、陆建德教授的补充。

武汉国际会议使我确信，采用“他者”理论来构建我的研究项目主框架不仅能够满足论证需要，而且可以为库切研究提供一条创新途径。一年后的希腊雅典“语言与文学”国际学术研究会(2011)检验了我的这种想法。我在会上作了“后种族隔离时代的颠覆他者——对库切《耻》的研究”的发言，通篇采用上述思路，得到与会者好评。不过，让我印象深刻的并非专家学者的赞美声，而是与会者的提问，尤其是来自南非开普敦大学教授们的问题。他们在肯定我论文观点的同时，提出如何界定传统与非传统的问题，还提出何为南非文学传统的问题。这实质上从一个侧面为我的库切研究提供了实证的路径。经会后修改过的论文(1.2万余字)于2012年11月发表后，得到学界充分肯定，于2013年被中国人民大学复印报刊资料《外国文学研究》第4期全文转载。项目研究成稿后，我有幸得到上海英美文学国际研讨会组委会邀请，于2013年4月赴会作库切研究主旨发言。我的题为“库切小说‘他者’多维度研究”演讲反响热烈，先后得到张定铨、李维屏、虞建华、乔国强等教授的高度评价。

本著作在研究与成书过程中，得到过许多人的帮助，其中最为重要的帮助来自如前所述导师李维屏教授。他以其丰富的学识与研究经验建议我以一个文本为一个专题进行深掘式研究，从不同维度展开对库切小说“他者”的研究。这种高屋建瓴式的意见使我受益良多，不仅使我的库切研究得以顺利进行，也为今后继续研究、丰富库切研究成果打下坚实的基础。

此外，虞建华教授的热情鼓励与支持也对该项目的成功起到重要作用。他不仅帮助我评估库切研究方案，而且帮助通读成稿全文，提出很有价值的建议；王守仁教授在通读全书后给出热情洋溢的评论，同时提出格式修改建议，为本书的逐步完善提供了可能；我的英国导师、Bristol大学英语系前主任Timothy Webb教授持续关注着本人的研究，为本项目研究提供了很好的意见和建议，并在通读英文稿后给出中肯的批评意见，使我受益匪浅。

此书还得到过乔国强教授、何兆熊教授、戴炜栋教授、史志康教授等的指导和帮助，得到过我参加过的国内国际会议中各位专家、教授的帮助，在此，我谨怀感恩之心，向所有指导、帮助过我的人们表示深深的谢意。对于上述会议的发起者杨金才教授、蔡圣勤教授、Gregory T. Papanikos教授，也表示崇高的敬意与诚挚的谢意，是他们的会议成就了这部书，使我近几年的学术生涯得以充实。

无法忘怀的还有在本项目研究资料搜集过程中给予我慷慨无私帮助的人们：其中包括南京大学与英国谢菲尔德大学联合培养博士姜礼福，他为我在英国收集了大量相关资料；博士生王静为我在苏州大学搜集并复印了研究需要的资料。为了获取第一手资料，我还数次前往澳大利亚，在悉尼大学、新南威尔士大学、悉尼科技大学等大学图书馆留下了足迹。悉尼大学胡晨、余佳祺，新南威尔士大学贾建伟、悉尼科技大学张哲昊等帮我搜集到大量有关后殖民、后现代理论以及有关库切研究的资料，在此，谨向他们表示由衷的感谢。

最后，我将谢意送给我的家人，是家人一直默默地、坚定不移地支持着我。夫人作为全国重点大学图书馆业务主管，不仅承担着图书馆业务管理工作以及图情专业硕士研究生指导工作，而且多年如一日地包揽了她工作以外的全部家务，同时还在资料查阅方面给予我不时的帮助；远在万里之外异国他乡的女儿女婿对我资料方面的要求做到有求必应、全力以赴，让我无时不感到家庭的温暖和幸福，感受到精神支持的力量。我为有这样和谐温馨美满的家庭而倍感幸运与自豪！

本书虽然取得一些阶段性成果，但是，限于水平，舛误与疏漏在所难免，恳请方家不吝赐教。

图书在版编目(CIP)数据

库切小说"他者"多维度研究 / 石云龙著. —南京:南京大学出版社,2013.12
ISBN 978-7-305-12547-8

Ⅰ. ①库… Ⅱ. ①石… Ⅲ. ①库切,J. M. —小说研究 Ⅳ. ①I478.074

中国版本图书馆 CIP 数据核字(2013)第 291358 号

出版发行 南京大学出版社
社　　址 南京市汉口路 22 号　　邮　编 210093
网　　址 http://www.NjupCo.com
出 版 人 左　健

书　　名 库切小说"他者"多维度研究
著　　者 石云龙
责任编辑 郭艳娟　施　敏　　编辑热线 025-83592148

照　　排 江苏南大印刷厂
印　　刷 常州市武进第三印刷有限公司
开　　本 787×960　1/16　印张 21.5　字数 337 千
版　　次 2013 年 12 月第 1 版　2013 年 12 月第 1 次印刷
ISBN 978-7-305-12547-8
定　　价 50.00 元

发行热线 025-83594756　83686452
电子邮箱 Press@NjupCo.com
Sales@NjupCo.com(市场部)